FAILSTATE

JOHN W. OTTE

MARCHER
LORD
PRESS

FAILSTATE by John W. Otte
Published by Marcher Lord Press
8345 Pepperridge Drive
Colorado Springs, CO 80920
www.marcherlordpress.com

Scriptures quoted are from THE HOLY BIBLE, NEW INTERNATIONAL VERSION®, NIV® Copyright © 1973, 1978, 1984, 2011 by Biblica, Inc.™ Used by permission. All rights reserved worldwide.

The author is represented by MacGregor Literary Inc. of Hillsboro, OR.

Cover Illustrator: Carlo Garde
Colorist: Katja Louhio
Cover Designer, Typesetter, Editor: Jeff Gerke

Library of Congress Cataloging-in-Publication Data
An application to register this book for cataloging has been filed with the Library of Congress.
International Standard Book Number: 978-1-935929-48-2

Printed in the United States of America

Advance Praise for *Failstate*

"Now, this is what's missing from bookstore shelves. John Otte's Failstate *combines mystery, action, humor, romance, and faith all in one rip-roaring superhero tale. Readers will cheer for Failstate—a rookie hero without a license—as he tries to solve a murder, control his unstable powers, and not get voted off the show* America's Next Superhero. *Otte provides short, cliffhanger chapters, deep characters, and a breathless pace that will keep young readers up all night."*

—JILL WILLIAMSON, CHRISTY AWARD-WINNING AUTHOR OF BY

DARKNESS HID

*"Multiple mysteries must be plumbed before a nefarious plot can wreak havoc on an unsuspecting world—young super-heroes learn to deal with their budding powers—strong Christian content and a splash of romance—*Failstate *isn't just a coming-of-age story. It's a "super" debut for John Otte."*

—KATHY TYERS, AUTHOR OF THE FIREBIRD SCIENCE FICTION SERIES

"FAILSTATE and its superheroes barrel onto the Inspirational YA market, ensnaring teens and adults alike! A refreshing and adventurous read, Otte's debut novel resonates with a power all its own. Interwoven with supernatural elements, deadly villains, heart-stopping action, and powerful images of redemption and forgiveness, FAILSTATE will not soon be forgotten."

—RONIE KENDIG, AUTHOR OF THE DISCARDED HEROES SERIES

John Otte's debut novel Failstate *can kind of be described as* Sky High *meets* The Incredibles, *with twists that Disney wishes they'd thought of . . . It's the classic underdog story rewritten in a fresh way in a fun genre . . . Otte's debut packs quite the punch, delivering a fun read with some thoughtful themes. Wholesome, wholehearted, and wholly entertaining,* Failstate *continues the Marcher Lord Press tradition of offering up the very best in Christian speculative fiction."*

—JOSH OLDS, BOOK REVIEWED FOR FICTIONADDICT.COM

"FAILSTATE made me almost miss a flight. I was so caught up in John Otte's novel, the flight attendant had to call my name twice over the airport speakers just to get my attention. And it's no wonder. This book has everything I love in a novel: compelling characters, terrific writing, a solid plot, and a brilliant hook . . . The only thing I don't like about FAILSTATE is how jealous I am that I didn't write it myself."

—CHRISTIAN MILES, CHRISTIAN YA AUTHOR

For Isaiah
One of the greatest heroes I know

CHAPTER
1

BEING A SUPERHERO was hard enough. Being one on reality television . . . Why had I thought this was a good idea?

The production assistant, a young Asian woman in her late twenties, poked her head into the green room and called my name. I followed her out of the room. You'd think after four weeks of competition, they would give me a little credit for being able to find my own way, but no. They couldn't let the contestants get lost.

We walked down a corridor made of beige cinderblocks, one dotted with metal doors. Florescent lights buzzed and snapped overhead. Backstage personnel rushed around and brushed past each other and me in barely controlled panic. Their infectious rush only built as we approached a doorway with a burgundy curtain hanging in the frame, the dividing line between the backstage area and the set. A red light hung over the door. It would turn green in a moment to signal when it was my time to enter. Even though I had walked this route half a dozen times in previous weeks, each step still sent my heart slamming into my ribs.

A slow throb grew between my temples. Oh, no. I stopped short and screwed my eyes shut and willed the ache to go away. I had to keep my power in check.

Please, God, let everything work tonight. Give me focus, give me calm, give me control. Just don't let me break anything.

I braced myself against the wall and took a deep breath. I tried to ignore the hum of the lights, then blew it out slowly. A relaxing tingle dribbled through my chest, down my arms, and down to my legs. The ache unraveled. When I looked up, I realized the production assistant had gone ahead without me. I jogged after her and darted around a corner, almost running into the show's executive producer.

Helen Kirkwood was a woman in her late fifties with a hatchet face, all sharp corners. Greying brown hair was twisted back in her usual tight bun, and horn-rimmed glasses perched on her nose, which was upturned just enough to give her a snobbish look. I'd never understood why she'd been chosen to be one of the judges. But then, she was Alexander Magnus's personal assistant and his company, Magnus Communication Group, produced the show.

Her eyes, grey as steel, flashed as she spoke into her cell phone. "I don't care what he says! He can use the old units for the finale . . . Because I have a different use for them, that's why!" Her gaze landed on me with enough force to knock me back a step. Helen's eyes narrowed. "Get in position, Failstate. And don't break anything tonight. We can't replace any more cameras."

The throbbing surged. I barely restrained the power spike. I managed a curt nod.

"Get going and good luck." From Helen's tone, I knew she wanted me to have anything but. Her voice chased me as I took my place. "How's the construction going on the finale set? . . . Unacceptable!"

The production assistant came back and took me by the arm. She steered me through the halls and to the stage entrance. After a few seconds' wait, the red light blazed.

"And now, Failstate!" The announcer's voice boomed from the set.

I took a deep breath and pushed the curtain aside and walked onto the set. The bright lights blinded me. The set, scaffolds built out of gleaming steel, was supposed to look futuristic but resembled a shattered disco ball. The stage poked out into the audience, who sat on large bleachers. Toward the back of the stage was a raised platform with a long table and three high-backed leather chairs. Normally the judges sat there, but since they hadn't been introduced yet, the dais was wreathed in shadows, silhouetted by the thirty foot tall video screen behind it. Even though loud rock music blared overhead, the low murmur of the crowd still filtered through.

I stepped to downstage center. The weight of the audience's scrutiny slammed down on me. It didn't help that a dozen different cameras, some of them perched on high crane arms, all stared at me with their glassy lenses. I counted to ten and walked to my right and took my place. I glanced at the big screen to see what new biographical tidbit about me the producers had decided to share with the audience. I skimmed through the personal data: sixteen, a local resident of New Chayton, five-five, a hundred fifty pounds. That hadn't changed.

Failstate once spent an evening trapped in an elevator after foiling a bank robbery. Oh, wonderful. They would have to choose that one!

"And now let's welcome Gauntlet!" Before the announcer even got the name out, the crowd bellowed. I groaned. Same as last week, same as always. He was here.

Gauntlet strode across the stage and waved to his screaming fans. As always, he wore his usual blue spandex, complete with golden greaves and shoulder armor. His rising star symbol blazed brightly on his chest. His sandy blond hair poked out of the top of his costume, complementing his green-gold eyes.

He paused for a moment, fists jammed into his hips. The girls in particular seemed to love his posturing, as the squeals pitched higher with each flex of his muscles. Finally, a stagehand waved at the glory-hog to take his place. Gauntlet did so, blowing kisses to the audience as he walked.

I glanced down at my costume, such as it was. I looked through the black scrim of my Halloween hood at the grey sweatshirt with a large grease stain on my right arm and well-worn cargo pants, both cotton. I struggled to keep my shoulders from slumping. It wasn't fair.

When I looked up, Gauntlet stared at me, his mouth twisted in a wry smirk. He nodded. He always seemed to know I was looking at him in spite of my mask, a full hood with black scrim to conceal my features. Although the crowd continued to chant Gauntlet's name, his chuckle rang underneath the din.

"Here's Lux!"

Lux practically bounced onto the stage. She was about my age and wore her usual shimmering silver costume that clung to every curve. Long brown hair partially obscured her face, but that didn't hide the sheer energy that boiled off of her as she waved and flashed brilliant smiles at the crowd. Her power was that she could generate light, different colors, different intensities, hence her name.

Heat flashed through my cheeks, as it always did when I saw her. Maybe I'd get up the courage to talk to her after tonight's show and . . . Who was I kidding? I'd stay mute like usual. Probably safer that way.

"Blowhard!"

Blowhard's name described his powers, if not his personality. How the taciturn hero remained in the competition remained a mystery. He was in his in his mid-thirties, and not handsome either, with a large nose and a scraggly beard. Maybe viewers liked his pirate costume, a long black coat over a ruffled white shirt, complete with a red-and-blue bandana he had tied over the top of his head to form a mask.

"Veritas!"

Veritas's expression was unreadable through his mask, which covered his entire face except for his eyes. He wore vibrant red and blue tights that covered him from head to toe, save for a shock of wild red hair that poked out of the top. He wasn't bulky by any stretch of the imagination, but he was in better shape than me. He probably worked out so much to try to compensate, since his power was being a living lie detector. He could see the truth of any situation, even read people's minds. He bowed to the audience and then walked to other end of the stage.

"Kid Magnum!"

Kid Magnum whirred and clanked as he strutted on-stage. His metallic armor, painted a mottled grey and black, shone under the stage lights. He wasn't a true hero, in my opinion. Instead of superpowers, he had an arsenal of destructive weaponry grafted into a suit of nearly impenetrable armor. You didn't have to be a hero to operate machinery. I had no idea how old he was, since he had never removed his helmet in my presence.

"Prairie Fire!" the announcer said.

Prairie Fire slunk on stage, her shoulder slumped and her arms wrapped around herself. She wore a shimmering black outfit crisscrossed with violet lightning bolts. I could never figure out why she chosen that as her name. She threw bolts of electricity, not flames. And she came from the swamps in Louisiana, not the Midwest. I suspected she worked as a cook in New Orleans. She always smelled of Cajun spices.

"Titanium Ram!"

Titanium Ram, or T-Ram, sauntered to center stage. He wore a fairly simple costume, a blue coverall jumpsuit that appeared more like something a car mechanic would wear rather than a superhero. But he also wore a gleaming chrome helmet. He was in his late twenties and built like an English bulldog, squat and muscular. He could propel himself at incredible speeds and smash through just about anything.

Everett Thompson, the show's host, bounded on stage. He wore his trademarked zebra-print suit and gaudy smile. He swept an arm in our direction. "And here they are, America! The remaining eight heroes! Which one will be *America's Next Superhero?*"

The crowd went wild. Most of them chanted Gauntlet's name.

Everett let the chaos reign for a few more moments and then waved the crowd into silence. "But before we can proceed with tonight's festivities, we need to send one of these brave young heroes home. As always, the three contestants who received the fewest votes since the last show will have one last chance to demonstrate their heroic acumen—in the Chamber. But America's voice matters most. The hero who had the least votes will be eliminated. So here's our chief judge, Helen Kirkwood, to deliver the voting results from last week. Helen?"

A rhythmic *pock-ting* of heels on steel preceded Helen's arrival. The crowd fell silent except for a few boos.

Helen waited for the few naysayers to settle down, her mere presence creating a chill that hung over the whole studio. She took the microphone from Everett and turned to the audience. "Over twenty million votes were cast, and the results are in." She paused, her gaze sweeping over us. Did she linger on me? No, it had to be my imagination.

Rhythmic music, driving and mysterious, began to play, sounding like a fast-ticking clock.

Helen pulled a small envelope out of her suit pocket and cracked it open. "The three heroes with the fewest votes, the three in danger of being sent home tonight, and the first of the three heroes facing the Chamber is . . . Veritas."

Veritas bowed his head for a moment but walked across the stage. He shook hands with Everett, then turned to face the audience. The audience cheered, and a few people shouted his name.

Helen waited for the noise to die down. "Next is . . . Prairie Fire."

Prairie Fire jumped, and a small shower of electrical sparks erupted from her shoulders and cascaded down to the floor. She scurried to stand next to Veritas. Everett didn't offer to shake her hand. Probably didn't want to risk getting electrocuted.

"And the third and final contestant who will try to keep his or her chances alive to win the government vigilante license is . . ." an ominous fanfare thundered overhead . . . "Failstate."

The audience roared, some shouting for me to say goodbye, others yelling my name. I accidentally sucked in a mouthful of my hood and choked. I somehow managed to stumble forward. I limply shook Everett's hand and took my place next to Prairie Fire.

Helen turned to face the three of us. "Tonight, your goal in the Chamber is simple: Take out one criminal within ninety seconds. Good luck."

A camera on a crane arm dove and whizzed past the three of us as the audience cheered and screamed. Hopefully not all of them were out for our blood. I tried to stand straighter, strike a heroic pose.

Being in the bottom three was not good. It meant I could have been voted out already, but I wouldn't know until after the Chamber. Technically, even if I did amazingly well in the Chamber, it couldn't change my fate if the audience had decided to eliminate me. It was more a chance for the two who were spared to redeem themselves, show what they could do. But the fact that I had wound up in the bottom three at all was a bad sign. It could all end right now, and then where would I be? Still wearing second-hand costumes and busting petty criminals

And never able to make up for what I'd done.

I tried to muster enough concentration to pray. All I could remember were the words of Psalm 103, my Bible study from earlier that day. *Praise the Lord, O my soul, and forget not all his benefits—who forgives all your sins and heals all your diseases, who redeems your life from the pit and crowns you with love and compassion, who satisfies your desires with good things so that your youth is renewed like the eagle's.* I didn't know if the Chamber qualified as a pit or if winning a reality show counted as being crowned with "love and compassion." So I just summed up my desires in one word: Help!

"How will Prairie Fire, Veritas, and Failstate do in the Chamber? We'll find out, right after this!" The announcer's voice could barely be heard over the audience.

The lights dimmed, and stagehands herded the three of us toward the Chamber. I shot a look at Veritas and Prairie Fire. Veritas remained unreadable, hidden behind his mask. Prairie Fire crackled as she walked. Sparks skittered up her arms and across her face. She glanced in my direction and smiled, a nervous twitch of her lips.

We left the studio, the audience's cacophonous din falling silent as thick metal doors thudded shut behind us. We walked down a cement ramp and into another beige hallway. A short walk past doors labeled "Costumes" and "Props" brought us to the doors of the Chamber, black metal without windows. Someone had helpfully taped a page of yellow legal paper to the door with the name "Chamber" scribbled on with black marker, complete with a skull and crossbones. Good thing there were no cameras back here.

The stage manager, a portly guy in his late fifties, paused for a moment and listened to the voices on his headset. He leveled a finger at me. "You're first up."

My heart jackhammered against my ribs. The throbbing behind my eyes spiked. I clenched my fists and willed my breathing to remain steady.

If the stage manager noticed my agitation, he didn't let on. "The 'criminal' is on the far side of the room. Bring him down and get these cuffs on him before the horn blows. Remember, ninety seconds go by really fast in there."

The stage manager handed me a pair of zip-cuffs, two plastic loops that could be pulled tight quickly. I tugged at them to test their strength. Two stagehands hauled the doors open, and I stepped into a darkened room. The doors slammed shut behind me.

An overhead light snapped on and bathed me in a small ring of light. I squinted. The Chamber, the size of a basketball court, had probably started as a corporate gym but had since been painted black. I could still hear the creak of hardwood floors beneath my feet, the same sound I heard in gym at school. The smell of dust hung in the air, mixed with the odor of stale sweat. Small pods, concealing cameras, dotted the brick walls. Various stage lights dotted the ceilings, shifting and rotating. I swallowed my rising panic. No way I wanted to fry this much equipment.

Then another light snapped on across the room. A solitary figure stood wreathed in light, a mannequin wearing a black and red zoot suit, a large-brimmed hat slouched over its face. I laughed. This was my criminal? Had I been transported back to the '20s?

"Failstate, stand ready!" Helen's voice blaring out of speakers nearly made me jump out of my boots. "In three . . . two . . . one . . . begin."

I dashed forward. I'd just tackle the mannequin, bring his arms together and . . .

That's when the firehoses appeared.

Nozzles popped out of the walls. Water slammed into me, knocked my feet out from under me, and rolled me into the wall. I coughed and spit a mouthful of water through my hood's fabric. I should've known it wouldn't be that easy. I inched my way forward and held up my arms to shield myself from the freezing spray.

Just as quickly as the assault started, it stopped, the water cutting off. I stumbled, unsteady on my feet, and I looked across the room. The mannequin still waited. I had to—

Thunder exploded next to me, a flash of yellow and white very close to my head, sparks raining down on my soaked clothing. I staggered backward, momentarily deafened. Were they crazy? Who would put pyro that close to anyone, superhero or not?

I braced myself for another assault. I summoned my powers. Maybe I could keep the next explosion from happening if I short-circuited the flashpots. Nothing happened. I snorted and started for the mannequin again.

A series of clicks echoed around me, and panels slid open on the wall behind the mannequin, revealing two large fans. My shoulder slumped. Oh, great.

The fans' blades picked up speed until high winds swirled through the Chamber. It picked up loose newspapers and plastic bags. Where had all this trash come from? My hands snared the edge of my hood to keep it from blowing away. I took an unsteady step forward but then realized I had dropped the plastic cuffs! Even if I made it to the "criminal," I'd have no way to subdue him. I looked around, surprised at the sheer amount of trash that filled the air. I couldn't cut through the debris and find the cuffs, not before . . .

Through the howling wind, I thought I heard something that might be a horn blast. No! I couldn't have—

The wind died, and the fan blades stilled. The doors to the Chamber popped open. I had lost. I groaned and balled my fists, and I stalked out.

Veritas's eyes widened when he saw me. Prairie Fire looked about ready to throw up. The stage manager patted me on the shoulder and then pointed to Veritas.

"Good luck," I said to him.

Veritas had to wait for the Chamber to be reset. Then he stepped through, and the doors shut him in. Helen's countdown was muffled to my ears in the hallway, as were the sounds of the hoses, the explosions, the fans. Prairie Fire jumped at each one, the electrical jags dancing across her body spiking and flaring.

The stage manager signaled to his helpers and they opened the doors. Veritas strode out. He dusted his hands against each other, his costume still dry. It didn't even look like his hair had been touched. I gaped at him.

As the crew worked at resetting the Chamber for the final run, I stared at Veritas. How had he done it? I wanted to ask him, but he had never been all that forthcoming in previous episodes.

"Prairie Fire, you're up," the stage manager said.

She squeaked and darted through the doors.

I tried to track Prairie Fire's progress based on the sounds. After the hoses kicked in, blue light flashed through the door's cracks, a storm that intensified with each second. The overhead lights flickered and static electricity tugged at my hair. Then the horn blared from within the Chamber. The doors opened and Prairie Fire stomped out, smoke rising from her hands. Her sour expression spoke volumes about how she had done.

The stagehands escorted us back to the studio.

We stepped onstage, and the audience yelled. I tried to hold my head high, but it was difficult, especially with the others staring at us from the left side of the stage where they sat on high stools. Veritas, Prairie Fire, and I took our place side by side at the center of the stage.

Helen stood to our right. Her eyes were stern, and her lips pursed into a tight line.

"Only one of you managed to defeat the Chamber. Veritas!"

The crowd roared its approval. Veritas waved to them once before clasping his hands behind his back.

"But that ultimately does not matter," Helen said. "Only the votes do." She produced an envelope from her suit pocket and ripped open the seal. She glanced over its contents and looked up, her gaze locked on me.

Oh, great. So I not only made a fool of myself in the Chamber, but now I'm eliminated too. I could already hear Gauntlet's laughter. He would love that.

"Prairie Fire, you came to us with such promise. You called yourself the human taser, able to stop violent criminals without killing them. And yet, week to week, we have seen your potential squandered as you have failed in basic tasks. This was your third time in the Chamber. Will it be your last?

"Veritas, no one can deny your abilities. The judges have commented on your tremendous potential. But you seem to struggle most with connecting with America. On this show, votes matter. Have you earned enough this week to remain safe?

"And Failstate. You have contributed each week, but far too many people seem to think you're simply squeaking by. We have yet to see you take charge and show us what you're truly capable of. Will you get that chance in the future?

"So who has been eliminated? We'll find out . . . after these commercials."

The lights overhead dimmed, and the crowd screamed. My stomach, already twisting and churning, felt ready to crawl up my throat and out my mouth. Prairie Fire wrung her hands, and electrical jags danced between her fingers. Veritas, on the other hand, didn't seem affected at all. He bowed his head, his eyes closed. Praying? Maybe I should try that again.

When the lights came up a few minutes later, Helen turned to face the cameras. "Welcome back. Let us find out the results of tonight's elimination." She looked at the envelope. As she did, the same clock-ticking music from before began to play, only more insistent and driving. "The eliminated hero is . . ."

I held my breath. I fought to keep my powers in check. It wouldn't do to have them spike when . . . *if* Helen said my name.

"Prairie Fire. Your journey ends here. Good luck with your own heroic endeavors."

The music turned warm and somewhat sorrowful. The audience cheered and chanted Prairie Fire's name. My head snapped around to stare at Prairie Fire. She sniffled and wiped away tears. The audience had eliminated her? Why?

But then I realized what else that meant: I was safe for another week! That was great—except that it was terrible. Now I would have to participate in whatever nightmare the production team cooked up for us. If I did well enough, more people might vote for me, and I wouldn't enter the Chamber again. I could maybe even win the whole thing. I'd be able to make a difference, fix things instead of breaking them.

Prairie Fire cleared her throat, her hand stuck out for me to shake. I did and stepped away. She shook Veritas's hand and waved to the audience and then Helen escorted her off the stage.

Everett took his place in the spotlight. "There we go, friends! Failstate and Veritas are safe. Stay tuned, because they and the other five will face new challenges in their quest to become *America's Next Superhero!*"

As the lights dimmed, I breathed out a sigh of relief and a prayer of thanks. Veritas clapped me on my shoulder and shook my hand as well. I nodded as we walked back to our fellow competitors.

Gauntlet stared at me, his eyes narrowed but his lips curled into a smiling snarl. I could read his expression all too easily. He would make sure I lived up to my name. And, as much as I hated to admit it, I probably would.

CHAPTER 2

WITH THE ELIMINATION ROUND out of the way, the show could continue. Everett waved for the audience to quiet down. "So who's ready to see which of these heroes have what it takes to be a champion?"

The audience roared in response.

Everett flashed them a dazzling smile. "Then we'll get started. Let's welcome Helen back to explain tonight's festivities and remind us what this is all about."

Helen emerged from the wings. "Tonight, the heroes will be divided into two teams—Alpha and Beta—to take on an obstacle course. But, if you've watched our show very long, you know it won't be just *any* obstacle course."

Even though her lines fell flat, the audience still laughed and yelled their approval.

"The winners will receive immunity from the next elimination voting. The losers will face possible expulsion from the competition." Helen held up a small purple card. "And remember that at the end of the entire competition, the winner will receive this! A vigilante license that will allow him or her to join the ranks of such distinguished figures as Raze, Etzal'el, and Meridian!"

The big screens along the back wall flashed a picture of Meridian in his prime. The broad-chested man wore his classic red and black costume, cape, and half-mask with a radiant starburst on his forehead. Electricity shot up my spine. To be in the same league as Meridian or Etzal'el . . . It was exactly what I wanted. What I needed. With a license, I could actively fight crime full time. I could make up for—

No. I couldn't think of Dad. Not now.

"And now, the teams." Helen's voice snapped me out of my reverie. "The first member of Alpha Team is . . . Blowhard!"

Blowhard waved to the audience, who responded with a chorus of "Yar!" and "Yo Ho!" He walked to downstage right and waited for the next name to be called.

Helen waited for the crowd to die down before she continued. "The first member of Beta team is . . . Titanium Ram!"

T-Ram smacked his helmet a few times before howling. He charged to the opposite end of the stage from Blowhard.

"Joining Blowhard on Alpha Team will be . . . Lux!"

She smiled, a brilliant flash of teeth, and dashed to Blowhard's side. She hugged him and jumped up and down. She shrieked along with the crowd.

"Next up for Beta Team . . . Kid Magnum!"

Kid walked over to T-Ram and fist-bumped him, producing an audible clank.

"The third member of Alpha Team is Veritas."

So much for a "random draw." It was common knowledge that Veritas worked with Lux outside the show on the streets. That could give Alpha team a small advantage, unless . . .

I double-checked the numbers. If we had been divvied up fairly, Alpha Team would still outnumber Beta by one. There was only one way to balance the teams. I closed my eyes and swallowed a groan. I tried to offer a desperate prayer that I would be wrong. But before I could summon the words, Helen confirmed my suspicions.

"Failstate will round out Alpha Team, leaving Gauntlet to join Beta!"

Once again, the crowd screamed Gauntlet's name. He strode over to his teammates and exchanged high fives and fist bumps.

I stumbled over to my teammates. We were doomed. Even though Alpha had an extra person, Beta had the "strappers," the heavy hitters. We had the "boosters," glorified sidekicks. Sure, we had Lux and Blowhard, but since they couldn't do heavy damage, they were second-tier. Then we had Veritas, whose mental abilities made him a "cognit," also no good for grunt work. And me? I didn't fit into any category, although people considered me a cognit by default.

"In just a few moments, our heroes will enter the obstacle course. Their objective is to find the villains' hideout and breach their defenses. The first team to find the villains' inner sanctum will be declared the winner!"

Oh, great. Breaching defenses? That was the work for strappers, not boosters and cognits!

Someone touched my hand. I looked up, startled, into Lux's eyes. Her lips pursed into a smile, and she winked. "We'll be fine. We'll just work smarter. Now wave to the crowd."

My unenthusiastic wrist-flick probably didn't inspire the audience's confidence. I could already imagine the bloggers dissecting our chances. Abysmal. Nonexistent. Snowball's chance in . . .

But then I saw her. A girl sat in the front row of the audience, her perfectly sculpted face framed by curtains of black hair. Ice blue eyes tore into my brain, setting off a riot of sparks. I froze. She ducked her head, as if embarrassed, and her smile grew wider. When she looked up again, she winked at me.

Warm light bled through my mask.

Lux waved to the audience and globes of light burst from her hands. They grew larger until they popped. The radiance orbited Lux and stretched out in ribbons of light that bound Alpha Team together. The audience gasped collectively and then exploded in cheers and screamed for Lux and by extension, all of us.

"Showoff." Even though only Veritas's eyes only peeked through his red and blue mask, I could tell he was smiling.

The lights dimmed, and the crew ushered us from the stage. As Beta Team passed us, Kid Magnum shouldered Veritas out of the way, muttering, "Cognits."

I wanted to confront him, but the stagehands ushered us out of the studio and toward the launch point into the obstacle course, a room the size of a large closet with metal doors at one end. My teammates didn't look too enthusiastic. Kid Magnum's insult must have stung them too.

Maybe I could hold an impromptu pep rally. "All right, guys—and girl—let's go out there and do our best, okay?"

Blowhard harrumphed. "Our best? Beta's got the strappers. What do we have?"

"Heart?" If only I could inject more excitement into the word.

Lux glared at Blowhard then smiled at me. "I'm with you. So's Veritas. Right?"

I blushed underneath my hood. She was with me? I mean, I knew she meant the team, but still. It was a nice thought.

Before Veritas could answer, a siren blared, and with a ponderous groan, the door slid open. I bounded out onto a city street.

Or at least, it was supposed to be one. The back lot of the studio had been transformed into an urban wasteland at night. A series of gutted shops made of cracked red bricks lined both sides of the pot-holed pavement. Most of the windows had been boarded over, and colorful graffiti decorated the walls. Three broken-down cars that appeared to have been burned were parked at random points on the street. Large scaffolds rose behind the buildings, bearing lights, cameras, and in some cases, even crewmembers.

I took the lead and we crept along the side of the buildings. We tried to stick to cover. Pops echoed in the distance. Gunfire? Probably, but whether it was from an obstacle or Kid Magnum was hard to tell. Would they use live ammo in an obstacle course? I hoped not.

"Watch it!" Lux shouted.

A brilliant light flashed behind me, and I whirled. Lux pointed to a rundown storefront, a weak glow clinging to her finger. Three silhouettes crouched in the windows of the nearest building, weapons at the ready. I got ready to charge them, but the cardboard cutouts retracted, indicating that Lux had hit them.

Lux blew the tips of her fingers as if they were smoking gun barrels. "Got 'em. I'd say that's the direction to go."

I nodded. Our group of four jogged across the street and to the steps. Barring our way was another metal door, smooth, without any handles. Inset in the wall on the right side was a keypad.

Blowhard groaned. "Now what?"

"You could huff and puff and blow the door down," I said.

Blowhard's jaw snapped shut. "Step aside."

He took several deep breaths and then his mouth popped open, far wider than any normal person's mouth could open. Gale force winds slammed into the building. Loose newspaper and other debris swirled through the air, and for a moment I thought I was back in the Chamber. The walls creaked but the door didn't budge. Blowhard collapsed, gasping.

"A good effort." Veritas wrung his hands together. "Maybe this will slow down Beta Team too."

A loud boom echoed down the street. Some of the scaffolding between the courses swayed in response.

"Unless T-Ram is using his particular gifts," Veritas added hastily.

Another boom. The vibrations tickled the soles of my feet. "So what are we going to do?"

"Leave it to us." Lux smacked Veritas on the back. Then she cupped her hand over the keypad. Blue light spilled from her fingers and bathed the keys in an eerie glow. Smudges appeared on individual keys, the three, six, and eight. Would the combination have only three digits?

Veritas's eyes went slightly unfocused, as if he were looking past the wall. "The correct order is . . . eight, three, six, three."

I tapped in the combination. Sure enough, the door slid open with a muted sigh. Blowhard whooped and Lux clapped me on the back.

A third boom echoed in the distance, followed by a metallic shriek. One of the scaffolds between the courses collapsed, spilling lights and equipment. That'd be expensive. At least Helen couldn't blame that one on me.

We moved into a dim hallway inside the temporary building. The walls were grey and stained, the floors covered in dingy tiles. I choked on the overwhelming stench of oil. The overhead lights barely worked, but I saw a couple of shadowed spots where the cameras were probably nestled.

Lux took the lead. Her body glowed, casting dim light on the walls and in front of her. "The way looks clear."

Panels in the ceiling opened, and three small black orbs the size of basketballs dropped. Small doors opened on their sides to reveal gun muzzles. Before they could extend to shoot at us, I lashed out with my power and destroyed one of them. Then a blast of air slammed them hard into the walls. One broke, green circuitry spilling over the floor. The other dropped, a large dent smashed in its side.

I glanced at Blowhard. "Nice save."

"Glad to do my part."

" . . . help me . . ." The faint voice was barely perceptible.

I held up a hand.

" . . . help me . . ."

"Did you hear that?" I turned back toward the door.

Lux shook her head. Blowhard shrugged.

"Someone's calling for help," I said. "Was anyone on the scaffold that fell over?"

"I didn't see," Veritas said. "It's probably part of the obstacle course."

" . . . please, help!"

I looked down the corridor. We had to be close to the end. The show favored shorter challenges they could sandwich between commercials.

"We don't have time for this," Blowhard said. "Whoever it is will be fine. We have to keep moving."

That made sense. EMTs were on duty for each taping in case something went awry. Surely the crew was already helping whoever it was . . .

But something wouldn't let me take that chance.

"You guys keep going," I said. "I'll check this out."

Blowhard groaned. "Will you forget it? What if we need you to get into the 'villain's inner sanctum'? If you're off doing who knows what, how will we—"

Lux shot him an angry look. "Catch up quickly."

Once outside the temporary building and back on the street, I paused to listen for the person to shout again. Sure enough, a plaintive cry came from the direction of the collapsed scaffolding. I sprinted to the edge of the obstacle course

I paused when I came to the twisted wreckage. Large pieces of metal snaked from a pile of splintered wood, looking like a crouching spider. A smashed door stuck out from under an I-beam. A storage shed?

"Hello? Is anyone here?" I shouted.

A muffled cry came from underneath the wreckage.

I pulled twisted girders, scraps of corrugated metal, and splintered 2x4s out of the way. Where were the EMTs? "Hang on! I'm coming."

I pulled aside another large sheet of metal, only to find a loud speaker with large scratches on it.

No way. It couldn't be . . .

23

"Help me!"

The voice came from the speaker.

A trick! I should have known! I dropped the metal and raced back to the building.

Lux stood on the steps and waved me on. "We need your help!"

We raced past the broken sentry orbs to a pair of metallic doors that had sealed the hallway and blocked our progress. Veritas stood inspecting the seam between the doors and wall. Blowhard lay on the floor, his chest heaving.

Veritas glanced at me as I ran up. "Triggered by an infrared eye, I think. Control circuitry is too far into the walls for us to access. Think you can . . . well, you know?"

The throb behind my eyes grew worse. "Maybe. Are the doors only metal?"

"I think so."

"Let's find out."

I pressed my hands against the doors. The throb intensified. I envisioned pushing that pulsing power outward toward the doors.

Lux whooped. I opened my eyes. A small divot had appeared in the door, and it grew bigger with each passing moment. I worked my jaw. Had to keep the energy working as it ate through the door.

The gap widened. Sweat stung my eyes. Maybe I should wear a headband under the mask. That wouldn't look as good, though. I shook my head. This wasn't *Project Runway*. Worry about fashion later. A pinprick of light appeared in the hole's center. I'd made it through to the other side! The door had to be about two inches thick. Only metal. Good. Now to make the hole big enough for everyone to wiggle through . . .

A horn blasted, cutting through my concentration. Lights flared around us

Everett's voice blared overhead, "Beta Team wins!"

I didn't want to face the judges. They glared down from their tribunal, engaged in what was charitably called "the Debriefing." In reality, it was a public dissection, flaying open all our failures for the audience.

First we watched Beta Team's success on the monitors. As much as I hated to admit it, they had done their job well. Kid Magnum had taken out both silhouettes and the sentry orbs, Titanium Ram had made short work of the first door. And Gauntlet had not only coordinated their efforts, but he'd ripped the final doors open with his bare hands. We hadn't stood a chance without scrappers. I didn't want to think about it, but the teams had felt stacked

I risked a glance at the judge's panel. Helen Kirkwood perched in the center, flanked by the Howling Vibe and Gal Strife, two retired heroes. As the replays of both teams' efforts wound down, Helen turned her cold gaze on me.

"You left your team at a crucial time, and they lost. Do you have anything to say?"

"I thought someone was in trouble." I kicked at my reflection in the floor with the toe of my boots. "I had to help."

"Admirable, but pointless in this case," Howling Vibe said. "You abandoned your team, endangering the mission. You lacked focus. Only the objective mattered."

Gal Strife shook her head. "No way, dude. The kid did what he thought best. Sometimes ya gotta go off the rez, y'know? Mix it up a little, especially if you think someone is hurt."

Helen rolled her eyes. "Do any of the other contestants have anything to add?"

Kid Magnum raised his hand. "I do. I think Lux cheated."

"Excuse me?" Lux's eyes flashed red. "We cheated but we lost? Really?"

"You expect us to believe that light could knock out those bad guys? I mean, in the real world, what harm would a flashbulb do?"

Lux smiled sweetly. Veritas leaned closer to me and whispered, "Close your eyes."

Even with my eyes shut, the brilliant flash cut into my head. When I looked again, Kid Magnum rolled on the ground and held his face.

Lux stood over him. Her hands glowed. "Still think I cheated?"

The audience shouted their approval. Howling Vibe tried to shout over the din, calling for peace. Gal Strife only laughed uproariously, leaning back in her chair and kicking up her heels on the table.

With a roar, Kid Magnum threw out his arms and gun muzzles popped out of his wrist armor.

Lux flicked her hand toward his face. A flurry of sparks exploded from her fingers, bursting around his head.

Then she was gone, replaced by Veritas, who flowed around Kid Magnum. Kid Magnum threw a wild punch at Veritas, but Veritas ducked and grabbed Kid Magnum's arm and toss him over his hip.

T-Ram dropped into a three-point ready stance, lowering his head for a charge. Blowhard took a step forward, sucking in a deep breath.

"No brawling!" I shouted. "You guys know that. Back down." I dove between Veritas and Kid Magnum. I snared Kid Magnum's wrists and my power flared. Kid's wrists twitched, and one of his wrist cannons fired. I whirled around in time to see Gauntlet snatch the projectile, which looked like a riot-control beanbag, out of the air.

"You heard him." Gauntlet tossed the beanbag over his shoulder and stepped forward, his hands raised. He stood at my side and glared at the members of Beta Team. "Kid shouldn't have questioned Lux, especially since the judges didn't. And we all know brawling is forbidden, both on the show and in real life. Gracious winners, okay?"

Gauntlet clapped me on the shoulder, much too hard, and took his place on the sidelines. The combatants stood down, and the judges wrapped up their comments. I didn't listen to Everett's final thoughts as the show ended.

"And . . . we're done," the stage manager said. "Good show, everyone."

The audience streamed for the aisles. Many of them clamored for autographs, most of them shouting for Gauntlet. I waited for a moment to see if anyone wanted to speak with me. Maybe the girl I'd spotted earlier?

Guess not.

I headed backstage. The production assistant from earlier escorted me to the confessional booth, a small room with pictures of the different contestants dotting the black walls. I sat before a camera and shared my thoughts from earlier in the night, basically telling the story from "my perspective." This would give the director footage to intercut with what actually happened, so that when the episode finally aired, our comments would come at all the right moments. After a half hour of trying to act upbeat about Alpha Team's shellacking, I was dismissed. I headed for the backstage door.

But Lux blocked my way.

"Thanks for sticking up for me back there," she said. "I couldn't believe Kid Magnum actually drew his weapons on me."

I shrugged, my mouth suddenly dry.

"So listen, I'm going out on a patrol tomorrow night, and I was thinking that . . . Would you want to come with me? It's just a swing through Hogtown, but maybe you would want to . . ."

She kept talking, but her words didn't register. She wanted to go on patrol with me? Why? I stared at her, drinking in the luminous, burnished skin glowing under her mask, her bright eyes, her brown hair.

I frowned. "What about Veritas? Will he mind?"

She laughed, sheer music, and green light exploded around her. "No, don't worry about him. We work together, but it's not like that at all."

Better say something. "Uh, yeah . . . That sounds . . . Wow, yeah."

She smiled, her face lighting up even more. "Great. Corner of Seventh and Ballast, say around 11:00?"

"I'll be there."

"See you then."

She practically sashayed away, and I caught myself staring after her. Was that a spring in her step? Couldn't be. Not if she'd asked me on a . . . well, not on a date, exactly, but pretty close.

I shook my head and escaped the studio. I stepped out into the cooling evening air. The studio was located in the north end of New Chayton in an inner ring suburb called Havensbrook. Winter was still trying to hold on to New Chayton and doing a fairly good job of it. I stuck to the shadows to avoid the traffic that filled the streets as fans left the studio and headed for home. I darted down the darkening street and into a nearby alley. A quick double check and then I reached behind a dumpster. The duffel bag was still there. Good.

Within a few minutes, I had changed from my costume and into my civvies. Then, from the bag's side pocket, I pulled the necklace.

I turned it over in my hand. It didn't look like much, a braided hemp rope holding a blood-red crystal, but I hated it. I resisted the urge to throw it in the dumpster and walk away. But I couldn't. Without this necklace . . . Well, without it, many bad things would happen.

I sucked in a deep breath and tied the necklace in place. For a moment, nothing happened, and then the throbbing behind my eyes shattered. The pieces ricocheted through me like hot needles. I wrapped my arms around myself and ground my teeth together.

On the heels of the pinpricks came the all-too-familiar dull ache that permeated every inch of my body. I blew out a shaky breath and touched the skin of my face. Smooth once again. No hint of what I hid beneath the mask.

Failstate was gone. Robin Laughlin had taken his place.

I jogged out of the alley and checked my cell phone—9:30. Production had gone late again. Mom wouldn't be happy.

I rounded the corner of Sixth Street and there Mom was, hunched over the steering wheel of the minivan. I kept offering to drive myself, but she insisted she needed the van. She glanced in my direction and her expression soured. I groaned. So which Mom was she tonight? Sniper or snubber? I shook my head and chided myself for my attitude. I knew all too well why she felt like this, and really, I couldn't blame her.

I opened the door up front but Mom's glare sent me to the back as usual. I slid into place and looked in the rearview mirror. Mom stared out the windshield. Snubber it was then. We pulled out from the parking space and drove for the library.

"So, any sign of Benjamin?" Mom finally asked.

Thanks for asking about my evening. "No, not yet."

We pulled to a halt outside the brick building. After a few moments, the door across the seat rolled open, and Ben slid in, tossing his backpack on me like I wasn't there.

Mom turned in her seat, a brilliant smile on her face. "How'd the study session go, sweetie?"

"Great, Mom. Sorry I'm late."

Mom waved away his apology. "No problem at all. Robin was fifteen minutes late already, so at least you didn't have to wait outside. That just isn't safe."

Pain exploded on my arm. Somehow Ben always managed to hit the same spot with his secret punches.

"You know you shouldn't keep Mom waiting," he said.

I glared at Ben. Green-gold eyes glinted back at me, his lips twisted into that all-too-familiar wry smile. I glanced down at his pack and saw a little corner of blue spandex sticking out. I tucked it back inside and set it between us. No brawling, I reminded myself.

Like I told him earlier.

CHAPTER 3

ANOTHER SLEEPLESS NIGHT in the Laughlin house.

I couldn't remember the last time I'd slept more than an hour or two. Not since I'd gotten my power. I'd always struggled with how to occupy my time. Late night television, which had once held an almost mythic quality, didn't help. Once the unfunny talk shows wound down, vacuous infomercials took over, and I would try to find something, anything to kill time.

Like now—

I could always rearrange my room. I glanced at the twin bed covered in a rich blue comforter, one that blended with the blue walls, three of which were a light baby blue, one just a shade darker. Mom called it an "accent wall." I didn't care for it, so I had done my best to cover it up with posters and pictures. The two biggest depicted Meridian and Etzal'el.

A wooden desk with a sadly outdated computer was pushed against a narrow window that overlooked our front yard. I could have switched my bed and desk around and moved the posters, but the last time I'd done that in the middle of the night, Mom had chewed me out for waking her up.

Reading? My gaze skipped down my bookshelf. Nothing jumped out at me. I should have gone to the library earlier in the week.

My gaze landed on my Bible. It was technically Saturday morning, but I liked to save my daily study for sunrise, the true start of the day.

Maybe a video game? No, I'd probably do terrible and that would just remind me of my poor showing at the taping.

That left me with one idea: Learn more about Lux.

After checking the doors to both Mom's and Ben's rooms, I went back into my room and settled in at the computer. I shifted in the chair, trying to find a comfortable position. Aches radiated through my chest, shadowed by intense itches. My fingers touched the necklace. Stupid thing never let me get comfortable, but taking it off wasn't an option. Who knew what my power would do to the desk or the chair? And a badly timed spike could wreck the computer. Mom wasn't bluffing when she'd said I'd have to buy the next one.

An Internet search brought up hundreds of articles on Lux. She had been busy. The oldest article was from three years ago, when she and Veritas had busted up a bank robbery. Reporters had speculated about their possible ties to Yale University, due to their names. Others had wondered if it was wise for such young teenagers to be working as vigilantes. But over time the critics had fallen silent as Lux and Veritas had racked up impressive statistics. Dozens of criminals caught, thousands of people saved through their efforts. I whistled, low and quiet. My career was pitiful in comparison.

One video I found online drove that point home. Apparently a girl named Michaela had been kidnapped. In the video, Lux and Veritas tracked down the gang responsible. Onlookers recorded the confrontation. While Lux fought half a dozen men much larger than her, Veritas pinned another gang member to a wall, his hands clamped on the sides of his face. After staring into his eyes for a few moments, Veritas revealed where Michaela was being held. Apparently he had read the truth from the gang member's mind. The person who had posted the video noted that Michaela had been rescued by the pair half an hour later and had been returned to her parents unharmed.

My next stop was a site that called itself "Cape Town." It was a blog dedicated to all things heroic. It was maintained by some guy who called himself GyFox. I had no idea who he was, but GyFox somehow managed to get spoilers from the show tapings and insider gossip.

I had to scroll past his latest post, a rant about how the world was spiraling out of control and needed to be reformatted and rebuilt from the ground up. Pretty wild stuff, but below that post, I found what I was looking for: pictures of Lux. Lots were screen captures from previous episodes. I opened up the first gallery and clicked past the group photos. There she was, standing by herself, her smile radiant. I leaned forward to drink in every detail . . .

Only to lean back, my discomfort growing, but not from the necklace. I was cyberstalking someone, and it didn't feel right. Why couldn't I just go to Hogtown tomorrow night and meet her, get to know her that way?

The picture was answer enough. Luxurious chestnut hair, which seemed impossibly long, cascaded down past her shoulders. I considered scrolling the picture down to see more of her form, but I stopped myself. I knew how tight her costume was. No need to torture myself with the knowledge.

Instead, I stared into those unnaturally violet eyes, surprised at how luminous they looked even through the computer screen. I could almost hear her melodic laughter. I closed my eyes and smiled, envisioning how the night might go. Pleasantries exchanged, a few petty crimes stopped and we would take a break on a rooftop somewhere, maybe with a good view of the moon. I could risk a few personal details, maybe get her to open up. I could say it was chilly, slide closer. And then . . . and then . . .

And then I'd have to take off my mask.

I blanched, a sour taste gagging me. No way she'd want to stick around after getting a look under my hood. Maybe I could slip on my necklace. It'd be tricky, but doable.

I leaned back, lacing my fingers behind my head, a movement that caused my chair to creak. As I did, I caught my reflection in the mirror over the dresser. I froze. No way she'd want to see how my necklace disguised me: pudgy cheeks, dirty blond hair that never stayed tamed, brown eyes that didn't quite fit the rest of my face, and a spattering of freckles that appeared more dirt than alluring.

I blew out a long breath and turned back to the computer monitor. Lux smirked at me, so warm and inviting. Maybe how I looked wouldn't matter to her. Maybe . . .

"Oh, dream on!"

My eyes snapped open and I almost lost my balance in my chair.

Ben steadied me from behind and leaned over my shoulder. "This is what you choose to do all night? Fantasize about someone out of your league?" Ben punched my shoulder with enough force to almost shove me out of the chair again.

Normally I'd accept Ben's shots. But not today. "As a matter of fact, I'm going out on patrol with her tonight."

Ben's eyes almost popped out of their sockets. "What kind of dirt do you have on her? You must have something, or she'd never agree to go out with you."

"She's the one who suggested it, not me." I was still enjoying the shock I'd seen on his face.

Ben's eyebrows twitched, and his mouth popped open for a split second. But his apparent surprise melted away in a heartbeat, and his usual smirk reasserted itself. "Pity. That's all it is. She knows you're cannon fodder on the show, and she wants to soften the blow when you finally crash and burn."

I whirled around and met his gaze. "If anyone's going to crash and burn, it's you."

"Oh, yeah? How do you figure?"

I stood up. "Because I know you haven't told the producers the truth about your power. What do you suppose will happen when everyone finds out you've been lying this whole time?"

Ben's frown froze. Then he pushed me back into the chair and marched out of the room.

I'd gotten off light that time. I had no idea what would happen when I proved him wrong about Lux. But I knew one thing for sure: It would be worth it.

CHAPTER 4

THE BUS JOLTED to a halt, and I almost pitched out of my seat. The smeared window did little to hide the rundown neighborhood. In many ways, it looked like the obstacle course set from the previous night: rundown buildings, boarded over windows, broken-down cars, all illuminated by flickering street-lights. Trash blew through the streets. The major difference was that this was real. Hogtown was never pretty, especially not at night. I pulled my knapsack close and rose.

A rough looking man, all stubble and grime, sneered at me. "Sit down, kid, this ain't no place for you."

I forced a cool smile to my lips, squared my shoulders, and started for the doors. Only I tripped over my own feet and spilled onto the foul-smelling floor of the bus. The man who warned me burst out laughing. So did a few of the other passengers. Heat erupted through my face. I scooped up the bag and dashed out of the bus.

The cool night air slapped me. Hogtown's rancid odor slithered up into my nose. Although most of the slaughterhouses that had given the neighborhood its name had closed a decade earlier, somehow their stench still lingered. No other industry had taken its place, and the neighborhood had spiraled into absolute decay. Normal people didn't visit Hogtown, especially at night.

Except for the occasional superhero who wanted to prove himself. Meridian, Gal Strife, even *El Defensor de Medianoche* had established themselves in Hogtown first. Many of us worked the streets at some point.

I ducked into a dark alley between two brick buildings and hunkered behind a bank of dumpsters to get into my costume. Shirt, pants, hood, tuck the civvies in the bag. I fingered the necklace. Then I untied it and tucked it away. The irritation swept through me, balling together and coming to rest as a throbbing behind my eyes. I groaned and clenched my jaw, trying to rein in the surge.

Too late. A hole burst in the dumpster, spewing wet garbage across the alley. I scampered backward with only a small spray across my boots. Not an auspicious start to the evening, especially compounded with the fall on the bus, but it could have been worse.

I cut through Hogtown, wary of any sounds. This was Blue Eclipse Boys territory, and those goons didn't tolerate heroes. Car engines, muted conversations, sharp laughter drifted past me. Nothing indicated that I had been spotted. Crossing from block to block proved tricky, what with the passing traffic and the occasional working streetlight.

My stomach twisted, but not because of my environment. What should I say to Lux when I saw her? Worse, what would

I say if Veritas was with her? No way I wanted a chaperone tonight.

I poked my head out of the alley. The streets were clear so I could risk moving a bit faster. I broke out into a jog and darted down the sidewalk and into another alley. For a moment, I imagined what would happen if I somehow won the show. I would stand center stage, and confetti would pour from the rafters as they crowned me *America's Next Superhero*. Etzal'el, in his signature billowing black cloak, would deliver the license. And Meridian too! He'd come out of retirement just long enough to congratulate me. But best of all would be Lux. She would beam, both literally and figuratively, sidling up to me, wrapping those lithe arms around me and then . . .

I jogged onto Fourth—

Right into the path of a running man. We went down in a tangle of limbs. My hood twisted across my eyes and blocked my vision. I mumbled apologies and straightened my costume.

When I could see through the scrim, I realized that the other man wore a red t-shirt and jeans. I also saw that he wore a half mask. His was made of leather that covered the left side of his face but left his lips exposed. I studied his features for a moment. His mask did nothing to conceal them. Thick face, bulbous nose, thin lips. Pale, sweaty skin. Brown eyes wide . . . bloodshot. It almost appeared as if steam rose from his massive body.

"We have to get out of here!" The shout came from farther down the block.

I glanced toward the intersection. Two men, dressed in black, waved frantically, either at me or the man I'd collided with, as if urging one or both of us to join them. They too wore half masks. One covered the top of the wearer's face and his hair. The other covered the right side of the wearer's face.

The fallen man knocked away my hands and scrambled to his feet. He disappeared with the other two down the street.

Weird. But then Hogtown had a few nightclubs and numerous bars. They were probably clubbers.

I felt cold on my hands, and I looked down. Ice bled through my gloves. Frost coated my fingers. Where had that come from? I flexed my hand and shook it out, trying to work some warmth back into them. It felt as though I had plunged my hands into a freezing river. The sensation soon passed, and I set out again.

I crossed the final street to Fifth and Ballast.

Where was Lux? Not on the corner. I checked my watch: 11:05. I glanced at my surroundings. A burned-out hotel, a closed grocery store, a vacant lot strewn with broken cinderblocks, weeds, and empty bottles. The whole mess was surrounded by a rusted chainlink fence. It didn't seem like . . .

Wait. I caught a flash of bright cloth that looked out of place in the grungy lot. What was that? A hand, someone's arm poking out of a small depression in the dirt.

It twitched.

Crime victim? Why else would someone be lying in that field?

A break in the fence allowed me to enter. I darted for the person—

Only to have my feet fly out from under me. I pitched face-first into a pile of snow.

I shook loose flakes from my mask. Snow? What was that doing here? The field was free of snow. It was only bare dirt in the moonlight. Yet I knelt before a two-foot drift. Behind me was a sheet of ice three inches thick.

No time for meteorology. I got to my feet and skirted around bare bush and a pile of broken bricks to get to the person on the ground. How close was the nearest hospital? An ambulance could probably be here in less than ten minutes.

I glanced toward the victim. Flashy clothing hugged lithe curves. A young woman, covered in blood. Another clubber?

"Don't worry, ma'am, help is on the way." I pulled out my cell phone. I'd have to destroy it after calling the cops, but it was a disposable phone, easy to replace. No one could trace the call back to Robin Laughlin.

"Failstate?" The victim's voice, weak and thready, was all too familiar.

I turned toward the woman and my mouth ran dry. Staring up at me, blood spattered across her mask and face, was Lux.

CHAPTER

5

NO, IT COULDN'T BE. A look-alike? An impersonator? Had to be. It couldn't possibly be . . .

"Lux?" I whispered.

She coughed and nodded, a bare twitch of her head.

The cell phone slipped from my fingers. I dropped to my knees. Multiple injuries across her torso, a few in her arms and legs. How much blood had she lost? I could rip my sweatshirt to shreds, use the strips as . . . bandages, tourniquets maybe? I didn't know.

Her hand caught mine. "Don't. Too late."

"Don't say that. You'll be fine." I scrambled for my cell phone to call 911. Was there a code for injured superheroes?

"Fail . . ." She fell back into the dirt. Her face contorted beneath her mask.

I ignored the tinny voice in the phone, scuttling across the dirt to her side. "I'll get help, okay? Then we can . . . Or is

Veritas somewhere around here, can he get help? I mean, we have to—"

Lux's head flopped to one side. "No, he's not here. Just you. Just me." Her arm snaked out again, her fingers entwined through mine. "Don't leave me. Not now."

I pulled her hand closer. "I won't. I promise. Just hold on." I held the phone up to my ear. "Send an ambulance to Fifth and Ballast now!" I dropped the phone and clasped her hands with mine. "The cops are probably tracking my cell phone now. GPS, you know?" I looked around the vacant lot, spotting the pile of snow in one corner. Any passersby? No! Where was everyone? Shouldn't someone have found us by now? "And then—"

Her grip tightened. "Tell Ver . . . magma . . ." Her breaths burst out in bare puffs and then the tension drained from her body.

"Lux? Lux!" This wasn't real. Couldn't be. Some sort of trick. A clone, a hallucination, a hologram, because if this was real, then Lux had just . . .

The throbbing behind my eyes intensified. I dropped Lux's hand and clawed at my temples. I couldn't let this happen, not now. Had to keep the power reined in. I couldn't afford to . . . let . . . it . . .

I stumbled headlong into the dirt. The throbbing turned to thrumming, then to rattling, then to a tremor radiating from my brain down my spine and into my feet.

My control shattered.

Fire rippled through me. Darkness clouded my vision. And destruction flowed out of my body, coursing through every fiber of my being. An invisible, intangible aura that cut through the field. I gasped with equal parts horror and relief. I knew my power was wreaking havoc in the vacant lot, destroying everything around me, but I couldn't stop. I'd have better luck stopping a fire hydrant with my hands. My back arched and I cried out, fingers raking the dirt. The outpouring couldn't last much longer, could it?

God, please! Make it stop!

After what felt like an eternity, the burning faded, and the steady throb behind my eyes returned. Fatigue slithered through my body. I took a few ragged breaths and rolled onto my back. I had to move. Check on Lux. See what kind of damage I had done this time.

First things first. Mask still intact? Yes. Holes had appeared in my shirt, my pants. I pushed myself into a sitting position and one of my boots crumbled.

My head swam, and I had trouble focusing. Most of my memories of the evening had turned into an impenetrable haze. I remembered a bus ride . . . hiding behind a dumpster . . . and then . . .

I looked around at my surroundings. It looked like this vacant lot had been scoured. Had I done this? Bits of memory filtered through my mental fog. The lot had been blasted by something . . . probably my outburst. Instead of the rough rise and fall of dirt, the ground appeared to be made of glass. The loose debris had been consumed. Well, not all of it. Small islands of normalcy jutted up at random points, mostly consisting of dead bushes and clumps of grass.

So what was I doing here? Going on patrol? In Hogtown, by myself? That was a recipe for disaster. No, I must have been meeting—

"Lux," I whispered.

A small pile of cinderblocks, worn smooth as if by a high wind, had offered her some shelter, but large portions of her costume had been destroyed. I averted my eyes, not so much for her privacy but because more of her injuries had been exposed, angry puncture wounds. Her eyes stared up at the sky, her mouth open.

Hot tears stung my eyes. I should do something for her. Cover her, close her eyes, something. I knelt down next to her. Should I say something? Offer a prayer? What?

The distant wail of sirens echoed through the streets of Hogtown, and within moments, flashing red and blue lights bathed the field. People crunched through the dirt behind me.

"Just hold it right there. Turn around slowly and put up your hands."

I did as I was told, turning to face the two police officers. They had weapons drawn, although I could read the nervousness in their expressions.

The cop on the right's eyes widened. "Holy crow, Jeff, do you know who that is? It's Failstate! He's on that show, right?"

"Shut up." Jeff's voice was little more than a guttural growl. He didn't lower his weapon but his gaze flicked past me to the body. "Whoever he is, he's got a lot of explaining to do."

CHAPTER 6

AT LEAST THEY TOOK the handcuffs off.

This precinct's interrogation room had muted earth tones on the wall, an almost stain-free beige carpet, a few potted plants along one wall, plus the obligatory mirror that dominated the wall to my right. A large wooden table filled the middle of the room, surrounded by three chairs. A small camera pointed down from one corner. I shifted in my chair. How much longer would they keep me? I had already been questioned three times. Sunlight had just started trickling in through a high window. Had Mom noticed I was gone yet? Was she worried? I snorted.

The metal door opened, and an older man strolled in, flipping through papers in a manila folder. He looked to be in his forties, broad face, sharp chin lined by brown and grey stubble. He wore a tight sweater that revealed a barrel chest and thick, tree-trunk arms. He sat down across from me, still studying the file's contents before looking up at me with flinty eyes. "Do you know who I am?"

Another detective, probably.

"I'm Agent Sexton with the Vigilante Oversight Commission." The man dropped the file and leaned over the table. "I assume you know what that means?"

I did. The VOC kept tabs on the superhero community. They granted the licenses. If a hero went rogue, they took him or her down. Nobody crossed the VOC. Nobody.

Sexton's eyes narrowed. "You've been jerking the cops around all night, kid. You claim you and Lux were going on patrol together but you found her body in that field. And then you 'accidentally' destroyed every shred of forensic evidence afterward. That it?"

I hesitated. I had told the story of what I could remember several times now, but I had a nagging feeling that I was forgetting something important. I had shown up where I was supposed to meet with Lux, found her dying, blasted everything in my grief. What else was there? Try as I might, I couldn't remember anything else. But I doubted Sexton would understand. I splayed out my fingers on the table top. "That's what happened."

Sexton slammed his fist into the table. "You think I'm stupid? You think we're all stupid?"

"No, sir."

"Then we're going to go over it again, got it? But first, the mask. Lose it."

Ice sluiced down my back. Not good.

"I don't have to cite the Vigilante Act, do I?" Sexton asked.

He didn't. I knew what it said. If an unlicensed hero were suspected of a crime, he or she had to unmask if told to by a law enforcement official. The VOC and its agents definitely qualified.

I fingered my hood's fringe. Other officers were probably watching behind the mirror. They might even be videotaping this discussion. If an image of my unmasked face leaked . . .

"I'm not gonna ask you again, kid. Take it off. Now."

I had no choice. I pulled off my mask, set it on the table, and waited.

The color drained from Sexton's face. He started to say something but gagged. What feature had caused his reaction, I wondered? My ruined and almost non-existent nose? The parchment-thin, furrowed skin that highlighted the path of every blood vessel? My inky black eyes that bled black fluid down my cheeks? Whatever it was, Sexton darted out of the room.

"This is pointless." I pulled on my hood and rose. Time to go. I'd leave and wouldn't look back. That's what Gauntlet would do. He'd even toss off a jaunty wave at any cop who tried to stop him. I stood and crossed the room. My fingers hovered over the doorknob. One twist and I'd walk through to freedom.

And Lux's killer would never be found.

That thought froze me. Sexton had said I had destroyed all the evidence. While a vacant lot probably would have been a nightmare for crime scene techs anyway, they could have sifted through it all. Now they had nothing.

Because of me.

I shook my head. Ridiculous. Sure, the forensic evidence would have helped but the cops could still dredge up other leads. A horde of officers were probably canvassing the area, looking for witnesses. They would find somebody who saw something.

Except folks in Hogtown didn't have a great reputation for cooperating with the police. And I hadn't seen anyone around the field.

My forehead thudded against the door. What choice did I have? I walked back to the chair and, with a sigh, dropped into it and waited.

Sexton reentered, dabbing at his mouth with a white handkerchief. The VOC agent glared at me.

I shrugged. "You asked."

Sexton laughed, a harsh bark. "So I did. Now, let's talk about Lux. When did you first meet her?"

"After I was cast in the show," I said.

"Never before that?"

I shook my head. "I'd never had the pleasure."

"You're both locals though, right? Both from New Chayton?"

"That's what I understand."

"So did the two of you hang out a lot on set?"

"Not until this past week. The producers want to keep us at each other's throats." Oh, shoot. Poor choice of words.

Sexton's eyebrows arched. "Really? In what way?"

My mind scrambled through possible answers. "They . . . Well, they're always reminding us there's only one license, you know? There's no prize for second place."

"You've wanted a license for while, right?"

"Who hasn't?"

"Badly?"

"Enough to join a reality TV show and humiliate myself."

Sexton's eyes narrowed with a predatory glint. "Enough to kill?"

My head snapped back as if punched. "Absolutely not! Lux was my—" What? Potential romantic interest? Fellow reality show contestant? Frenemy? "—friend."

"How about everyone else on the show? Everyone else so friendly with Lux?"

"Am I supposed to be able to read everyone else's mind? I'm not telepathic."

Sexton opened the file and produced a pen. He clicked it open and flashed his teeth. A starving wolf would have been friendlier. "Too bad. That would've made this a whole lot faster."

When I stumbled out of the precinct, the sun had risen considerably. I glanced at my watch. 10:30. Not good. Mom would notice my absence, especially since I'd missed church. And now I had to retrieve my civvies on foot. Not good.

People stared and a few passing cars honked as they zipped by. If only I had been able to retrieve my civvies and change. Best to ignore them. I had to get home. The faster, the better.

"Hey, Failstate. Got a minute?"

I whirled around. Two brutes in black suits stood by a sleek red sports car. Mirrored sunglasses obscured their eyes. The one on the left had blond hair trimmed into an almost military cut. A thick mustache perched over his mouth. The other was shaved bald, and the sunlight glinted off his burnished skin.

"Do I know you?"

"No, but our boss wants to get to know you better. So you'd better come with us."

I looked between them. The speaker crossed his arms over his chest, twisting his face into a sneer. The other opened the back door to the car and motioned for me to get in.

"Forget it," I said. "And the '70s called. They want their facial hair back."

"Cute," Blond Brute said. "But we insist."

Both drew guns. I rolled to the right, lashing out with my power to destroy their weapons.

I missed.

Brightly colored darts landed on my chest. A feeling like lead dribbled down my arms and legs. I took a faltering step forward, only to pitch to the sidewalk, diving into darkness before my face hit the pavement.

CHAPTER
7

A STING ON MY CHEEK WOKE ME.

Blond Brute towered over me. He scowled. "'Bout time you woke up." The man's voice rumbled like an avalanche. "The boss wants to talk to you."

Where was I? Looked like a lavish living room. The walls were covered with dark wood. A rich burgundy carpet lined the floor. Arched windows allowed sunlight to pour over some of the nicest furniture I had ever seen: at least a half-dozen plush chairs around an ornate coffee table, a matching couch set in front of a fireplace made of grey stone. Hanging over that was a large painting of a wooden sailing ship cresting a wave in a stormy sea. Dozens of mounted animal heads stared down at me with glassy eyes. Lots of exotic critters, very few that I could actually name.

"Yeah, the boss likes his trophies." The goon leaned in close, so near that the heat of his breath seeped through my mask's fabric. "You cooperate with him or I'll add your head up there, *capiche?*"

A clichéd threat, but cold sweat erupted along my brow anyhow. The goon crooked a finger at me and led me through massive wooden doors into a hall.

He led me through a hallway filled with black and white pictures of unsmiling people. Then we entered a study. Large bookshelves, packed with leather-bound books, small statues, and other decorations lined the walls on either side of me and reached toward the vaulted ceiling. Two large easy chairs were pushed into one corner, next to a black iron lamp with a colorful glass shade. A crystal chandelier hung overhead.

At the opposite end of the room stood a massive wooden desk, its top bare save for a solitary pen in dead center, a complex phone with dozens of buttons, and a blue crystal under a glass dome. A high-backed leather chair faced a large window, like a cathedral window but without the stained glass. It overlooked a large tree and an expansive backyard. The morning looked like it would be a hot one. A man sat behind the desk, but he was turned away and looking out the window.

The goon cleared his throat. "Failstate, as ordered, sir."

The chair swiveled around, and out from behind the desk stalked Alexander Magnus.

I gasped in spite of myself. I never thought I'd be this close to Magnus, even though *America's Next Superhero* was produced by his company. When I had seen him on TV or in magazines, he'd appeared god-like. In person, Magnus wasn't nearly so impressive. Sure, he stood a head taller than me, but the lines and creases in his face pulled his features into a perpetual scowl, made all the more severe by the greying widow's peak that pointed to dark eyes. Magnus's charcoal suit hung like a rumpled curtain as he scuffled around the desk, leaning heavily on a black cane topped with a snarling gargoyle's head.

Magnus stopped mere inches from me and his gaze roamed over my mask, down my costume. "Hard to remember why we cast you. Had I known the fuss you'd cause, I would have ordered Helen to axe you in auditions."

So much for my hero worship. I opened my mouth to protest, but Magnus held a hand in my face.

"Not a word until I ask you a question." He hobbled toward the window. "So did my boys rough you up too badly? I told them to go easy, but they said you resisted."

Was that an invitation to speak? Might as well risk it. "If they would have said you sent them, I'd have come."

Magnus laughed. "Uh-huh." He looked over his shoulder, his lips twitching into a snarl. "So why'd you do it? Jealousy? Thought she'd get the license instead of you?"

"I didn't!"

"Oldest story in the world, Failstate. You a student of American history? The Battle of Gettysburg ring a bell? The Galena Tanner finally confronts the Rebel Yell and the two tear it up for three days. Wrecked the town, killed thousands of their own troops before it was all over. It's happened dozens of times between heroes since then too. One's more powerful than the other or is more popular or more successful, and before you know it, one of them winds up hurt . . . or worse."

Instead of Lux, an image of Gauntlet preening for the audience flashed before my mind. I shook my head to clear it. "It's not like that at all."

"Really?" Magnus's eyes narrowed. "I think you're holding something back. That's why I sent out a few of my boys to pick you up. We're going to get to the bottom of this right now."

"Mr. Magnus, I'm sorry about what happened. I know Lux was a big draw for the show."

Magnus's head snapped around and he stared at me. Then he burst out laughing. He doubled over and staggered to his chair. Tears formed rivers through his wrinkles. But then he stopped, fire replacing any mirth in his eyes. "Nice try. Let's review, shall we?" He fiddled with something under his desk and the lights in the study dimmed.

A hologram flared to life in the middle of the room, pale green lines from the chandelier tracing out the vacant lot in Hogtown. The position of Lux's body was marked, as were details of how I had destroyed everything.

My stomach lurched. "How did you get this information?"

Magnus smirked. "Folks on the inside will tell you just about anything you want to know if you have the right contacts. For example, I have some preliminary reports from the coroner's office. Want to see what's there?"

He adjusted the controls again, and the hologram zoomed in on Lux's body. I closed my eyes. I did not want to see any gory details. But when I looked, I realized the hologram wasn't an image of Lux. Instead, a wireframe image of a young woman hovered in the air, lines tracing paths through her body.

"The medical examiner found fifteen different entry wounds. Two-thirds were through-and-throughs. But they can't find any projectiles. None. Which leads me to two possible conclusions. Either the killer used an energy weapon or . . . someone's power dissolved the ammo." Magnus steepled his hands. "So tell me, Failstate, how lethal are your powers again?"

"I can destroy organic material, but it takes a while. There's no way I could do it with that precision."

"But you could have destroyed the projectiles that killed her, yes?" Magnus's voice was little more than a whisper.

His question slammed into my gut. "Yes."

"So at the very least, you've muddled the investigation. At the worst, you're covering up a crime by destroying incriminating evidence. Way to go, rookie. I'd say you owe somebody an explanation."

"If you've got the cops' report, you already know everything I do."

Magnus snorted. "You'll forgive me if I don't take your word for it."

I took a step closer to the desk. "So now what?"

"Leave it to my team."

One of the bookcases pitched forward, swinging on a hinge. A false door? What lay back there?

The familiar pock-pock of Helen Kirkwood's footsteps echoed from the hidden hallway and, sure enough, Magnus's assistant emerged. She glared at me as she crossed behind the desk. Figured she would be here.

But then a person wearing a blue and red costume followed her into the room. My heart dropped into my stomach.

"Veritas?"

CHAPTER 8

VERITAS SHUFFLED IN after Helen, his head bowed. He appeared almost crushed, as if by a great weight. I could only imagine what he was feeling, having just lost his partner. But why would he be here? Had he been abducted as well?

"I believe you know everyone." Magnus's gaze never strayed from me. "So let's get down to brass tacks. Failstate, you're withholding information. I want it. Veritas will make sure you give it to me."

Veritas flinched and leaned closer to the billionaire. He tried to whisper, but I heard what he said. "I'm not comfortable with—"

Magnus held up a hand, almost hitting Veritas in the face. "As I was saying," Magnus spoke through gritted teeth. "Veritas will find the truth. I suggest you don't resist."

Veritas's shoulders slumped. He plodded to me and finally met my gaze. "I'm sorry. Relax, and we'll get this over quickly."

I tried to step away but bumped into something. Beefy hands clamped on my shoulders.

"Hold still." Blond Brute tightened his grip.

Veritas pressed his fingers against my temples. A faint tickle danced across my skin and into my hair, its cadence synching with my heart. Feathers drifted through my mind.

"What are you—" My words were little more than a gasp. Then the bottom fell out of my mind.

I free-fell through a frigid void. I tried to hold it together. I even tried to help. Maybe by using his power, Veritas would be able to uncover whatever I was missing about that night in the lot. Dark shapes flashed past, too quick to fully discern. The vacant lot, Lux's body, the route I took from where I hid my civvies to . . .

The hiding place! Was Veritas trying to dredge up my secret identity? I tried to focus on something else, anything. I pictured the obstacle course. The silhouetted bad guys Lux incapacitated, the way she and Veritas had cracked the security code, Blowhard . . .

Light exploded around me. The memories I had conjured spun off into the darkness, only to be replaced by images of Hogtown alleys, leading back to the dumpster I had used to stash my backpack.

Veritas was getting too close. Try to dovetail again, lead him down a false path? No, that didn't seem to work. A distraction then. Something to break Veritas's concentration.

I tipped my head back and looked at the chandelier. I stretched out, marshaling my destructive energy. I couldn't touch the crystal itself—Blond Brute might notice. No, shunt the power around, gather it next to the cable, and thrust . . .

The chandelier smashed to the floor in front of Magnus's desk. Veritas jumped and broke contact. I shoved him away. His arms pinwheeled and he fell into the broken remnants.

No time to make sure he was okay. I whirled and formed an intense field between Blond Brute and myself. Sure enough, the goon had drawn his gun and fired. The darts shredded before they could touch me.

I leapt onto the desk and looked out the window. How high up were we? Didn't matter, had to get out. There was a tree outside the window. I could probably leap that far and catch a branch.

I slammed onto the desk. My breath exploded from my lungs. Helen slammed her forearm into my throat, holding me down.

Had she swept my feet out from under me? I shoved at her arm, trying to free myself, but I couldn't get her to budge. She certainly didn't look this strong.

"Wait!" Veritas emerged from the chandelier's wreckage. He brushed off some of the debris and took a wobbly step toward the desk. "He's clean. He doesn't know anything else."

"You're sure?" Magnus asked.

"Positive. Let him go."

Magnus's glower gave way to what I could only call relief. Magnus collapsed into his chair. "Get him out of here."

Helen stepped back. Blond Brute snagged my arm and dragged me off the desk. Something pricked my back and hot lead coursed through my limbs.

"Not agai . . ." I murmured before darkness swamped me.

• • •

I woke up in the alley across from the vacant lot. The sun was dipping toward the horizon. I shook off the lingering cobwebs and jogged to where I had hidden my civvies. I pulled the pack from its hiding spot and pawed through the contents. All there.

A minute later, I emerged from the alley, necklace in place, and ran for the bus station. I didn't look forward to explaining my absence to Mom. Or Ben.

I ran through the door at 9:00 that night, braced for a hurricane of wrath with my mom as the center. "Hello?"

No answer. I frowned. Light from the TV in the living room flickered across the hall's wall. I followed the noise of canned studio laughter into the living room, where Mom sat in the overstuffed easy chair. A bag of chips was open on the floor next to her.

"About time you came down from your room." She didn't look away from the TV. "I was about to send Ben in after you."

My room? I stared at her, my mouth swinging open.

She turned in the chair to glare at me. "You going to take out the garbage like I asked you to or not?"

I looked through the living room door into the kitchen. Sure enough, a garbage bag stuffed full leaned against the back door, ready to go out. Numbly, I stumbled for the kitchen and picked up the bag.

Before I opened the back door, I turned back toward the living room. "Mom?"

"What?" Her voice was sharp enough to cut me.

I winced. "Never mind."

CHAPTER 9

SOMEONE POUNDED ON my bedroom door. I shuffled over and popped it open.

Mom glared at me. "Get out to the van, Robin. I'm not going to tell you again."

I tried to put on my best "sick" face. I couldn't remember the last time I had actually been sick, so I mostly had to imitate how Ben acted the last time he was sick. I offered a few coughs and sniffled loudly.

It was low, and I knew it, but after the weekend, the last thing I wanted to do was go to school. A day to lie low, gather my thoughts, and regroup—that's what I needed.

Mom cocked her head to one side and glared at me. She stuck her hand on my forehead. "You're not even close to being warm. Nice try. Get your bag and go to the van."

I had no other choice, then. I collected my backpack and headed out of the house and climbed into the minivan. Ben was already waiting for us. He munched on a toaster pastry. He smirked at me as I slid into the back seat.

We rode in silence to Lincoln High School. As we pulled up to the curb, my gaze roamed over the sprawling red and white brick building. Our classmates streamed up the steps and into the building, greeting each other with hugs and high fives.

Ben popped open the door. Before he slid out of the van, he leaned over and kissed Mom on the cheek. "See you later, Mom. Have a good day at work." He bounded up the stairs and bellowed greetings to his friends.

I frowned. No one was waiting for me, I just knew it. Three months alone.

"You going or not?"

Mom actually spoke to me?

"Uh, yeah." I scooped up my backpack. "See you later, Mom, okay?"

She didn't even look in my direction. I barely got the door shut before Mom gunned the engine and swerved back onto the street, almost like she couldn't wait to put as much distance as possible between her and me..

I faced the building. Might as well get it over with.

The flow of students streamed up the steps and through the doors and I fell in with them, just another anonymous drone. Lincoln's hallway walls were a dull puke green bordered in white, with large black-and-white photos of past students in class and sports.

I wound through the halls and into the auditorium for the assembly that marked the first day of the semester. The walls had been painted a deep blue, with a rich red curtain closing off most of the stage. A large podium stood in the center. I found a seat off to one side, closer to the front than I liked but it guaranteed me some privacy. As I sank into the plush cushion, I glanced around the auditorium and nodded to a few of my acquaintances. I stifled a pang of loneliness.

And then Ben made his entrance. His friends announced their presence with boisterous laughter. Ben bestowed his most dazzling smiles on some of the freshmen girls before the entire pack settled in the center of the auditorium. He even kicked his feet up on the seat in front of him and threaded his fingers behind his head. He glanced in my direction and his brazen smile grew slightly. I turned away. He was a ham in costume and out.

Within moments, Principal Steven Beckmann ambled on stage, waving and smiling like a movie star on a late night talk show. Some students clapped politely. A few added mocking cheers. Beckmann didn't seem to care.

"Good morning, ladies and gentlemen! It is wonderful to see you all with us again. I want all of us to consider this next semester a clean slate, a new start for all of us."

I rolled my eyes. He had the same speech every semester. I knew what would come next: encouraging us to academic excellence, peaceful co-existence, and general perfection, all achievable with the right attitude.

I tuned him out. Instead, I pulled my new schedule from my backpack. Another course in geometry. Great. I dreaded the impending nightmares of angles, rhombi, and parallelograms. English Lit. U.S. history. Spanish III. Chemistry. Plus a study hall first period.

Someone dropped into the chair next to me. A Japanese kid, newcomer by the looks of him. He wore a black t-shirt with red symbols and the image of a wide-eyed cartoon girl with an impossibly large smile. Baggy jeans spilled down his legs to his beat-up shoes. "Don't even know why I bothered coming," he said. "The aliens are going to get me pretty soon."

I worked my jaw for a moment, trying to think of the right response to that. "I'm sorry?"

"Don't be, it's not your fault." The kid stuck out his hand. "Name's Haruki. How about you?"

"Rob. You're new here?" Obviously. I think an alien abductee would stand out, even at Lincoln High.

"Just moved here from Canada. My family had been living with my aunt but she kicked my folks out." Haruki shook his head. "Stupid aliens must have gotten to her too."

Might as well risk it. "Aliens? As in little green men?"

"I can't speak to their size, coloration, or gender, but you've got the right idea. They've been hounding me for the past two years or so, causing me all sorts of problems."

Thankfully, Beckmann wrapped up his remarks and dismissed the students. I grabbed my stuff. "Sorry to hear about that. Good luck with the new semester."

Haruki smiled, a hint of sadness in his eyes. "Hope I make it all the way through."

I escaped up the aisle and headed for the study hall room, a large classroom with fifty desk chairs in crooked rows beneath buzzing fluorescent lights. One wall was nothing but whiteboards, grimy with echoes of previous words and drawings all over it. The back wall was covered with a yellow case, filled with random books and papers. I found a chair in my favorite sort of spot, one with a good view out the window, and took my place. More students filtered in, and then the bell rang. Mr. Yvers, the study hall monitor, glared at us but then settled in at his desk, reading a paperback novel.

Within ten minutes, I couldn't sit still. My legs bounced, drumming out a random rhythm. I tried to find something to distract myself, a book or something, but my mind kept drifting back to the field.

Lux. I frowned. What was happening with her body now? Had her family been notified? That could be tricky. Would her true identity be released to the press? That happened sometimes. Had the VOC found any leads? Worst of all, her voice kept echoing in my mind.

Tell Ver . . . magma . . .

What had that even meant? Tell Veritas something, but what? I dug out a notebook and flipped to an empty page. I wrote the word "MAGMA" across the top.

Well, she hadn't been burned, so probably not real magma. Were there any villains who called themselves that?

Or maybe I misunderstood her. I had been badly freaked out, on the edge of panic. So what else could she have been saying?

Magnus? As in Alexander Magnus? Maybe, but what would his motive be?

A thought occurred to me. I wrote "Magnum." Kid Magnum? His arsenal surely included a weapon or two that could have caused her wounds. He and Lux had argued at the show taping. Maybe Kid Magnum had overheard where she was going and ambushed her in the vacant lot. Maybe they exchanged words, things got out of hand, and before Kid Magnum knew what had happened . . .

I sat back in my chair with a grunt. A lead? Maybe. I'd have to pursue it later.

The loudspeaker crackled for a moment. "Would Robin Laughlin please report to the office?"

A few students snickered. I blushed and darted from the room. How many times had I told the office not to use my full name? I'd have to remind them again. Or I could just destroy the P.A. system. That would show 'em.

I stepped into the office, a brightly lit room with a whole forest's worth of plants pressed up against one wall. A counter divided the room in half, with offices opening into the space behind it. Mrs. Bennett, the school secretary, beamed at me from her desk behind the counter as I entered. "How was your break? Do anything fun?"

I almost laughed. "Not really, no."

"That's too bad. Look, I was hoping you could do me a favor. I was hoping you could act as tour guide for a new student."

I forced myself to smile. It had to be Haruki. Now I'd spend the rest of first period leading him around the school, listening to weird stories about aliens. I turned to see where Mrs. Bennett was pointing.

A girl with raven hair rose from the chair, dimples popping in her cheeks.

My heart threatened to leap up my throat and throttle my brain.

It was the girl from the show taping!

"Thanks for doing this." She took my hand. "Elizabeth Booth."

A charge shot up my arm and set my heart racing. I sputtered for a moment. I should say something witty. I opened my mouth. "Why me?"

That wasn't it. Elizabeth's eyes lit up with silent laughter. I could have kicked myself. Smooth. Really smooth.

I turned to Mrs. Bennett. "I mean, don't you usually take the new students on the tour?"

"Yes. I usually do." Mrs. Bennet's voice had taken on a sing-songy tone. Her eyes sparkled. "But today, I just thought maybe you might like to do it."

Oh, great. She must be thinking of a set up. She did that sort of thing. Most turned out to be abysmal failures, like the time she'd tried to get the head cheerleader to go out with the winner of the school's Grammar Rodeo. Utter disaster.

I glanced at Elizabeth. Then again, maybe this wouldn't be such a bad idea after all.

CHAPTER 10

SHE COULDN'T BE REAL. A hallucination caused by aftereffects of when Veritas had been rummaging around in my brain? Some sort of practical joke? As corny as it sounded, I considered pinching myself. Elizabeth dipped her head and smiling as we walked.

"First stop, your locker." I winced at how loud my voice was. Dial it back, Laughlin. "Which is . . . ?"

"523."

As we headed for her locker, I did the math. That number meant she was a junior, like me. We might even have some classes together. Her locker was nowhere near mine though. Stupid alphabetical order! I wondered how much it would cost to legally change my name . . .

"So you're new to town?" I asked.

She nodded. "Just moved here last week."

I pointed out the sports trophy case, crammed with dusty relics of past glory. "Where are you from?"

Should I take her down by the cafeteria? Maybe. I could already smell the pizza wafting down the hall. No, I didn't want her distracted.

She smiled and twirled her hair around one finger. "Lots of different places. My parents moved around a lot before . . ." Sadness crept into her voice, so much I could feel it coil around my own heart. "Well, *before*—"

I nodded and led her down the hall to her locker.

She fumbled with the combination and put her backpack inside. Then she unzipped her jacket and revealed an *America's Next Superhero* t-shirt.

I blinked and a smile jumped to my lips. I shouldn't have been surprised, since she had been at the taping.

Elizabeth glanced at me and her smile grew broader. She glanced down at her shirt. "Are you a fan too?"

I stuttered for a moment. "Um . . . Not really. You know, I just watch it when I'm flipping channels. That sort of thing."

"Uh, huh. Sure." Her eyes sparkled. "So who's your favorite?"

My mouth went dry. Just a week ago, I would have said Lux. But after what happened, I knew I couldn't trust myself to say her name. Besides, her death hadn't been announced yet, so I couldn't reveal I had insider knowledge. Instead, I said the first thing that popped into my mind.

"T-Ram."

Her jaw dropped, and she burst out laughing. "Are you kidding me?"

"Yeah, sure. Why not? He's got a certain . . . indefinable greatness I just like."

"You mean he's got an uncrackable skull he uses in every situation. Like the time he rammed a tree to get a kitten out of it?"

My cheeks flushed. I had forgotten about that.

She snickered and hung her jacket in the locker.

"So who's your favorite?" I regretted the question as soon as I asked it. Stupid, self-serving. But I had to know.

She tipped her head. "Well, I think Gauntlet is cute. Something about his eyes . . . I sound really silly, don't I?"

I shook my head even though I was screaming in my mind. "Not at all. I can see why people might like him."

"Yeah, but that's really shallow, right? I'll tell you who I'm rooting for, though." She leaned in close. "Failstate."

No way.

I somehow kept my expression neutral. At least, I think I did. "Really?"

She nodded. "Yeah, I know. Something about him really resonates with me, you know? Like this past Friday, I was at the show's taping, and in the middle of running this obstacle course, Failstate ran off to help someone he thought was trapped even though it meant his team lost."

"You don't say."

"Now you're teasing me. So you don't like him because he's a cognit, is that it? I've never thought it's fair the way people use that word as an insult. I mean, it's what they are, not a—"

"No! It's just . . . I've always liked the licensed heroes better than the wannabes, you know?"

"Okay then." She crossed her arms. "Who's your favorite *licensed* hero?"

"Etzal'el, obviously. I mean, the guy just exudes cool."

69

She shuddered. "Creeps me out, truth be told. So dark."

"Yeah, I know." Hopefully she didn't think I was completely stupid. "And then there's Meridian. I love him. Really awesome."

At the mention of his name, shutters slammed down behind her eyes. Her face froze in an inscrutable mask but I got the feeling I had committed some taboo.

The cold look thawed almost instantly, replaced by a dazzling smile. "Let's keep going with the tour." She closed her locker door.

I practically vibrated as I led her down the hall, pointing out where most of the classrooms were, the stairs that led to the auto shop classes, the performing arts wing, the media arts center.

"So what's down here?" She pointed down the hall that led to the gym. Before I could answer, she was off.

I wracked my brain for something else to talk about. But my thoughts refused to organize themselves in a coherent way.

Then she entered the weight room, and I couldn't help but groan. The last place I wanted to take her.

The odor of old sweat slapped me as I stepped through the door. The weight room wasn't very large, with a wall of mirrors on one side trying to make it look larger. Three treadmills faced the mirrors, with a rack of free weights against another wall. But Elizabeth stood with a crowd in the center of the room. They were watching something, or someone. Oh, please no.

Sure enough, it was Ben. His cronies were shouting encouragement as he lifted a loaded bar over his head, held it for the cheers, and then slammed it back into place. He sat up and accepted the high fives and accolades from his sheep.

Then he saw me. "You lost, Robin? Or did you come down to humiliate yourself?"

Elizabeth glanced at me and mouthed my name, laughter shining in her eyes.

I wanted to escape. Leave the weight room and head back to study hall. Maybe go through with that name change idea and just leave town entirely. But I had promised Mrs. Bennett, and I definitely didn't want to abandon Elizabeth to Ben and his friends.

Ben's smile broadened into a brilliant flash of teeth. "And who do we have here?" He strutted up to her, swaying his body to flaunt his well-toned biceps. "I'm Ben Laughlin, Robin's brother. You're new here?"

"Yes, I—"

"I knew it. Beauty like yours is a rare commodity. I would have noticed you before now."

Elizabeth gaped at him, and my stomach curdled. Hopefully she wasn't lactose intolerant, given the sheer amount of cheese Ben was spewing.

"Well, that's very kind of you." Elizabeth's smile matched Ben's in sheer intensity, and her cheeks flushed ever so slightly.

Wait, she was actually falling for Ben's smarmy behavior?

"Allow me to introduce you to my colleagues." Ben's hand rested lightly at the small of her back as he steered her away from me.

Elizabeth didn't seem to mind. I felt as if I were shrinking, growing smaller and smaller in the doorway.

Ben's friends swarmed around Elizabeth, creating a living wall between her and me. I wanted to be angry, but the irritation died. She was laughing, enjoying herself. And really, that was for the best. Ben would be better company than me anyway.

He hadn't gone through what I had. She'd fit in better with his little mutual admiration society. Besides, the bell would ring soon and I'd have to move on to my next class. Ben would take over, and Elizabeth probably wouldn't mind at all. Probably wouldn't even remember the other guy who had been with her earlier.

The rest of the day whizzed by. At one point, I caught my reflection in a window and my hand involuntarily touched my necklace. I knew I should be grateful for the bead's ability to change my appearance. But if it was going to change me, why couldn't it make me look . . . less average?

I trudged to my locker to gather my things. When I opened the door, a folded piece of paper tumbled out. Frowning, I bent to retrieve it. A note, written in flowing script:

Sorry we couldn't finish the tour. I'll make it up to you.

I stared at the words for a few moments. Then a smile tugged at my lips. I refolded the note and tucked it into my pocket.

Then Ben jogged past me, landing a well-aimed blow to my arm. He paused for a moment and frowned at me. "What are you smiling about?"

Should I tell him? No, best to savor the small victory. "Nothing at all."

CHAPTER
11

I SHOULD HAVE GONE HOME. But instead, I caught the bus to the Hawkeye Mall to go costume shopping. My outburst in the field had done too much damage to my old one. Maybe I'd cobble together something nicer. It was pitiful: an alleged superhero who wore sweats and a Halloween mask? In that getup I looked like I was going to perpetrate the crimes rather than stop them.

I breezed through the glass doors and walked into the food court. Geometric skylights dotted the roof which allowed shafts of light to dance over the clusters of tables and chairs. The various restaurants bordered the central dining area in a loose arc. A large arch led to the stores beyond. The odors of different foods blended together and sent a rumble through my stomach. A few dozen people were seated at tables scattered throughout the food court, their conversation blending together into a low buzz.

I skirted around the edge of the tables and followed a white line set in the green tiles. Mr. Johnson, the owner of Krakatoa, the mall's only coffeehouse, waved to me and turned back to a customer.

Dropping into the human traffic that flowed out of the food court and into the shops felt like dipping into a warm bath. I could get lost in the anonymous flow past the multi-colored and bright stores. I ambled along, studying the usual collection of older walkers, gaggles of giggling girls fresh from school, and families pushing strollers with kids in the middle of tantrums. And nobody looked my way at all.

"Hey, you!"

I froze. No way. I turned and was blinded by Elizabeth's smile.

She rushed to my side. "What are you doing here?"

What could I say? Going shopping to replace my worn-out superhero costume at the second-hand store? Yeah, that would go over well.

"Window shopping." I motioned toward one of the stores, a jewelry boutique.

"Do you come here often?"

I shrugged. "I suppose."

"Great!" She shoved a stack of papers into my hands. "Which of these is the best?"

"What?" I shuffled through the ream. Job applications from just about every store in the mall. I had no idea which one to choose for her. Did she just want a discount to go shopping? "You're not wasting any time getting plugged in, are you?"

She nodded. "My mom. She insists I need to be more responsible and earn my own spending money. Parents, right?"

My smile froze in place. That was a topic I didn't want to broach. Not yet anyway. "Yeah. Absolutely." I handed the applications back to her. "Look, forget this stuff. Just follow me. I know where you want to work."

I led her back to Krakatoa. Mr. Johnson had decked out the interior with a lot of Tiki decorations. The tables were made of bamboo, the chairs all wicker. I don't know if his coffee had anything to do with the actual island of Krakatoa, but there was no denying that Mr. Johnson had the best coffee in South Bend, our little corner of New Chayton. The coffee house was always packed. A large plastic volcano stood behind the counter, the different flavors and prices written in neon colors on the side, almost as if they were lava running down the side.

Mr. Johnson waved at me, his face bright. "Rob! Your usual?"

"Absolutely." I set my money on the counter. "And a job application."

"What?" Mr. Johnson turned to one of the baristas. "A caldera East of Java, extra foam, dash of cinnamon." He grinned at me. "You're finally caving in? Going to work for me?"

"Not yet," I said. "It's actually for my friend, Elizabeth."

"Ah, a potential pretty barista, huh?" He turned a critical eye to her. "Ever work in a coffee shop before?"

She shook her head.

"Ever want to?"

She bit her lower lip. "Honestly? No. I mean, I'd never thought about it until . . ."

Mr. Johnson laughed, a hearty guffaw. "Well, let's sit down and go over the application. Rob," he said, passing me a steaming Styrofoam cup so big I could barely wrap my hands around it, "see you later."

I considered waiting to see how things went, but I knew Mr. Johnson would talk Elizabeth's ear off and get her to sample every flavor. She could wind up in Krakatoa all afternoon. Best to get my shopping done while she was tied up.

"I'll be back, Elizabeth."

She smiled and waved, looking a little nervous as Mr. Johnson led her to an empty table.

I slipped out of the coffee house and wound through the mall, heading straight for the thrift store.

The Turnaround wasn't crowded, and I knew my way around it. I found what I needed toward the back: two darker sweatshirts, a pair of black khakis, a new pair of work boots. One bin held a dark glove I could pull halfway up my arm. It fit perfectly, but its match was missing. I left it behind and paid for my purchases.

Next stop, a nearby electronics store. I pulled the last bit of cash out of my wallet and paid for a new disposable phone. I eyed some of the other electronics lining the wall. Sound amplifiers, a night vision scope. I could spend a small fortune here. But knowing my luck, I'd wind up breaking all of it before the week was out.

A glance at my watch propelled me back to Krakatoa. Sure enough, half a dozen cups littered the table in front of Elizabeth. She glanced in my direction and waved. I waved back. But it didn't appear that Mr. Johnson was anywhere close to being done. As much as I wanted to stay, I couldn't. I had to wrap things up and get home before dinner hit the table or I'd rouse the sniper for sure.

I waved again and headed home.

• • •

Our kitchen wasn't much to look at. Old counters with dull cabinets that were pulling away from the wall. A small wooden table was pushed into one corner, piled high with bills and books and other debris. Mom and I sat at the center island on stools that were on the verge of collapse. I glanced up from my tuna casserole at Mom. She didn't meet my gaze. She remained focused on her meal.

"So how was work today?"

She mumbled something. It might have included the word "Fine," but I couldn't tell for sure. I shoved noodles around the plate, not really wanting to eat them but not sure what else to do.

At one point, she took a deep breath and looked up at me. She appeared to be on the verge of speaking.

I leaned forward, trying to keep anticipation from my face.

Then her mouth snapped shut. She frowned and then nibbled at her Texas toast.

I studied my own barely eaten meal for a few moments. "Mom . . . when you were my age, did you ever lose someone . . . close to you? A friend?"

Her gaze darted up to meet mine. Heat flashed down my spine. Stupid question. Maybe asking her about this wasn't a good idea.

"When I was about your age, I had a friend named Naomi." Mom squinted at the far wall, as if the story had been printed there. "Naomi Harrison. When we were sophomores, she came to school and we could tell something was wrong. At lunch, she told us she had just come from the doctors and the news wasn't good. Leukemia. Her doctor had missed the early warning signs and so Naomi didn't have long. Just a few months."

77

"Were you two close?"

Mom smiled, tears misting her eyes. "Kind of. She'd been my best friend in middle school, but we'd drifted apart. But she was still my friend." She frowned, picking up her toast and then setting it down again. "Why are you asking about this?"

I gritted my teeth. Technically, Mom didn't know what Ben or I did. I think she suspected. It'd be hard not to put the pieces together. But she never asked and I never told.

"There's this girl I know and . . . well, she died this past weekend. In an accident. And I guess . . . well, I'm wondering . . . Do you ever get over it?"

Mom's gaze dropped to the table and she whispered, "No."

And I knew she wasn't talking about Naomi anymore.

Thankfully Ben chose that moment to come home. He breezed into the room but stopped in the door. "Is everything okay in here?"

Mom swiped away her tears and beamed at him. "We're fine. Good day at school, sweetie?" She stood and got a plate, dishing up some food for Ben.

"Not too bad," he said. "First day of the semester, you know. Not much going on. I did meet a pretty neat girl, though."

That last comment was directed at me. I shoved a bite of casserole into my mouth, forcing myself to chew both it and the retort I wanted to make.

"She's new. Really smart, really nice. I think she said she lived near here."

"That's great, Ben." Mom set the plate in front of him.

And so it went. With Ben home, all attention gravitated to him. I disappeared from Mom's radar completely. They continued to chat about Elizabeth, then moved on to Ben's class schedule and how his shift at the local library went. After another fifteen minutes, I excused myself, depositing my plate in the sink.

I sequestered myself in my room, fishing a copy of *Brave New World* from my school backpack. I plopped down on the bed and started reading, not bothering to get out Mr. Gordon's reading guide. I had plenty of time to see what the book said on its own before I started looking for what Harrison wanted me to get out of it.

I had gotten thirty pages in when someone knocked at my door. I sat up. Could it be Mom?

"Yeah?"

The door opened, and Ben slipped inside. "You check with the studio yet?" He didn't wait for me to answer. "We're supposed to head in Wednesday night for a special taping. Confessionals about what happened to . . . well, you know."

I set my jaw. They were going to include what happened to Lux in the show? It'd probably really boost the ratings. Classy. Real classy.

Ben kicked at a small pile of clothes creeping out of my closet. "Look, I don't know where you've been, but are you okay? What happened on Saturday? Were you there?"

"Not really. I came up on the scene after . . . well, after. And I wound up answering a bunch of questions with the cops and the VOC."

Ben's eyes narrowed, and he scrutinized my face. I fought to keep my expression neutral.

"Well, whatever, I'm glad you're okay." He whacked one of my feet and turned to leave the room.

"Hey, Ben?"

He turned around.

I pointed to the edge of his sleeve. "Your costume is show-ing. You might want to be a little more careful, Gauntlet."

He smirked. "Always am, bro. Don't you worry." And with that, he was gone.

I collapsed back on my bed, breathing a sigh of relief.

You know, God, I never thought that things would ever be this messed up. Can't I catch a break for once?

But no answer was forthcoming. Like always.

I waited until I was sure Mom had gone to bed before I snuck out to the garage.

The musty aroma wafted over me as I slipped through the door. I didn't know what caused the distinct smell. It was the normal scent of gasoline mixed with a tang I couldn't identify. No other garage ever smelled quite like this. I didn't mind. It reminded me of Dad.

Uneven concrete crunched underfoot as I walked past the snow blower and lawnmower. I wrapped my arm around myself to ward off the chill. The wooden walls were thin, the frame of the lone window rotten. That didn't matter. This was where I came when I needed to be alone. In the back of the garage was a large table made of 2x4s and a chipped plywood board. I ran my hand over the workbench's gouged surface. Dad had built it himself. Faded paint worked patterns over the wood. I leaned heavily against it, bowing my head and closing my eyes, trying to recapture the feeling. Dad and me, hiding out here, testing my power, seeing what it could really do.

My face twisted at the sharp pang. *God, why did it have to happen? Why couldn't You stop it?*

I wiped tears from my eyes. Enough of this. I removed the necklace.

The spot behind my eyes began to pound. I winced as a pang jangled down my spine. Once I was sure the transformation was complete, I turned to a stack of papers on the bench.

Oldest order first. A woman from Las Vegas wanted me to carve a bust of her deceased husband. I looked over the requested dimensions and the provided photo. Nice enough looking guy. Difficult, but not impossible.

I pulled out an old orange crate filled with assorted rocks and bricks I had collected. I found a good candidate, a chunk of granite almost as big as my head. I studied the pictures again, envisioning the general shape of the head, taking into account his nose, his ears. Then I cupped my hands around the rock, channeling my power to eat away at the rock.

The first pass roughed out the general shape of a man's head and shoulders. I tightened my fingers, drawing them closer. A bead of sweat stung my eyes. The second pass brought out even more features, nobs for ears, the general shape of a nose.

I sat back and studied my efforts, then compared it to the photos. Not too bad. Channeling my power to the tip of my finger, I traced patterns over the rock's surface. Eyes emerged, followed by a recognizable nose. The ears were delicate work, but I got every curve just right. Within an hour, I had finished. Not a bad likeness.

I carefully set the bust aside and checked the invoice. Another hundred bucks. Not too shabby. Maybe I'd splurge and buy that surveillance equipment after all.

Next order, someone wanted a crystal poodle. I winced. I had a few pieces of quartz in my box, but working with crystal always worried me. Too many chances for the sculpture to shatter if I didn't do things just right.

I started to work, but for something like this, the garage was too quiet. I needed some sort of a distraction. Dad had put an old TV in the garage. I fumbled for the remote and flipped on a 24 hour news channel, setting the volume low, just enough for a background buzz.

Two passes and the quartz resembled a four-legged animal. I stroked away bits to bring out the finer details. Not too bad, if I said so my—

My picture flashed on the screen.

I froze, glancing at the TV. It was me, all right, in my costume. The shot switched back to the talking head, but the text running across the bottom of the screen said something about whether or not *America's Next Superhero* was a good idea. I turned up the sound just in time to hear a group of "experts" debate not just the show but the whole vigilante system. One of them, some sociology professor from out east, argued that the VOC, the masked heroes, all of it, was a big mistake and that we it should all be abolished.

"This business with Lux just proves it," the professor said. "How old was she? Sixteen, seventeen years old? The only thing she should have been worrying about was what party she'd be attending Friday night, not bleeding out in a vacant lot. And another teenage so-called 'hero' was somehow involved, that Failstate moron? Please. If they had left fighting crime to the actual police, this wouldn't have happened. And the licensed heroes are no better! This is why we need to get rid of them all. They're dangerous."

Oh, not good. Not only had I failed Lux, but now I had also failed the rest of the hero community.

Grim resolve flooded through me. I'd have to step up my game then. Fix this. With a certainty that surprised even myself, I suddenly knew what I had to do.

I would find who killed Lux and prove that we weren't dangerous.

CHAPTER 12

I LIGHTLY BANGED MY HEAD against the window of the van. Mom insisted I had to go to youth group. How was Ben allowed to go out and "study," as he put it, and I wasn't was beyond me. I glared at the squat brick building that housed Mount Calvary Christian Church.

At one time, it had been a school, and it still showed. Large glass windows of former classrooms looked out over a grassy lawn. A large box, the gym, rose on the left. A newer sanctuary, whose bricks were a little darker than the rest, was to my right. Someone had added a black metal scaffold with a cross to the roof.

This was the last place I wanted to be tonight. Not that I had a problem with the church or youth group or anything like that. But I should be investigating Lux's murder or preparing to question Kid Magnum.

I stumbled out of the van, and Mom gunned the engine and practically tore out of the parking lot. She didn't even touch her brakes as she left. Hopefully she'd remember to pick me up when the meeting ended.

A few of the youth group members waved at me as I approached the building, but they closed ranks, making it pretty clear I shouldn't join their conversations. No problem. I walked up the stairs to the gym.

The gym itself looked fairly ordinary, large enough for two basketball courts, a large stage cut into one wall. Large banners flanked the stage, the one on the right depicting Jesus on the cross. The other showed Jesus washing Peter's feet. A rough semi-circle of blue metal folding chairs had been set up at the edge of the stage. The praise band was tuning up their instruments, occasionally playing a lick or a riff or whatever it was called.

Most of the members of the youth group hung back on the other side of the gym, clustered in small knots.

Pastor Grant laughed with some of the other kids. Then he glanced in my direction and his face lit up. He charged up the aisle to meet me. He reminded me of T-Ram with his enthusiasm: head-first into anything. "Bob! We missed you on Sunday!" He cuffed my arm, the same spot Ben always hit.

"Sorry about that." I tried to hide the pain. And my annoyance that he couldn't remember to call me *Rob*. "I wish I could have been here."

Pastor Grant, or P.G., as he called himself, was in his mid-thirties, somewhat thick around the waist, with thinning brown hair and a poorly trimmed beard. He wore faded jeans and an unbuttoned shirt over a t-shirt with some cartoon character from the '80s on it. He radiated cheese. Still, youth group was always well attended with thirty or forty kids from different schools around New Chayton.

"Were you sick or something?"

"Something like that, yeah."

"Awesome!" Another slap to my arm. Uncanny aim. "Look, I've gotta get ready, but be sure not to miss this Sunday. We're going to start an in-depth study on the book of James, okay?"

"Sounds good."

And he was off, bellowing greetings to another new arrival. I looked around the gym to see if I could find anyone to sit with.

Standing by herself in a corner of the gym was Elizabeth.

She hugged herself around the waist, looking around with wide eyes. Nervous energy poured off her. She glanced at her phone and tucked a stray lock of hair behind her ear.

I moved before I was really aware of it. "Elizabeth?"

Her gaze met mine, and she smiled. She rushed to me and grabbed my hands. "Thank goodness! Someone I actually know!"

"What are you doing here?"

She laughed, a frantic giggle. "Ben invited me to come yesterday. He said he'd meet me here twenty minutes ago." Her smile faded. "He's not with you."

"No, he's not."

Her expression crumbled further. "And he didn't tell you I would be here?"

"Uh . . . no, he didn't."

Her head dipped and her cheeks reddened. She flipped open her phone and started a text. She mumbled something about needing a ride home.

For a moment, my hands spasmed into fists. How could Ben do this? He had run out of the house after dinner, allegedly for a study group. But I knew the truth. There'd be news reports about Gauntlet saving people from a fire or stopping a mugging. Sure, he'd do some good out there, but how could he do this to Elizabeth?

Then a thrill shot up my spine, exploding into my mind. I had her all to myself.

"Ben does this sometimes. Truth be told, he's kind of flaky. But I'm here. Why don't you stick around?"

Her hand hovered by her ear. Had she hit "send" yet? Didn't look like it.

"Please," I said, pointing at the folding chairs. "It'll be fun. I promise."

A booming guffaw ricocheted through the sanctuary. P.G. was practically doubled over with laughter, but given the expression on the faces of those around him, he was the one who had told the joke and the only one who found it funny.

"At least, I think it'll be fun. Only one way to find out, right?"

A smile teased the corners of her mouth. She clicked the phone shut. "Why not? Besides, I'd hate for Carson to make an extra trip."

I quirked a brow at her. "Who's that?"

Her lips twitched into a tight smile, and her gaze dropped. "My step-dad."

Touchy subject. Okay. "I see."

She smiled again, a brilliant flash of perfect teeth. My heart hammered against my ribs. Even the constant irritation from the necklace faded, if only for a moment. In fact, if I hadn't been wearing my necklace, I probably would have blown every light in the building.

"Hey, Rob! What are you doing here?"

I had heard that voice only once, but recognized it immediately. I closed my eyes. No way.

Sure enough, Haruki grinned at me. He glanced over my shoulder and his eyes widened. "Hey, who's the *bijin?*" He stepped around me and extended a hand. "Takahashi Haruki at your service."

"Elizabeth Booth at yours, good sir."

Haruki laughed. "I like you." He turned to me. "I like her. You have dibs?"

I froze. Elizabeth's eyes grew wide. Then Haruki burst out laughing. I quickly joined in. Soon so did Elizabeth.

We found an empty row of chairs about three-quarters of the way back. P.G. hopped up onto the stage and greeted everyone. I glanced around. After a few brief introductory remarks, P.G. waved for the band to start up.

I stifled a groan. This was the worst part of the night. Oh, the band was fine. Pretty good actually. But they led us through a fifteen-minute set of what I called "seven-eleven" songs. Sing seven words, and repeat the phrase eleven times. Repeat ad nauseum. For a moment, I wished we could sing songs like I had back when—

A sharp pang lanced through me. My skin burned. No, don't think of that. Not now.

Elizabeth glanced at me. "Are you okay?"

"Yeah, I'm fine." I joined in the singing with as much enthusiasm as I could muster.

Once the band finished, P.G. leapt from the stage to lead us across the gym to a community-building game. I came to a halt when I saw what was set up.

Ropes were strung between ladders, along with a row of sawhorses and tape on the floor. An obstacle course? A familiar twinge tugged at the back of my mind. It almost looked like . . .

"That's right, ladies and gentlemen, we're going to do an obstacle course tonight!" P.G. swept his hand over the room. "You know that *America's Next Superhero* is filmed in New Chayton. Well, you're all pretty heroic to me. So get into teams."

The other kids laughed and chuckled. A few of them started jockeying into potential teams. P.G. took control immediately, divvying everyone up.

I couldn't believe it. Now that I looked over the set-up, I recognized it. This had been a challenge from the show's third week. We had each been sent in to navigate through a course filled with snares and traps. Fastest time won immunity.

I had been the third person in. Typically, within two minutes, I had been dangling upside down from a foot snare. My power had flared, shorting out the lights. It had also eaten through the snare. I was about to drop, but Lux had barreled into the course to help me down.

That one thought of Lux sent my mind careening back to the vacant lot. I could smell the blood again, feel the dirt between my fingers . . .

My stomach lurched. I dashed for the nearest exit, down the hall, and then burst through the doors into the cool night air.

Who was I kidding? I was supposed to be a superhero, but a simple memory could defeat me? What would happen when it really mattered? I kicked at some stray rocks from the landscaping. With a groan, I collapsed onto the church stairs and massaged my scalp.

"Needed some air?" Elizabeth smiled down at me. Without waiting for me to invite her, she sat down and scooted close. "You okay?"

Deep breath, Rob. I nodded. "I think so."

"Want to talk about it?"

Laughter escaped through my clenched teeth. "I wish I could. It's private, you know?"

She studied my face. Oh boy. How was I going to explain this? Food poisoning from supper? An emergency late night study session? Maybe my religion prohibited obstacle courses? No, that was stupid, seeing as we were in my church.

"Okay." She sat beside me and patted my knee. "I just had to check up on my hero."

Her what?

"I mean, you did show me around school. You got me a job at Krakatoa. And you convinced me to stay tonight. The singing was pretty cool and P.G. seems really nice."

My head swam. I felt like I was spinning out of control, spiraling into her eyes. She was so close. A tremble wormed through my legs. I could put my arm around her. Would that be too forward?

"Hey, knock it off, you two!"

We jumped apart.

P.G. glared down at us. "Hey, Bob, you know we've got a no PDA rule here. I don't care if you sit out of the game, but stick with the group, okay?"

Elizabeth murmured an apology and darted back into the church.

I tried to follow but P.G. stopped me. I thought he would chew me out more but instead, he smiled and cuffed me on the arm.

The rest of the night was a blur. I rejoined Elizabeth, and once the game was over, we went back to the folding chairs. P.G. talked about the heroes honor roll in Hebrews 11, as he called it.

"But notice what it says in chapter 12. 'Therefore, since we are surrounded by such a great cloud of witnesses, let us throw off everything that hinders and the sin that so easily entangles, and let us run with perseverance the race marked out for us. Let us fix our eyes on Jesus, the author and perfecter of our faith, who for the joy set before him endured the cross, scorning its shame, and sat down at the right hand of the throne of God. Consider him who endured such opposition from sinful men, so that you will not grow weary and lose heart.'

"Think about what the author wrote! We don't idolize these heroes. Instead, their examples spur us on to greater heights, greater good! And we keep Jesus as our goal, our purest example, the one that we try to emulate the most."

Once he was finished, we sang a few more songs and we were dismissed. Elizabeth waved to me as she climbed into her step-dad's van. I returned the gesture.

Mom picked me up a short while later. I didn't mind the silent ride this time, though. My head was too full. I couldn't wait until I got home. Ben had some explaining to do.

CHAPTER

13

BEN'S WINDOW SCRAPED OPEN. I glanced at my clock. Past midnight. So much for our school-night curfew. I walked across the hall and opened Ben's door.

He was climbing through his window. He froze when he saw me. His eyes widened for a moment but then a lazy smile tugged at his lips. "Hey, Robin. What's up?"

"Good night on patrol?"

"Kind of boring, actually. I stuck to Pressville. Two muggings and a car chase."

"Car chase?" I winced. "How much property damage did you cause?"

He shrugged. "Just smashed the engine of the car."

"What if it was stolen?"

Another shrug. "That's what insurance is for, right?"

Silly me. "So did you forget about anything tonight?"

He frowned. His eyes darted back and forth as if consulting an invisible calendar. "I don't think so. Why?"

Heat flashed from my feet up through my chest. "What about youth group?"

"Mom was cool with me skipping."

"What about Elizabeth?"

He actually dared to look confused. "What are you talking about?"

"You invited her to youth group tonight. She showed up, but you were out on patrol. Classy, Ben, real classy."

"What are you talking about? Yeah, I mentioned youth group to her, and I said it'd be great if she wanted to come along someday, but we never made definite plans."

"Then why was she there?"

"How should I know? Maybe we got our signals crossed. Maybe she thought she'd surprise me." A wistful smile flickered across her face. "Would have been a nice surprise."

I snorted and stormed back to my room. I tried to shut the door but he blocked it open.

Ben slid in after me. "Why are you so bent out of shape over this? It's not like I'm in the wrong here. Bad guys, remember?"

"Oh, of course, because you never are in the wrong, are you?"

"Rob." Ben's voice was so quiet, I wasn't even sure he had spoken. "Rob, I know what this is about. It's about Lux, isn't it?"

Guilt shot through me. I closed my eyes.

"I understand. She was special. I was thinking and . . . Look, you and I know the cops have their hands full. The VOC too. Why else would they let Magnus give away a license on the show? So why don't we try to find out who killed Lux? We team up. We'd be unstoppable."

I looked at him. It was a tempting offer. I wasn't all that powerful in a fight. Having him backing me up could come in handy if things turned violent.

Ben must have read the uncertainty in my eyes. "C'mon, you know it's the right thing to do. You backing me up, taking down the killer. It'll be so much fun!"

My stomach curdled. Fun? Lux was dead. Ben wouldn't think it was so great if he had been the one in that vacant lot. Or maybe he would.

"Just think about it. The Laughlin boys, working together. No one could stop us."

The way Ben was talking, it seemed that he expected the bad guys to just roll over. A nice fantasy, but unlikely. "I suppose we could always recruit a few more people," I said. "Maybe some of the other contestants?"

Ben waved away my words as if he were shooing a gnat. "We've got this covered. No worries, no problem. We'll tear through this in no time."

"Or it'll tear through us," I said.

Ben rolled his eyes. "That's defeatist talk. We'll be fine."

"Lux isn't."

My quiet declaration hung between us.

Then Ben nodded sagely. "True. But we will be."

I saw the smile lurking behind his eyes. Ben wasn't taking this seriously. That meant there was a good chance that one of us would get hurt.

That thought alone sent ice slicing through my veins. What if Ben got hurt? Whoever was behind Lux's murder obviously didn't have a problem with killing heroes. As much as I might gripe about Ben, I didn't want to see him injured—or worse. Neither would Mom. I could already imagine how she'd be with me if Ben and I did team up and something happened to him. She'd never forgive me. Just like with Dad. Even worse.

I forced a brave smile. "I appreciate the offer, but I think I've got this."

Ben studied my face for a moment before shrugging. "Well, hey, no problem. Just let me know if you change your mind." He left my room and shut the door.

I blew out a breath and collapsed into my desk chair. Crisis averted for now. But I'd have to make some headway soon or he'd suggest it again. I powered on my computer and pulled up the web browser to continue my research into Kid Magnum. He was still my prime suspect in Lux's death. Maybe something in his past would give me a clue as to what happened or grant me some insight into the way Kid thought.

It turned Kid Magnum had a checkered past, that was for sure. He'd first appeared in Kensington, Pennsylvania, about ten years ago, armed from head to toe. He'd made a name for himself by raiding a hostage situation in an office park. Nobody had died, but in the process he'd caused close to half a million dollars in property damage.

The next major cluster of articles dealt with the death of a criminal who'd called himself the Blank Specter, who had died while being pursued by Kid Magnum. Kid hadn't denied that he had killed Blank Specter, but he'd claimed it had been done in self-defense. VOC crime scene technicians had disputed his version of events. In the end, the VOC had chosen not to act since no definitive conclusion could be reached.

The worst blot on his record, though, dealt with a 40-year-old drug addict named Blaire Thornton. Thornton was the on-again, off-again girlfriend of a minor crime lord, a crime lord Kid Magnum had apparently desperately wanted to find.

According to Blaire's version of events, when she wouldn't cooperate with Kid's investigation, he'd roughed her up. Photos of her had flooded the Philadelphia press, showing her face bruised and cut, supposedly from a beating Kid Magnum had administered. Kid had denied it, of course, but the VOC had started an investigation.

Then, a week later, Thornton had withdrawn her allegations, claiming her boyfriend, not Kid, had beaten her. Nevertheless, several commentators had said that Kid's reputation had been tarnished. They'd said he would need some big redemption to boost him into the ranks of licensed heroes.

I checked the date of those articles. The Thornton brouhaha had settled down a month before *America's Next Superhero* had begun taping.

If Kid Magnum had already been sore and in need of a big win, and if he'd thought he wouldn't win, especially because of how Lux had humiliated him at Friday night's taping by taking him out with a "flashbulb," as he put it . . . A stretch? Maybe, but it was all I had. I'd find out the next night.

"Hope you're in a talkative mood, Kid" I whispered.

CHAPTER 14

THE NEXT NIGHT, Mom had to work late at the hospital so Ben and I had to fend for ourselves to get to the studio. Public transportation was the only option, as much as that rankled. I left earlier than Ben. It wouldn't do for us to be seen arriving together.

I took a circuitous route through New Chayton. I kept an eye on the other passengers on each bus and at each stop. No familiar faces. Nobody seemed to be following me. The final bus took me to downtown New Chayton and the Magnus Communication Group Studios.

I switched into my Failstate gear in my usual hiding place, a nearby alley, and I headed for the studio. The guards at the front gate nodded to me, raising the yellow-and-black traffic arm to let me pass. I threaded through the back lot, heading for the large studio building. For once, I was thankful for my costume. The night was unseasonably cool. The extra layers helped keep me warm. When I grabbed for the door to backstage, I wound up touching someone else's hand.

I looked up and groaned. Gauntlet stared back at me, surprise shining in his eyes.

"Just great," I said. "We're not supposed to arrive together. Didn't you take any precautions?"

He snorted and pulled the door open. I sighed and followed him in.

As I entered, a group of men in overalls charged down the hall. They pushed a cart filled with wooden crates. I jumped back as the heavy wheels missed my toes by inches.

"Figures the shipment would be this late," one of them muttered. "And you know Kirkwood ain't gonna pay us overtime."

"Just hurry up. Faster we get this stuff to the finale set, sooner we can get out of here," one of his companions said as they rounded a corner and disappeared. As the men's complaints faded, I moved on to the green room.

The room itself wasn't green, but a soothing tan, so I didn't know where it had gotten its name. A small TV hung in one corner, flanked by large green plants. A cappuccino machine sat on a counter near the entrance. The other contestants sat in plush chairs. It always felt weird, seeing so many costumed vigilantes just lounging in Laz-Y-Boys. They didn't talk to each other. As a matter of fact, most of them didn't even seem to be aware that the others existed. T-Ram was subdued for once. He had a small bottle of vitamins out and was sorting through them in his open palm. Kid Magnum had removed his wrist guns and was carefully cleaning them. Blowhard waxed and twisted his moustache into a tight curl. No sign of Veritas yet.

I took the only available seat in the room, a rickety folding chair that had seen better days. The metal creaked as I sat down, and I was pretty sure it gave an inch. Kid Magnum glanced in my direction. At least, I think he did. It was hard to tell with his featureless faceplate. Unnerving.

Then the door popped open, and Veritas slid inside.

He looked horrible. His costume was wrinkled, and it hung loose, almost as if he had lost weight since I'd seen him a few days earlier. He shuffled to a corner, not meeting anyone's eyes.

"Are you okay, man?" Titanium Ram asked.

"If there's anything we can do, you let us know, okay?" Blowhard's words overlapped T-Ram's.

I kept quiet, watching Kid Magnum's body language. He strapped his wrist guns into place, his head down. Then he pushed out of the chair and walked toward Veritas. "Tough break. I'm sorry it happened."

"Yeah, right."

Heads snapped around, and everyone's eyes bored into me. Had I actually said that out loud?

Kid Mangum took a step toward me. "You got something to say to me?"

Better get this over with. I squared my shoulder. "Yeah, I do. Where were you on Saturday night?"

Kid Magnum froze stock still, like a gleaming metal statue. A gasp ricocheted through the room. I peeked over Kid Magnum's shoulder at Veritas. He stared at me with wide eyes.

"What are you implying?" Kid's whisper was barely audible.

"You and Lux brawled Friday night," I said. "You were pretty mad when she humiliated you."

Kid's armor rattled. Was he shaking? "I'm no killer."

"Says the 'kid' with all the artillery. Tell me, this past Friday, how many of the shots you put into those silhouettes would have been lethal?"

"Those were paper cut-outs, not real people. And I was firing bean bags!"

"What about Blaire Thorton? What about the Blank Specter?" I took a step closer. "Why not come clean about all of it?"

Kid took a few steps back. His head swiveled to face the others. Then he jabbed a finger in my direction. "You shut up."

"Not until you tell me where you were on Saturday night."

Kid Magnum roared and took another step back. Barrels popped out of his wrist plates and he took aim at me.

I lashed out with my power to form a destructive field that was flat and thin, like a knife blade. I drove it between his armor plates.

A second later, most of Kid Magnum's armor clattered to the floor, the straps cut from within. He froze, his head tipped at the pile of metal at his feet.

T-Ram charged, his head lowered.

I sent a spike of power into the floor in his path, carving out a divot. T-Ram stepped right into it and, with a cry of alarm, slammed face first into the floor.

Then large hands squeezed my arms and pinned them against my side.

"What are you doing, man?" Gauntlet whispered.

"Knock it off, all of you!"

The bellow cut through everything. Alexander Magnus stood in the door, Helen at his side. He walked in, and it felt as if we had all been pushed away from him, as if his mere presence took up most of the room. Gauntlet let me go and snapped to attention. Magnus's gaze sliced through each of us. But then he whirled on Veritas. "What was going on in here? Couldn't you have done something?"

"Sir, I—"

"No excuses!" Magnus ran a hand through his hair and sighed. "One of you morons is supposed to win that license, but given what I've just seen, I'm not sure any of you deserve it. Brawling? Over what?"

"Failstate accused me of killing Lux," Kid Magnum said, his voice sulky.

"Really?" Magnus's eyes narrowed at Kid Magnum, a predator's gleam flashing through them. "Did you?"

Kid Magnum sputtered for a moment. "No! I didn't!"

"You've got an alibi?"

"Not exactly, no. After the taping, I went home to Philly and I spent Saturday night on patrol. By myself."

"No one saw you?"

"Not that I know of. Quiet night, not even a speeder."

Magnus rubbed his jaw. Then he turned to spear his fiery gaze through me. "You have proof to back up your accusation?"

Under Magnus's intense gaze, my so-called case dissolved into mist. Lux's last words, Kid Magnum's past, the near-brawl last Friday, none of it really added up to what anyone could even charitably call an inkling of proof. Lots of conjecture and too many deductive leaps.

"I guess not," I whispered.

"Okay then. Shake and put it behind you."

Kid nudged the pile of armor at his feet. "You gonna replace that, cognit?"

I ground my teeth but nodded. I'd have to do a lot of extra orders.

"Good thing I have an extra suit." Kid thrust out his hand, and I clasped it briefly.

"All right, now that the histrionics are over, let's get down to business." Magnus rapped his cane on the floor and leaned heavily on it. "Lux's . . . *passing* was unfortunate and has left us in a bit of a lurch. But I've met with the producer, and we've hashed things out. For starters, no one will enter the Chamber this week."

Was that supposed to be good news? I glanced at the other contestants. Veritas in particular looked ready to crumble in on himself. Only Blowhard looked happy.

"And tonight, you will visit the confessional with Helen, record some thoughts. We'll air what was filmed on Friday and use what you say tonight in a tribute in the next episode."

How could the man be so nonchalant about all this? A hero had died, so far as I knew no one had any new leads, and he was trying to somehow spin it for good ratings? It was cold, heartless . . .

My eyes widened. Of course! Lux *had* been trying to say "Magnus." He had her killed.

Given Veritas's participation in my unorthodox "interrogation," he and, by extension, Lux, must have had some connection with Magnus. But why would he do this? A ratings stunt? Possibly. If *America's Next Superhero* wasn't doing well, this sort of controversy would bring in lots of new viewers and bring many previous viewers back into the fold. Or maybe there was some connection between Lux and Magnus I didn't know about.

I looked around at the others. We had all put our trust in Magnus and his production team. How did we know he wasn't trying to wipe us out one by one? Any of us could be a target.

Magnus glanced in my direction. His lips twitched into a snarl, but then he turned and stalked out of the green room.

Gauntlet elbowed me, hard enough to blow the air out of my lungs. "You listening or not?"

I blinked and looked around the room. Helen had crossed her arms over her chest and was glaring at me. "I'm sorry—what?"

"Failstate," she said, sounding exasperated, "you're up first in the confessional."

I followed her to the small room and sat down in the usual chair. Helen took her place behind the camera. I tensed, remembering how easily Helen had taken me down in Magnus's house. Suddenly the camera looked much more sinister, the lens a barrel of a high-caliber weapon.

If Helen noticed my apprehension, she didn't let on. "So how have you been coping with the news of Lux's death?"

"I haven't been coping with the news that well. In some ways, I can't believe she's actually gone."

We covered some basics, like how I was feeling after Lux's death, my favorite memories of her from the competition. Confessional taping was always weird. Helen would ask me questions, but I had to rephrase her questions in my answers and make it seem like I'd thought up what I was saying on my own.

"Is it true you were the one who found Lux?"

Sweat beaded across my forehead. "I was the one who found Lux. We were supposed to go on patrol together the night this happened. But . . . well, that never happened."

"Tell us if you've been doing any investigating."

Not good. If Magnus knew I suspected him, I could be his next target. Better phrase things carefully.

"I'm sure the VOC and the New Chayton police are pursuing their own leads. This might be one of those times when it's best to leave things to the professionals."

Helen smiled, her lips thin and turning white.

I tried to relax but couldn't. What if Helen were in on it too? How high did this thing go? What if they were trying to garner some great ratings and get rid of us heroes all at the same time? There was only one way to find out. I'd have to act fast though. For all our sakes.

CHAPTER 15

THURSDAY EVENING, I could have watched what the network called "an unforgettable and explosive new episode of *America's Next Superhero.*" Instead I spent my time more productively, by planning a break-in at Magnus's mansion.

The timing wasn't a problem. According to the society page of the *New Chayton Register*, Alexander Magnus would attend a museum opening on Saturday evening. Helen would probably be with him. As near as I could tell, she rarely left his side.

But breaking in, finding the evidence I needed, and escaping unobserved—that was far beyond anything I had ever done before. Worse, I was skating on legal thin ice. Technically what I was planning was breaking and entering. If my hunch didn't play out and I was caught, I'd probably have another intimate chat with Agent Sexton or one of his VOC cronies. Even if I found evidence linking Magnus with Lux's death, that could happen.

I had to chance it. I could pass on my suspicions to the cops or the VOC, but given Magnus's connections with just about everyone in New Chayton, I doubted it would go anywhere. But I had to do this. For Lux. I had to take down Alexander Magnus.

I went to the web site of *Celebrity Homes*, a show dedicated to snooping around the mansions of the rich and/or famous, and found the episode featuring Magnus's house. I couldn't glean too much. The host seemed more interested in the flashy decor and high-end toys. But I found that, by watching the show in slow motion, I could put together some rudimentary floor plans. But every time I reviewed the footage, I found an inconsistency in my rough sketches: a missed doorway, a hall branching the opposite direction, windows where walls should be. This was not going to go well.

About 9:30, I heard the sound of car doors slamming and muffled hoots outside. I glanced out the window. I recognized the beat-up minivan parked in front of our house. It belonged to Derek Hewitt, one of Ben's friends. Ben tumbled out the side, actually rolling across the lawn. He leapt to his feet and laughed loudly enough that I could hear him through the closed window. He sauntered back to the house, pumping his fist in the air. Derek responded with a fusillade of horn blasts and then tore away from the curb.

Ben tromped up the stairs and poked his head in the door of my room. "So what are you up to tonight?"

I quickly switched off my monitor. Last thing I needed was for Ben to piece things together. He'd try to stop me. Or worse, come with me.

"Nothing," I said. "Just some homework."

"Uh-huh. Like you have to worry about that."

He threw himself on my bed, landing with an exaggerated bounce. He laced his fingers behind his head and crossed his feet. Ben grinned at me even as his wet shoes soaked into my bedspread. I sighed. Might as well play the game to get him out of my room that much quicker.

"So how are the boys?"

"Oh, they're all fine. They send their regards."

I bet they did. "So what'd you do tonight?"

"Not too much," Ben said. "Went to the Hawkeye Mall, picked up some girls, and then headed to Riverside Park and just hung out."

I started to say something but his cell chirped. He held up one finger and pulled it from his pocket. He read the text and chuckled, his fingers flying over the keypad for a few seconds.

"Sorry, just touching base with one of the gals I saw tonight. Friend of yours, actually. Liz."

It took a moment for me to couple the name with a face. Elizabeth? What was she doing with him?

"Yeah, we ran into her as she was leaving Krakatoa. Figured I had to make it up to her after ditching her at youth group. She's really nice, isn't she?" He slapped his thighs and rolled off my bed. "Well, goodnight. Some of us still need to sleep."

I stared at the door as it closed and then mechanically turned back to my computer. I turned on the monitor again and tried to focus on the pictures of Magnus Manor, but all I could see in my mind was an image of Ben and Elizabeth, sitting together in a dusky park.

CHAPTER 16

THOUGHTS OF MAGNUS MANOR chased me through the next day at school. Every time I tried to focus on my classes, images from my research danced across my eyes. I doodled possible entry strategies in the margins of my notes. In the middle of Geometry, I tuned out Mrs. Dennison completely, envisioning the route I'd take through the mansion. Nothing snapped me out of it until Haruki collapsed into the chair next to me during lunch. He sighed and poked at his burger with a fork, and then he pushed his tray away.

"Are you crazy?" I asked. "The food's actually edible today."

"I don't have much of an appetite." Haruki ran his hand through his hair, but rather than smooth it out, his hair twisted even more. "The aliens are coming tonight."

This again? "That's too bad."

Haruki shrugged. "I'm used to it. They've been harassing me for years. Same pattern every time. The inspection, the injection, the collection, and finally, the rejection. Then wait a few months and the fun starts all over again. Lucky me, tonight is 'injection' night."

His tone, muted and dull, broke me out of planning mode. Haruki slumped in his chair, his eyes almost vacant.

I touched his shoulder. "Is there anything I can do to help?"

He shook his head and forced a smile as fake as the hamburger meat. "I appreciate you asking, though. Don't worry about me. It's annoying, but I'm used to it." With that, he picked up his burger and started eating, although he didn't seem all that enthused.

We made small talk after that, chatting about the weather, our teachers, our mutual distrust of organized sports. Haruki was a good guy, even if I didn't totally understand his love of anime. He asked me if I'd be at Mount Calvary that weekend for services, I promised I would.

As I walked out of the lunchroom, I mulled over my conversation with Haruki. Did he really think that aliens came to abduct him? He seemed genuine enough, but then, it could all be a joke, his way of breaking the ice. Or could it be some sort of mental condition? Maybe. I could do some research, see if there was a mental illness that caused people to believe they were abductees.

I shook my head. Forget it. I had too much on my plate as it was, especially with the show taping that evening. Some mysteries would have to solve themselves.

• • •

At least Ben got the timing down. He arrived at the studio fifteen minutes after me, plenty of time for me to get situated in the green room and wait for instructions.

The other contestants trickled in slowly. Blowhard nodded in my direction. Kid Magnum and Titanium Ram conferred quietly in a corner, their armor casting reflections that danced across the walls and the floor. Probably discussing the best way to do as much bodily harm to a suspect without killing him.

But then T-Ram pulled out a bottle of vitamins and shared some with Kid Magnum. T-Ram glanced at me. "Hey, Failstate? You need a little boost, dude? I got some all-natural supplements here that'll charge you up."

I shook my head. Gauntlet strode into the room and T-Ram fist-bumped him. Veritas walked a little taller when he came into the green room. He didn't appear nearly as fragile. He sat in a chair near mine.

The familiar cadence of heels against the floor announced Helen's arrival. Sure enough, she breezed into the green room, her face set in her usual impassive mask, although I noticed a flash of irritation when she looked at me. "We have something of a situation," she said. "Our show is being put on hiatus."

My head snapped back. The other contestants grumbled. Veritas seemed to deflate in on himself.

"Why?" Kid Magnum asked.

"The network has received a number of complaints from the public, especially after what happened to Lux. With the VOC's on-going investigation, the network decided it would be best if we went off the air until her murderers are brought to justice. We were unable to plead our case." The other contestants started to grumble again. Helen held up her hand. "But we're planning on giving the network a great episode tonight, one that will show them that what you're doing here is vital. Okay? Stay loose, and be ready for anything."

With that, she marched out of the room.

A moment later, the stage manager came to get us. "Okay, kids, time to get going. Let's stay safe out there and have some fun!"

I didn't rise right away. There was an eagerness in his voice that said we would have trouble doing either.

The audience seemed muted as we made our entrances. They weren't nearly as enthusiastic as they had been the week before. I scanned the crowd. Was Elizabeth here this time? A sea of faces swam in front of me, more than I could count. No sign of her.

Everett Thompson made his entrance next. He mugged for the crowd and practically blinded everyone in his suit. This time, the white stripes were made of bike reflectors, which cast weird reflections all over the stage. After a few moments, he got the crowd to settle down and then took his spot downstage center.

"Now I know you're all here to see the heroes and what they can do," he said, "but first, we'd like to observe a moment of silence on behalf of Lux. I know I'm not the only fan who will miss her, right?" He folded his hands and bowed his head.

Most of the crowd stood and mimicked his posture.

God, I know I failed her. I know I messed up. Help me do better tonight. Make me the hero You want me to be.

For a moment, I envisioned myself standing at the start of a race, hunkered down and looking down the field. A lone figure stood in the distance, urging me on. Warmth swirled around my mind, buoying me. A presence, calmer than anything I had ever felt, trickled through me but then was gone. The crowd chanted Lux's name.

Everett broke through with a bellowing guffaw. "Let's get down to business! You may have heard the rumors and unfortunately, they're true. The network is taking us off the air for a little while." He allowed the audience to boo. "We decided to go out with as big of a bang as possible. We want all of you to see our heroes in action, doing what they do best. That's why tonight . . . they're going out on patrol!"

The crowd roared.

I stared at Everett, unsure whether I had heard him correctly. He had to be kidding. Most nights I went on patrol were boring. Even when a hero found crimes to fight, it was usually purse-snatchings, attempted muggings—nothing that would make for great television.

Everett mugged for the camera as if he had announced we would engage in an epic battle between good and pure evil. "We're going to take a little while to get our heroes ready. And once they are, you'll be able to watch the fun on these screens!"

With that, music crescendoed, pyrotechnics went off, and the stagehands hustled us to a waiting bus. We took our seats and glanced at each other. T-Ram's legs bounced enough to shake the bus. Kid Magnum kept flicking his wrists, popping and retracting the barrels in his wrist cannons.

The bus lurched and, once we were going, the director appeared at the head of the bus.

"Okay, here's the deal. We're heading for the warehouse district. Each of you will be dropped off at a random point and equipped with this—" He held up a blaze orange backpack. "It's a combination GPS and camera pack. You will wear these through the entire event. They're well nigh indestructible but that doesn't mean any of you should try to break it."

Those last words were directed at me. The throb behind my eyes grew. I tamped down on it, hoping I wouldn't cause the bus's engine to die. The bus rolled forward, and I relaxed. So far, so good.

Within fifteen minutes, we had pulled into New Chayton's warehouse district, a collection of ugly brick and cement buildings. Not a lot of street lights, not much in terms of human activity. We passed a few restaurants and bars but otherwise, there weren't that many open businesses.

I was called first. The director strapped the pack to my back and shoved me out of the bus with a half-hearted, "Good luck, kid."

Two cameras emerged from the pack on flexible stalks. One wrapped around to get a close-up shot of my face. Thanks to my hood, that'd be pretty boring. The other extended a full three feet into the air, tipping down to look at me.

I looked around. Two large buildings flanked the street. One was a food warehouse. The other seemed abandoned and empty, boards over the broken-out windows. A parking lot next to the vacant warehouse was overgrown with weeds and filled with trash. It reminded me a bit too much of . . . No, I wouldn't think of that. I had to focus.

With a dull grumble, the bus pulled away. I broke out into a jog and darted deep into the district. Might as well get this over with.

CHAPTER 17

I LEANED OVER THE EDGE of the fire escape and scanned the empty streets. Still nothing. A car alarm brayed in the distance, answered by a barking dog. I had gone deeper into the district and clambered up the side of a warehouse, hoping to find a better vantage point. All I could see were rows of brick buildings, cars parked at random spots on the street, and not much else.

This was silly, hiding on a rooftop in the middle of a reality show challenge while a real villain could be plotting to kill more heroes. For all I knew, this challenge could be part of Magnus's scheme. I should slip away, get out of the warehouse district, and continue my investigation. A quick burst of power and the backpack would be gone . . .

The cameras! The pack shifted on my back and I became acutely aware of the whirring of lenses within the stalk-like appendages. Anything I did would be witnessed by the director and Helen. Even if I shucked my camera pack, they'd notice my absence.

I tensed and resisted the urge to look at the cameras staring over my shoulder. I couldn't abandon this now. If I did, Magnus would become suspicious. I had to fly under his radar a bit longer.

So back to "patrolling." Great show we were giving the audience. The producers would probably edit together the best of whatever happened, but what were they showing the studio audience right now? How long would they stick around if the rest of the contestants were giving them the kind of gripping footage I was providing?

"Hey!" The voice came from the bottom of the fire escape. I saw T-Ram standing there looking at me. He scrambled up the ladder and plopped down next to me. "Seen anything yet?"

"Nothing requiring our help. A lady was locked out of her car about forty-five minutes ago, but she had already called for help when I found her."

T-Ram snorted. "Figures. Hey, you want some energy vitamins? Might be a long night."

"No thanks." I stood up and stretched. Maybe I should keep moving, leave T-Ram at this lookout. It couldn't hurt. I . . .

A low boom echoed in the distance. I froze.

"What was that?" T-Ram asked.

The sound had come from my left. Car accident? It wouldn't make for award-winning television, but it would be better than this.

Another boom and smoke rose from the street three blocks over. I turned to T-Ram to suggest we check it out, only to find him halfway down the fire escape. By the time I reached the bottom, T-Ram was a block away. I groaned and jogged after him. He would get the good footage, no doubt.

A few seconds later, I almost crashed into him. T-Ram stood like a statue, frozen in place. I could understand why.

Next to a warehouse crouched a massive robot. Its body was black and shaped roughly like an upside-down boat. Its six burnished legs glinted in the streetlights, two piston-driven arms battering the building's walls. Rust chewed at its flanks. The robot's head swiveled back and forth, gears whirring loud enough I could hear them across the street.

Well, this certainly changed things, but I wasn't sure for the better. I squinted at the warehouse. Its sign was burned out, but I thought it said something about being owned by the Magnus Corporation. Wasn't that an interesting coincidence?

Once it had opened a big enough hole, it reached inside with a massive claw and pulled out a safe. A compartment opened in its chest and it dropped the safe inside.

"Well, that's not something you see every day," T-Ram murmured. With a war cry, he charged.

The robot whirled, lights snapping on and illuminating T-Ram, who dropped his head and aimed for one of its legs.

The robot swung a arm and smashed T-Ram aside and into a nearby parked car. He groaned and slid to the pavement, leaving a massive dent in its side.

Okay, so a frontal assault was out of the question. The massive machine turned back to the hole and went back to rummaging around in the building. It withdrew a canister painted bright yellow with a radioactive symbol stamped on its side. I blinked. Who would bring hazardous materials into the warehouse district? Something wasn't right here.

T-Ram stumbled to my side. "Thanks for the help, cognit."

"Thanks for running off without including me in your plan."

The robot continued dropping bits and pieces into its chest compartment. Since it didn't press the attack on T-Ram, it was probably programmed not to attack but just to defend itself if someone tried to interfere.

Best to test that theory. I slowly approached the robot. Its head swiveled and regarded me for a moment with its lone eye, a twenty year old video camera. I stood still and waited. The camera swiveled down, then up. And then the robot went back to pulling junk out of the building. After another second, I backed away to T-Ram.

"Do you plan on just watching while it rips off that warehouse, cognit? Or are we going to actually, you know, do something heroic?"

"You go ahead and try again if you want." I motioned toward the robot. "Your first plan was epic."

T-Ram's expression soured. "Coward."

"It's not cowardice if we want to catch a bigger fish. I'm willing to bet it'll go home to roost pretty soon."

T-Ram cracked his knuckles and scowled. "How do you figure?"

"Do the math. The chest compartment can't hold a whole lot more. Robo-thief will have to go drop that stuff eventually, right?"

T-Ram studied the robot for a moment or two before nodding. "Okay. So we follow it?"

I nodded.

T-Ram smiled, a predatory flash of teeth. "And then we'll squarsh whoever sent it, right?"

"Absolutely." I hoped T-Ram or the audience didn't pick up on the uncertainty boiling through me. I didn't like the situation. Obviously the robot was our challenge for the night. But with Alexander Magnus behind this, there was no telling what could happen. It might not be a carefully controlled situation, not if he wanted to kill more heroes. We had better finish this fast.

CHAPTER 18

I PRESSED UP against the brick wall of a warehouse. The robot still lumbered down the middle of the street, its legs whining and creaking as it stomped along. The robot's head swiveled from side to side, reminding me of a tourist taking in the sights.

"Why is it moving so slow?" T-Ram asked.

"How should I know? I didn't build the stupid thing!"

He had a point, though. The robot had traveled four blocks over ten minutes and didn't seem to be in much of a hurry. I could probably outrun it.

The temptation to disappear surged again. I could leave T-Ram to track the robot and claim I was going to go look for other crime. It'd be a stupid move in terms of the show, but really, with Lux dead, who cared about the show anymore?

No, the timing still wasn't right. I could feel the cameras boring into the back of my head. It wasn't just their gaze but

Magnus's. He would see. He would know. Any other contestant would finish this challenge. I had to keep playing the game.

The robot appeared to be heading for a three story warehouse made of white cement. It knocked a few cars out of its way. The robot's head swiveled in a full circle. A loading dock in the warehouse slid open and the thing tromped through. About time. Now maybe we could get to the bottom of this.

T-Ram darted past me. We sprinted across the street to the closing garage door. T-Ram skidded through the opening. I imitated his move but was nowhere as smooth. I banged my elbows and knees as I rolled and then slammed into T-Ram and knocking him off his feet.

"Watch it!" He pushed me away and got to his feet.

The loading dock was shadowed and dark but empty. The robot had disappeared. The only exit was a large doorway that led into long hallway lit by flickering fluorescent lights. The robot turned a sharp corner into the darkness beyond. I glanced up at the ceilings. Girders and struts held the roof up, with power lines snaking across the ceiling. No visible security, but that didn't mean we weren't being monitored. I turned to tell T-Ram to proceed carefully only to discover that he had already taken off in a silent jog down the hall.

"Oh, great," I muttered.

I didn't like this. It was the perfect spot for an ambush. Large air ducts ran along both walls providing numerous shadowy alcoves. Not only that, but I passed by four doorways that opened into darkened rooms. My eyes widened at the thought. Maybe that's what Magnus intended: an "accident" in the warehouse district. I choked on my breath. T-Ram could have run right into the teeth of Magnus's scheme. Or I could be the target.

The throbbing behind my eyes spiked, which caused my backpack to emit a loud squeal and erupt in a shower of sparks. Heat flashed over my back.

I ripped off the pack. A quick inspection revealed what I already suspected. I had fried it. I groaned. Helen would kill me.

I shook my head. I had to keep up with T-Ram. We had a giant robot—and whoever had unleashed it—to deal with. I spotted T-Ram crouching at the end of the hall, so I took off toward him. He motioned for me to slow down and keep quiet. I poked my head around the corner to see what we were dealing with.

Like the loading dock, the rest of the warehouse was mostly empty. It was huge. The ceiling soared overhead. Stacks of wooden crates lined three of the walls. Set up against the far wall was a dais dominated by a stack of large computer monitors along with a tarnished control panel at least thirty feet long. The robot knelt before the dais.

Standing before it was a portly man in a stained red lab coat, his spindly arms and legs barely able to fill out the coat and well-worn khaki slacks. What little grey hair he had frizzed out in an incomplete halo, a pair of black goggles strapped to the top of his head. His skin was peppered with age spots. The guy appeared to be in his seventies. He looked familiar.

"Very good, my pet. *Da*, very good indeed!" His voice, thick with a Russian accent, wheezed through the space. "Soon your brothers shall return with their *grebyesh* and my master plan can come to fruition!"

My jaw dropped. Who talked like that in real life? He had to be an actor hamming it up for ratings. And who was he talking to? The robot? Oh boy. This was going to get ugly.

"Let's do this," T-Ram said.

We charged around the corner. Blinding lights flared on. The robot whirled on us, red lights rimming its camera eye.

"Titanium Ram and Failstate, I presume!" the Russian guy said. "*Koneshna*, I should have known that *geroe* would try to interfere! Radius, attack!"

The robot charged, its joints shrieking. I dodged to my left. T-Ram shot forward, dropping his head for impact. With surprising quickness, the robot evaded and T-Ram smashed through a far wall. He didn't emerge from the wreckage.

Was he okay? I wanted to go check on him. But the robot had other ideas. It focused on me, its red lights flaring. Not good. I took a step back involuntarily.

It swung a massive claw in my direction. I lashed out, channeling my destructive field into a flat blade. I partially sheared through its arm. Hydraulic fluid sprayed across the floor and the claw went slack.

The robot swung again, using the broken arm as a club. I tried to fire off another disintegrating bolt but missed, scoring a long trench in the concrete floor. I ducked only barely in time, the arm slicing air above my head.

Then it darted forward. It thrust out with its other claw, knocking me to the ground. I tried to get up, but it pinned the edge of my pants with one of its feet. I scrabbled at the floor but couldn't escape.

"Ah, too bad. I had hoped you would be more of a challenge. Radius, *poka*." The old man waved at me like he was shooing a fly.

The robot reared back and raised its useless claw. I winced, sure the killing blow would come at any moment.

Instead, a wall disintegrated, sending broken bricks and wooden splinters raining down around me. What was that?

The robot spun as if distracted, its camera tracking the dust cloud billowing into the room. That was all the time I needed. I reached out with my power disintegrated a portion of the foot that pinned me in place. It scrambled to maintain its balance, and I wiggled free.

I had half-expected to see T-Ram emerge from the newly made hole in the wall. But instead, another robot like the one that attacked me thrashed on its back, gears whining as it tried to right itself.

Before it could, something smashed into its head. All I saw was a flash of blue and gold, but that was enough to know who it was.

Gauntlet ripped the head off the downed robot. He crushed it and tossed it aside like a piece of crumpled paper. He set one foot on the now destroyed robot and pointed at the old man. "I don't know who you are, but your scheme ends now!"

"Me? You do not know me? I . . . am Krazney Potok!"

I blinked. Krazney Potok was one of the villains Meridian had fought early in his career. He had been captured in the early '90s and sentenced to at least a century in prison—because dozens of people had died in his last scheme. This was no actor brought in to play the villain. In fact, maybe this wasn't part of the show at all. My hands spasmed into fists.

This had to be how Magnus was going to kill another hero. Why else would Krazney Potok be here? And the heroes he might kill would include my brother and me.

Gauntlet didn't seem phased. "It's time you faced justice."

"Hmph. I have heard similar sentiments from better vigilantes than you!" Krazney Potok tapped some commands into his console.

Lights flared around us, the warehouse suddenly bright as day. Out from the shadows stepped six more robots. We were surrounded. Worse, a buzzing filled the air as drones dropped into the room. They looked like basketballs with propellers spinning around their center, perched on top of an orange crate. A little ridiculous, especially with the hammers and sickles painted crudely on their sides. But the gun muzzles that sprouted along their bases were no laughing matter. The drones aimed at my brother.

I darted from my hiding place and speared one of the drones with my power. It fell to pieces. Gauntlet nodded at me and turned on the others.

Then a ninth robot joined the party. Just what we needed. But instead of going for Gauntlet or me, this one smashed into one of the other robots, and both went down in a shrieking pile of twisted limbs.

"So I didn't miss anything?"

The voice came from so close to my shoulder that I nearly leapt out of my costume. I turned and found Veritas next to me.

"Don't do that!"

Veritas shrugged. "You prefer to have those two back in the fight?"

I looked at the fallen robots. "You did that? How did you—"

"When I realized the robot wouldn't attack me, I jimmied a hatch and hacked its systems. Rode it back here and set it loose. So what's going on?"

"Apparently this has all been orchestrated by Krazney Potok."

Veritas's head snapped back as if struck. "Potok? He's here?"

I pointed toward the dais. Veritas squinted at the old man.

Gauntlet climbed atop the wreckage, a plucked robot eye in his hand. "Stop gawking and start fighting, you stupid cognits!"

I winced. He was right.

Gauntlet smashed the eye into one of the robots, putting a colossal dent in its chest. He swung up and around its arm and pulled as hard as he could. The limb tore free in a shriek of ripping metal. He then hefted it up like a javelin, aiming for Krazney Potok's dais.

The old man threw up his hands. "No!"

Gauntlet hurled the severed arm. It smashed into the console, coring a hole straight through. Sparks shot across the dais. With a low moan, the apparatus went dark. The robots shuddered and then stiffened, the red lights around their cameras shifting to blue.

Potok grasped his head with both hands. He made several incoherent sounds and then whirled on us. "You idiot! Do you realize what you've done?"

Gauntlet struck a heroic pose, fists on his hips. "I've put an end to your scheme."

"*Nyet*! You've ruined everything!"

Confusion danced across Gauntlet's face for a moment. "What do you mean?"

Potok pointed toward the console. "You destroyed my safety module. Now the robots will revert to their hardwired programming." He shook his head. "I told him this would be a bad idea, but did he listen? No, of course not."

"What are you talking about?" I asked.

Potok collapsed on the dais, his head in his hands. "The VOC came to me with a deal. They are saying they will allow me to return to Mother Russia if I play the 'bad guy' on television. They are giving me access to my old technology. I am giving them good show, then I am going home. But they are giving me only one week, they find only these out-of-date monstrosities. These *robotui*, they are hard-wired for death and destruction. I am telling them to find more modern units, but they refuse. I had to cobble together—how you say?—failsafe, *da?*—module to override their primary programming. Now module is gone." He glared at Gauntlet. "Without module, *robotui* will soon reboot with original mission parameters."

"Which are what?" Veritas asked, his voice low.

Potok regarded the three of us with tight lips, tension radiating from his eyes. "Killing of heroes."

Gauntlet laughed. "Oh come on. This is a joke, right?" He turned to Veritas. "He's lying. This is all part of the show. Just another riddle for us to solve."

"No." Veritas looked at Potok, his eyes slightly unfocused. "He's telling the truth. Unless we do something fast, we're all going to die."

The robots stood in a tight circle like cars on a showroom floor. But even as we watched, they began to whir and lurch as their operating systems came back online.

My heart dropped, encased in lead. Now Magnus would claim even more victims.

CHAPTER 19

"THEN LET'S GET OUT OF HERE before they finish rebooting!" Gauntlet brushed concrete dust from his costume and turned to leave.

"It is too late for that, *tovarich.*" Krazney Potok trembled, suddenly appearing fragile in his labcoat, like a soap bubble about to burst. "They have filed you in memory. Fleeing will not stop them. They will hunt for you until you are dead or they are destroyed."

The robots still shuddered. Their blue lights now flashed in a sequence that quickened with every second. Who knew how much longer we had?

"What about the rest of that console?" Gauntlet shoved the villain toward the dais. "I only destroyed half of it. Can't you jury-rig something that could—"

"Idiot! Did you not listen? Commands are hard-wired. Actual override module was small. The rest, only fancy blinking lights for show." Potok sighed. "I do not know if you are religious, but now is good time for praying."

"No." I shouldered my way past Gauntlet to face the robots. A solution churned in my mind—dangerous and crazy—but I couldn't think of any other way out. "T-Ram is still under that rubble. You two find him and get out of here. Put as much distance between you and the warehouse as you can in the next six minutes. I'll handle the rest."

"Look, little boy in Halloween mask, you are not understanding gravity of situation," Potok said.

"I understand all too well. Either we stop them here or lots of people will get hurt or die." I turned to the robots and looked over their positions. They were still clustered together in a tight circle, just at the foot of the dais. "Tell me, if I'm the only one here when they activate, what will they do?"

"They are to be swarming you."

"Good. Now go."

Potok didn't need any more prompting. He jogged for the nearest exit, Veritas close behind him.

Gauntlet frowned at me. "Ro—" He caught himself. "Failstate . . ."

"Get out of here," I said. "One of us needs to make it. I'll be fine." I wanted to say more, to tell him to take care of Mom. I couldn't, though. Dozens of cameras could be recording us. No way I'd tip off Magnus about Gauntlet's true identity.

Gauntlet took a step closer. "You can't—"

I held up a hand to stop him. His mouth snapped shut. He sighed and nodded, and reluctantly turned aside. He sprinted to Titanium Ram, threw off some rubble, scooped him up and darted out through the hole in the wall of the warehouse.

The robots' lights flashed at a dizzying speed, and the hum grew louder, as if they were discussing their course of action. I wove through their legs, finding a spot in the center.

A tremble shimmied up my spine. I blinked back a tear. Only I could take out all of the robots at once. That was the sort of thing heroes did, right? Sacrifice themselves for others? During his career, Meridian had faced down tougher odds than this. If I wanted to be like him, I couldn't run now. Who knew—maybe I would live.

I glanced around the darkened warehouse, wondering if the cameras were zooming in on me, trying to catch some hint of doubt in my body language. "You want a show? I'll give you a show."

The robots' hum turned to an ear-splitting shriek and their lights flashed from blue to red. With a sputter of their engines, the flying drones took to the air. They wobbled a bit as they righted themselves. I stood my ground. The drones hovered outside my range. I wanted to make sure to get them too.

Then, as if on some unspoken command, the robots charged. I had positioned myself well. Two slammed into each other, their legs tangled. The drones dove in, guns spitting fire at me. A bullet zinged through my sleeve, followed by a flash of burning pain. I was committed now.

"See you soon, Dad," I whispered. Then I spread my arms and unleashed my power.

Waves of destruction flowed from me, slamming into the oncoming robots. The robots stumbled, paint boiling off their surfaces. The propellers fell off a drone and it crashed to the ground, splintering into pieces.

But that was it. The robots regained their footing and charged me again.

Not good. I could channel my destructive field into intense bursts, but evidently I couldn't take down all the robots at once. The throbbing behind my eyes intensified and I pushed. The throbbing transformed into a jagged spike of pain that bored deep into my skull. I winced, grinding my teeth together. "Aaagh!"

The arms sheared right off one of the robots, followed by its legs. It collapsed in a heap, sparks erupting from its head. The lights around its camera died. The other robots hesitated, as if startled by their companion's demise. They seemed to notice for the first time that their extremities were boiling away under my assault. Nevertheless, they scrambled after me again.

Sweat soaked my hair. The air I sucked through my mask burned my throat. *Lord, help! These things need to be destroyed, and I'm not strong enough to do it. Help me, please!*

The throbbing dropped from my head and moved into my chest, shattering into a million jagged pieces that ricocheted through me. From some source I'd never tapped before, a blast of concussive force burst from my body, slicing off the robots' feet.

Liquid fire flowed from every pore, sweeping away my enemies. The robots crumbled to dust, their remnants blown away on unfelt winds.

And still the destructive energy came, slicing through the floor, peeling it away. The lights inside the warehouse flickered and died. The remnants of Krazney Potok's console flared and then disintegrated. Large girders rained down from above, one of them smashing a robot to bits.

My power slackened and I collapsed to the floor. The warehouse swam in my vision. I had destroyed everything around me.

I took long, deep breaths, and finally the world settled. The robots were gone—without a trace. I stood in a small crater carved out of the concrete floor. Gashes dotted the walls. But what caught my attention were the large chunks missing from the steel girders that held up the roof.

The ceiling groaned and shifted. This building was coming down. I ran for the door and debris rained down around me. I tripped on the crater's lip and fell. The sky collapsed over me in a thunderous roar, and darkness swallowed me.

CHAPTER 20

DARKNESS PRESSED AROUND ME. Dust coated my tongue. A cough burst in my throat and I groaned. My hands probed my surroundings, but not far. I didn't have a lot of room. Rough concrete pieces on every side, although the floor underneath me felt smooth.

At least I had obliterated the robots. Granted, leveling the building was overkill, but they were gone. I seemed to have escaped relatively uninjured. And I'd definitely given them a show they'd remember.

How much rubble lay over me? Maybe I could burn through it. I reached deep into myself and thrust out with my power.

Nothing happened.

I frowned in the darkness, groping for any indication that I had made a difference. Nothing. Had I destroyed even a bit of the wreckage?

Panic bubbled up my throat. I took several deep breaths, closed my eyes, and tried again, picturing a wedge of destructive

132

energy tearing through the debris. In my mind, light poured through the new hole, guiding me to the surface.

But when I opened my eyes, I was still trapped in darkness. I couldn't find even the smallest dent in the rubble above me.

God, this isn't right. I took out those robots and probably saved a lot of people. How can things end like this?

I frowned. In the distance, someone shouted my name. I tried to answer but all I could muster was another cough.

Eventually the pile above me shifted. Rocks clattered against each other. Metal shrieked as it was pulled away. Then a shaft of light stabbed my eyes. I squinted and tried to roll away.

A silhouette appeared in the hole. "Failstate!" It was Veritas. "Are you okay?"

My answer stuck in my throat. Soon the hole above me widened as more and more pieces of rubble were cleared away.

Before too long, Veritas dropped down next to me. He looked me over for a moment but blanched. "Failstate, your face . . ."

Oh, no. My hands darted up and touched my ruined cheeks. My mask had been destroyed. I looked down and realized that most of my costume had been shredded as well. I groaned. I had just bought this one! Looks like I had to make another trip to the thrift store.

"I'm sorry," I whispered. "It's a bit much to look at, isn't it?"

Veritas's eyes widened. "You mean you always look this way?" He actually laughed. "That's a relief. I thought the building's collapse did this."

Nice. Real nice.

I tried to sit up but he stopped me.

"There are EMTs up there who can check you out." He produced a roll of bandages from his pocket. "But let's cover your face first, okay?"

I consented, propping myself up as Veritas unrolled the bandage, winding it around my head.

"Where's Gauntlet?" I asked.

Veritas snorted. "Helen has him talking to the cameras, giving his version of events."

Some of the tension drained out of my body. "And everyone else?"

"They're all fine. Just a few bumps and bruises. Nobody else got hurt." His eyes dropped to his lap and he fiddled with the bandage roll. "Thanks to you."

It was strange, but it almost sounded as if there was disappointment in Veritas's voice. Why would he be upset?

I gagged on the bandage. Could Veritas be in on it? That would explain why he had participated in Magnus's interrogation. Sure, he had acted all broken up about Lux's death but maybe that's all it was: an act. Clever and convincing but still fake.

I took the bandage roll from his hands. "Look, I appreciate it, but I'm good. Thanks for finding me, but I'll take it from here."

His eyes narrowed for a moment. "Okay. If you're sure."

I nodded. He shimmied back out of the hole. I finished as best I could, leaving holes for my eyes and mouth. I stood up, gingerly testing my legs. No pain there. While my costume had been shredded, it held together enough to protect my modesty. I supposed that was as good as I would get.

I clambered up out of the hole and into the glare of lights. Firemen and police crawled over the rubble, shifting some of the bigger pieces out of the way. A corner of the warehouse still stood, its edges smooth and sharp, a long talon stabbing up into the air. At least a dozen emergency vehicles surrounded the ruins, their red and blue lights flashing over the scene. Several cops ran to my side, hustling me out of the building and into the street.

Reporters shouted questions at me, most of which I couldn't understand. I winced and turned my head away from the bright lights. The cops kept me moving, through the gaggle of reporters and toward a building across the street to a small mom-and-pop restaurant.

A long counter stretched across the back of the room with a dozen small tables and chairs scattered throughout the restaurant. Deactivated neon signs dotted the walls. Men in suits talked with my fellow contestants. Three of them surrounded Krazney Potok with grim expressions.

Oh great. VOC.

"So, we meet again." Agent Sexton's gaze flicked toward my face and for a second, he turned green. "First you wipe out our crime scene, and now you bring down a warehouse. What's on deck for you next, boy?"

So much for *Thank you.* "I didn't have anything to do with Lux's death. And I didn't have much choice here," I retorted, "since your boys dropped the ball."

Sexton's head snapped back as if I had slapped him. His eyes narrowed. "We'll see."

He stormed away.

I sank into a nearby chair. I closed my eyes and rested my head in my hands.

I haven't had the chance to thank You yet, Lord. I didn't think I'd actually make it out of there, but I did. Thank You.

"Where is he?" Magnus's voice boomed over the hushed conversations. The billionaire shouldered his way into the restaurant. Helen dutifully followed in his wake. Magnus glared down at me with fiery eyes. "What do you think you were doing? You destroyed a perfectly good warehouse and all of Krazney Potok's robots! Do you know how much this will cost me?"

I stared at him for a moment. Had he just admitted he was behind the robot attack? I'd better proceed carefully here. "You didn't seem too concerned when his robots bashed holes in the sides of your buildings."

Magnus waved away my words. "Those buildings were scheduled to be demolished anyway. You nearly got everyone killed after you disrupted the cameras!"

I frowned. "What are you talking about?"

"There was some sort of weird power spike in the warehouse right after you and T-Ram arrived," Helen said. "All of the embedded cameras were taken out."

"So in the end, we've got nothing. Not one single bit of usable footage of your confrontation with Potok, not any of the fight," Magnus said. "This was supposed to help us go into hiatus on top! Instead, we'll be the laughing stock!"

Before I realized what I was doing, I popped out of the chair and stepped in close. "I know it was you. I know you had Krazney Potok released for this stunt. Too bad you didn't give him the time or the equipment he needed. I'm going to make sure you pay for that."

Magnus's eyes narrowed into dangerous slits. "You're welcome to try, kid." With that, he marched away.

I glared after him. More pieces of the puzzle were coming together. He must have had Lux murdered to boost ratings and then, just to make extra sure, hatched this ridiculous plan. All I needed was proof. He hadn't denied being behind Potok's little attack. That was a start.

I knew just where to find the proof I needed. And I also knew Magnus probably wouldn't be home for the next few hours.

CHAPTER
21

I CROUCHED IN THE BUSHES across from Magnus's mansion, waiting for a few stray cars to pass. The house itself sat on a tall hill, the grounds sloping down to a tall rock fence. Small copses of trees dotted the yard. I half-expected to see a peacock ambling around the grounds.

I found a loose rock under the bush. I concentrated on it and willed it to disappear. It boiled away in my hands. My powers had come back. Good thing too. There was no way I'd do this without them.

I glanced at my watch in the darkness. It was already two in the morning. I grumbled to myself. If only I hadn't had to run home to get a different costume. I didn't know how much longer Magnus would be occupied in the warehouse district. I had to go. Now.

The last car disappeared around a corner, so I darted across the street. As I ran, I focused on the nearest streetlight. With an audible pop, sparks erupted from the bulb. Then I was up against the wall surrounding Magnus's grounds.

The wall itself was old—dingy rough stones with crumbling mortar. According to my research, Magnus's mansion had been in his family for generations. The wall had originally been built in the late nineteenth century. Iron spikes atop the wall jutted toward the sky. No one would want to climb over those.

Not that I intended to.

Magnus had likely added sensors, or alarms, or perhaps had even electrified the spikes. The wall itself, though, probably didn't have any modern enhancements.

I focused my power against a small area of the wall. A hole wormed its way through the stone. In a matter of minutes, I had created a tunnel, just big enough for a person to wiggle through. Taking a deep breath, I squirmed through to the other side.

The mansion, a large stone mansion three stories tall, stood two hundred yards away. It was a long way to run undetected. The windows were dark. The one thing I hadn't been able to determine in my research was how much security Magnus might have. An alarm for sure, but I didn't know if he had any personnel like Blond Brute and his mute partner on site.

"Well, best get it over with," I muttered.

I sprinted across the open, grassy space, weaving between the heavy pine trees. Hopefully the relative darkness of the grounds would obscure me from any cameras.

Finally, I slammed into the house's wall and waited. No alarms. Good sign.

I funneled my power around my fingers and drove my hands a few inches into the wall, carving out hand-holds. I crawled up the wall, passing the first and second floors. The house's security would likely focus on the main floor. Most thieves wouldn't scale the building or enter through an upper window. At least, I hoped that was true.

A third story window looked into a long hallway. There'd be sensors on the window, which meant I couldn't break the glass. Carving a hole through a wall wouldn't be subtle either. Time for the riskiest part of my plan.

Closing my eyes, I tried to picture the sensors—wired into the window. The wires would lead back to a central hub that monitored the entire security system. I willed the hub to break, not badly enough to summon the authorities, just enough to give me an hour or two of uninterrupted snooping.

A warm sense of satisfaction spread from my head to my toes. Had it worked? Only one way to find out for sure.

I focused on the window's lock, dissolving it. The glass swung open, and I slipped into the house. A motion sensor hung in one corner, seemingly inert. So far, so good.

If Magnus had any information I could use, it'd probably be in his study. Slight problem: I didn't know where that was exactly.

I popped my head into the first room I found. It was a bedroom The walls were light brown. A large four poster bed filled one corner, decked out with a gauzy white veil. A desk sat underneath a high window, covered with piles of papers and school books, the corner of a laptop poking out of the mess. I spied racks of clothes through an open closet door. An enormous teddy bear lurked in the opposite corner, almost as big as I was. A girl's room?

I should have kept going, but I slipped inside. At first, I thought the occupant of the room was a girly-girl, but there was a pretty sweet electric guitar with a good-sized amp in another corner, along with a whole pantheon of photos taped to the wall in a huge collage. A teenage girl, about my age, posed with different celebrities. Movie stars, rock stars. This chick got around.

She looked familiar. Her face was round, her nose upturned a bit, but with an infectious smile. I finally shook my head. She probably just had "one of those faces." Definitely cute. But I had to keep moving.

In the next bedroom, clothes were strewn across the floor, creating an island around a bed with a deep blue comforter. The walls were dotted with posters for some sci-fi show I had never heard of. Two immaculate guest rooms rounded out the floor.

Down the stairs to the second floor. Magnus's bedroom suite, another guest room, a lavish family room with a TV big enough to fill a wall. One room was filled with wrapping paper, rolls of it. I considered doubling back to Magnus's bedroom, but decided against it. I was no forensic specialist but I doubted the evidence I wanted would be there. That left the ground floor.

Past the foyer, animal heads leered at me from their spots in the living room. Bingo. I slipped through a dining room with a wooden table that sat twenty and found a kitchen bigger than my house. Then finally, I stumbled into Magnus's study.

The room had become more ominous since I'd last been here. Odd shadows cast by the tree outside the window danced across the walls. Large bookshelves towered over me on either wall, funneling me through the room to the massive desk before a large window. Definitely the sort of room a supervillain would hang out in. I skimmed the shelves first, my gaze dancing over the leather-bound books. There must have been hundreds. I grimaced beneath my mask. If any of them were fake, if Magnus had used any of them to conceal what I sought, I was out of luck. It would take me hours to sort through them.

The desk was even bigger than I remembered, its surface still clean except for the one pen and the prism under glass. I frowned. The prism had been rotated since the last time I had been here—a quarter turn.

The top left drawer was empty. Huh. I supposed Magnus could afford to be quirky like that. But when I pulled open the next drawer, it too was empty. So was the third. The drawers on the right didn't hold anything either. I frowned. What was the point of an empty desk? Maybe there'd be something in the middle drawer.

I pulled it out and reached in deep. My fingers brushed against a switch set in the underside of the desktop. A thrill surged up my spine. Why hide a switch unless it triggered something incriminating? I pushed it and leapt back.

A muted buzz sounded behind a wall. Then, with a click, a bookcase to my left popped forward and swung open. I glanced through the hidden door.

The bookcases had swung aside and revealed a small room, one cluttered with papers and files. The walls were covered with a cheap wooden siding, dinged and scuffed. The lights looked as if they had been scavenged from an old grade school, their long bulbs humming. A whiteboard covered by scribbled multicolor notes hung on one wall, most of the notes incomprehensible. Lots of numbers, long strings of letters. Some sort of code?

On another wall was a framed picture. In it, a group of pilgrims had been drawn on brown parchment. At least, they looked like pilgrims, conversing with each other. But the way they were looking over their shoulders at the artist made me think they weren't saints. Why would Helen have that? Did she come from Massachusetts? Or maybe she had ancestors who landed at Plymouth Rock? It was a mystery I couldn't puzzle over. There was still too much to do.

Filing cabinets lined the other wall. And on the last . . . I groaned. There was a door that led to the hallway. Did that mean this was Helen Kirkwood's office? Sure enough, a quick look at the topmost papers revealed a few with her signature on them.

I walked back into Magnus's office. Maybe I would have to take the time to search each book individually. I glanced at my watch. Two thirty. Not good. Magnus could be home at any moment.

Wait. What was that?

Faint light shone underneath a bookcase on the opposite wall from the entrance to Helen's office. I cocked my head to one side. It almost looked like light spilling out from under a . . .

My eyes widened. Another hidden door. But where was the doorknob? I ran my hands down both sides of the frame, underneath every shelf. Could there be a switch hidden in or under one of the books? That seemed a bit cliché.

The door to Helen's office had opened with that switch in the drawer. I turned back to the desk and my eyes fell on the prism. My hands trembled and I gave the base an experimental twist, rotating the whole thing to the right.

Something groaned behind me, and I turned. The bookcase swung out, revealing stairs descending into barely lit gloom. My heart jackhammered against my ribs. This could be it. The proof I needed was down there, I was sure of it.

The stairs went down for a long time, deeper than any basement I'd ever been in. It felt as if I had walked down at least four flights, maybe more. The walls felt like brick but I couldn't find any sort of lights. Still, light was coming from below. The steps ended in a long, brightly lit hallway. Little nooks, each six feet long and ten feet high, were cut into the wall, flanked by metal pillars and lit by floodlights. I crept down the gallery, glancing from side to side. What was this, some kind of museum?

A set of shelves in one nook held a dozen metallic clamshells, silver with a crimson slash down their centers. Upon closer inspection, I realized they were severed robot heads. More of Krazney Potok's creations!

Each little area between the pillars contained similar artifacts, remnants of supervillain plots. I recognized some of them: Mind Master's Staff of Cognitive Domination, Serpentina's headdress, Typhoon's manacles. I couldn't believe it. Owning any of this weaponry was illegal. What reason could Magnus possibly have for having it?

Then I came face to face with the answer.

At the end of the hall stood a circular glass case, taller than me, and inside was a full costume. I easily recognized the red and blue breastplate, the sweeping black cape, and the full mask complete with starburst between the eyes.

The strength drained down through my legs. I almost collapsed right there. Suddenly the pieces came together.

"Failstate?"

A teenaged boy, dressed in faded jeans and a green polo shirt, stared at me with wide eyes. He mouthed a few words before taking a step forward, his hand outstretched.

I bolted away, tearing through the gallery and back up the stairs. I cursed myself and prayed frantically, asking for some way out of this.

As soon as I rounded out of the hidden entrance, a brilliant burst of light smashed into me, so intense I felt like I had been punched in the eyes. I shrieked, falling to the ground and clawing at my mask. I was vaguely aware of footsteps around me.

In a few moments, my vision cleared enough to recognize that Alexander Magnus stood over me, his usual scowl fixed in place. Helen Kirkwood stood at his side.

At that point, there was really only one thing I could say. "Hello, Meridian."

CHAPTER 22

ALEXANDER MAGNUS WAS really Meridian.

Even though his hands still glowed from the photonic blast he'd just fired at me, even though that explained how he'd obtained the items in his museum, and even though I had seen his costume with my own eyes, my mind refused to accept it.

I had studied Meridian's exploits. He had been one of the greatest heroes New Chayton had ever known. His example had inspired me to become Failstate in the first place. He was my idol. That this sour grump was really the Master of Light . . .

But Magnus hadn't denied it when I'd called him Meridian. And Helen didn't seem at all surprised by my accusation. Instead, they exchanged an uncertain look.

Then Magnus sighed and offered me his hand. "What, exactly, are you doing here?"

"Well, sir, it's like this." The whole story tumbled out of me: my suspicions, my planning, how I had gotten inside. I didn't even consider lying.

About halfway through the story, the teen I had seen downstairs joined us. The first thing I noticed was the striking resemblance he bore to Magnus, though the boy's skin was a bit paler and his red hair more messy. He stood in one corner, his arms wrapped around him like a shield. I had seen someone stand like that in Magnus's office before.

My eyes widened and my story screeched to a halt. "Veritas?"

The boy's head snapped back. The rest of the pieces flew together. The girl's bedroom, the familiar photos . . . My mouth dropped open.

Lux and Veritas hadn't been just partners—they had been brother and sister. And their father was Alexander Magnus, Meridian himself.

"You seem to have us all at a loss, kid," Magnus said. "You know who each of us are. Me, Helen, my son." The last word was sharp enough to cut. "Back in the day, when a hero unmasked another, it was only polite to reciprocate. *Quid pro quo.*"

"I don't think that's a good idea." The words were out before I could really consider them.

Magnus's face hardened. "You broke into my house. I could call my friends down in the VOC."

My fingers twitched. I wanted to unmask, but something didn't feel right, especially since I had left the necklace back with my civvies. *Quid pro quo* aside, I doubted Magnus would want to puke all over his study floor.

"Dad, come on." Veritas's voice, normally so resonant and sure of himself on the set, sounded hollow. "You know that's not true."

Redness shot through Magnus's cheeks. "I suppose. Come to think of it, the Azure Shrike figured out who I was, and she never unmasked for me." He glanced at Helen. "Do we know whatever happened to her?"

"Still unknown. Last sighting was in Barbados, if I remember correctly." Helen's lips twitched into what almost passed for a warm smile. "Do you want me to track her down?"

Magnus laughed. "That'd be asking for trouble, wouldn't it?" His smile grew broader. "Remember that time we were both chasing . . . Oh, who was it? Mind Master? She wanted the reward. I wanted him to 'face justice.' We had him cornered but got into an argument about who would take him in and we wound up brawling for close to two hours." He sighed. "Stupid. Double-M got away and we wound up in Dutch with the VOC. Almost lost my license over that." His gaze shifted in my direction and the mirth fled from his expression. "Anyway, let me see if I have this straight. You thought I was responsible for the death of my own daughter?"

Put that way, the whole thing did seem ridiculous, but of course I hadn't known the family connection at the time.

"Yes, sir." I could barely mumble the words.

Magnus collapsed into his desk chair. "Well, that's a new one. But I suppose I would have thought the same thing." He leaned forward, fixing me with an intense stare. "Okay, so let's clear the air completely. Now that you know who I am, and if you're not going to unmask, is there anything else you've been holding back about that night?"

I wracked my brain, trying to think of any details. "Just maybe her last words. I thought she was trying to tell me you were responsible. She said something like, 'Tell Ver . . . '" I paused as it all came together. "She was trying to tell me who you and Veritas were."

Magnus stroked his chin for a moment. "Okay, here's what we're going to do. I want to find Lux's murderer, obviously. And you will too, given the scuttlebutt I've heard from my sources at the VOC. They still like you for her murder. So since we both want the same thing, I'm suggesting a team-up—"

I sucked in a deep breath. Had Meridian just suggested I work as his partner? How could I say no to that?

"—with Veritas."

Oh. I glanced at Veritas. It was odd seeing him out of costume and still knowing his identity. At the moment, he didn't look much happier at the suggestion, but he did summon a small grin for me.

Best to make the most of it. "All right," I squared my shoulders. "But first, do you mind if I ask you a few questions?"

Magnus's eyes flashed, a red glow that turned his face skeletal. "I'm still a suspect?"

Heat shot through through my cheeks, made hotter as it reflected from my mask. "No, of course not. But obviously you've got enemies. While Lux hadn't been at this for as long, she probably had a few too. I'm wondering which group we should focus on."

Helen stepped forward. "I don't think this is a productive discussion to have now. Perhaps Failstate and Veritas can continue this at a later date." She glared at me. "I presume next time, you'll be polite enough to let us know you're coming first?"

I nodded.

Magnus slapped his thighs and rose from the chair. "Good enough for me. Veritas, show our guest out."

Veritas led me out of the study, down the hall, and through the front door. But on the front steps he touched my shoulder. "Hang on a second." Veritas disappeared into the house and then returned, pressing a slip of paper into my hand. "Give me a call tomorrow morning."

The massive door closed and clicked shut. I glanced at the paper. He had scribbled a phone number on it.

As I headed back to where I hid my civvies, I wasn't sure how to classify tonight's mission. Not a success, not really. Not a failure either, though. For me, that was progress worth celebrating.

CHAPTER 23

"YOU'RE ALMOST HERE?" Vertias's voice sounded hollow on the other end of the cell phone.

I glanced out the bus window. Magnus's house flashed by as we rounded a corner. "Looks like it."

"Good. Head to the park and follow the easternmost trail. Stay alert for a dirt path about twenty yards in. Follow it and you'll do fine." The line went silent.

A minute later, I stepped off the bus outside of Hightower Park. A dingy bronze plaque near the open gate detailed the park's history: the land had been donated by Alexander Magnus in the early '70s, developed and landscaped to his exacting specifications, and given to the residents of New Chayton for their recreation and pleasure. Black paved paths wound through hills and trees. The morning sunlight filtered through the trees, and I took a moment to breathe in the pine-scented air. Thankfully no one else seemed to be using the park.

Toward the back of the park, I found the dirt path. A low chain hung across the entrance, a faded and rusted sign hanging from it warning off unauthorized personnel. I glanced around. Nobody seemed to be watching. I stepped over and jogged down the path.

A small copse of trees provided me the perfect cover to change from my civvies into my costume. I considered taking off my necklace but decided against it. Who knew what kind of valuable equipment Magnus would have in his house? If Veritas and I ended up back there today, there was no way was I going to risk damaging any of it.

I stashed my pack and continued down the path. I came to a small shed tucked into one corner of the park's walls, just a rickety building made of corrugated metal with painted-over windows. A small garage butted up against one of the stone walls, its door misaligned. When I approached the shed, part of the wall peeled back to reveal a small video screen. A silhouette appeared on it.

"Come on in." The voice had been distorted, warbling and low.

The shed's door opened with a soft whoosh, revealing a darkened interior lit by a single flickering bulb over a wooden chair. Broken shelves lined the walls, none of them level. I stepped inside, and the door shut behind me. I sat down in the chair and waited.

Suddenly the cabin's interior lit up. I shielded my eyes as the room spun around me. No, not the room, but the lights. Bright spotlights rotated around my body. Then the floor opened up beneath the chair. My fingers clamped onto the chair just as it dropped through darkness. Then it shuddered to a stop.

Veritas, wearing a t-shirt and jeans and no mask, stood in an open door, his hands tucked behind his back. "Sorry for the over-the-top production. Dad is a little fanatical about security, especially when visitors come to his command center."

"That's okay." I had trouble prying my fingers from the chair. "I'm surprised you didn't wear your costume."

"Not much point in that, seeing as you've seen me without it, and you know who I am."

My face reddened beneath my hood as I stood up. I hadn't thought of that. "If it's any consolation, I haven't done any prying about you."

"I appreciate that." Veritas hesitated. "It probably will get kind of stuffy down here with your mask on. You could remove it. And don't worry about how you look. I've seen worse."

My insides flash froze. I worked my jaw, no sounds escaping from my mouth.

Then Veritas laughed, a short bark that didn't convey any mirth. "You know what, forget I said anything."

"No, it's okay. Like your dad said, *quid pro quo*, right?"

I fingered the hem of my hood. Once again, my fingers rebelled, refusing to take hold. I swallowed several times, trying to keep down my rising panic. But this was the right thing to do. With a quick tug, the mask slipped off.

Veritas stared at me for a moment. "Wow, that's some good makeup."

I touched the necklace. "It's actually this. When I wear it, I look like this, and my power is shut off."

"I see. Well, at least it's an improvement, right?" Veritas winced and ran a hand through his shaggy mane. "Never mind. Let's get going."

We walked down a darkened tunnel. The heavy darkness pressed in around me, and I swallowed my rising panic.

"Sorry." Veritas's voice floated around me. "Dad always produces his own light and I've gotten used to the dark here."

"No problem," I lied.

"My name's Mike, by the way."

"What?"

"I thought you might like a name to go with the face—my real face." His voice trailed off expectantly.

In for a penny . . . "I'm Rob." We shook hands as we walked. I tugged at the edge of my sweatshirt. "So how are you doing . . . with everything?"

"I've been better. Her funeral was yesterday."

I nearly tripped over my own feet. "And you went to the taping anyway?"

"Dad's idea. He's always said that people in our line of work can't let anything stop us. Not even . . ." His voice hitched.

We continued on in silence. Then a pale green light flashed over us. I jumped backwards and dropped into a defensive crouch.

"Just another security check, Rob. Don't worry."

Part of the wall opened, and the bricks retracted, revealing a good sized bunker, one lined with dingy black bricks.

"Welcome to Meridian's Lighthouse." Mike swept his hands out around him.

The room—more like an aircraft hangar—was massive, easily the size of a football field, the ceiling thirty feet overhead. The room had been divided into different areas by low walls. A large bank of monitors lined one wall, with several computers underneath. A bank of lockers dominated another, towering over a number of exercise machines. A small kitchenette was tucked into one corner.

My legs wobbled beneath me. Everyone in New Chayton had heard about Meridian's Lighthouse. When I was a kid, I used to draw pictures of it. To actually be standing in the Lighthouse, with Meridian's permission . . . I suddenly couldn't breathe.

Mike led me over to the computers and motioned for me to sit in a high-backed leather chair. I sank into it, and he sat behind a keyboard.

"So where is your dad right now?" I asked.

"At a meeting with the network and the mayor. Apparently last night's taping ruffled some feathers."

"Gee, I can't imagine why."

Mike pressed his lips together in a thin line. "Let's get to work. Any thoughts?"

I leaned back in my chair. "Has your dad heard anything more from the VOC about what happened to Lux?"

Mike shook his head. "They still don't know what caused her injuries, although they're pretty sure it wasn't a conventional firearm. The police canvassed the neighborhood three times, but nobody is coming forward. And there wasn't any forensics." His gaze bored into my forehead. "Do you have any more information?"

I frowned. Every time I tried to remember that night, it remained a jumbled mess. Some sort of information danced at the edge of my memory. I shook my head. "Sorry. I wish I could. Lux was really special."

"She was, at that. And you can call her Elena. I don't think she would have minded."

The name hit me like a blow to the gut. I hadn't wanted to know. Somehow it made my failure even heavier. "What was she like?" The words escaped my mouth before I could think. But they continued to spill out. "I mean, I don't have a sister, so I don't really know what it's like."

"Elena was . . ." He laughed. "She was a pain sometimes. Always late. But you never cared. She was . . . she was light itself." He swiped at his eyes. "Look, this is a little too early. Let's just . . ."

I held up my hands in surrender. "Right, sorry, I didn't mean to—"

"It's okay, really. I just . . . it's hard, you know?"

I didn't know, but I nodded anyway. "So could it have been one of her enemies? Had she started any real feuds?"

Mike gritted his teeth for a moment. "Well, kind of. We'd been tangling with the Blue Eclipse Boys lately. Some of them have superpowers, so I'm thinking—"

"If the Blue Eclipse Boys really killed a hero, don't you think they'd be bragging about it? You'd think that the police would have heard something about that by now."

Mike frowned at me. "So what do you think?"

"Maybe it was one of your dad's enemies. They found out who he really is and took revenge on Lux?"

"I suppose that's possible. Dad didn't make a lot friends in his career." Mike turned from the computer to face me. "It's a long list, Rob."

I sighed and leaned back in my chair. "Well, then we'd better get started. Your dad's archnemesis was Mind Master, right? "

Mike snorted. "It's not Mind Master."

"How can you be so sure?" I said.

"Well, for starters, he's in prison serving fifteen consecutive life sentences—"

"He could have escaped. Or he could have used his powers to bring someone under his control."

"No way," Mike said. "Not possible. Trust me."

"All right, fine. Who do you think it was?"

Mike typed something into the keyboard and the screens lit up. A flowchart, shaped like a pyramid, appeared. Individual boxes contained names, dates, data.

"The Blue Eclipse Boys pretty much control Hogtown. Drugs, prostitution, protection rackets, they're into it all. Elena and I tried to take them down but their leadership rarely surfaces." He waved his hand, indicating the lowest row of boxes on the flowchart. "We took out about half a dozen of their foot soldiers. None of them rolled on their bosses. But recently, Elena thought she had unearthed some data on one of the Boys' top lieutenants."

One of the boxes zoomed in. Instead of a picture, a black silhouette filled the left side. No real data to speak of, just an alias, "Pyrotrack." Weird name, but then, who was I to judge?

"If this 'Pyrotrack' heard that Elena was closing in on him, he might have ordered a hit," Mike said.

"Have the Blue Eclipse Boys ever killed a hero before?"

"Not to my knowledge, no."

I crossed my arms over my chest. "Why would they start now? I still think it's one of your dad's enemies, like Mind Master . . ."

"I'm telling you, Mind Master did not do this."

"How can you know for certain?"

Mike sighed and pushed himself away from the computer. "You're not going to drop this, are you? All right, let's go see Mind Master."

My eyes snapping open wide. "Wh—what?"

"You heard me. Let's drive down to Kidron and see him."

My mouth went dry. Kidron, a small suburb to the south of New Chayton, was home to the Valley Correctional Facility, a prison designed to contain supervillains, the worst of the worst. I had always assumed I'd visit Valley someday, probably while bringing in a captured villain. But not so soon.

Mike stared at me expectantly.

I swallowed and nodded. "All right, let's go."

"We'll take the car."

"Car?"

"The one my dad designed for Lux and me to use on our patrols. Hang on, let me change."

My nervousness dissolved, replaced by a wave of excitement. Meridian was famous for his "Photon Cycle," his preferred method of transportation. As Mike went over to the lockers and rummaged through one of them, I remembered the news stories, detailing how Meridian would blow into a situation on the Cycle, scattering everyone in his path. I couldn't wait to see what Magnus had cooked up for his kids.

Once Mike was in uniform, we went down the hall and bypassed the chair elevator and rounded a corner. I tensed, ready to be wowed.

Instead, sitting in a pool of light, was a puke green Plymouth Reliant. Rust bordered the doors, random scratches trailed down its side, and a crack snaked down the edge of the windshield. The antenna had been snapped off, leaving a six-inch stub in its place. The front license plate hung at an almost forty-five degree angle. This had to be a joke.

Apparently not. Veritas popped open the driver's side door, which swung open with a metallic shriek. "Get in."

"This is your ride? Shouldn't it be flashier, like the Photon Cycle?"

"No way. Dad tells me that while he used the Cycle, it was stolen twice, smashed five times, set on fire ten times, and egged more times than he could count. But with this baby, you can drive it into a neighborhood and not worry about anyone messing with it. Don't let the exterior fool you—Dad tricked it out. Top of the line engine, a remote control, armored all around. And the stereo is awesome."

Huh. If even half of that were true, I bet it'd be a fun car to drive. Maybe I could ask him to let me go for a spin at some point. At the same time, there was something disheartening about getting into a car that appeared ready to disintegrate without my help. I opened the passenger door, and a pile of fast food wrappers and empty soda cans spilled out, clattering across the floor.

"Sorry about that," Veritas said. "Part of the camouflage."

"Uh, huh." I slid into the passenger seat. "Maybe you shouldn't try so hard."

"Helen says the same thing."

Veritas reached up to the visor hit what looked like an ordinary garage door opener and the whole car shuddered. I looked out the window in time to realize that the floor itself was rising. Within a matter of moments, we were in a garage with three rickety wooden walls and one of rough stone. We faced the stone wall. Much to my surprise, it pulled open and revealed daylight and an alley. Veritas carefully pulled out of the garage.

"So what's the deal with your dad and Helen?"

Mike snorted. "What does that mean?"

"Well . . ." How should I phrase this? "I mean, aside from the show, she's always with him. When you guys questioned me and last night, and probably now. Are they . . . well . . ."

"Oh, no. Nothing like that," Mike said. "They're close, sure. She's worked for him for close to thirty years now. Days, some nights, lots of long weekends."

"Your mom didn't mind that?"

Mike fell silent for a moment. The corners of his eyes glinted. Tears? Oh no. I must have strayed into painful territory.

"Not as much as you might think," Mike whispered. "It's like Dad always said. You have to have someone."

Then he fell silent and I didn't mind, because I couldn't help but think of my own dad. And I wished he was still there for Mom.

CHAPTER 24

"WELL, THIS WAS YOUR IDEA," Veritas said. "You coming in or not?"

My gaze roved over the squat building. The grey concrete looked like a blister poking out of a field of brown and barely green grass. To even get to the parking lot, we had had to pass through three concentric stone walls, each one dotted with guard towers and sparking razor wire and manned by armed guards. Now we faced the main prison complex, its narrow windows glaring at me like the eyes of an accusing god. Danger oozed through the bricks, spilled across the parking lot, and lapped at my feet.

Veritas stepped into my field of vision. "Look, I know it's intimidating. The first time we came here, I nearly needed to change my costume. But the guards are the best the VOC has and the security is top notch. But you might want to take off the necklace. Just in case."

"Just in case of what?" I winced at the squeak in my voice.

"Well, nothing is foolproof. One time, Dad was bringing in the Golden Slinker—and no, I don't know why anyone would call themselves that—when a prison riot put Valley in lockdown for three days. Dad was trapped with everyone else."

My guts turned to ice. That was supposed to reassure me . . . how?

"Anyway, I'm sure we'll be fine, but better safe than sorry."

I fumbled with the necklace but finally got it off. I gasped as the irritation rushed through my body and became the steady throb behind my eyes. I tucked the necklace into my pocket and fell in step behind Veritas. "You do realize that without my necklace, I tend to break things accidentally. Like security systems?"

Veritas didn't say anything, but he did slow down as we approached the front doors.

Two burly guards in crisp white uniforms stepped out of the gatehouse, their badges glinting in the light. But what caught my attention were the large guns on both hips.

"Hold it right there, fellas," one of them said, holding up a hand. "Identify yourself."

"Veritas. And this is my colleague, Failstate. I believe you have my credentials on file."

The first guard's eyes widened for a moment. "Oh yeah! I thought you two looked familiar. Sure, yeah, hang on a sec."

He went back into his booth and came out with a security wand of some kind. "Sorry about this, guys, but you can't be too careful, y'know? Lots of baddies in here."

"Of course." Veritas held out his arms parallel to the ground.

The two guards took turns waving it over Veritas and me, running from head to toe. I gritted my teeth as the wand skimmed my arms and down my side. Concentrate, keep the power in check. It probably wouldn't help our case if I fried the security scanner.

"Hey, that was a tough break last week with the obstacle course," the first guard said as he worked. "I really thought you guys were going to make it. Say, I almost hate to ask this, but if it isn't too much bother . . ."

He held out a piece of paper to me.

I stared at it, unsure what I was supposed to do. Then I realized what he wanted. An autograph! Wow! I smiled, even though he couldn't see my expression, and took the paper.

"Could you get me Gauntlet's autograph? That guy is so cool!"

I had to fight to keep from crinkling up the paper. "I'll see what I can do."

"Awesome!" Both guards stepped aside. "Head to the main lobby and check in."

We passed through the thick iron doors into the lobby beyond. Scuffed green and white linoleum lined the floor, clashing with the beige tiles that crawled up the lower half of the walls. Veritas led the way to the visiting office. A frumpy looking lady in her mid forties barely glanced at us as we entered the office.

"Name of the prisoner you wish to see?" she asked.

"Mind Master," Veritas said.

The woman glanced up at us. A smile blossomed on her face. "Oh, hey, Veritas. No problem. You know the drill, right?"

Veritas nodded and reached over the counter, pulling out a thick binder labeled "Visitor's Log." He flipped through the wrinkled and torn pages to a fresh sheet where he scribbled his alias and a few more details.

I followed suit. I tried to disguise my handwriting as much as I could. That wasn't easy. I kept wanting to write my true name. The end result was a barely legible jumble of lines.

The woman typed something on her computer, then looked up at us. "Mind Master is on his way to the visitation room. Take care, guys!" Her voice was a sunny chirp.

We walked out of the office and Veritas led the way through twisting halls and past windows covered with thick iron bars. We swung around a corner and almost collided with a pair of barrel-chested guards.

One of them cracked his knuckles loud enough to be mistaken for gunshots. "Head on in. You got ten minutes." He slid his ID card through a reader.

The door, made of steel three inches thick, rolled into the wall. We stepped through to an even dingier hallway and the door slid shut with an ominous *thunk*. Every muscle in my arms and legs stiffened. The throbbing behind my eyes became more insistent.

"We're okay." Veritas's murmur set my nerves even more on edge. "The really bad cases are housed in a separate level, deep underground."

We stepped through the door and into a small room, maybe twenty feet at its widest, ten feet across and high. A narrow window near the ceiling allowed a feeble amount sunlight to trickle in, just enough to offset the absolute coldness of the room. Dull white walls made opf painted bricks wrapped around us. A metal table filled the middle of the room with four plastic chairs set at odd angles around it. A large sliding metal door dominated the wall opposite us. Veritas motioned to one of the chairs. I sat down, not really relaxing. My heart ricocheted off my ribs.

Then the large door slid open and a man in his mid-fifties shuffled in, wearing a dull grey jumpsuit with a long string of letters and numbers on his chest. Although he wasn't burly or muscular, he appeared taut and ready to strike at any moment. His salt-and-pepper hair was pulled back in a tight ponytail that reached down to the middle of his back. His face, lined with wrinkles, still carried a youthful air. His eyes, blue chips of ice set deep in his skull, flashed with menace. A cold tendril slithered up my neck.

"Ah, Veritas. And you brought a friend."

"Mind Master, meet Failstate," Veritas replied.

Mind Master, the villain who was Meridian's arch-nemesis sat down on the edge of his chair. The cold tentacles crawling across my scalp dug into my brain. Was that him? Was he probing my mind already?

"So pleased to make your acquaintance." His voice, a soft coo, echoed in the suddenly chilled room. "It's so rare that heroes bother with me anymore. And yet now, here are two. To what do I owe the honor?"

Veritas nudged me between my shoulders. He wanted me to take the lead? Oh, great.

"We, uh . . . we have some questions for you."

"Undoubtedly, else you would not be here." Mind Master's smile turned to a grimace, as if he were readying himself to swallow me whole. "Ask away, my young friend."

The words caught in my throat. "I thought—that is, I thought perhaps you might know something about what happened to Lux. Y-y-you've heard about that?"

"Oh, yes." His lips drooped and he looked out the window. "All of Valley is abuzz over her death. A true pity, that."

He actually sounded sad. But why? A guilty conscience maybe?

"So has anyone in particular been buzzing? Like someone who is responsible for what happened?"

Mind Master's eyes widened and he laughed. "Surely you do not believe I am to blame? How could that be possible?"

"Oh, I don't know. Maybe you planted the suggestion in a guard or another visitor. They went out and did it, but you were the one who set things in motion."

A smile twitched at the corner of his mouth, just a little half-grin that did nothing to disguise the malevolence in his gaze. "Am I? Do you really believe I could do something like that?"

And suddenly, those icy fingers dug into my mind. I tensed as they bored in, as if someone were trying to rifle through my thoughts.

Mind Master's smile had frozen in place but an eerie light shone in his eyes. "Now, Failstate, answer my question. Do you really believe I am capable of such a thing?"

My arms twitched. I glanced at Veritas, but he seemed frozen as well. Had Mind Master already gotten him? My neck twisted involuntarily and sharp pins dug deeper into my brain.

Maybe I could block him somehow. I tried to imagine myself erecting barriers, thick walls that would keep him at bay. The sensation lessened for a second, but then the storm exploded through my skull. My fingers balled into claws. I had to do something to stop this.

I lashed out with my power and sheered through the legs of Mind Master's chair.

His eyes widened in surprise and he toppled. His arms lashed out to stop his fall, then he tumbled to the floor.

Alarms blared in the distance. I couldn't wait for the guards, though, not now that I was free. I exploded out of my chair, vaulting the table. I landed on Mind Master's chest, my arm cocked to punch him.

He stared up at me for a moment and then laughed. "Oh, I *like* him!"

CHAPTER
25

VERITAS LAUGHED TOO. "I thought you might. Get off him, Failstate."

I turned and glared at Veritas. "How can you say that? It felt like he was tearing my brain out."

The two guards burst through the door, weapons drawn. Mind Master held up his hands.

Veritas shooed them back out. "We're okay, really." He turned to me. "He's not a threat."

"It's true, boy, I'm not. If you would kindly stop sitting on my chest, I would be happy to elaborate."

Veritas nodded, so I stood and stepped over the fallen supervillain. The guards went back out and closed the door.

Mind Master sat up with a groan, but he remained on the floor. "I understand your concerns, but they are unfounded—for two reasons. First, my powers have deteriorated. At my prime, I could have done as you suggested to Lux. But now I have become too clumsy. You may have noted my lack of subtlety just now. Second—and, I believe, more importantly—I would never do such a thing, especially not to the lovely Lux."

"And why's that?" I demanded.

"Because, my boy, I have, as you might say, 'gotten religion.' I converted to Christianity five years ago."

I stared at him, his words not registering. When they finally made sense, I turned to Veritas. He nodded. Huh. I would have never figured that.

"So you're saying that Christians can't commit murder?" I asked.

"No, not at all. Any of us is capable of great evil. I, better than most, understand what it means to squander our God-given talents and use them for nefarious purposes." Too bad Mind Master didn't come with subtitles. He stood and nudged the remains of his chair with his toe. "The warden will not be pleased with you. As I was saying, my becoming a child of the Light does actually exempt me from your list of suspects. I could never harm Lux or her intrepid partner, because I have come to care about them too much. Isn't that right, my boy?"

"True enough," Veritas said, leaning against the wall.

I looked between them for a moment and then sighed. "So which one of you will explain it to me?"

"I'll let him," Veritas said. "He makes the story sound classy."

Mind Master chortled. "You do me a great injustice to tease me so, but I shall do as bid. As I am sure you're aware, twelve years ago, Meridian brought my career to an end. The jury at my trial, in their wisdom, saw fit to sentence me to . . . Oh, I lose count. Eighteen consecutive life sentences? Nineteen? The numbers do not matter. The fact that I would never leave Valley alive does.

"For the first seven years, I festered in my cell. Brooded. Plotted my revenge. I tried many times to escape so I could wreak vengeance upon Meridian, the judge, the jury, everyone even remotely connected with my trial. It left me hollow, but I didn't care. I refused to see how it had been I—me—who had ruined my life."

Mind Master settled into one of the other chairs and studied the ceiling. "Most inmates in this squalid excuse for a prison knew to avoid me. But there was one pie-eyed optimist who refused to let me go. The chaplain. I heaped such scorn on him as to cause a lesser man to crumble. He didn't. He kept coming back, insisting that God loved me and offered forgiveness. I wouldn't have anything to do with it."

"What does this have to with Lux?" I asked.

Mind Master held up a hand. "Patience, my boy, patience. As I said, the chaplain didn't leave me alone. Neither did the Holy Spirit. They wore me down, as it were. And then one night, I understood. How does the Scripture go? 'If anyone is in Christ, he is a new creation. The old has passed away; behold, the new has come.' I was reborn, my past sins washed away."

My face scrunched into a scowl. From anyone else, I'd think it was a ruse to get out of prison. But Mind Master seemed so sincere . . .

"Still, while my sins may be gone, their consequences are not. I have left a trail of suffering and heartache in my life. So many people ruined because of me." He pursed his lips. "I suppose you cannot sympathize with a visceral need to make up for past mistakes."

I shifted uncomfortably in my chair.

Mind Master spread out his hands as if to embrace the room. "I deserve to be in Valley, making amends as best as possible. But I realized there was one person I had wronged most: Meridian.

"Our chaplain put in a request through the VOC for Meridian to come. For months I received no word. But then one day, we met, face to face, in this very room, and I sought his forgiveness and offered him anything I could." He turned toward Veritas and leaned forward, threading his fingers together. "Do you remember what happened next?"

Veritas chuckled. "How could I forget? Meridian brought Lux and me to see Mind Master. I was scared half to death, thinking we were going to be brainwashed. But instead, Meridian told Mind Master that if he wanted to make things right with him, he should tell us everything he knew about fighting supervillains such as himself."

"And so began an instructional course that lasted two years," Mind Master said, leaning back in his chair. "In that time, I came to be quite fond of my pupils. They became . . ." his voice hitched for a moment. "—like my children. So you see, Failstate, I could never have participated in Lux's death. Truth be told, I hope you find the beast and put him or her in here with me." His smile evaporated and, for a split second pure malice shone in his eyes. "My powers may be weak, but they would suffice."

My brow quirked up. "That's not very Christian."

"No. But it is human."

I sighed and looked at Veritas. He'd convinced me. Mind Master wasn't Lux's murderer. There had to be some way to redeem this visit, but I couldn't think of anything. "I'm sorry we wasted your time."

Mind Master stood. "Not at all, my boy, not at all. It was a pleasure to meet you. Veritas, I am sorry for your loss." He hesitated, indecision flitting through his eyes. "Tell me, will you see *her* today as well?"

For a split second, I thought Mind Master was asking if Veritas were going to visit Lux's—Elena's—grave.

But Veritas reared back, his spine straight. A twitch tugged at one eye. "C'mon, Failstate, let's go." He marched out of the visitation room before I could answer.

I tried to follow him out, but Mind Master grabbed my arm.

"Before you leave, I hope you would agree to a little exchange of favors with me as well, Failstate."

I turned to face him and expected to feel his telepathic fingers rifling through my thoughts again. But there was nothing, just his earnest eyes.

"Meridian asked me to do more than instruct his protégés," he said. "He also wanted me to focus on Veritas. For some reason, he wanted me to encourage Veritas to meet with one of my fellow inmates. Delphi. Have you heard of her?"

I shook my head.

"I have been less than successful in this. Perhaps you might take up the gauntlet?"

I ground my teeth. Bad choice of words. The request didn't sit well with me. If Veritas didn't want to speak with her, whoever she was, who was I to interfere? But Mind Master looked so earnest, almost vulnerable. Maybe he was messing with my head again, but I found myself nodding.

"Excellent. Then I suggest you hurry along before Veritas realizes we have conspired against him." With that, Mind Master turned and walked to the opposite door. It ground open. He glanced once over his shoulder to smile at me, and then he was gone.

We walked back through the layers of security, and I wrestled with my promise to Mind Master. What could I say? Veritas obviously didn't want to meet with Delphi, but what were the chances that we'd ever be back to Valley together? Even though it seemed a now-or-never kind of deal, I couldn't bring myself to say anything.

Veritas led me back out to the parking lot. We didn't speak on the ride back to the Lighthouse.

Once Veritas parked the car, he turned to me and I caught the barest hint of a smile through his mask.

"So should we keep going then?"

I glanced at the clock in the car. It was almost four in the afternoon. I winced. Not good. Mom would expect me home soon.

"I can't." Then an idea occurred to me. "But hey, what are you doing tomorrow morning?"

"Nothing, why?"

"Why not come to church with me? I mean, we won't be able to talk about the case, but it might be cool to hang out, you know? Talk about other stuff? I don't know about you, but I get kind of . . . well, lonely."

I winced. Stupid. What was I thinking? Mike stared at me for a moment. Cold sweat burst across my forehead. Was he seeing through me? Finally, he nodded. "Sounds good to me."

I gave him directions to Mount Calvary. Mike then escorted me back through the shed and let me out again. I found my pack and changed back into my civvies and then headed for the bus station. I glanced over my shoulder at the shack and smiled. Small steps were good enough sometimes.

CHAPTER 26

THAT EVENING I BOLTED from the dinner table the moment Mom excused me, and I headed up to my room.

I almost had the door shut behind me when Ben shouldered it open. He studied me carefully, his arms crossed over his chest. "So where were you today?"

My eyes narrowed. Alarm bells clanged through my mind. "Out."

"Uh-huh. Doing what, exactly?"

"Shopping. I have to replace my costume thanks to Krazney Potok, remember?" Hopefully he wouldn't catch me in the lie.

"And yet you didn't come home with any bags."

Shoot. It was stupid of me to think he hadn't noticed.

His arms unwound so he could crack his knuckles. "So where were you?"

I almost laughed at him. What did he think I was, a criminal in need of interrogation? "With a friend," I said.

"Patrolling? Investigating? Or what?"

The phone rang downstairs and I hoped that Ben would leave to see if it was for him. It usually was. No such luck. He cracked his knuckles and his lips twitched into an almost feral grin.

"It's none of your business," I said.

"Maybe I should make it my business."

"Rob, get the phone!"

I blinked. Who could that be? I hadn't given Mike my number. But at that point, I'd talk to just about anyone. I dove backwards and snatched up the phone. "Hello?"

"Hey, you."

My eyes widened at the melodic voice. "Elizabeth?"

"So you do remember me." She chuckled. "I was beginning to wonder."

Ben's face twisted into a glare. His fingers curled into fists, his knuckles turning white.

I almost suffocated on the hostility that flooded the room. But with Elizabeth on the phone, I felt a bit bolder than usual. I covered the phone's mic and returned Ben's dirty look. "Do you mind? This is private."

Ben ground his teeth, but he stomped out of the room.

"Sorry about that," I said into the phone.

"No problem. So have you heard about what happened at the taping?"

Oh. She only wanted to exchange gossip about the show. I should have known. I collapsed in my chair and wheeled myself over to the desk. "No, I haven't."

"Well, I heard things didn't go according to plan. From what I've read, they sent the contestants into the warehouse district and . . ."

As she continued her story, my eyes fell on my computer. It wasn't that I didn't want to listen to her. Far from it. Her voice was the soundtrack for my dreams, sweet and breathy all at once. But I had lived what she was telling me. So maybe I could do some research while she shared her gossip.

I wiki-ed "Delphi." It turned out she had been a hero during the mid '90s and had started her career in Los Angeles. Her power was "instant cognitive awareness of limited potentialities," whatever that meant. Probably some fanboy wrote that trying to look smart.

" . . . and then T-Ram smashed through the legs of one of the robots and brought it down on top of himself!"

"Uh, huh." I skimmed Delphi's career highlights. Nothing indicated a connection between her and Veritas or Meridian. The article wrapped up by saying that her license had been revoked years ago in the wake of a scandal. But whoever wrote the article hadn't provided any links or sources. I glared at the "citation needed" notice. I'd have to keep looking.

" . . . and apparently it was some Russian dude who broke out of prison . . ."

I did a search of news articles next. There were a lot to sift through, the usual write-ups in Los Angeles newspapers or national magazines. I went back to the search engine and entered her name and Meridian's.

" . . . then the robots went out of control! They could have destroyed all of New Chayton . . ."

Huh. The search engine actually turned up a few articles. Apparently Meridian and Delphi had partnered for several months, not only in Los Angeles but also in New Chayton.

And then I saw the picture.

It was grainy and poorly focused and taken at night. Weird shapes loomed out of the darkness, but I could make out two people, partially obscured by shadow. A well-muscled man held a lithe woman in his arms, tipping her head back, their lips close to touching. A paparazzo in L.A. claimed the photo was of Meridian and Delphi kissing.

"No way!" I whispered.

"I know!" Elizabeth said. "Thankfully Gauntlet showed up and he was able to help . . ."

I leaned back in my chair. No wonder Veritas didn't like Delphi. He had to have seen this picture. I had no idea how I would have reacted if I found out that one of my parents had had an affair.

" . . . and then Gauntlet destroyed all of the robots!"

That snapped me back to reality. "What did you say?"

She sighed. "Weren't you listening? Gauntlet destroyed a dozen rampaging robots and saved the city!"

"Who told you that?"

"I read about it on a blog," she said. "Cape Town? The author calls himself 'GyFox.'"

A few keystrokes brought up the Cape Town website. Sure enough, GyFox had interrupted one of his usual apocalyptic rants to give Gauntlet the credit for saving the day. Great. And since GyFox had been so reliable in the past, everyone would believe his version, especially since none of the footage had survived.

"So did you only call me to share this news?" I asked.

"Well, no, not exactly." She sounded a little hurt. "I know we've got church tomorrow, but I was wondering if maybe . . . you and I could go out and get some coffee or something afterwards?"

A thin thread of hope twanged inside me. Just her and me? Alone? Like on a . . . I couldn't bring myself to label it. I didn't want to come off too eager. I leaned back in my chair and tried to still my stammering heart. "Oh, sure, yeah. You know, I've got a friend coming with me, but once he's gone, I'm sure we could do something."

"Great! I'll see you tomorrow then!"

She hung up. I stared at the phone in my hand. Then I looked up toward the ceiling and mouthed the words *"Thank you!"*

Ben was waiting for me outside my room when I emerged. He glowered at me. "What are you smiling about?"

I paused in the doorway. "Nothing. Nothing at all."

CHAPTER 27

I SHIFTED UNCOMFORTABLY on my feet, back and forth, and checked the entrance to Mount Calvary's gym for the third time in as many minutes. More people filed through the door, chatting and laughing, finding their friends and taking their seats around the stage. Then Mike came through the door, wearing a pair of khakis and a striped button-down shirt. For a split second, I forgot he was Veritas; he blended in with the crowd all too well. He tapped his hands against his legs and looked around. I waved to him and he smiled.

"Glad to see you could make it," I said.

"Me too. Dad almost locked me in the house today. He wanted me to catch up on my training." A bitter edge crept into his voice. "If it were up to him, I'd spend my whole time either doing homework, at 'work,' or . . . in the basement. Great way to spend a Sunday, huh?" Then he smiled. "So what do we do now? Just hang out, or is there some sort of program?"

I led him from the doors toward the chairs. "The service will get started in a few minutes. Right now we're supposed to 'fellowship' with each other. At least, that's what Pastor Grant says we're supposed to do."

"Did someone say my name?"

I nearly jumped out of my shoes. Pastor Grant grinned at me. He wore a polo shirt with a small Jesus-fish embroidered over his heart, and he carried his Bible tucked under his arm. He shifted his attention to Mike. "So who's your friend, Bob?"

"Pastor Grant, this is Mike Ma—" I said.

"Mike Rickman." Mike stuck out his hand.

I blinked, surprised. If P.G. noticed my hesitation, he didn't say anything.

"It's great to have you here!" P.G. pumped Mike's hand. "Listen, I'd love to stay and chat, but I have to get the band going. Mike, be sure you stop by our visitors' table and pick up a free book. We've got a lot to choose from, okay?" And with that, he was off, bellowing the name of another student.

"Rickman?" I asked. "Why the alias?"

"Who says it's an alias?"

Before I could keep questioning him, I noticed movement out of the corner of my eye.

Ben ambled over to us. He sized up Mike for a moment before turning to me. "Who's this?"

"Mike, this is my brother, Ben Laughlin. Ben, this is Mike Rickman."

Ben slapped Mike on the arm. "Good to meet you, Mike. So what are you doing hanging out with my little brother?"

"Rob invited me to come."

"Really." Ben considered me, then turned back to Mike. "Do you go to our school?"

Mike shook his head. "Not unless you go to Briarton."

"We couldn't afford one class there, let alone a whole year." Ben's eyes narrowed. "You look really familiar."

Mike's gaze sharpened as well. Then he blinked and took a step backwards. "I get that a lot."

"Huh. If you want to meet some of the guys here, let me know, I'll introduce you around, okay?" Ben sauntered away.

Mike whirled on me. "We have met before, haven't we?"

Uh-oh. Revealing my secret identity to Mike was one thing, but technically I shouldn't expose Ben. But Mike would know if I lied to him.

"Um . . . can I plead the Fifth?" I said.

Mike laughed. "Fair enough."

We wandered around the edge of the chairs, making small talk about traffic, the weather, and our schools. We were comparing classes when I noticed a disturbance through the crowd. People scattered as if a radioactive monster moved among them. Then the mass of bodies parted, and I recognized who they were avoiding.

"Haruki?"

He looked horrible. Red sores blotched his skin, which was much paler than usual. His eyes were bloodshot and seemed a few shades lighter. His hair appeared brittle, as if it were made of glass and ready to break. He smiled wanly.

"Are you okay?" I rushed to his side, and Mike came with me. Had Haruki been beaten up on the way to church? Been in a car accident? No, his marks weren't bruises.

"*Sukoshi warui no ja nai.*" He waved me away. "I'm fine. I look a lot worse than I am."

"Are you sure?"

He nodded. "Yeah, it's just because of the aliens. Happens all the time." He looked down at his hands. "Well, not this bad usually."

"Should you go see a doctor?" Mike asked.

Haruki glared at him. "Hey, why didn't I think of that? I don't have a fever or nausea or anything like that, and the moment I tell them why I look like this, they'll want to check me into some psych ward. Not gonna happen. Now, if you'll excuse me, I'm going to go find a seat." He brushed past me and headed for the chairs.

I would have followed but the band started playing. I lost Haruki in the shuffle so Mike and I found seats toward the back. P.G. bounded up on stage and greeted everyone enthusiastically. He challenged us to worship hard enough to disturb the service in the main sanctuary. Then the band was off, starting their fifteen minute set.

I tried to sing along as best I could, but I kept checking on Mike throughout the service. For all I knew, this could be his first time in a church. I wanted to be sure I was ready if he had questions. He followed the words on the big screen. At one point, he met my gaze and smiled, but I could read an uncertainty in his eyes.

"I know all of you spent some time chatting with each other before worship began," P.G. said, "but now I want you to greet each other in the name of the Lord. Let's make sure that everyone here knows they matter to us and to God." P.G. hopped off the stage and headed for the nearest worshiper.

I turned to greet Mike, but he was already chatting with a doe-eyed girl. Someone tapped me on the shoulder and I turned.

Elizabeth smiled and hugged me. "It's good to see you."

Warmth shot through me. But much too quickly the embrace was over.

She tucked a stray black lock behind her ear and looked over my shoulder. "So this is your friend?"

Mike turned from the doe-eyed girl and saw Elizabeth. He froze for a moment, a frown flitting across his face.

His expression matched Elizabeth's. A clearly fake smile locked on her face, but then her eyes softened and she stuck out her hand. "I'm Elizabeth Booth."

"Mike Rickman."

"Well, it's good to meet you," she said. "Any friend of Rob's is a friend of mine."

"Glad to hear that."

She focused her exquisite blue eyes on me. "Well, I'll see you in a little bit, okay? I'm going to go say 'Hi' to Ben." And with that she was off, weaving through the crowd.

"She's cute." Mike's frown deepened. "Are you and she . . . well . . . ?"

My cheeks burned. Was I that easy to read? "No. At least, not yet. Uh, we're supposed to go out after church."

Mike's eyebrows shot up. "Interesting."

Why did he sound so cautious?

At that moment, P.G. called everyone's attention back to the stage. He read a passage from James and then launched into his lesson, pacing the stage and waving his arms wildly while he regaled the crowd with stories from his youth, references from the latest TV shows, and a few really corny jokes. I tried to pay attention, I really did, but I couldn't help checking on Mike's expression, trying to read him. And more than once, I tried to see if I could spot where Elizabeth was sitting. She had disappeared, but I noted with some satisfaction that she wasn't sitting by Ben.

After P.G.'s message, we sang another round of songs. During that time, ushers walked the aisles and passed out prayer request cards. I didn't bother taking one. There was a lot of divine help I needed: figuring out who killed Lux, self-control for my power, help to not make a complete dork of myself on my date with Elizabeth. But I couldn't ask P.G. to pray for any of that.

Much to my surprise, Mike took one of the cards and scribbled something on it. He didn't meet my gaze.

The worship set wound down and the ushers handed the cards up to P.G. He led us in prayer, reading off the requests. Now I was doubly glad I hadn't filled out a card with my requests.

" . . . And now, Lord, we pray for Mike and his family." P.G. said. "Mike recently lost his sister in a tragic accident and his father's struggling with it. Lord, just comfort this hurting family with Your presence. Grant them the peace that only You can give and let them trust in Your divine grace . . ."

I glanced at Mike as P.G. moved on to the next request. Mike had his head bowed and tears glistened in the corner of his eyes. I turned away, not wanting to intrude on his grief.

And that was when I saw Ben. He had turned in his chair and was looking straight at us, that all-too-familiar glint in his eyes. I looked away immediately but I knew it was too late. Ben had figured it out.

I had gotten a good start on my panicking by the time P.G. wrapped up his prayer and faced the crowd.

"You know, we sing a lot of songs here. Well, I got nostalgic recently and decided I wanted to go old school this morning.

Really old school. Like eighteenth century. To close out our service today, I asked the band to prepare one of my favorite hymns from when I was growing up. So let's give this a shot, huh?"

The guitar player started an up-beat tune I sort of recognized. Had I sung this hymn before? Maybe. It would have been a while. The first verse appeared on screen, and I saw that it had something to do with blessing what had been sown for God's glory.

Then the words appeared for the second verse and I almost fell over.

To You our wants are known From You are all our powers. Accept what is Your own and pardon what is ours. Our praises Lord, and prayers receive And to Your Word a blessing give.

The band then started an extended instrumental riff. I stared at the screen where the words gleamed across a brilliant white field. "From you are all our powers"? Wow. What would P.G. have said if he'd known that three superheroes had been worshiping here today? It was almost as if he had known . . .

The third verse sped by and the service was done. I glanced at Mike.

He smiled at me. "This was great, Rob, really. I'll have to come back some time. Call me later so we can keep working on . . . that project, okay?"

I nodded. He disappeared through the door. I turned to Elizabeth.

She smiled and my heart jack-hammered against my ribs. "So, Mr. Laughlin," she said with a giggle, "what shall we do now?"

CHAPTER 28

ALL I COULD THINK OF was a movie at the mall. Not very creative, and not the ideal first date, but Elizabeth's brilliant smile didn't waver when I suggested it. She said good-bye to her friends and we were off.

Happily, the mall was within walking distance of our church. As we walked down the sidewalk, I stole glances at Elizabeth. Why would she want to go out with me? Elizabeth should be going out with someone, well . . . someone much better looking than me. More popular. More Ben-like. My necklace seemed to squeeze my neck. I ran my fingernail along its rough string. Why couldn't it give me a chiseled jawline and striking eyes—something other than my pudgy, freckle-spattered cheeks and dull brown eyes?

Elizabeth must have noticed. She touched my necklace and ran her finger across the hemp rope. Her touch left a trail of fire across my skin beneath it. "What's with this necklace? It's looking a little ragged. Maybe we could buy you something nicer while we're at the mall. My treat."

Her finger tucked under the bead. Immediately the itching tingle swept through my body and lodged between my eyes. My skin crackled and my lips began to shrivel. No! I jerked away and the bead dropped back into place, arresting the transformation before it could truly begin.

Elizabeth stared at me with wide eyes. But then an uncertain smile tugged at her lips. "I—I'm sorry, I didn't mean to—"

Ah, *man!* I had already screwed things up.

"It's not your fault. It's just . . . this was a gift from my dad and . . . well, I guess I'm a little overprotective about it."

The cars rushed by on the street, not that either of us were saying anything. Elizabeth wouldn't meet my gaze and heat crept up my cheeks. I wasn't lying, not really. Dad had made my first necklace, but I had outgrown that one years ago. The fib didn't sit well with me but I really didn't have any choice.

"So what, that necklace has something to do with your deep, dark secret?"

Heat trickled up my cheeks and into my scalp. If I hadn't been wearing the necklace, my power would have spiked from my embarrassment, I just knew it. "What makes you think I have a deep, dark secret?"

"Oh, everyone has one. Even me." She took a step closer to me, her voice suddenly husky. "So what's yours?"

My thoughts snapped back to my duffel bag, hidden under my bed. Should I tell her? It'd be so easy. And she was a fan, my fan! She'd be so excited . . .

. . . until she would want me to prove it. Then I'd have to take off my necklace and she'd see my true face. That would be the end of us. Besides, secret identities didn't stay secret very long if they were shared with people we didn't know very well.

In my desperation, I latched on to the only thing I could think of. "I like show tunes?"

She laughed. "That's your big secret? Come on."

Oh great, she didn't believe me. I'd have to really sell this. "Oh, yeah. Broadway musicals are my passion. Every time there's a . . . a . . . ." What was the right term? " . . . a traveling show I'm right there in line to get tickets front and center. Yeah. If you were to look at my iPod, nothing but show tunes."

Okay, time to shut up, genius.

"I would have never guessed that." She grinned before she started across the intersection, a noticeable bounce in her step.

She bought it? I jogged to catch up with her. "So what about you?" I asked. "What's your big secret?"

She giggled. "Um . . . would you believe I've never been kissed?"

"Oh, come on!"

Elizabeth nodded. "It's true. It's never happened, not even close."

I stared at her, my mouth slack. "How is that possible? I mean, have you seen you lately? You're gorgeous! I'd think there'd be guys lined up for the chance."

She ducked her head, hiding behind her hair. "That's sweet of you. The truth is that I've never really wanted to kiss anyone before. Nobody's ever caught my eye."

She glanced at me and a warm fog descended on my brain.

Wait . . . did she want *me* to be her first kiss? My mouth went dry, all the moisture in my body draining to my palms. Here, on the street? No, don't be a moron. This isn't what she'd want. Not in public. But maybe at the end of the date. I could escort her home and then, before she went in, I could lean in, and . . .

"So, tell me about your dad."

Her question jolted me out of my reverie. "Excuse me?"

She shrugged. "Well, you said he made that necklace for you. And I've never heard Ben or you talk about him much."

A flash of anger shot through me. How often had she been talking to my brother? Had she told her secret to him? "He died."

Her hand stroked my arm for a few moments. Any jealous thoughts I may have had about Ben fled under her caress. "Rob, I'm so sorry."

"It's all right. It happened eight years ago."

Unbidden memories danced before my mind. Dad's rough but gentle hands, his encouraging laughter as we worked in the garage. I closed my eyes, trying to will the memories away. I didn't need to go down this road, not right now.

"How?"

"Car accident on his way to work." I wanted to tell her more, but I knew I couldn't. If I said anything else, I could reveal too much about what happened. And that would lead her to questions I couldn't answer. I forced myself to smile and glanced at her. "How about you? What happened with your parents?"

Her face closed, her eyes going dead. "That's a long story."

One she wouldn't tell, apparently. We walked the rest of the way to the mall in silence.

Elizabeth brightened as the parking lot came in view. "I'm not that hungry, are you? Why don't we just go catch a movie and get some popcorn?"

"Sounds good to me."

The parking lot stretched before us. We crossed it in silence. I savored her presence beside me. I worried that if I said anything, I'd snap back to reality. This had to be a dream. How else could I be on a date with someone like Elizabeth? Even the greasy smell of the food court wasn't sickening today. Why else would the sky be so vibrant, rich with blues and whites? Why else would three ratty men be clustered around a car in a secluded corner of the lot?

Wait. What were they doing?

Two of them stood guard, their backs to the expensive sports car, the third working with a tool to pop the door open. In the middle of the day? I came to a halt. My hand crept toward my necklace. Maybe I could pull my shirt up to cover the bottom half of my face . . .

Elizabeth grabbed my arm. "Let's go!"

The tension drained out of my body. How stupid was I? I couldn't do anything while Elizabeth was with me. I let her lead me away from the car but as we walked, I grabbed my cellphone and started dialing. I might not be able to stop them directly, but I could at least call the police.

"Hey! What do you think you're doing?"

My head snapped around. One of the look-outs started across the parking lot, a determined scowl on his face. I fumbled with my cellphone, my fingers suddenly unable to find the right keys. Elizabeth whispered my name, pulling on my arm.

The criminal walked even faster, his lips peeling back into a snarl. "You better drop that phone—"

His words dissolved into a shriek as his body stiffened, his arms shooting out. I stared at him, dumbfounded. He was in some kind of convulsions. Then I noticed the thin wires, leading from his side back to a gleaming column standing in the parking lot. I squinted and raised a hand to protect my eyes.

With a whirring of motors and the clank of his boots, Kid Magnum strode forward, the wires leading into one of his wrist gauntlets. "Never fear, citizens. I have the situation under control."

The criminal who had threatened us collapsed to the ground. The other two stared at their fallen compatriot with wide eyes.

Kid whirled on them. "Get down on the ground before I decide to use you for target practice." Kid raised his arms, multiple barrels popping out of his arms.

The one who had been working on the car did as he was told, diving to the pavement and putting his hands behind his back. The other look-out ran. Kid made a scolding sound and fired.

A beanbag smashed into the back of the fleeing criminal and knocked him onto his face. The criminal skidded to a halt and squirmed, clutching at his back and groaning.

"Can you believe this?" Elizabeth asked, sounding thrilled.

No, I really couldn't. What was Kid doing in New Chayton? With the show on hiatus, he should be home in Philadelphia.

A small cluster of men and women trotted up behind him, one of them carrying a professional video camera. Kid cuffed the three suspects then he turned and clanked over to us. "Are you two okay?"

Ice sluiced through me. What should I do? If I spoke out loud, he could recognize my voice. That could lead to uncomfortable questions, especially with Elizabeth standing next to me. I ducked my head and scuffed at the pavement.

"We're fine," Elizabeth said. "Thank you for your help."

"It's what I do, young lady." He then turned to the camera crew. "You get that?"

The man holding the camera nodded. "Every last bit of it."

"Good." Kid rolled his shoulders. "About time something happened. I was beginning to think today would be a complete waste."

"We did get footage of you rescuing that kitten from the storm drain."

Kid snorted, a burst of static through his faceplate. "Big deal. I'm sure that's going to win me the license."

My head snapped up. "What?"

Kid's head swiveled in my direction. "What rock have you been living under? The vigilante license on *America's Next Superhero?*"

I swallowed my frustration at his condescending tone. "Yeah, but that show got cancelled, didn't it?"

Kid laughed. "No, it's just on hiatus. Besides, the way I figure it, maybe I can still win. You know, go out there and right some wrongs and do it with my own camera crew. That way, when the show comes back on, I can hand over some sweet footage of me in action." He clapped his hands together with a clank that hurt my ears. "Then the license will be mine. Now if you'll excuse me." He turned his back on us and walked back toward the camera.

I stared at him, unable to move.

Elizabeth gently tugged on my arm to get me walking again. "What a loser. Everyone knows he isn't going to win. No wonder he's trying a stunt like this—he's desperate."

I tried to find comfort in her words, but I couldn't shake the queasy feeling in my stomach. What if it worked? What if Kid did get the license because he was doing this sort of thing? Sure, I had an in with Mr. Magnus, but what had I really accomplished since the show had gone on hiatus? A bungled search of the wrong person's house, an interview with a super criminal that hadn't led anywhere. At least Kid was still trying.

We walked through the doors and into the mall's food court. As we walked by Krakatoa, Mr. Johnson came rushing out to us. "Elizabeth! Thank goodness you're here! Three of the baristas called in sick today and I'm in desperate need for help. You could use the extra hours, right?"

Elizabeth blanched. "Well, yeah, the money would be nice, but Rob and I—"

Mr. Johnson looked at me, almost as if he hadn't noticed me before. "Oh, sorry, Rob. I don't mean to interrupt your plans." He walked back into the coffee shop.

A line snaked out the door and a lot of the waiting customers didn't look happy, tapping their feet or consulting their watches.

"He'll be okay," Elizabeth said, uncertainty in her voice.

"Oh, I'm sure."

We started for the theater. I tried to muster some excitement but Kid Magnum's words taunted me as we walked. And Elizabeth looked over her shoulder twice. I sighed. I doubted either of us would really enjoy ourselves anymore. "Look, why don't you go back and help Mr. Johnson."

Elizabeth smiled, just a hint of relief painted across her face. "Are you sure? Because I've been looking forward to spending time with you, but I really could use the extra—"

"No, it's okay. Really. We can do this another time. "

She grabbed a handful of my shirt and drew me close.

I choked on my own breath. She was so close. If I leaned in just a little, brushed my lips against hers . . .

"I'm holding you to that, Laughlin. Call me." With that, she turned and hurried away, but not without casting a sad look over her shoulder.

I blew out a shaky breath. Should I have kissed her when she had me by the shirt? We had been so close. All I would have had to do was lean in, brush my lips against hers.

A shake of my head dislodged those thoughts. If I kept following that train of thought, I'd wind up chasing her down. Instead I headed for the exit.

Outside, I paused to scan the parking lot. No sign of Kid Magnum, but he couldn't have gone far with his entourage in tow. For a moment, I considered calling Mike to see what his take on Kid's plan was. But I kept walking for the bus stop. I could handle only so much mental torture in one day. Ditching Elizabeth more than met my quota. I looked skyward as I walked.

C'mon, God. Just a tiny break, please? I'm not asking for much.

But there was no answer, just the first few drops of a cold early spring rain.

CHAPTER 29

LINCOLN HIGH WAS a ghost town the next day.

More than two-thirds of the student body were missing. So were half the teachers. Eventually the rumor mill caught up with me. The missing people had all caught colds. Nothing serious, but just enough to knock everyone on their collective rears. No one had gone to the hospital or anything like that. The remaining teachers and subs didn't bother with actual lessons. Each class turned into a *de facto* study hall. The novelty wore off after the first two periods. If I had known, I would have brought a book or something.

Toward mid-morning, my cell phone vibrated. I glanced at the teacher, a young sub who was completely engrossed in a magazine. He probably wouldn't notice. I fished the phone out of my pocket. My eyes widened. The caller ID was Mike. I turned from the front of the classroom and huddled for privacy. "Hey, what's up?"

Mike hacked. "Seems I've come down with a cold."

"Yeah, a lot of people are sick here too," I said.

"Anyway, I just wanted to check in with you. How are you feeling?"

"I'm good. I don't get sick."

There was a long pause. "Ever?"

"No."

Another silence. "Huh. Well, I'll give you a call when I'm feeling better, okay? We don't want the trail to get any colder than it is."

"Okay. Bye." I put the phone away and glanced at the sub. He sent me a glare but then turned back to his magazine. I slid lower in my seat and sighed. I had to find something to do before I went out of my mind with boredom.

The bell released me from academic purgatory. I walked through the halls, passing only a few students. None of them seemed in any hurry either.

On my next class, no other students had shown up. Only Mr. Sinclair, the teacher, waited for me. I sighed.

"I know, Mr. Laughlin," he said. "I've been informed by the office that you are the only student I can expect for this period."

"Then can I go down to the computer lab?"

He shrugged. "I suppose that'd be okay."

I snagged the hall pass and headed through the deserted corridors to the lab. I settled in at a desk far from yet facing the entrance, partially shielded by a half-wall partition. I clicked over to a search engine and started digging for more information about Delphi.

I started with the paparazzo photo and settled back in the chair. According to the accompanying article, the photo had been taken in 1993. Had Magnus still been married to Mike and Elena's mother at the time? I hated to do it, but Mike probably wouldn't give me the information and there was no way I would ask his dad. So that left me with news archives. I did a search for anything on the Magnus family from around the same time period to see what I could find.

Lots of society page photos. I called up the first I found, one from 1991: Magnus and his wife Carissa at a charity event, he in a sharp tux, she in a sleek evening gown, all blue and sparkly. She was pretty with luminous eyes and an impish smile, the same one Lux had given me the night before she . . . I couldn't dwell on that. I scanned the article and my brows shot up.

The reporter, some gossip columnist, had filled the article with speculation about whether or not Carissa Magnus were pregnant. I checked the photo again. I didn't see anything, but the reporter seemed pretty confident. And sure enough, the next article I found confirmed it: The Magnus family officially announced that a child was on the way.

I scrolled through the rest of the articles, detailing numerous high society baby showers and charity events. No wonder Magnus relied on Helen so much—it seemed like he was always out and about. A few articles dealt with the rumors that the baby would be a girl. Others speculated about possible names.

The next article from the *New Chayton Gazette* was about a hospital fire.

I frowned. What was that doing in the mix? Maybe the search engine had glitched. I was about to flip past it when I noticed the accompanying picture, not of Alexander Magnus, but of Meridian. His normally sterling costume was covered in soot. He sat on the edge of a sidewalk, almost as if he had collapsed there. He cradled something in his arms, a small corner of fabric draped over his massive forearm. A baby? I read the caption: "Meridian holds newborn Elena Magnus after rescuing her from the disaster."

I sucked in a deep breath. No way Meridian would allow himself to mess up like that, unless . . . My gaze flew over the article. On August 24th, 1992, an explosion had rocked New Chayton Mercy Hospital, setting most of the building on fire . . . officials weren't ready to speculate on the cause . . . Meridian was immediately on hand to help survivors from the blaze . . . there had been seventy injured and sixteen deaths, including . . .

I dropped back in my chair, feeling as if I had been punched in the gut.

Including Carissa Magnus, wife of billionaire Alexander Magnus, who had given birth to the couple's daughter, Elena, mere hours before the disaster.

Numbness trickled from my brain through the rest of my body. That photo didn't show simply a man exhausted from having saved innocents from a fire. It showed a man crushed with grief, clinging to his daughter. Had he tried—and failed—to save Carissa? I could only imagine what he must have been thinking and feeling.

The door to the computer lab banged open. I panicked, fumbling with the mouse to clear the screen. Too late. The newcomer appeared around the corner.

"Rob?"

I looked up. "Haruki?""

The strange splotches that had dotted his skin the day before had disappeared and he looked relatively healthy. But now he looked haggard and crushed. His clothing hung on his body like he was a child playing dress-up in his dad's closet. His face appeared as if gravity were trying to drag it to the floor.

"I just wanted to find a place I could be alone. There weren't too many people in my class and none of them were talking to me anyway, so I'd better just—"

"What's wrong?"

His face scrunched up. "It's nothing, really. I'm just, well, I'm just worried about everyone who's sick, that's all."

I frowned. "Why? It's just a cold. Creeping crud. We get that a lot this time of year."

"This much?" Haruki sighed. "At least nobody's died this time. So far. Sorry, Rob, I should really go. Talk to you later, okay?"

And with that, he left, the computer lab door slamming behind him. I stared after him, my confusion mounting. What did he mean by "this time?" Had he seen something like this before? I had intended to research Lux's career, get some idea of who might want to hurt her. But at that moment, I had other questions that needed answering.

I called up a search engine, entering Haruki's name. Not surprisingly, I didn't find anything unusual. So I searched for "strange disease outbreaks." Again, nothing relevant. I mopped my hand over my face.

Maybe I should narrow the search. Haruki had spent time in Japan and Canada before moving to New Chayton. I started with Japan first, narrowing my search to Haruki's early years, the late nineties. One result caught my eye—a mini-epidemic of rubella near Aso on Kyushu in 1997. Three hundred people had been infected, even though they had all been inoculated. Ten had died. Officials had no idea what caused it. The city had braced for the worst. Only the outbreak burned out quickly.

On to Canada. A similar search brought up a bizarre story. Five years earlier, an outbreak of tetanus, diphtheria, and polio had hit Swift Current, Saskatchewan. Some of the victims had caught all three at once. Like the outbreak in Japan, officials in Canada hadn't been able to pin down a source. This time, thousands had been hit by the diseases, and hundreds had died. And just like in Japan, the mini epidemic had ended as quickly as it had started.

I leaned my head in my hands, staring at the screen, my face pinching into a scowl. Had Haruki lived in those areas? That could explain why he was worried. But everyone in New Chayton had caught a minor cold only, not a serious disease.

I shook my head. As much as I wanted to help Haruki, he wasn't connected to Lux's death. At least, I didn't think he was. I wasn't sure of much anymore. I closed my eyes and leaned back in my chair.

God, I need Your help here. The answer's staring me right in the face, I know it. Just give me some insight here, please.

As I sat in the computer lab, a stillness descended on me. I could feel the different threads drawing together, weaving into a pattern. Haruki and Lux, the show, Veritas and his family, they were all related by . . . what?

The bell rang, jolting me so hard I nearly tipped over in my chair. I ran a hand through my hair. As much as I wanted to stay in the lab, I knew I had to move on to my next class. I closed the browser and headed for the door, but not without one last look at the computer. I had been close. With any luck, I'd be able to piece it all together again.

CHAPTER 30

"HELLO?" I SLIPPED THE DOOR SHUT behind me. Mom had had a bad headache when I'd left for school. She had skipped work, a rarity for her, and she wouldn't be too happy about her lost wages. Best not to antagonize her further.

Ben trudged from the kitchen to the living room, still in his pajamas even though it was late afternoon. He sniffled loudly and glared at me as if his illness were my fault. But then he started coughing, almost bent double.

"Should you even be out of bed?"

He growled, then hacked a bit more. "I'm starting to feel better." In spite of his protests, he threw his arm over me and let me steer him back to the living room. He collapsed onto the couch with a groan.

"Do you need anything?" I asked.

He shook his head and groped for the TV remote. "What was school like today?"

"Dead. No real classes. Almost no one there. In Spanish, Smithson tried to teach all both of us, but he gave up after twenty minutes."

Ben started flipping channels. He tossed the remote from hand to hand. It spun and tumbled crazily, almost hovering in mid-air each time. "Was Liz there?"

I ground my teeth and swallowed hard. "No, she wasn't. Why?"

"When I heard how many people were out sick, I tried calling Liz. Never heard back from her." He cleared his throat, snorting and hacking, and then winced. "So you're all chummy with Veritas now, huh?"

I jumped, startled by Ben's quiet question. He wouldn't meet my gaze, staring at the flickering images on the screen. But in spite of the tension in his jaw and the hard edge to his eyes, I could still read the disappointment in his eyes.

"I don't know what you're talking about."

Ben laughed, a harsh bark that ended with a hacking cough. "Please. I'm not stupid. How else would you have hooked up with a kid from Briarton who recently lost his sister in an accident?" He settled deeper into the couch cushions. "So you two are investigating Lux's murder? After I offered to help you? But whatever. Still, I'd be willing to bet you two could use a strapper, right?"

As much as I hated to admit it, his offer was tempting. Even though we hadn't crossed paths with the Blue Eclipse Boys yet, I knew we'd be in for a fight when we did. Who knew what kind of muscle they had? Help, even if it was Ben, would be welcome. My head began to bob.

Ben smiled, sitting up straighter on the couch with his chest puffed out. "This is going to be awesome! Too bad there won't be any cameras, huh? Just think of the footage we could have gotten for the show."

That's what he was thinking? That this would just be an act? He looked so cheesy, so cartoonish, I knew he wasn't taking this seriously. Any eagerness I had for his help evaporated. No way did I want to add Ben's name to the list of people I'd hurt. Mom would never forgive me.

"You know what, forget it. We've got this."

"Are you sure?" Ben asked.

I nodded. "Trust me."

"Suit yourself. Hope you cognits do okay without a real hero to back you up." Ben glowered at me.

Pathetic. He looked like a three year old who had been told he couldn't play with his favorite toy.

As I trudged up the stairs, I tried to purge my conversation with Ben from my memory. But one thing stubbornly clung with me. Elizabeth. Had she really been incommunicado all day? That couldn't be good. For a split second, I considered barreling back down the stairs and out the door to go check on her. Even sick, she'd be radiant and so happy to see me. We could pick up where we had been the day before. I couldn't get sick, so I could even kiss her today.

Before I did anything, though, I had to check on Mom. I crept to her room. The sounds of her TV drifted through the closed door. I slowly pushed open the door and poked my head inside. "How are you feeling, Mom?"

She lay in her bed, wearing a ratty t-shirt, mountains of pillows ringing her head. In the flickering light of the TV, she looked pallid and waxy, like a copy of my mother instead of the real thing. She groaned. "I'm okay. What are you smiling about?"

Had I been? I guess the thought of seeing Elizabeth again so soon buoyed me. "No reason."

Mom blew her nose and settled deeper into the pillows, casting an annoyed look in my direction. I should retreat, leave her to rest and feel better. The fact that she wasn't hanging out with Ben probably meant she didn't want company right now. Certainly not mine.

Would Elizabeth? The thought froze me in place. Maybe going over to see her wasn't such a good idea. If she were this miserable too, she might not appreciate the gesture.

"Mom, can we talk?"

"Not right now, Robin."

"It'll only take a minute."

She sighed. "What?"

"I was just wondering . . . Suppose there's someone you like and you're pretty sure they like you too. And she's not feeling well. Do you think it would be cool to just stop by and make sure that person is okay?"

"Oh." She fell silent and for a moment, I thought that maybe she had fallen asleep. But then she spoke, her voice low. "If this person really likes you, I'd think she'd be happy to see you no matter what." She sat up straighter in her bed and our gaze met. Her mouth opened, as if she wanted to say more. Her gaze flicked to her nightstand, where a picture of Dad smiled up at her. Her face fell and she settled deeper into the pillows. "Get out of here. I need my rest if I'm going to work tomorrow."

"All right, Mom. Good night." I walked to the door. I paused before I stepped through. "I love you."

Silence. I forced myself to leave. At least she had talked to me.

I headed back downstairs and grabbed my jacket but I paused at the door. If Elizabeth were sick, it might be nice to bring her a present. Maybe she'd need some more tissues? Oh, sure, really romantic. Chicken noodle soup? No, that was almost as bad. Flowers? Too cliché, especially for someone as special as Elizabeth.

My thoughts drifted out to the garage. I smiled. I had just the thing.

Elizabeth didn't live in what I'd call a nice part of town. It wasn't as rundown as Hogtown but it was close.

The glass in the apartment building's front door was covered with spiderweb cracks but was still locked. I punched the button for the Booths' apartment and waited. The speaker blatted at me in an odd imitation of a ring tone. On the third jolting screech, the speaker clicked. Was this thing even working?

"What do you want?" The tinny voice nearly deafened me.

"I'm here to see Elizabeth." I didn't know why I was shouting.

"She ain't feeling well. Neither am I, so buzz off and wait until she goes back to school."

"I've got something for her. I won't stay long, I promise."

Was that static from the speaker or muttered cursing? But the lock buzzed.

I yanked the door open. "Thanks!"

"Hey, hold the door for a second?" A delivery guy in a blue jacket jogged up the sidewalk, carrying a large object wrapped in brown paper.

I propped the door open and let him through.

"Thanks, man."

The delivery guy disappeared up the stairs. A nervous thrill shot through me. I couldn't wait to see her, even if she was sick. I dug in my pocket and pulled out my gift, a small rose blossom I'd just cut from a piece of quartz, no bigger than the palm of my hand. The crystalline flower glinted in the hallway light, sparkling and looking like it shimmered. But as I slowed on the third floor, I frowned. It looked like something had smudged one of the petals. What was that? Pocket lint? I stopped to take a closer look, but someone was stomping up the stairs after me. I ducked into a corner, gently poking at the petal with my fingernail. I brushed the debris free.

According to the directory, Elizabeth lived in apartment 315. I glanced at the nearby doors. Lower three hundreds. Down the hall, the delivery guy knocked on a door, which opened a second later. "Got some flowers here for an Elizabeth Booth. She lives here?"

"Liz!" A man's voice, possibly the one from the speaker.

I pressed myself into a doorway. I don't know why, but for some reason, I didn't want Elizabeth to see me.

"Who are these from?" It was Elizabeth's voice. She sounded sick but happy. Paper rustled.

"There's a card inside," the delivery man said.

A few seconds later, the door shut. The delivery man clomped down the hall and gave me an odd look as I emerged from my hiding place. Once he disappeared into the stairwell, I hustled down the hall to the door. Sure enough, apartment 315.

I chewed on my lower lip. Who were the flowers from? Should I even bother with my little gift? I looked at it. Sure, I was proud of my work, but what was a hunk of rock carved by an amateur compared to real, actual flowers?

I pressed my ear against the door. The conversation was muffled, Elizabeth talking with an adult, something about three dozen tulips, her favorite, and I definitely heard the name "Ben."

My shoulders slumped and the quartz rose slipped from numb fingers. It thudded to the ground. I didn't even care if it broke.

I turned and stalked out of the apartment and back to the van. When I started up the engine, the radio blared annoying pop music. I shut it off with a jab of my finger. I'd rather drive home in silence than listen to syrupy dreck.

Once home, I stomped into the living room. Ben napped on the couch, the flickering light of the TV dancing across his features. My lips twitched into a snarl. He wasn't going to get away with this.

But my voice caught. A quiet voice chided me. It wasn't like Elizabeth and I were going steady. We hadn't even had a whole date. And while I thought she had flirted with me, she hadn't exactly declared her undying love.

And really, if it came down to her choosing either Ben or me, it would be no contest. Ben had the looks, the physique, the charm, everything I lacked. About all I could offer was my relation to him. I sighed, loudly enough to wake him.

He glared at me. "Where have you been?"

"Just wasting my time."

CHAPTER 31

SCHOOL WAS CANCELED the next day due to the mini-epidemic sweeping through New Chayton. I spent the day in the garage, filling sculpture orders. We didn't have youth group that night either—apparently Pastor Grant was still under the weather.

But school was finally back in business on Wednesday. I liked being able to disappear into a crowd again. The empty halls had been too creepy.

Between first and second periods, I took a few moments to bask in the normalcy of the crowd. Small knots of my classmates flowed through the halls, laughing and chatting, comparing notes about symptoms and what they'd done with their days off. I didn't even mind the fact that no one seemed to notice me.

But there was one person I didn't want to see. Elizabeth. I tried to psyche myself up. At first, I was relatively sure I could fake nonchalance, pretend like I didn't care or even know about the flowers. But the more I envisioned how our conversation would go, the more I realized I couldn't do it. So I did my best to avoid her.

That proved difficult. After second period, I sprinted toward my next class, but I spotted her. She was leaning against a wall, giggling and twirling her finger through her hair. She was radiant and I could feel myself drifting in her direction. A haze descended over my mind. I didn't care that my brother had sent her flowers. We were meant for each other.

Then the crowd parted and I realized she was speaking to Ben. Her eyes sparkled, and she batted at his arm. Her hand lingered on his shoulder, stroking his arm. He smiled and leaned in so close I was sure they were going to kiss. It didn't happen—she tipped her head away. But she still pursed her lips as if inviting him.

A chasm tore through my chest. I spun away and fought through the crowd. I had to come up with a new way to get to my next class, and I wound up a minute late.

The image of Elizabeth inviting Ben to kiss her pursued me through the rest of the day, taunting me. By the end of the day, the memory had become a miniature movie, played out in awful slow motion. The flirting. The touching. The lean in. The near kiss. And worse, my mind provided the dialogue.

"Oh, Ben, I'm so glad you sent me those flowers. Otherwise I would have wound up dating that loser brother of yours."

"That would have been a disaster for sure! You really liked them?"

"Let me show you how much . . ."

By the time the final bell rang, I wanted nothing more than to get home. Maybe the tormenting vision would stay behind here in the halls that had spawned it.

I ran to my locker and practically tore the door from its hinges. I shoved books into my bag. I had to get out of the building, fast.

Then the hair on my neck rose. I could feel someone looking at me. I looked over my shoulder and relaxed. It wasn't Elizabeth. Instead, Haruki smiled wanly at me.

"How are you feeling?" I asked.

"Better now that it's all over." He looked even smaller than usual, wrung out and limp as he leaned against the wall. He studied the crowd with dull eyes, almost as if he were searching them for lingering signs of sickness.

I winced. The questions that had plagued me earlier about him echoed in my mind. I had to find out. "Where'd you say you were born?"

Haruki's face pinched into a frown. "A small town near Aso on the island of Kyushu. Why?"

A cold wave crashed through me. "And you moved here from Canada?"

"Yeah."

"Where'd you live in Canada?"

Haruki's face hardened and his eyes narrowed. "A town you've probably never heard of in Saskatchewan."

"Try me."

"It's called Swift Current."

I had to steady myself against the locker.

Haruki stared at me a few moments more and then took a step away from me. "This wasn't my fault." The fear in his voice sliced through me.

"I never thought it was. I was just curious—"

"Rob, don't get messed up in this."

I held up my hands, hoping to keep him calm. "I'm just curious. These aliens, how long have they been visiting you?"

Haruki's eyes fell to the floor. "I don't know. Maybe two or three years."

"Why haven't you gotten anybody to help?"

Haruki laughed ruefully. "What am I supposed to say? 'Hey, these aliens keep bothering me and every now and then, a bunch of people get sick afterwards.' Can you imagine how people would react?"

"Well, you're telling me now. When are the aliens supposed to come back?"

Haruki shifted on his feet and his gaze locking with mine. "This Friday. It's collection time."

"Okay. Well, that doesn't give us a lot of time—"

"What are you going to do about it?" Haruki asked. "I don't know what you could do. Not unless you have a bunch of superheroes on speed dial or something."

Now that you mention it . . .

I swung my backpack over my shoulder, the weight of my books throwing me off balance for a moment. "Isn't it good to get it off your chest?"

"Not really, no." He sighed. "Look, Rob, I appreciate the support, but this is just something I need to deal with on my own. Thanks anyway, okay?" With that, he disappeared into the milling crowd.

I watched him go and then turned back to my locker, retrieving my jacket and backpack. I slammed the door shut and then almost ran into Elizabeth.

She smiled at me and my heart stopped beating. I stared into her eyes for a moment, suddenly unaware of anything but her. A wave of numbness crashed over me, as if I were falling, drifting, circling through her presence.

"Hey stranger. I haven't seen you all day," she said. "Were you avoiding me or something?"

"No." The word escaped my lips before I could think of another answer. I didn't want to hurt her feelings, after all.

"Good." She took a step closer to me, her body almost touching mine. "Listen, clear your schedule for tomorrow night, okay? I'm coming over to your place to watch the last episode. Can you believe they put that show on hiatus? They must be crazy."

"Sounds good to me." It did? Since when? But once the words slipped past my lips, I knew they were true.

"See you then." And then she was gone.

I blinked a few times. What just happened?

I shook my head sadly. Who was I kidding? I couldn't stay mad at her. I slung the backpack over my shoulder and headed for the door.

CHAPTER 32

I HADN'T BEEN BACK to Hogtown since the murder. My stomach roiled as the Reliant pulled up to the curb across from a small grocery store a few blocks from the vacant lot. Mike stared out the windshield, his eyes unreadable.

"You okay?"

He blinked a few times. "I'm good." He turned to face me. "I've got some informants in Hogtown, people I've helped out. They said that this guy, Benin, would be making collections for the Blue Eclipse Boys tonight."

"Who's Benin?" I asked.

"Mid-level enforcer, nobody really special, but still not someone an average person would want to tangle with. I figured this would be a good chance to lean on him, find out if they had anything to do with what happened to Lux."

I studied Veritas's profile for a moment. "Why didn't your dad just give you the license?"

His head snapped around. Although his face was obscured by his mask, his eyes registered his surprise. "What?"

"I mean, you obviously know what you're doing. You have informants, the equipment, the training. Why go through all the nonsense of the TV show?"

Veritas settled back in his seat. "A couple of reasons. First of all, Dad thought he could make money from the show. He has a business to run, after all. Second, he wanted us to earn the license." He fell silent for a moment. When he spoke again, his voice had dropped to a mere whisper. "And if he was going to give it to anyone, it wouldn't be me."

My eyes widened.

Veritas wouldn't meet my gaze. Instead he stared out the windshield, tears forming in the corner of his eye. He cleared his throat. "We'd better settle in. It might be a long wait."

I threaded my fingers together, tucked my hands behind my head, and sighed. It was hard to get comfortable in the Reliant, especially in full costume. I wanted to remove my hood and breathe some cooler air.

Veritas glanced at me from the driver's side. "He can't be too much longer."

"Uh-huh." He'd told me that a half hour earlier.

I glanced over at my . . . well, I suppose I could call him a partner. Maybe even a friend. He lounged in his seat, staring through the darkened windows.

"So let me ask you something," I said. "What's with Elena and your names? I mean, I get that 'Lux' means light and 'Veritas' means truth. But why Latin?"

Veritas smiled. "Dad's idea. I think it was a joke. He went to Yale. That's their motto: 'Lux et Veritas.' Light and Truth." He drummed his finger on the door's arm rest. "So my turn. Why 'Failstate?' The name doesn't exactly inspire a lot of confidence."

I winced as the memories flooded back. "That was my dad too, believe it or not. Back when I was ten, he brought me to meet this scientist at New Chayton University. Dad put me in a mask, refused to identify himself or me. I showed the scientist what I could do. The scientist theorized that my power created a 'potential failstate within covalent bonds at a molecular level,' whatever that meant."

"No one ever figured it out for sure?"

"No. That scientist probably would've tried, but then my power spiked and I wrecked the lab's scanning electron microscope. The scientist wasn't happy and Dad got us out of there as quick as he could."

Veritas stared at me for a moment and then burst out laughing. I scowled at him, even though he couldn't see my expression.

"Oh, come on," he said, "that's kind of funny."

I didn't see the humor. When Mom found out what happened, it had sparked yet another argument. One that led . . .

I didn't need the distraction, not tonight. I derailed that train of thought.

But Veritas wasn't done yet. "You haven't said much about your dad. What happened?"

I ground my teeth together. "He died in a car accident a couple of years ago."

"Oh." Veritas stared at me. No, he stared *through* me. Shoot, he was probably reading me like a book. If I didn't stop this now, he'd hit on the truth and that was the last thing I needed.

"What aren't you telling me?" Veritas's voice was quiet, so much so that I almost wasn't sure he spoke.

"What's that rule you guys have? *Quid pro quo*? I'll tell you about Dad if you tell me about Delphi."

That worked too well. It was as if steel shutters slammed down behind Veritas's eyes. He turned away and looked out the windshield.

Big mistake. I shouldn't have done that. I'd be lucky if he spoke to me at all again, let alone worked with me.

His shoulders slumped and he fell back into the seat. With a groan, he pinched the bridge of his nose through his mask. "You've got a deal."

I jumped in the car seat. I hadn't expected him to speak again, much less agree.

"But you go first," Veritas said.

I coughed, trying to speak. "Like I said, he died in a car accident. What I didn't say that it was an accident that . . . I might have caused."

Veritas frowned. "How do you mean?"

"When Dad found out about my power, he liked to goof around with me, see what I could do. Mom wouldn't let us experiment in the house, so we always went out in the garage." I smiled beneath my hood. "We destroyed all sorts of stuff. We had a great time."

"It sounds like it."

"But Mom didn't find it so funny. She hated the fact that Dad let me take off my necklace and try out my powers. If it was up to her, we would have implanted it into my skull so I'd be 'normal.' I mean, you saw what I look like without it."

Veritas's eyes remained unreadable, but he shifted in his chair, leaning away from me ever so slightly. Oh yeah. He remembered.

I touched the fringe of my hood to make sure it was still there. "They started fighting about it. A lot. And after one of those fights, Dad took a drive to cool off . . . and he never came home."

Silence descended on the car.

"What happened?" Veritas asked.

"His brakes failed. For a while there, the police thought someone had cut them. They actually took a hard look at Mom. But then they concluded it had been a catastrophic failure, that the line broke because . . ." tears choked me. "—because of poor maintenance, as if something had eaten through it . . ."

I pushed a hand underneath my hood and wiped the tears from my eyes. Stupid. I should have known better than to talk about this. "So you can guess who Mom blames for what happened," I stared down the long dark streets of Hogtown. "Not that she's far wrong."

"Oh come on, you don't know that."

"Yes, actually, I do. Dad and I spent hours in that garage, right next to his truck. You know what my power does. Do the math."

Veritas touched my arm. "Have you ever talked with anyone about this?"

"Like who?"

"How about the youth pastor at your church?"

I snorted. "Pastor Grant? Oh, sure, like he'd understand any of this."

"You might be surprised," Veritas said. "I've been talking to him."

"You have?" I didn't know why I thought I'd know about such things first, but I was still surprised. Well, this was good, wasn't it?

"Yeah, since Sunday. E-mails, on the phone. I haven't told him everything, obviously, but he's good, and I'm really glad that you introduced me to him. Think about it, okay?"

I almost laughed out loud, but then I remembered how P.G. talked with the other youth group members. One night, he spent the entire evening with the family of a girl who had just lost her grandmother. And as cheesy as his devotions were, I never doubted his heart. "We'll see." I blinked a few times to drive away the tears and sat up straighter. "All right. Your turn."

"Fair enough." His fingers wrapped around the steering wheel. "What have you figured out so far?"

"Well, I did a little digging. Sorry. I found out that, shortly after your mom died, Meridian was spotted kissing Delphi. I figured that your dad was having an affair with her."

Veritas stared at me, his eyes blank. "That's not—I mean . . ." He sighed. "Well, here's the rest—" He leaned forward in his seat. "Hang on." He jerked his chin toward the window. "This will have to wait until later. Here comes Benin."

A large man emerged from a storefront and sauntered to a nearby bar. My stomach curdled at the sight of him. He was a walking boulder, so large I wondered who would win if we rammed him with the Reliant. Probably him. He was dressed in an impeccably cut black business suit with a colorful handkerchief poking out of his breast pocket. He was out of place in Hogtown, that was for sure. He turned and disappeared into the bar.

"Let's go." Veritas and I scrambled out of the Reliant and headed for the entrance. Veritas held up a hand as we crossed the street, his eyes slightly unfocused. "He'll be heading out the back into the alley."

"Does he know we're here?"

"I don't think so. Probably just S.O.P. C'mon, we'd better hurry."

We rounded the building into the darkened alley. Even though there were four garbage bins and a dumpster, bags of trash spilled across the ground. A row of crumbling apartments bordered the other side of the alley. A few of the apartments had lights on. Hopefully the residents wouldn't look out their windows anytime soon.

Veritas pointed to a streetlight. I focused on it and channeled my power into it, creating a loud pop and shower of sparks as the light died. We were plunged into semi-darkness. Veritas silently directed me to hide on one side of the door. He took the other.

A few moments later, the door banged open and Benin stepped outside, thumbing through a stack of dollar bills. I froze at the sight of him. He was even bigger up close. His chest was so large I probably couldn't have wrapped my arms around it.

"Hello, Benin." Veritas stepped out of the shadows. Benin whirled and, with a roar, swung at Veritas.

I was stunned by the reaction. If the punch had been aimed at me, I would probably have taken it on the chin. But Veritas seemed ready for it. He snatched Benin's fist, stepped in to get a better grip on the man's arm, and tossed Benin over his hip. The mobster slammed into the pavement, sounding like an avalanche running over a ski chalet.

Veritas planted his boot on his neck. "Don't bother getting up. You know who I am?"

Benin clawed at the boot for a few moments. Then he relaxed. "Yeah. You're Veritas."

"Then you've also heard what happened to my partner." Veritas removed his foot and knelt down next to him. "I want to know who did it."

Benin chortled. "What makes you think I know anything about that?"

"You're a Blue Eclipse Boy, aren't you?" Veritas opened Benin's suit coat and pushed his sleeve up to the elbow, revealing a tattoo of a sunburst obscured by a blue moon on his forearm. "I thought nothing happened in Hogtown without your guys' say-so. So who said so?"

"Go fish, Captain Underpants. I've got nothing to say to you."

Veritas glanced up at me, then back at Benin. "That's too bad. See, I've got a new partner. You ever heard of Failstate before?"

"From the TV show?" Benin laughed, a guttural rumble. "What's that loser cognit gonna do?"

"Oh, but you've never seen his power up close, have you?" Veritas asked, his voice laced with menace. He nodded at a spot on the ground near Benin's head. My eyes widened. He couldn't be serious. His eyes narrowed, and his gaze darted toward the ground again.

I sent a spike of power into the ground, raking it up past Benin's ear. A two-inch deep gouge appeared in the pavement.

Benin snapped his head to the side. He scrambled to his feet and tried to dart out of the alley but Veritas cut him off. Benin backed into a corner, terror in his eyes. I shifted my weight back and forth, my stomach flipping. This wasn't right. What would Veritas do if Benin didn't talk? Have me try to vaporize his head?

Veritas crossed his arms over his chest. "Imagine what might have happened if he'd aimed two inches to the left."

Okay, this was getting out of hand. I cleared my throat, but Veritas held up a hand, never taking his eyes off of Benin.

"Now I'm going to ask you again. Who killed Lux?"

Benin laughed, this time with a harder edge. He took a step out of the corner. "Who you tryin' to kid, kid? We've known you two were trying to 'clean up the streets' or whatever. What did you think was going to happen when you trespassed on someone's territory?"

"You hear that, Failstate?" Veritas said. "He's just admitted that the Blue Eclipse Boys had something to do with Lux's death."

"I ain't sayin' nothing like that." Benin adjusted his suit. "But you wannabes try to 'right wrongs' and 'set things straight.' Down here, we got a different idea of right and wrong, you know? Your partner was an idiot if she thought she could come into Hogtown and stir up trouble without facing some sorta blowback. You ask me, she got exactly what she deserved."

For a split second, ice encased me. Veritas and Benin looked flash frozen as well. I didn't know if Benin even realized what he had said. He certainly couldn't have understood how personal his remark was.

Veritas's hands clenched into fists and his arms tightened. He slammed Benin into the wall of the bar. They tumbled to the ground, Benin trying to keep Veritas at bay. But he couldn't.

Veritas flipped him onto his back and straddled his chest, his fists working like pistons, smashing into the mobster's face over and over again. Benin tried to curl into a ball but Veritas wouldn't let up. Wet smacks filled the alley. Soon, Benin's shouted protests turned into moaning.

I shook myself free of my paralysis and dashed forward, hooking Veritas under his armpits and dragging him off Benin. He kicked and swung, trying to get back to the mobster. I tightened my grip, wrapping my arms around his chest. I managed a half-spin and tossed Veritas away from him. I stepped into his path, blocking him from getting back to Benin. "That's enough!"

Veritas ran into me and I had to push him back. He glowered at me.

"Get out of here." I injected steel into my voice.

Veritas stomped out of the alley. I blew out a breath and turned back to Benin. He had rolled over onto all fours and was struggling to get upright again. I squatted next to him. He winced, but then glared at me out of puffy eyes.

"You kids stay right here. I want you to meet my boys."

"No way. It's time to come clean with me."

"After what just happened? Forget it!"

"Have it your way." I rose. "But here's the thing. You're upset with one or two heroes poking their noses into your territory?"

"Yeah."

"Fair enough. But what do you suppose will happen if I let it slip that the Blue Eclipse Boys had something to do with Lux's murder? You think it's bad that two of us are asking questions, 'trespassing on your turf?' What if dozens of superheroes started poking around? I put in a call, and we'll have Gauntlet, Titanium Ram, and Kid Magnum all over Hogtown. Imagine the problems that will make for your boss."

Benin clenched his jaw and although I saw a glimmer of fear in his rapidly blackening eye, I knew I hadn't pushed hard enough. I took a step closer to him and tried to summon my most menacing voice.

"And with that many amateurs in one neighborhood, how long do you think it'll take before the licensed superheroes take notice? Sure, you Boys might be able to fend off us 'wannabes' for a while, but what will happen when Raze or Dr. Olympus come to Hogtown?" I lowered my voice even more. "Or do you think the Blue Eclipse Boys could take on Etzal'el?"

That did it. The color drained from Benin's face and his legs shook. He mopped his forehead. "What do you want from me?"

"The truth," I said. "Who ordered Lux's death?"

Benin opened his arms wide. "How am I supposed to know that? I just collect protection! The bosses don't exactly keep me in the loop."

"But it is possible they gave the order?"

"Well, yeah, I guess . . ."

A thrill shot through me. I took a step closer to him and tried to crack my knuckles. It didn't work, but Benin seemed a bit more freaked out nonetheless. "So who would I have to ask? Pyrotrack?"

Benin chuckled nervously. "If you think I'm going to rat out him, you're crazy."

"Fine. Give my regards to Etzal'el when you see him." I turned to leave.

Benin moaned. "All right, all right! I'll tell you what I know. It ain't much, but it'll have to do."

I faced Benin and crossed my arms over my chest.

He glanced around for a moment and then leaned in close. "Pyrotrack wasn't exactly sad when Lux died. Matter of fact, he wants to hold a special meeting tomorrow night to figure out how to take advantage of the situation."

"Where?"

Benin's mouth twisted into a scowl but then he sighed. "You ever hear of the Penguin's Claw? They got a back room there. The meeting's gonna go down at ten."

Ice sluiced through my veins, chased by heat. Elizabeth was coming over to watch the show tomorrow night at eight. I'd have only an hour to meet up with Veritas and get to Hogtown. And that would mean leaving Elizabeth with Ben, the thought of which twisted my stomach. I closed my eyes and dismissed the thoughts. I didn't like it, but I'd have to do it. I glanced at Benin, who studied his feet.

For a moment, I wanted to call Veritas back into the alley to confirm what Benin had said was true, but that probably wasn't a good idea. "All right, get out of here."

He fled from the alley, disappearing into the shadows. I breathed a sigh of relief as the tension drained from my body. I left the alley to find Veritas.

I found him sitting on the hood of the Reliant. His hands were curled into fists and pressed onto the hood. He didn't even acknowledge my arrival.

"Are you okay?" I asked.

His head snapped around, and he glared at me. "Don't you ever lay your hands on me again, do you hear me?"

I held up my hands, afraid he would attack me. But instead, he turned his head away.

"What was I supposed to do, let you keep beating on him?"

"He deserved it!"

"That's not a decision for us to make! For crying out loud, Veritas, what would happen if the VOC found out you were beating up a suspect? You'd never get your license. They'd probably throw you in prison!"

He shrugged. "You think I care about that stupid license? He said she . . . she . . ." He choked for a moment. "And now we don't have anything!"

"That's not entirely true. Pyrotrack is going to have some sort of party tomorrow night at the Penguin's Claw. I was thinking about crashing. You want to come?"

Veritas stared at me, his eyes dead. I wasn't even sure my words were registering. Then he slid from the car hood and got in my face. "You'd like that, wouldn't you? Keep riding my coattails for a little while longer? I know what you're doing. You were pretty quick to sidle up to me once you found out who I was and who my father is. You've been trying to undercut me this whole time!"

Who was this raving lunatic? Had I dropped into an alternate reality?

"Mike! That's not true."

"Oh, isn't it? You think I don't know the truth? Poking at me, prying into my past, trying to get me to doubt myself. And it's working too! Dad keeps asking about you, you know. 'How's Failstate?' 'You two close to catching her killer yet?' 'I bet you two will succeed because Failstate has what it takes.'"

Whoa, Meridian had said that about *me*? I wanted to bask in the second-hand praise, but Veritas wouldn't let me.

"You know what, I'm done. You just go home to your family and leave mine alone, okay?"

"Now wait a minute—"

Veritas grabbed the front of my sweatshirt and spun me around. I slammed into the side of the Reliant hard enough that pain spiked through my spine and ribs. "Don't you get it? This is all your fault! *Yours!* If you hadn't agreed to go on patrol with her, this would have never happened. She would've stayed home and been safe. Lux would still be alive, and you would be nothing!"

His words cut into my chest. Veritas tossed me onto the floor. I rolled across the pavement and came to a stop in the middle of the street. He ripped open the driver's side door and climbed inside. He tossed my duffel bag onto the street. The Reliant peeled away from the curb in a screech of tires, leaving me alone in Hogtown.

CHAPTER 33

BUSES IN HOGTOWN in the middle of the night were sporadic at best, so I wasn't able to make it home until close to two thirty in the morning. I should have done something to relax, but I couldn't. I wound up pacing the house all night, never settling in one spot for long.

I didn't want to go to school in the morning. I could have played sick, claiming I'd caught the cold a few days late. But I knew that wouldn't work. I never got sick.

When I reached the study hall for first period, I wanted to bury my head in my arms and just shut out the world, but my mind wouldn't stay still. So, just as I had during all that pacing, I replayed the previous night's events, Veritas's angry words slamming into my chest, me slamming into the Reliant's side, over and over again. At first, I felt sorry for myself. But then anger tore at my self-pity.

Veritas was out of line, accusing and blaming me. He wanted nothing to do with me? Fine! But I wasn't quite done with him yet. I had one last mystery to unravel.

I snagged the hall pass and headed for the computer lab. I found the same terminal I'd used before.

As soon as the search engine came up, I pulled up all the information I could about Delphi, focusing on the end of her career. Something must have happened that had upset Veritas so badly and I was determined to find out what.

Nothing presented itself immediately. The biographies I found made oblique references to her final months as a licensed vigilante, citing "excessive force" and "erratic behavior." But I couldn't find anything concrete. One author wondered if her decline had something to do with Delphi's "missing year," an eleven month period during which she had disappeared.

I leaned back in my chair, frowning. I called up the paparazzo photo again. The photo had been taken in 1993— and the missing year was in 1994. So about six months after Meridian and Delphi had been spotted kissing, she had fallen off the face of the earth for close to a year . . .

My eyes widened. I hunched over the computer, typing furiously. I had to find out what happened before she was arrested. There had to be a record somewhere, a news story, an eyewitness account. I'd even take a poorly written blog post at that point.

The last entry was from an L.A. newspaper. The headline screamed that Delphi had been arrested by the VOC. I clicked on the article, calling up the information. According to the article, Delphi had holed up in an Echo Park apartment with an infant, refusing to come out and attacking those who approached her. Finally the VOC, assisted by Meridian, had stormed the apartment, bringing an end to the standoff.

One line in particular caught my eye: *Bystanders reported that while being removed, Delphi spouted "prophecies" about the infant. She claimed that only she could protect him from a dark future.*

The last picture I found of the incident was of Meridian, slumped in the building's main entrance, cradling the baby in his arms.

My head spun. It looked so much like the picture of Meridian with Elena that it couldn't be a coincidence. Meridian had the same sorrowful expression. I skimmed the articles, trying to find something, anything, that would confirm my suspicions.

Buried in an account of Delphi's trial was a name: The apartment's occupant had been a "Stephanie Rickman." Authorities at the time had believed that Delphi had commandeered Stephanie's apartment for her standoff. But in that moment, I knew the truth.

Delphi had been in her own apartment. She was Stephanie Rickman. And she was Mike's mother. No wonder Veritas was so touchy about Delphi. I would be too.

I should have felt satisfied. But instead, I only felt hollow. Mike's mother was in prison. Now he'd lost his half-sister. His dad probably didn't understand . . .

Without really thinking, I plucked my cell phone from my pocket. Should I text him? No, this was too important to condense down to letters and characters on the screen. I hit Mike's number. After two rings, it clicked over to voicemail. "Hey, Mike, it's . . . it's me. Look, I know you probably don't want to talk to me, and that's fine. I understand. But I want to talk to you about . . . well, about your mom." I winced. Was that a good idea, revealing what I knew? Probably not. Too late now. "Look, just call me, okay?"

As I left the computer lab, I saw Elizabeth down the hall. She smiled and waved. "See you tonight?"

"Looking forward to it." Although, truth be told, I found myself glancing at my cell phone instead.

CHAPTER 34

I WATCHED BEN spend most of the afternoon straightening the living room, even going so far as to vacuum. Then he prepared some show-time snacks. Nothing too fancy. At least, I didn't think the nacho chips and salsa were anything special. All he had to do was rip the bag and open the jar. But the way Mom went on, you'd think that Ben had crafted a culinary masterpiece, refined cuisine fit for Olympian gods.

They were so wrapped up in the preparations that they missed the doorbell. That left me to play doorman. I sighed. Might as well get used to the feeling. I wouldn't do much better than "third wheel" all evening.

It was Elizabeth. She looked incredible. She was bundled in a caramel wool coat that reached her knees, a white knit cap on her head. Her eyes lit up when I opened the door and she rushed inside. "It's freezing out there," she said with a laugh.

"Are you kidding? It's gotta be in the fifties. Great weather."

She shrugged out of her coat. At which point I nearly choked. She wore a homemade Failstate t-shirt. A cartoon version of me crouched in an alley corner. I looked vicious, coiled, ready to strike. Awesome if a bit detached from reality.

Elizabeth glanced down at her shirt. "Did I spill something?"

"Uh, no. Not that I can see." I took her coat and hung it up in the front closet.

"Hey, I got something for you." She pressed a CD into my hands.

I looked it over and laughed. A "Best of Broadway" compilation of show tunes. I held it up. "What's this for?"

"It only seemed right. After all, you've been my knight in shining armor plenty of times the past couple of weeks. And then I found a sculpture in the hallway outside our apartment earlier this week and I thought maybe you . . ."

My breathing turned ragged. She looked at me so expectantly. I couldn't speak. Whatever I had wanted to say had become a jumble in my mind.

She shrugged. "Anyway, I saw that at the mall and thought of you. Hope you like it."

And then Ben and Mom descended on her. Ben swept an arm around her and escorted her into the living room. Mom made sure we were settled in, and then she excused herself to go to work. Before she left, she glared at me, and I could almost hear what she really wanted to say. *Don't screw this up for Ben the way you do with everything else.*

But she never actually said that, even if she did think it really loud.

Much to my relief, Elizabeth curled up in the big overstuffed chair by herself. Ben flopped down on the couch, positioning himself so I couldn't join him. I found a spot on the floor and used the end table as a backrest, enduring the sharp corner that dug in between my shoulders.

"Comfy?" Ben asked with his lopsided smirk.

"Just fine." I had to force the lie through my clenched teeth.

Ben flipped on the TV just in time for the opening credits of *America's Next Superhero*.

The music was overdone, some overwrought big band piece, and the graphics were late nineties at best, but I still got chills when each contestant appeared on screen, striking a dramatic, heroic pose. Everyone looked so noble, larger than life. Except of course when halfway through, there was me, dressed in my second-hand clothes and Halloween mask, looking like an amateur among avenging angels. I tucked my knees under my chin.

Helen Kirkwood appeared on screen, seated in what I guessed was the show's control room, though I'd never seen it. "Good evening. By now, I'm sure most of you have heard the tragic news regarding one of our contestants. Last week, our own beloved Lux was murdered while out on patrol in a neighborhood of New Chayton called Hogtown."

"Whoa," Ben said softly. "Look how broken up she is."

Tears glinted in the corner of Helen's eyes. Not all that surprising, given her connection to the Magnus family. But Elizabeth didn't know that and apparently Ben hadn't deduced Lux's true identity either. I kept my expression neutral.

The first few moments of the show were dedicated to Lux. News clips emphasized Lux's impact on New Chayton in her brief career. Then it was back to Helen, who had taken the time to fix herself up—a bit cheesy, since this was all prerecorded, and she could've had five days to dry her tears if she'd wanted to. More likely, she did it right away in order to preserve her fragile mood. Tears were good for reality TV ratings.

"We here at *America's Next Superhero* debated what kind of response would be appropriate, given the situation," Helen said. Gone were the almost-tears and the tremor in her voice. "In the end, we decided, to borrow the old show business phrase 'The show must go on.' Lux chose to be a hero. She knew the risks. Therefore, our search for America's next superhero will continue. But we here on the show will always remember the sweet girl we knew only as Lux."

The show cut to the confessionals, each contestant talking about Lux and their experience with her. Each one rang false. The way they gushed, you'd think that they had been best friends with Lux for years. Kid Magnum especially laid it on thick, going on and on as to what an intense and honorable competitor Lux was. He was probably just trying to cover his tracks after his near brawl with Lux.

Gauntlet's confessional followed Kid Magnum's. He sat tall in his chair, he looked into the camera, and smiled warmly. "You could tell from the beginning that Lux was destined for greatness. She had a truly indomitable spirit. She never gave up, even when the odds were stacked against her." The show cut to footage of Lux from previous episodes, laughing, helping, fighting. Gauntlet's words continued over them. "This isn't just a loss for our show. It's a loss for everyone."

The show cut to footage of Lux and Gauntlet working together on a challenge from the third week. He boosted Lux up and over a wall, and then scrambled after her. When his feet hit the ground, Gauntlet jammed his hands into his hips and threw out his chest. Lux laughed but clapped him on the back.

I glanced at Ben. He had tucked his hands behind his head and his smirk had grown even bigger.

"What a ham," Elizabeth punctuated her statement with a snort. "If you ask me, he should be the one called 'Blowhard.'"

I guffawed but immediately regretted it. Ben would kill me for that. His smile froze in place. I could almost hear the wheels locking up in his mind. I swallowed my smile and hugged my legs closer, burying my mouth in my knees.

We were spared any rebuttal as the show cut to Veritas. I leaned forward a bit more. Veritas looked on the verge of tears himself. He stumbled through a few words and then excused himself.

And then I appeared on camera. I winced at the image. I hated seeing myself on the show. I never looked quite right, even behind a disguise. This time, the bottom of my mask was tucked into my sweatshirt collar. Why hadn't anyone said anything? Compared to Gauntlet, I looked ridiculous.

"I really liked Lux a lot," I said on screen, shifting in my chair. "You know how some people, you meet them and you feel like you've been friends for years? That first day . . . she greeted me by name, she seemed genuinely excited to see me. She knew it was a competition and that only one of us could win, but that didn't matter to her. It's going to sound cliché, but she could literally light up a room when she walked in." I remember how I choked up at that point, and apparently the producers had decided to keep that part in, because there I was, choking up on screen. "I'm going to miss her. If this weren't a competition, I'd be her number one fan."

I stifled a groan. How cheesy was I?

And yet I heard Elizabeth sniffle. She had leaned forward too, and now her eyes were bright with tears.

Ben glared at me, his annoyance more than plain.

Thankfully, the doorbell rang at that moment. I leapt to my feet and headed for the door. "Who is it?"

"Pizza delivery."

I frowned and turned to Ben. "You order pizza?"

He shook his head.

I opened the door, ready to send whoever it was away. "Look, there must be some—"

The door exploded inward. I fell back, and Elizabeth shrieked.

Four men in ratty clothing charged into the house. All of them wore ski masks and had automatic rifles drawn and ready.

"On the floor! All of you!" one of them shouted.

I splayed out my arms. Ben hit the floor as well, but anger flashed in his eyes. He wanted to do something. So did I, but what could we do? Anything we did would expose ourselves.

Plus there was Elizabeth to worry about. She had curled up in a ball on the chair, her eyes wide and her whole body quaking.

One of the men shoved her to the floor. "Keep quiet now and we'll get this over with quickly."

One of the others produced a roll of duct tape and started with me, twisting my arms behind my back and taping them together. I winced, biting my cheek. I glanced over at the TV.

Gauntlet was on screen again.

"You know, sometimes you just need a hero."

I closed my eyes. Truer words were never spoken. I just never thought they'd be so true for me.

CHAPTER 35

HEAVY FURNITURE CRASHED upstairs, followed by the sound of shattering glass. I winced. Angry voices carried down the steps. Criminals had invaded my own home, and the only thing I could think about was how upset Mom was going to be when she returned.

"We're going to have to do something soon," Ben mumbled.

I glared at him. What could we do? The invaders had shoved us in one corner and then torn the house apart, bringing whatever valuables they could find to the kitchen.

Ben was right, though. My costume was hidden under my bed upstairs. I didn't know where Ben kept his. If the criminals found them, the situation would get a lot uglier. If Ben and I had been home alone, this would have been over already.

But what could we do with Elizabeth in the house? We couldn't let her—or the burglars—know who we really were. Elizabeth had curled up in a ball and was crying softly. Searing energy flared up my spine. Who knew what else the criminals might try with her here? Ben and I had to act. Now. I nodded to Ben.

A loud rip cut through the living room and Ben's hands were free. He balled up the length of duct tape and tossed it aside.

Elizabeth whimpered. "What are you doing?"

Ben shushed her.

I froze, not daring to even breathe. Had the invaders heard anything?

Smaller thuds ricocheted across the ceiling, followed by more angry cursing. Apparently not. And they probably hadn't found the costumes yet either.

Ben scuttled over to me and ripped my tape apart as well. Then he went to Elizabeth's side and looked at me. "Get her out of here, Robin."

"No way! You're going to need my help!"

He ground his teeth but turned to Elizabeth. "I need you to go to the neighbors. Call the cops."

"You two are coming with me!" Panic pitched her voice higher. She grabbed at Ben's arms. "You're free, so let's go!"

He gently broke loose. "We'll be fine. Just go."

Her eyes pleaded with me and she motioned for me to take her hand.

My fingers twitched, and I had to struggle to keep my hands at my side. I wanted to carry her to safety, be her hero. But that would leave Ben outnumbered. As much as he might believe it, his power didn't make him invincible. I swallowed my rising fear. "Go."

She scrambled for the door and slipped out into the night.

"Okay, now what?" I whispered.

Ben looked around for a moment, his face set in a stony mask. "We're outnumbered two-to-one and they're armed. We need to tip the balance back in our favor. Kill the lights."

I blanched. "What?"

"You heard me. Take off your necklace and blow the power."

I cringed, already hearing Mom's angry words when she discovered I had used my powers in the house.

Ben grabbed my shoulder and squeezed. "Robin, I know you have problems controlling your power. But you can do this. I know you can." He sounded like he was encouraging a first grader to tie his own shoes.

Patronizing jerk. Of course I could do it. I untied the necklace and gasped as relief flooded through me, washing away the annoying itch.

Ben looked away. "Can't you cover up or something?" he whispered.

Heat flashed through my chest. "My mask is upstairs."

Ben still wouldn't look at me. I sighed. I picked up pillow and took off its case. A few quick blasts from my power ripped eyeholes in it. I pulled the makeshift mask over my head. "Better?"

"Great. Now do your thing."

I closed my eyes and visualized going down into the basement, taking a right at the bottom of the stairs. There it was, the circuit breaker box. All I had to do was focus, imagine a spike of my power driving into the circuits, disrupting them. Aha!

But when I opened my eyes, the lights were still on. I screwed my eyes shut and tried again. Come on. I had done this before. I had taken down Magnus's entire security system, for crying out loud. What was a lousy old breaker box compared to that? Break, stupid thing—break!

Nothing. Ben shifted back and forth, probably anxious to get into the fight.

C'mon, God, I know I can do this! Just let it work.

Another try. I pushed, straining every muscle in my body, trying to force the electricity to spike, for every breaker to trip at the same time. But it felt as thought I was pushing against a brick wall, trying to knock it down with only my strength. Then I tried to flip just half of them. Then just one. No luck. My goal was just out of reach, but try as I might, I couldn't . . . get . . . there . . .

I gasped and collapsed. I panted for a few moments, surprised at how sweaty I had become. "I . . . I can't do it."

Ben ground his teeth and nodded. "Then we do this the hard way. You take the two in the basement. I've got the two upstairs."

And he was off, darting in a crouch toward the hall. I lurched to my feet, trying to mimic his posture only to trip over my own feet. I scrambled the rest of the way into the kitchen and to the stairs.

I paused for a moment before descending, trying to gauge where in the basement my prey might be. Hard to tell. Snatches of conversation and laughter drifted up the stairs, but nothing that helped me fix their position. Maybe by the washer and dryer?

For once, the wooden stairs didn't creak. I crouched at the bottom and took a moment to calm myself. Thanks to a thin wall of fake wood paneling, the invaders wouldn't be able to see me, but my heart jackhammered anyway. I took a deep breath, bowing my head in an effort to calm myself.

I spotted a folded paper on the cement floor. I picked it up. A map—printed from an Internet site, maybe. Not the layout of our house, though. More like a neighborhood. I tucked it in my pocket. Thugs first, cartography later.

I glanced around the corner. My two invaders tore apart the boxes we kept by the washer. Boxes of my dad's stuff. The criminals pawed through it, dumping the contents. Their shirts rode up, revealing that they had tucked their guns in their waistbands.

One of them paused to survey the damage. "This good enough, you think? Boss only wanted us to kill 'em."

"Yeah, but he wants us to make it look like a home invasion first. Keep dumping."

They were here to kill us? My breathing turned ragged. Someone had figured out our secret identities!

A boom shook the ceiling overhead. Ben had probably just taken out one of the invaders. The two in the basement heard it and turned toward the stairs. They saw me and froze.

"Hey!" one of them shouted, raising his gun.

My power flared and this time I did finally kill the power. The basement went completely black.

A shot rang out but missed me. I lashed out in the direction of the muzzle flash, driving a spike of power deep into the gun. The man swore, and I heard metal clatter to the cement.

I found that my eyes were adjusting. Thanks to dim street-light creeping through a high window, I could sort of see the two burglars. I slashed out with my power again, disarming the second thug. Then I stabbed into the hot water hose behind them. Jets sprayed them from behind. They both jumped and turned toward the spray. Just what I wanted.

With a cry, I shot forward, throwing out my arms to tackle them both.

I connected with them, and one of the thugs smashed head-first into the laundry sink. He collapsed with a muted groan. The other, however, fought, our limbs tangled. I had to end this and quick. No way I'd win this wrestling match. I finally did the only thing I could. I kneed him in the groin. Not the most heroic move, but it got the job done. He rolled away, moaning. I flipped him onto his back and cracked my fist across his jaw.

Ow! Pain exploded through my knuckles. But the man didn't move. I grabbed a roll of duct tape and trussed up both thugs, hands behind their back, legs taped together. Then I raced up the stairs.

At the top, I almost knocked Ben off his feet. He steadied me quickly. "Are you okay?"

"Yeah, I'm good. You?"

"They're both down and out," Ben said. "You'd better get your necklace back on before the cops get here."

I nodded and rushed back into the living room. A burst from my power destroyed the makeshift mask. I'd have to think of an excuse to give Mom later. A quick knot, and it was back in place. I shuddered as the throbbing exploded into a thousand needles, pricking across my skin and through my body.

Just in time too. Red and blue lights bathed the room in an undulating pattern and two armed cops burst into the living room. Ben and I raised our hands immediately as they came in.

"You Ben and Rob Laughlin?" one of them asked.

"We are," I said.

"Where are the intruders?" the other cop asked.

"Two upstairs, two down," Ben said.

The cops glanced at each other and then at us. I could almost hear them doing the math. Two teenage kids taking out four home invaders? I wouldn't believe the story either.

"What happened?"

"It was Gauntlet," Ben said. "He must've been nearby or something. He just came in and took them out single-handedly."

Wait, what? My head snapped around and I gaped at Ben. He ignored me, his arms crossed over his puffed-out chest.

"That true, kid?"

The cops looked at me and waited expectantly. What could I do? Getting into an argument with Ben would only raise their suspicions.

I ground my teeth together and sighed. "Yeah, it's true."

The cops hustled us out of the room and onto the front yard. A small crowd of our neighbors milled about in the flashing lights of the police cars, some of them straining to get a look inside the house. Then a blur of color exploded from the mob. Elizabeth. She sobbed and laughed and rushed for us, arms open wide.

I winced. Here came the big romantic moment. Elizabeth would rush into Ben's waiting arms. They'd kiss. He'd reassure her. They'd walk away from the crowd to be alone. I stepped out of the way so as to not get run over.

Only she sprinted across the lawn and threw her arms around me.

Me.

CHAPTER 36

THE WORLD STILLED. I drew Elizabeth close. She clung to me, her sobs shuddering through my chest. I closed my eyes and breathed in her scent, savoring the smell of mangos in her hair. Her head fit under my chin perfectly as we rocked back and forth. The wailing sirens were a pale note in the background, the gathering neighbors nothing more than a buzz, the whole rotten burglary just a dream.

"Kid, we're gonna need to talk to her at some point."

The cop's gruff whisper snapped me out of the moment. Elizabeth let go, smiling up at me shyly. Then she turned to the policeman, who led her away, peppering her with questions.

Ben scowled at me, his fingers repeatedly balling into fists. He wouldn't physically attack me, not with bystanders, but he'd start some snide commentary pretty soon.

I kept my face neutral and I thrust my hands into my pockets. I took a few steps away, my back turned to Ben. If only

Elizabeth and I had been alone. I could have lifted her chin, tipped her head back, brought my lips to hers, and . . .

Wait. What was in my pocket?

I pulled out the crumpled map the invaders had dropped. I turned to give it to the cops, but as I did, I scanned its contents and frowned.

Like I suspected, it was a neighborhood map. A destination flag was marked in its middle. I looked closer. The flag was planted right on our house, circled in red ink. And our address was scribbled next to it along with the time the attack was to take place.

My eyes widened. This was no random burglary—they had targeted us! I suddenly recalled what the thugs in the basement had said: *make it look like a home invasion.*

The Blue Eclipse Boys! It had to be! Benin must have slipped some sort of tracking device on me yesterday. He could have put one on Veritas too. And if Benin heard our argument, then he knew . . .

The meeting! I forgot all about it. If Veritas went to the Penguin Claw, he was going to waltz right into a Blue Eclipse Boys trap.

I took off for the house. I tore up the stairs to my room and checked my watch. It was closing in on nine. Only an hour left. I dodged around police documenting the evidence of Gauntlet's "solo" fight with the home invaders. My room seemed relatively untouched. Apparently Ben had surprised them before they'd gotten there. I yanked the duffel out from under the bed and started down the steps again.

"Hold it, son." A uniformed cop blocked my way. "What's that?"

"It's mine." I gave an exaggerated look at my watch. "Look, I'm late for my shift at Burger Blasters. I already gave my statement. Can I please go?"

His eyes narrowed. Was he allowed by law to search my duffel bag? I didn't think he could—he was investigating the home invasion, and this had nothing to do with that. Finally he nodded and stepped out of the way.

I raced out of the house for the bus stop. Too bad Mom was at work, or I could've used the van. I looked at my watch again and did the math. I'd be cutting it close, and that was only if the buses were running on time. Too close, actually. But I was pretty sure I could get to Hogtown, find the Penguin's Claw, and . . .

Ben fell into step with me. "Where are you going?"

"I've got something I need to take care of. Me. By myself." He tried to snare my arm but I shook him off. "Look, someone needs to stay here and deal with the police and Elizabeth. And what will Mom think when she gets home and finds our stuff all smashed? You know she'll take this better coming from you."

Ben jogged after me as I kept walking. "But what if you need help?"

"I'll be fine." The lie came easily. We had gotten lucky this time; Ben hadn't been injured. But there was no telling what I'd find in Hogtown. Ben had to stay here, where he'd be safe. "Just . . . stay here, all right?"

And with that, I broke into a run and left Ben standing at the end of our block.

CHAPTER 37

THIS WAS STUPID. The whole situation was spiraling out of control. Maybe I should have brought Ben along after all. Too late for that now. What had I even been thinking?

Every jolt on the bus ride to Hogtown set my heart to beating faster. Every person entering the bus loomed over me, a potential bad guy to fight. Every second dragged into an eternity in which Veritas could be hurt . . . or worse. I kept checking my watch, dreading how close the hands were creeping toward ten. I would fail another member of the Magnus family. I couldn't face his father again.

The bus disgorged me into Hogtown. I hunkered behind the nearest dumpster and changed into my costume, not really caring if anyone saw. I tore the necklace off, the sharp pain spurring me out of hiding and onto the streets.

I sprinted through alleys and ducked between shadows until I found the Penguin's Claw, a dingy grey building with cracked windows and a flickering neon sign that looked about ready to short out completely. Single story, quite a bit smaller than my house, with a flat roof dominated by what looked to be an air conditioning unit and a small satellite dish. The two windows facing the street had been painted black. Muscular bouncer at the door. A few other thugs patrolling the exterior.

And there, on the roof, a figure in blue and red. Had to be Veritas. He disappeared behind the air conditioner housing.

How had he gotten up there? He didn't reemerge, so he must have gotten inside from the roof. How would I get in to help him? The bouncer at the front door looked big enough to tear a truck in half. No way I'd want to take him on face-to-face. Too bad my powers wouldn't let me chop through bones. Maybe I could find another way in if I circled around to the back of the building.

It took me close to ten minutes to sneak around the neighboring buildings and into the alley behind the Claw. My heart sank when I saw the back door. Two large men flanked the exit, chatting quietly. They wouldn't ignore a masked hero trying to sneak past them—even if I did look more like a homeless guy than a superhero.

I crept around the corner, shimmying through the alley between the Claw and the pawn shop that was its neighbor.

There! Two banks of windows lined the back wall of the Penguin's Claw. Judging by the height and the blurred glass, those windows probably led to restrooms. Perfect.

I found a wood crate for a quick step up. With hinges along the bottom, the window probably tipped outward. I could work with that.

I focused my power along my fingertip, imagining a blade of destructive energy poking out about three inches. Working carefully, I traced the top of the window, hopefully slicing through any locks. Then I ran my finger along the hinges. The metal dissolved under my touch. The window fell out of its frame, still attached by two swinging arms. I burned through those and lowered the glass to the alley. The resultant opening was just big enough for me to slip through.

A quick up and over, and I was in. The bathroom, though dingy and smelly, was also empty. I crept across the linoleum and cracked open the door.

A dozen rickety tables surrounded by mismatched chairs were scattered through the interior of the bar. A jukebox with flickering lights sat in one corner. A flat screen TV hung slightly off-kilter on the far wall. There appeared to be only half a dozen people in the main room. On my right was the back wall of the bar, with a door in the middle, twelve feet away. I guessed that was the entrance to the Claw's back room. How was I going to get there without being spotted?

To my left, the bar stretched away from me, a series of shelves lining the wall behind it, each one holding dozens of bottles. I smiled and reached out with my power.

I slashed through one of the arms holding up the top shelf. The metal fell away, and the shelf followed, spilling its bottles and smashing through the lower shelves. Everyone turned to the bar, some of them laughing, others shouting in surprise. The bartender whirled around. In the confusion, I darted out of the bathroom in a crouch and through the back room door.

Then cold, hard metal pressed against the back of my head.

"Get up, kid." The voice sounded like an earthquake.

Benin appeared in front of me, a gun leveled on me.

I raised my hands and slowly straightened. Whoever had the gun to my head poked me in the back, and I stumbled forward through a hallway and into a larger room, one lined with faded fake wood paneling with large I-beams that held up the ceiling. Posters of women in various states of undress dotted the walls, along with a large map of Hogtown.

Six thugs stood around the room, glaring at me, most of them wearing t-shirts cut to reveal different iterations of the Blue Eclipse Boys tattoo.

A grey metal desk stood toward the back of the room. At the desk sat a spindly man poring over a stack of papers. He wore a baggy sweatshirt and faded jeans. Odd geometric patterns had been cut into his red crewcut. It looked like some creature had taken chunks out of his scalp. He glanced up at me. His eyes, set in a ridiculously narrow face, weren't normal. Red corneas swam in an ocean of black. He smiled, revealing a row of sharpened teeth. "Ah, Failstate," he said. "We were wondering if you would show up. You can call me Pyrotrack. I believe you know my other guest."

The small crowd parted to reveal Veritas, tied to a chair. At least he was conscious, and I couldn't see blood on him anywhere. My escort rammed the gun into my ribs. I walked forward and two goons shoved me into a chair, twisting my arms behind me and wrapping my wrists with what felt like nylon rope. Great, tied up by bad guys twice in one night.

I leaned toward Veritas. "You okay?"

He faced forward. "I'm fine."

Pyrotrack slammed his fist on the desk. "Silence! Gentlemen, I don't think you realize the gravity of your situation."

"Well, let's see here." Veritas said, sounding surprisingly calm. "We're both tied up, I count six of your boys, all of them armed. And then there's you and your odd dentistry." Although his full mask covered his face, I somehow knew Veritas had a cocky smile on his face. "So what happens to us now?"

"Now we use you as a demonstration of why heroes should not mess in Blue Eclipse Boys business!"

Benin cocked his gun. Was this how I was going to end?

Veritas continued to stare at Pyrotrack with impassive eyes. Did he have a plan? Veritas coughed quietly and his gaze drifted toward the ceiling. I followed it and saw the rows of humming fluorescent lights. Veritas nodded, ever so slightly.

He wanted me to blow the lights? I glanced up at them, sweat coating my forehead. What if I couldn't do it again? But I had to. If I didn't cause a distraction, we'd be stuck! I took a deep breath to calm myself and I willed the lights to break, imagining the electricity disrupted, the circuit overloaded, whatever it took.

With an audible crack and a burning smell, the room plunged into darkness.

The gang members shouted in alarm, and I focused on the rope around my wrists. A second later, they fell away. I spun out of my chair and behind Veritas, slicing through his bonds.

"C'mon, let's get out of—"

Light flared. I winced. One of Pyrotrack's fist had burst into flame, casting odd shadows over his face while demented glee shone in his eyes.

"Oh, now that can't be good," I muttered.

"A nice try, boys." Pyrotrack crossed around the desk. He rubbed his hands together and then both fists were on fire. "But futile. I'm afraid I do have to kill you, or no one will heed the warning. Do you have anything to say before I fricassee you?"

"I do." Veritas crossed his arms over his chest. "Why didn't you do something more decorative with those I-beams holding up your ceiling?"

Pyrotrack frowned. "Why would you ask something like that?"

"No reason. Failstate, you have any questions you want answered?"

"Yeah. Do you have your insurance adjustor on speed-dial?"

Pyrotrack snarled. "Of course not."

"Too bad."

I lashed out with my power and sliced through the pillars. The ceiling tumbled down with the sound of thunder.

CHAPTER 38

SHOUTS, CURSES, AND DEBRIS rained down around me. Veritas yanked me back and a girder smashed into the floor where I had stood. We burst through the door and into the bar's main room. Patrons screamed. I sprinted for the entrance.

"Duck!"

Veritas's shout barely registered but I hit the ground anyway.

A ball of fire sliced through the air above me. Pyrotrack leaned in the open door. Blood dripped down his face. He clenched his fist, and another gout of flame traveled up his arm. We had to get out of there.

I scrambled for the door and smashed through to the street, Veritas right behind me. Another fire burst set the door ablaze.

The bouncer and one of his comrades tried to stop us. Veritas ducked a blow and threw the bouncer into the other thug, dropping them to the sidewalk. Then a wall of fire erupted in front of us. It traced a semicircle around the bar's front and cut off our avenue of escape.

"Now what?" I asked. "You got a fire extinguisher on you?"

Veritas made a show of patting down his costume. He shook his head. "We'll think of something."

"That's not reassuring."

"I didn't intend it to be."

I looked up and down the street for some kind of help. Rusty cars dotted the curb. A streetlight curved overhead. I spotted a fire hydrant and my heart zinged for a moment. But I didn't have the right tools to open it, and that would take time.

Pyrotrack emerged from the bar, his hands smoking. He grinned at us, a predatory gleam of teeth. "Did you think our business was concluded, boys? Not by a long shot."

"We wouldn't miss it for the world," Veritas said.

Pyrotrack laughed. "I doubt either of you have faced a man as powerful as me."

"Maybe not," Veritas said. "But then you've never faced heroes as great as us."

Pyrotrack guffawed and his entire body erupted in flames. He whirled his fists around each other. A large ball of fire formed between them, and he threw his hands out.

I dove to my right just as flames singed my mask. Veritas darted at Pyrotrack, ducking another fireball. He threw a few punches, none of which connected, but his attack was enough to keep the thin man distracted. A fire blast knocked Veritas off his feet, the front of his costume smoking. Pyrotrack turned on me.

I punched through the fire hydrant with my power.

Water gushed out but it fell to the ground far short of Pyrotrack.

He cackled, and his flames burned even brighter. "You missed."

"With that, maybe." I sliced through the nearby streetlight. "But not with this."

The pole toppled and clipped Pyrotrack across the back of his head. He crumpled and his flames went out. In a matter of moments, the hydrant's water rushed down the sidewalk and extinguished the ring of flames. Veritas scrambled to his feet and looked down at the smoking villain and then at me.

"Are you okay?" I asked.

He nodded. "Just a little singed."

My entire body felt like it was vibrating. But then slowly, the tingling swept away and suddenly echoes of our fight from the other night came back. I saw them return in Veritas's eyes as well. His anger stabbed into me once again. "Veritas, look, I'm sorry about what—"

"You're not the one who needs to apologize." He turned toward the sound of sirens in the distance. "Besides, that can wait. Let's go see what we can salvage from the back room before we have company, okay?"

We walked through the wrecked bar. Only Benin remained conscious, but when he saw us, he bolted for the back door. We let him run and stepped through the debris for the desk.

We reached Pyrotrack's desk. Veritas produced a flashlight and poked through the papers on top. He whooped. "Do you know what this stuff is?"

I shook my head.

"Everything we need to shut down the Blue Eclipse Boys. Nothing on Lux, but I'm sure it's in here somewhere. The cops are going to have a field day with this." The sirens grew closer. "Time to go. But first . . ." He scooped up a piece of paper and a pencil. He scribbled something across it and then set it carefully on the stack of papers.

I skimmed the note: *Courtesy of Veritas and Failstate.*

"Dad always said it helps to take credit for what you've done," Veritas said.

We darted out the back door and down the alley just as red and blue lights painted the dingy brick walls. No one would know we'd been there—until they found our note.

"So now what?" I asked.

"You have your duffel stashed somewhere?"

I nodded.

"Let's get your clothes and then I'll give you a ride home, okay?"

Within a half hour, we changed and were in the Reliant. Mike wanted to leave Hogtown, but I suggested we swing by the Penguin's Claw, just to see what was happening.

The fire department, cops, and even the VOC swarmed over the block. Pyrotrack and his goons, all of them cuffed, were loaded into different vans. A few local news crews surrounded the whole operation with some guy in a VOC blazer speaking to them. I smiled. Tonight had started a little rough, but at least it had ended well.

"Anywhere else you want to go?" Mike asked.

"Actually, now that you mention it . . ."

• • •

Mike pulled up outside Elizabeth's apartment and killed the engine. "Are you sure this is a good idea? I mean, it's almost eleven. Would she appreciate a late night visitor?"

Unlike the last time I had been here, just a few days earlier, this time I wanted to be here. Too bad I didn't have the crystal flower. I could have given it to her. I remembered her warmth, the smell of her hair. "I have to make sure she made it home okay."

"Fair enough. I'll be here."

I slipped out the door and jogged silently across the lawn toward the ugly apartment building. But when I realized that there were two people standing in the front door, I skidded to a halt and ducked behind some bushes. When I glanced out from behind my cover, I recognized who they were. Elizabeth's arms were twined around Ben's neck, drawing his head down to hers for a passionate kiss.

CHAPTER 39

NUMBNESS SWIRLED THROUGH ME. I couldn't breathe. I didn't even want to. Ben and Elizabeth? They kept kissing, for excruciating seconds. Or hours. Time had stopped along with my heart.

Elizabeth broke away from Ben, an uncertain look on her face. My heart stuttered, the tiniest bit of hope surging. Maybe Ben had kissed her without permission. She'd slap him, burst into tears, kick his shins, declare her love for me . . . something.

Instead she kissed him again, her hand on the back of his neck. She ran her hand down his chest before she disappeared into her apartment. Ben watched her go, then he seemed to drift back to Mom's van.

I stumbled out of my hiding place and walked back to the Reliant. I fumbled with the door and fell into the seat.

Mike frowned. "So is she okay?"

Not really, so far as I was concerned. But I didn't want to go into it, not now. "She's fine."

Mike's eyes narrowed. But if he saw the truth, he mercifully dropped the subject. "Look, are you in any hurry to get home?"

I laughed. Not if I had to face Ben. "No."

"Good." He tucked his cell phone back into his pocket and started the car. "Because Dad wants to see us both right now. You up for that?"

I laughed, a mirthless chuckle. "Ready and willing. Let's go."

Magnus waited for us in the long tunnel that led to the Lighthouse. He threw open his arms and beamed. Actually beamed. A small nimbus of light surrounded him, lighting up the shadows. "I can't believe it," he said. "If anyone had told me that Veritas and Failstate would bring down Pyrotrack and the Blue Eclipse Boys, I would have laughed in their faces. But here you are. Good job, boys. Great job!"

I shook his offered hand even though his words stung. Talk about your backhanded compliments. He probably would have "expected" Gauntlet to succeed . . . and get all the girls. No, I wasn't going to think about that.

"So, the Boys. Were they the ones who . . ." His voice caught.

Mike nodded emphatically. "I'm sure of it, Dad."

Magnus blew out a long breath. "Incredible. To think she was taken down by a bunch of hoods. But at least she can rest easy now." Magnus hugged Mike, but the embrace looked stiff and awkward, as if he were uncertain where to put his arms. Mike endured it like a block of ice, his arms at his sides.

Then Magnus walked deeper into the Lighthouse, his footsteps punctuated by his cane. "Come on, boys, let's head upstairs and get a snack. I bet you're starving. I know I was always famished after a fight."

I wasn't about to turn down the offer. Mike and I fell into step behind Magnus and we trotted up the stairs into Magnus's study.

As we emerged from the secret passage, Helen Kirkwood came out of her office, carrying a file in her hands. "Mr. Magnus, I was going over the figures for tomorrow's meeting . . ." She jumped when she saw us. The papers spilled out of her hands.

"That can wait." Magnus jerked a thumb toward the door. "Post-fight snack. You know how it is."

A thin smile pulled at her lips, and she reached down to retrieve her papers. "Of course. Will you need any further assistance?"

"No, I think we're good."

Helen nodded, but her gaze lingered on me for a moment. Then I realized I had come up from the tunnel in my civvies without my mask while wearing my necklace. It hadn't even occurred to me that Magnus and Helen would see me like this. But I swallowed my unease. After all, Magnus wouldn't say anything and Helen had kept her employer's secret for decades.

We crossed through the halls to the kitchen, and Magnus got busy, bringing out chips and dip, fruit and cheese, and bottled water. While he worked, I looked around. The kitchen was almost as large as our house, with dark granite countertops, a refrigerator that looked big enough to hold four people, and a center island the size of a dining room table.

Magnus insisted we tell him what happened. When we told him how the Blue Eclipse Boys had captured both of us he didn't look too happy, but any disappointment soon gave way to a smile and laughter, especially when we told him about how we took out Pyrotrack.

Magnus slapped the granite counter. "Excellent! This is exactly what I need for tomorrow!"

I frowned. "Why? What's tomorrow?"

"I'm meeting with the network again to convince them to not cancel the show. You two breaking the Boys is just the good press we need to convince those pinheads to let us finish what we started."

Mike nibbled on a piece of cheese. "Do you really think that'll work, Dad?"

Magnus's eyes narrowed at Mike, but then he gave a smile that looked forced. "Only one way to find out. We have to try. We've invested so much. What I'd really like to do is get things back on track so we can hold the finale as we planned."

I grimaced. The finale, where the winner would be presented with the license, was supposed to be held in six weeks.

Magnus stood up. "There's one more thing we have to do now that the snack is over."

Mike groaned. "C'mon, Dad, it's late, and Rob should get home."

"What's going on?" I asked.

"Dad has a tradition. After a night out, you have to spar."

"Gotta push yourself." Magnus shooed us out of the kitchen. "Let's go. Failstate, get changed."

I retrieved my costume from the car. By the time I returned to the Lighthouse, Magnus had changed into a tight-fitting black outfit. He led us to one corner of the Lighthouse. A padded mat filled the center. Racks of weapons and boxing equipment bordered the area, creating a space for sparring.

He jabbed a finger at the floor and looked at me. "You sit this one out first, okay?" He turned to Mike, who had somehow changed into his costume without me noticing, and beckoned with his hand. "Let's do this."

Veritas dropped into a ready stance, fists up, legs wide. Magnus took a few steps toward him but Veritas didn't budge.

"Think you know what I'm planning?" Magnus's lips twisted into a feral grin.

"I can see the truth of your actions." Veritas fell back a step, crouching lower.

"Uh, huh." Magnus launched at his son, his fists a blur.

Veritas knocked aside the blows and circled around, sweeping a kick at Magnus's feet. Magnus cartwheeled in midair and landed lightly. The old guy still had the magic. Then Magnus threw more punches—punches that Veritas either turned aside or ducked.

They separated, and Magnus's smirk grew wider. "Not too bad, kiddo. But out there, no one's gonna go easy on you."

Veritas rolled his shoulders. "I think I have a good idea of what's—"

Magnus interrupted with another flurry of punches. Veritas tried to counter but foundered on the last one.

Magnus slapped him lightly across the face. "Focus, Mike! I know you're tired—"

Veritas swept his dad's feet out from under him. He punched at Magnus's face, but Magnus rolled out of the way and kipped to his feet.

"Good! Enough warm up, huh?"

I couldn't keep up with their blows and counter-punches, their kicks and jumps. Light flowed through the room, blinding traces of greens, reds, and blues, burning from Magnus's fists and feet. If his age had slowed him down, I couldn't tell.

But Veritas kept up with his dad. He ducked most of Magnus's blows and even landed a few good hits himself.

In the end, Magnus caught Veritas in a choke hold. Veritas struggled for a few moments before going limp. Had he passed out? His eyes were open, resignation lurking behind them.

Magnus let him go, and his son crumpled to the mat. "Better. But not by much." He rubbed his forehead with his sleeve and then looked at me. "Okay, Failstate, you're up."

I blanched, my gaze darting from Veritas to Magnus. "Um, uh . . . no?"

"My house, my rules."

"I can't even do a quarter of what you two just did. No way I could go toe to toe with you."

"I'm not expecting you to." He beckoned me with an open palm. "But let's see what you can do."

I joined him in the center of the mat, straightening my costume to keep from getting twisted in it. Magnus dropped into a ready stance and beckoned me with both hands. Did he really want me to hit him? I doubted I could, but I tried anyway, swinging for his chin.

Not surprisingly, Magnus dodged. He poked me in the ribs. "You're telegraphing your intentions. Try again."

"Of course you can see what I'm going to do—you guys are telepaths!"

"Only Mike is, and not really. C'mon!"

I took another swing. Magnus blocked it. Frustration boiled within me.

Magnus kicked me in the shin, just enough to sting. "You haven't had any training."

"None."

He grunted. He retrieved two thick pads from the racks and he strapped them to his palms. "I can go over some basics with you tonight, but you might want to look into joining a dojo or taking boxing at the Y. We'll start with a simple pattern. Left, right, left, right. Hit the pads as hard as you can."

I followed his instructions, punching in time with his barked orders. Left, right, left, right. A musty cloud exploded from the pads at each impact, their thick odor choking me through my mask.

"You can do better than that! If you're going to hit me, hit me!"

I tensed. How often had Ben taunted me with similar words? I swung harder, my fist pounding into the bag. Magnus grunted but his face remained impassive. I kept the rhythm up, but now Ben's voice echoed in my mind. That only stirred up images of him . . . and Elizabeth. Standing on her doorstep.

I stumbled. The side of my face stung. I adjusted my mask.

"Where's your head right now, kid?" Magnus's voice was a growl. "You should have seen that coming." He held up the pads again.

I resumed pummeling them, trying to exorcize the images from my mind. But they came back, stronger, more insistent. How had they wound up kissing? Had it been his idea? Hers? Didn't she realize how I felt about her? Should she have? I mean—

Light exploded in my eyes. I stumbled and my arms pinwheeled to remain upright.

Red light poured over Magnus's body. The aura faded but his stern expression didn't. "Don't let yourself get distracted. Try again."

We resumed our drill. I managed to dodge his next hit, only to be smacked by his other hand. The throbbing behind my eyes grew worse. Magnus snapped a hand in my direction only to pause long enough for me to dodge, then he hit me.

The rhythmic thrum of my power trickled down my arms and collected around my knuckles. I channeled all my rage into one last punch into the pad.

Magnus yelped and shook the pads off of his hand. He rubbed his hands together and gave me a funny look. "What did you do?"

I frowned. "I'm—I'm not sure."

Uncertainty danced across his face. He held out his bare hand. "Try to do that again. Hit my hand as hard as you can."

I took a few swings at the air, trying to channel my power into my fists. Then I punched his open palm.

Magnus howled, dancing away from me and clutching his hand. He took several deep breaths before he shook out the hand.

"Oh, Mr. Magnus—I'm so sorry!" I'd injured Meridian, my hero. "Do you want me to get you some ice? I can—"

His howls of pain turned to howls of laughter. "Holy cow, kid! It's like all the pain receptors in my hand fired at the same time. With a punch like that, you could rank right up there with the biggest strappers of them all." He fanned his hand in the air. "Wow!"

Veritas shook his head but I'm pretty sure I saw a smile underneath his full mask.

Then I saw Helen. She stood in the entrance of the sparring room, her face set in her usual scowl. I smirked at her beneath my mask. She and the other judges had been so dismissive of me during the episode tapings. Maybe she'd have to readjust her opinion of me. I felt pretty good. It was almost enough to help me forget what I saw earlier.

Almost.

CHAPTER 40

I WISHED I COULD have carried Magnus's praise with me but it evaporated the minute I stepped back into our house.

Mom was stretched out on the couch in the living room, still in her scrubs. Even in sleep, her face was still pinched into a scowl. Had she been waiting? For me? I tried to imagine what she must have felt, coming home to a house in ruins, police everywhere. And then, on top of it all, I had left without telling her. She'd never noticed or cared before. Why now? Maybe I could make it up to her.

I walked through the house. A lot of it was still wrecked. Broken dishes littered the kitchen, clothing was scattered in the upstairs hallway, and cardboard boxes still soaked up the water in the basement. Well, it was only four in the morning. I probably had a few hours before Mom would wake up. Might as well do some cleaning.

I started in the basement and worked my way up. It was dreary work, but by the time the rising sun streamed in through the windows, I had most of the damage squared away. Ben would be up soon. Mom too. Maybe I should make breakfast for them. Why not? I got started on scrambled eggs and put on some coffee.

Once the aromas wafted through the kitchen, Mom stumbled into the room, bleary eyed and rubbing her head. She paused when she saw me at work. "If you think this is going to keep you from getting into trouble, you'd better think again," Her voice was still hoarse from sleep.

"I know. I'm sorry. I should have been here when you got home, but . . . well, a friend needed my help, and—"

"*We* needed your help, Robin." Mom's words took on an edge. "Our home is trashed, thugs almost killed both of you and Elizabeth . . . and I come home to a house swarming with police who won't tell me what's going on . . ." Were those tears? Mom wouldn't meet my gaze. She scuffed at the floor with her foot and swiped at her eyes. "If anything had happened to you . . ."

Where had this come from? Was this some new tactic to torture me? And yet her worry seemed so genuine. I scraped the eggs from the pan, trying to figure out how I should respond. Best to keep it simple. "We were fine, Mom, really. We made sure El . . ." Her name stuck in my throat. "Elizabeth was away. And we were able to handle ourselves."

"I know." Mom whispered. "It's just . . . it's hard. I don't want to know what you two do. I don't. But when you're out there, I worry. And I always hoped that we would be safe here. Our home should be . . . But now, after last night . . ."

I bit my lower lip. What could I say to reassure her?

"What smells so good?" Ben shuffled into the kitchen. He looked between the stove and me a few times. "*He's* cooking?

Well, I suppose it'd be good for him to have something to fall back on."

Heat flashed across my face. "You seem happy today. Anything you want to tell me?"

His smirk grew brighter. I knew what he was up to. He wouldn't say anything about Elizabeth, not now. He'd save it for the biggest impact. Well, two could play that game.

"Have a seat, the eggs are almost done."

Mom and Ben settled in at the center island. Ben looked around the kitchen. "Someone's been busy. The house looks great too."

"Had to find something to do. Taking out the trash seemed like a good way to spend the night."

I served the eggs, toast, and glasses of juice. Ben started in right away, shoveling the eggs down his throat. My manners weren't much better. The food tasted good after the night's excitement.

Mom stared at both of us. "How can you two eat? Aren't you upset about what happened?"

Ben shrugged. "Well, yeah, Mom. But the creeps that did it are in jail. I mean, it stinks, but it was just a random crime. Right, Robin?"

My grip on my fork tightened. That wasn't true, not even close. But since the real criminals responsible were in jail too, I figured it wouldn't hurt to reassure Mom. "Right."

Ben snatched up the remote and clicked on the small TV at the other end of the counter. "Let's see what's going on in the world today, huh?"

I nearly choked on my food. The eagerness in Ben's voice gave him away. He was hoping to see himself on TV taking credit for breaking up the home invasion by himself. But instead of the news, the screen displayed a weatherman walking us through the day's forecast. That gave way to a stream of commercials.

"So everything good with your friend, Robin?" Ben asked.

"Just fine. It was all pretty boring, actually." I took another bite and forced it down my throat. "How about you? Anything interesting happen last night after I left?"

Ben's smile widened, a wolfish glint in his eyes. "Not really."

Then the anchor reappeared on the screen. "Late last night, some of New Chayton's local heroes cleaned house in Hogtown."

Ben's smirk froze in place. "Wait . . . Hogtown?"

"Here with more details about the extraordinary fight is Tricia Olson. Tricia?"

The perky reporter appeared, standing in front of the Penguin's Claw, the entire area wreathed in yellow police tape. "That's right, Evan. According to eye-witnesses, Veritas and Failstate, local heroes who are participating in the reality show *America's Next Superhero*, scored a major victory against crime in New Chayton last night."

The details of what happened slowly unfolded, with Tricia speaking to different eyewitnesses. I clamped my mouth shut to keep from smiling but it wasn't easy. The people interviewed made Veritas and me sound larger than life—avenging angels in human form. One dingy young man seemed particularly thankful, saying he hoped the Blue Eclipse Boys would never come back.

Ben stared at the TV, his mouth hanging open. Several times he tried to say something, but no matter how hard he worked his jaw, he remained mute. Oh, victory was sweet. It didn't counterbalance the sweetness he had enjoyed with my would-be girlfriend, but it did feel good.

The report continued, showing mug shots of Pyrotrack. Then a spokesperson for the VOC publicly thanked Veritas and Failstate—me, in positive media coverage!—for our assistance.

The report ended, and the TV cut back to the anchor. He faced the camera. "Thank you, Tricia. With me here right now is Alexander Magnus, the executive producer of *America's Next Superhero*. Mr. Magnus, what is your opinion about what happened last night?"

Magnus appeared on screen. He smiled, a toothy flash. "I think this just illustrates how great our show is. We sought out the best of the best and I think we certainly found them in Failstate and Veritas. That's why I'm hoping we'll be able to come out of hiatus very soon."

The interview continued, but I couldn't pay attention to it. Ben had turned to face me, his jaw jutted out. His fingers tightened around the edge of the counter. I dipped my gaze to the plate and finished off the last of my breakfast. "Well, I think it's only fair that since I made breakfast, Ben cleans up. If you'll excuse me, I need to go get ready for school."

With that, I retreated from the kitchen, finally allowing the smile to blossom on my face. A Pyrrhic victory, maybe, but I'd take any win I could.

CHAPTER 41

I PLANNED TO AVOID ELIZABETH throughout the day. I knew I couldn't trust myself to behave rationally if I saw her. By now, the mental image of her kissing Ben assaulted me only two or three times an hour, a definite improvement. But when we arrived at school, I heard through the rumor mill that she was out sick again. Part of me hoped that whatever it was could be spread via kissing.

At lunch, I found Haruki seated by himself in one corner of the cafeteria. Thankfully, he appeared to be healthy and whole again. He greeted me with a shaky smile and went back to pushing his ravioli around his plate.

"Haruki, are you okay?"

He sighed and wadded up his paper napkin and tossed it into the sauce. "Not really, no. You know, the aliens . . ."

I nodded. "So what usually happens when they come to visit?"

He leaned away from me. "Why?"

"Because I'm worried about you. I want to make sure you're going to be okay."

Haruki sighed. "Happens the same way every time. About midnight, the *akuma* show up. They—"

"I'm sorry, the *akuma?*"

"It's Japanese. It means 'demons.' Anyway, one of them paralyzes me while another pokes me with needles. And then they're gone."

"What do they look like?"

"I don't know. I'm usually pretty out of it. They look kind of like you and me, I guess. I try yelling for help but I can't. Like one of those dreams. My folks say they don't hear me, so maybe I don't really make a sound. Or maybe they're just scared." Haruki poked at his food some more. He shoved his tray away. "What does it matter? Nobody's ever going to help me." He picked up his tray and walked over to the window to deposit it.

I watched him and nodded to myself. With the Blue Eclipse Boys out of business, I had a bit of free time. Maybe nobody had ever tried to help Haruki before, but tonight, someone would.

Mom had to work the night shift again, leaving Ben and me to fend for ourselves for dinner. We ate in different rooms, me watching TV in the living room, him in the kitchen. His cell phone beeped a few times as he received texts. I tried to lose myself in a documentary about Etzal'el's career, but I had seen it twice already.

Once dinner was over, I retreated to my room to prepare for my mission of the night. Hopefully Ben wouldn't follow me. Thanks to the hole in my wall from the burglars, I didn't have much privacy. My cell phone was charged and ready to go. I had a pair of binoculars and a sound amplifier from the local Radio Shack. The clerk had sworn I'd be able to hear a mosquito sneeze from two hundred yards away. I packed my bag and left my room.

I nearly collided with Ben as he left his room. We paused and regarded one another. He had changed since coming home. He was now dressed in a button-down shirt open over a plain black t-shirt. He stared at my duffel. "Where are you going?" His voice was hard.

"Out. And you?"

"The same." His eyes narrowed, his gaze never leaving my bag. "Going to see a sick friend."

Heat shot through my cheeks. That explained who he had been texting throughout dinner. "I see."

"And how about you? What's on your agenda?"

"Something similar." I shifted my duffel behind my back.

Ben snorted. "Right. Well. Have fun." He pushed past me.

I waited until the front door slammed, counted to thirty, and headed out. The last thing I needed was Ben sticking his perfectly-shaped nose into my business. As much as I hated the thought of him making out with Elizabeth, at least it would keep him distracted. It galled me, but I had to divorce her from my mind. So far as I was concerned, she was gone. Out of my life. She had to be.

CHAPTER 42

HARUKI'S HOUSE WAS a forty-five minute walk from ours. I kept my head down the whole way, bag slung over my shoulder. Although the spring night was still a bit cool, someone was barbecuing steaks. I could smell the charcoal drifting on the wind. I glanced at the grey clouds that hung overhead. The weatherman hadn't said anything about rain, but he was usually wrong.

Soon the modest houses of my neighborhood gave way to larger homes, sprawling mini-mansions with three car garages and immaculate lawns. I passed by a few late-night joggers, a family taking a stroll. Dogs barked at me for violating their territory. I ignored them all, focused on my mission: Find out who Haruki's aliens really were, if they actually existed, and send them packing.

I turned the corner onto Haruki's block and slowed down. I ambled, trying to look casual. The glares Haruki's neighbors gave me suggested I wasn't succeeding—even in my civvies. I walked past Haruki's house, a story-and-a-half box covered in faded wood siding. White paint peeled around the windows, the doors. Looked like servants' quarters in the middle of the luxurious homes surrounding it.

So where was Haruki's room? Upstairs? Hard to tell. The basement could be finished, with Haruki's room down there. I couldn't risk checking out the house from the alley. That'd bring the authorities down on me for sure. Instead, I had to find a place I could keep an eye on his house.

The neighbors' houses didn't offer many prospects for my stakeout. A few sparse bushes, a lone birch tree. I stood in the street and turned a slow circle. While all the other houses were lit up, the house directly across the street stood dark. Scaffolding wrapped around the two story house. Plywood filled the first story windows and bright white frames shone in the dark from the second floor. The house was being renovated or built. Either way, no one was home now. Perfect.

I changed into my costume in a nearby park bathroom, a small brick structure that reeked. Hopefully I wouldn't carry the stench with me back to my stakeout.

Getting into the vacant house proved easy. A quick burst of destructive energy popped the lock and I let myself in. I left close to thirty bucks in cash on the half-finished kitchen to cover the damages, then went upstairs to find a window over-looking Haruki's house.

The unfinished master bedroom provided the perfect perch. I popped open the window and set up my listening gear, aiming the microphone at Haruki's. I scanned the neighbor-hood. It didn't look like anything was amiss. The neighbors I had spotted earlier had gone inside. A lone woman jogged down the street, but she didn't even glance toward Haruki's house.

I tugged on the headphones for the listening device and aimed the microphone toward Haruki's house. For a few moments, I couldn't hear anything, and I worried that I had already broken it. But then I heard a hushed conversation in Japanese and the clink of what I assumed was silverware on plates. A momentary thrill shot through me. The device actually worked! But then I realized I was eavesdropping on Haruki and his parents. Not cool. At least I couldn't understand what they were saying.

Five hours later, I checked my watch. Coming up on midnight. I groaned. I hadn't expected this to be so boring. About the only entertainment I had was a dog that had been barking the entire time. Only that had grown old very quickly. Haruki and his parents had gone to bed two hours ago. At least, it sounded that way. I couldn't pick up any more noise from their house. Maybe I should have brought a book. Or a snack. Something. I twisted my neck around and rubbed my arms, trying to work a bit of warmth into them. I didn't want to stand up. The windows didn't have curtains and I didn't know if the neighbors would be able to see me.

The sound of a car's engine caught my attention. I looked over the window's ledge. A rusty grey Oldsmobile pulled up to Haruki's neighbor's house. The driver's side door popped open and a kid I recognized from school jogged around the car. Eric something, I thought. Played baseball. He opened the passenger door. An attractive girl stepped out. He put his arm around her waist as they slowly walked to the front door of the neighbor's house. On the porch, she turned to face him and took a step closer to him. He put his arms around her and drew her into a kiss.

As much as I wanted to, I couldn't look away. I even considered turning the listening device on them, just to hear the empty words of affection they whispered to each other. But seeing them there only made me think of Ben and Elizabeth. My stomach twisted and I banged my head against the wall, the dull ache synchronized with the throb between my eyes. If I wasn't careful, my power would spike and I'd fry the audio equipment. But I didn't care. I wondered if—

A wave of grogginess crashed over me. I fell to the floor, feeling as though a ton of cotton had been dropped on me. This was not normal drowsiness. It was almost like getting knocked out. I remembered the knock-out darts that Magnus's Blond Brute had shot me with. I gagged and sucked in breath through the mask.

What just happened? I checked myself for knock-out darts. Nothing. Was it something outside? I pulled myself up to look outside.

The young lovers lay unconscious on the front porch. I fumbled with my binoculars to look at them. It looked like they were still breathing, and I didn't see any blood. I switched on the listening equipment and scanned the neighborhood. Nothing. The dog had gone silent for the first time in hours. And I couldn't pick up anything other than the sound of quiet snoring. I shook my head to clear out the stuffiness. The movement helped, but not much.

Then an engine roared in my ears. I winced and yanked the headphones off. Even without them, the sound echoed through the quiet neighborhood. A dark cargo van rolled up outside Haruki's house. I could hear the passenger side door banged open, but the van kept me from seeing who got out. I fumbled to get the listening equipment's headphones back on.

"—they'll all stay asleep?" The voice was pinched and nasally, undercut with fuss and nerves.

"We go over this every time. Look, I've knocked out everyone in a six block radius." This voice was smooth, soothing, like rich chocolate clinging to the side of a mug.

"What about the kid? Never seems to work on him." The third voice sent ants made of ice marching up and down my spine.

"His naturally boosted immunity response could negate our friend's anaesthetizing ability," Nasal said. "Perhaps I could test this hypothesis and—"

"Stow it, Professor," Icy-Ants said. "Boss only wants us to follow through on our assignment. Or do you want to get zapped again?"

"Heavens, no!"

Footsteps shuffled up the sidewalk. Three men stood on the sidewalk. One, a stocky man with thin arms and legs, flowed through the darkness, as if he swam rather than walked. The second appeared as thin as paper, fragile and small. The third was huge, a strapper if I ever saw one. Steam rose from his body. They turned and went around the house and down the hill. It looked like at least one of them was wearing a mask. I could see the straps winding through his hair on the back of his head.

I rose, but my legs wobbled beneath me. I didn't really regain my balance until I was halfway down the stairs. If one of the "aliens" had knocked out the neighborhood, why was I still awake? Maybe because I didn't normally sleep. Maybe because I never got sick. No time to puzzle that out. I was too late to stop them from getting to Haruki but I could keep them from escaping.

By the time I made it downstairs and out of the house, I felt relatively normal.

The van was a large Chevy, uniform black or maybe dark blue. I scribbled the license plate number onto a scrap of paper and slashed through the tires with my power. I retreated to the shadows. Best to maintain the element of surprise for as long as I could.

A few minutes later, voices drifted from around the house, unusually loud even without the listening equipment.

" . . . hate the way he looks at me, all wide eyed and scared," Icy-Ants said.

"Well, your face is pretty intimidating." Smooth Voice chortled. "What we can see of it."

"I hope the boss will not be angry with us," Nasal said. "We didn't collect near enough. One of the pods must have released early. That might explain the mini-epidemic."

I knew it! Haruki wasn't being abducted by aliens. Somehow it was these jerks, and they were using him to do something horrible. The sickness proved it. My power seethed within me, and I was tempted to slice their van in half right there.

"We may have to subject Patient Zero to another round," Nasal continued.

Icy-Ants snorted. "The boss'll love that. You go right ahead and share that bit of information, see what happens."

"We wouldn't have reason to worry if it hadn't been for your temper!" Nasal shot back.

Three men dressed in black outfits, came around the house and walked for the van. My stomach flipped. Villains. One of them could put people to sleep. What could the other two do?

They were about halfway to the van when the stocky one darted forward. He swore and ran around the van. "Someone slashed our tires!" It was Icy-Ants.

I stepped out of the shadows. "Having car trouble, boys?"

They turned toward me. All three were carrying metallic cylinders about three feet long, each one marked with a bright biohazard symbol. They each wore odd half-masks. Smooth Voice wore one that covered his eyes and nose from over his forehead. Nasal's covered the right half of his face only. Icy-Ants had one that covered only the left side. The masks appeared to be leather with little hooks digging into their skin.

Wait . . . hooks?

I had seen this trio before. I stumbled backward as the memory came crashing over me in a rush. Hogtown, slamming into the big guy, the two of us going down into a tangle of limbs. The fog that had wrapped itself around my memories of Lux's death vanished, and I remembered.

They had been in Hogtown the night Lux had died.

CHAPTER 43

MY MIND LOCKED. The men from Hogtown . . . these were Haruki's aliens? What connection could there be between Haruki and Lux?

The other two joined the stocky man in the street. They dropped their canisters, which clattered against the street. Recognition blossomed over Smooth Voice's face. "It's the guy from Hogtown, from the night we—"

"Shut up, Madrigal!"

"Whatever you're doing to Haruki, it ends tonight!"

"Take a walk, mask." Icy-Ants crossed his arms over his chest. "This doesn't concern you."

"But isn't he the one who . . . ?" Madrigal asked.

"Am I the one who what?" I demanded.

"You had your chance." Icy-Ants cupped his hand and swung like he was pitching a ball at me.

Knife-like projectiles streaked toward me. I dodged, but one sliced through my hood, trailing cold against my cheek. What was that?

Icy-Ants cupped his hands, but I summoned a destructive screen in front of me, shredding his projectiles. He cursed and tried again, but I closed the gap and punched, trying to focus my energy into my fists, the way I did with Magnus the night before.

The impact barely registered on my knuckles but Icy-Ants yowled and stumbled backward. His hands tore at his face. He tripped over his own feet and thrashed on the ground.

I whirled on the other two and ran for the canisters. What had they been collecting from Haruki? I wouldn't be able to figure it out myself, but maybe if I brought it to the VOC, their labs could—

Madrigal, the thin man with the mask that covered his forehead, jabbed a finger at me. Warmth oozed over me. The world spun in and out of focus. I stumbled and fell to my knees. Every bone in my body had turned to jelly. Madrigal opened his hands and the sensation intensified.

"No." My tongue felt five sizes too large. I staggered to my feet. My legs buckled under me, and my power flared, ripping a gash in the side of the van.

The Professor spoke, his voice a high-pitched drone, but I couldn't understand his words. They were as indistinct as a swarm of bees buzzing through my skull. Madrigal replied, but his words were as the gurgling of a distant river. The Professor grabbed at Madrigal's arms, but the larger man shook him off.

I couldn't understand them, but I wasn't completely incapacitated. While those two were distracted, I gouged a hole in the pavement beneath Madrigal's feet. He stumbled, and the syrupy sensation in my head vanished.

I lurched forward and swung wildly. I knocked Madrigal's legs out from under him. He went down so hard his head bounced off the pavement.

I turned on the Professor. He hadn't done anything yet, so I didn't know his powers, but I didn't want to take any chances.

He raised his hands to block me. "Wait! I'm unarmed! I don't want anyone to get hurt."

"What about Haruki? What about Lux?"

The Professor's skin looked bleached against the dark leather of his half mask. "We didn't . . . I mean, we weren't supposed to—"

"Supposed to what?"

"It was an accident!"

My eyes widened. These three had killed Lux? Not the Blue Eclipse Boys? That meant that Veritas and I had risked our lives fighting Pyrotrack for nothing! We had been wrong, so wrong, the whole time! The throbbing in my head turned into spikes that clawed through my skull. Fire burned through my arms and dripped from my fingers. Large gashes appeared in the street around me. My control was spiraling away, but I didn't care. I would make these three pay. I would—

My feet went out from under me, and I skidded down the street, surprised at the sheet of ice that covered the pavement.

Icy-Ants rose from a pile of . . . was that snow? White powder fluttered to the ground. A cold blast of wind cut through me, pushing me farther away. Frost spread over his face, his hands. He drew back both hands and his eyes shone with malicious glee.

A blue and golden blur exploded out of the shadows and slammed into Icy-Ants from behind. The last vestiges of Madrigal's effects dissipated and I realized who my "savior" was.

Gauntlet rolled to his feet and jammed his fists into his hips. "Good start, Failstate, but I'll take it from here."

Before I could answer, Icy-Ants reared up, his face a rictus of rage. He slammed his hands together and thrust them out, and icy shards sliced through the air.

I shouted an incoherent warning. Gauntlet turned in time to catch the projectiles on his chest. But rather than rip into him, the ice shattered.

Neat trick. I'd have to ask how he did that.

Gauntlet swung at Icy-Ants. The villain ducked and took several steps back, but my brother kept after him.

Icy-Ants finally bent down to touch the ground. Ice snaked from his hand and encased Gauntlet's feet.

Gauntlet struggled but the ice crept up his legs. Within moments, it had swallowed his waist. Gauntlet's eyes met mine, and they widened as the ice consumed his head.

"So now you got a problem," Icy-Ants said. "We can keep dancing, or you can help your buddy before he suffocates. Choices, choices." He darted for his partners. "C'mon, Professor. Grab Madrigal and let's go."

They scooped up the canisters and ran off down the street. I wanted to chase them, but I couldn't. I rushed to Gauntlet's side. I had to get him out of there. Which worked faster, suffocation or freezing to death? My hands roamed over the ice. It had to be at least a foot thick. He looked like an ice sculpture of a grizzly bear. If it weren't so dire, it would've been funny.

I exerted my power and I directed it into the ice. But the surface of the ice remained smooth. Had I failed? I couldn't tell if the ice were dissolving under my assault. Maybe I was slightly accelerating the melting. I couldn't see. I had to move fast, I had to . . .

A crack ripped through the ice. It snaked from Gauntlet's arms outward and encircled the block until it exploded. I threw up my arms to protect my face from the flying debris.

With a groan, Gauntlet fell onto me and we both smashed to the ground. I shoved him off of me. He shivered, wrapping his arms around himself.

I rolled to my feet and took off after the trio, but there was no trace of them. I slapped my thighs and turned a full circle.

"So what was that all about?" Gauntlet dusted some ice out of his hair and shook himself.

I glared down at him. "Are you okay?"

He rubbed his arms. "I think so."

"Good, because I'm going to kill you."

Gauntlet laughed. "Nice gratitude."

"What should I be grateful for? You letting them get away?"

"That wasn't my fault. You just stood there."

"That's because I was worried about you, you moron!"

"Why? I had things under control."

I stared at him, dumbstruck. "You were encased in a block of ice! For all we know, you've got frostbite."

He shook his head and rose to his feet. "I'm good."

I glowered at him. It figured. He always did come out of bad situations unscathed. But this time, he had made a bad situation worse. The bad guys had gotten away with whatever they had come for, which meant they were free to harass . . .

"Haruki!" I started for the back of the house.

I made it halfway to the house but then paused. A large sheet of ice coated the ground where Icy-Ants had fallen earlier. I nudged it with my toe. It had to be at least four inches thick. Just like the drift of snow from the vacant lot. Why hadn't I remembered that before? Stupid, stupid, stupid. It was a minor miracle I could even walk and breathe at the same time.

"So what's our next move?" Gauntlet was right at my side.

"*My* next move is to check on Haruki. You can go home."

"No way! Let's go after those guys. We owe them for what they tried to do to us and Hooki."

"Haruki."

"Whatever. Let's go, man!"

"I thought you were supposed to be with a sick friend tonight."

Gauntlet waved away my words. "No way. This is a lot more fun."

My hands spasmed into fists and my power flared. A nearby power line threw sparks from its pole.

Gauntlet ducked and looked at me with wide eyes. "What's your problem?"

Like he had to ask? He blew off spending the evening with Elizabeth to mess up my night. I would have killed for the chance to be with her . . . well, maybe not kill exactly, but certainly maim . . . Okay, not that either. How could he be so insensitive when she needed someone?

"It's not as if it's that big of a deal. Derek will get over it."

An insult died halfway up my throat, choking me for a few seconds. "Derek? He's your sick friend?"

"Yeah. Who did you think I was talking about?"

I didn't say anything. I didn't want to speak her name, didn't want him to have any opportunity to rub it in.

But he must have read me anyway. A broad smile blossomed, his teeth flashing brightly in the darkness. "Liz? I offered, but she wasn't interested. Why would you . . ." His smile froze and became brittle, as if it could shatter in an instant like Icy-Ants's shards. We stared at each other for a few moments before Gauntlet laughed. "Are you serious? Did you really think you had a shot with her?"

I raised myself up a bit taller. "As good of a chance as you."

"Dream on, Robin! Why would someone like Liz even give you a second look?"

Fire surged up my spine and my power spiked again. Furrows tore through the sidewalk, radiating out from my feet and under the van, which dipped into the hole. I was going to destroy the whole block if I didn't get out of here fast. Still, I had to check on Haruki.

Gauntlet danced over one of the newly formed ruts.

I couldn't win this, so why did I even try? Nevertheless, I heard myself speak: "She gave me plenty of looks a week ago—"

"That's right, your big 'date,' the one *you* blew off. And when she was sick, at least I sent her flowers. What did you do?"

I thought of the crystal flower I'd dropped in her hallway. Sure, she had found it, but she still didn't know it was from me.

Gauntlet crossed his arms. "Out of the two of us, I'm the only one who's actually been there for her consistently."

Even last night. The statement, unspoken as it was, hovered between us. I tried to relax my fingers but the tension radiated up my arms and wrapped around my heart.

Sirens wailed in the distance.

Gauntlet looked over his shoulder and then back at me with that all-too-familiar smirk. "Fine," he said. "Tell you what. You want the spotlight? It's all yours. Have fun explaining this to the cops." He jogged into the night.

Leaving me to stand outside Haruki's home, wrestling with the fact that I knew he was right about how he'd been there for Elizabeth but I hadn't.

CHAPTER
44

"ALL RIGHT, LET'S GO over it again." The cop clicked his pen several times and scribbled something into his notebook.

I rubbed the back of my neck. He was just doing his job, but his repeated questions were causing a headache that bled down my skull.

Half a dozen squad cars and two ambulances had cordoned off this part of Haruki's neighborhood. Cops swarmed through the yard, taking pictures of the damage to the road and the van. Two EMTs sat with the young couple next door and checked their vitals while a cop took down their statement. At least they looked okay.

"I told you," I said. "Someone was harassing Takahashi Haruki, and I came to find out who. Three men went into his house. I confronted them in the street, and we fought."

"And they all had powers?"

"No, just two of them. Far as I could tell. One could put people to sleep. He said he knocked out everyone in a six-block radius. The other had an ice power. I don't know if the third one had any special abilities but he didn't do much." I glanced at the front yard. The snow from Icy-Ants had almost completely melted. The small drifts gave my story some credibility. My gaze fell on Haruki's house. "Can you at least tell me if the Takahashis are all right?"

The cop frowned at me. "They're fine. They don't remember anything."

"Not even Haruki?"

"The kid claims he didn't see anyone in his house."

That made sense. Haruki had never described these three as humans but as aliens. He probably didn't really remember everything that happened.

"Look, I just want to help," I said.

The cop scratched his forehead with the back of his pen. "The VOC is on their way to take over the case. And the city works people will be here soon to patch your . . . handiwork. Now don't touch anything." He walked over to a detective and the two of them conferred quietly.

I scuffed at the ground with my toe.

"Hey."

I gasped. Veritas stood next to me.

"I heard you got yourself into some trouble tonight," he said. "I thought I'd come see if you needed any help. The cops giving you any information?"

"Some. The VOC is on their way."

"Lovely." He tugged on my elbow. "Well, let's get out of here."

"What about the cops? Won't they get upset?"

"Did they arrest you?"

"No."

"Then you're fine. Let's head back to the Lighthouse. You can fill me in on what happened and we can take it from there."

We circled around to my hiding place so I could gather my stuff. Thankfully, the police didn't spot us. I doubted they'd be all that happy about my breaking and entering.

On the way to the Reliant, I filled in Veritas on what had happened. He listened quietly, occasionally interjecting a question or two. But then I told him about how they'd been there the night Lux had died.

He placed a hand on my chest and stopped me. "Why didn't you tell us about them before?"

"I honestly couldn't remember them. Maybe when my powers flared, it screwed up my memory somehow. I don't know. Nothing like that had ever happened to me before, at least, not on such a large scale. I'm sorry, Veritas."

Veritas sighed. "And I thought we had finished this with the Blue Eclipse Boys."

"Me too. But when I saw those leather masks they were wearing, that somehow broke through the block, and I remembered everything. And the Professor pretty much admitted to it."

"What masks?"

"It was weird. Three leather half-masks with hooks that dug into their skin. It almost looked like someone had chopped one mask into thirds and made them wear the pieces."

Veritas's eyes darted back and forth for a moment. He started walking faster. "Let's go. I've got something to show you."

• • •

"Are these the masks?" Veritas asked.

We were in the Lighthouse, sitting in front of one of the computers. An old photo popped up on the screen. The image was grainy, black and white, probably taken from a surveillance tape. Three men stood in a bank lobby, automatic weapons trained at the crowd. Sure enough, they wore what looked like the same half-masks. From the body shapes and postures, I could tell that these men weren't the same three I'd tangled with.

"What are they?" I asked.

Veritas tapped at the keyboard. The surveillance video disappeared and was replaced by a close-up of the three masks, set against a black-and-white grid. "They're called the Trifecta. About thirty years ago, Mind Master and Krazney Potok partnered to take down the licensed heroes. They combined their expertise and created these masks. They're not disguises so much as devices. They tap directly into a person's central nervous system and takes control of their minds."

I frowned. "That's it? Do they grant the wearers extra powers or something?"

Veritas shook his head. "Not that I know of. Those guys you were fighting had those powers before they put on the masks."

"So why did Mind Master and Krazney Potok think they'd be able to take down all the licensed heroes with only three masks?"

"They didn't. The original Trifecta were prototypes. They wanted to mass produce them, make an army. But the two villains had a falling out and they only made three."

"So who wound up with them?"

"Both of them, actually. They took turns. When one was caught, the other would use them." He frowned. "You said that two of the guys had powers. What about the third?"

I shook my head. "He seemed pretty freaked out. He never even tried to use a power, as far as I could tell."

"The one they called 'Professor?'"

"Right."

"What about the one who tried to put you to sleep—they called him 'Madrigal?' Like the music?"

I shrugged. I had never heard the term before so I had no idea.

Veritas's fingers flew over the keyboard. A red box proclaiming "No matches" flashed at him on the big screen. "Well, Dad doesn't have anybody with that name on file. Could be someone new. Let's see if we can't figure out who this 'Madrigal' is."

The flashing red box disappeared, replaced by a black screen with a vaguely human head-shaped blob.

"What's that?" I asked.

"It's a facial reconstruction program Dad's company made for the VOC. What kind of shape did this Madrigal's head have?"

"I don't know. Kind of like a square, I guess."

We set to work, sculpting the head, adding a nose, eyes, the right sized lips, and so on until, an hour later, the man's head rotated slowly on the screen.

"That's him," I said, astonished.

"Good." Veritas continued typing for a moment. "I'll call up a facial recognition program. Dad has taps in the VOC, the FBI, the INS, and a few other alphabet soup organizations. If anyone has this face on file, we'll find it." He entered a command and turned back to me. "Tell you what. Why don't we grab a few hours upstairs? Then we'll head over to Valley and chat with Mind Master about the Trifecta."

That sounded great to me, especially since it meant I wouldn't have to see Ben until I wanted to. Which, if I had things my way, probably meant I'd have to move into Magnus Mansion.

CHAPTER 45

MIND MASTER WAS WAITING inside the visitation room. Early morning sunlight trickled in through the high windows, painting the white bricks with brilliant colors. His face lit up with a genuine smile. "Twice in as many weeks?" He chuckled. "This can't be good."

"It's not," Veritas said. "The Trifecta's being used again."

The corner of Mind Master's eye twitched.

I nodded. "Twice I've seen the same men wearing them. We need to know more, like where you left them last."

Mind Master blew out a breath, almost a whistle, and leaned back in the chair. "When I was sentenced, I disclosed their location to the VOC. As far as I know, they retrieved and impounded them."

"Is there a chance Krazney Potok got to them first?" I asked.

"I don't quite see how." Mind Master stroked his chin. "Sergei and I weren't on speaking terms before my final capture. I wasn't about to share that kind of information with him."

"And no one else knew where they were?" Veritas said.

"To my knowledge, no." He shuddered. "If they are in use again, you must destroy them."

"There's one thing I don't get," I said. "I haven't seen those guys since the night Lux . . . Well, you know. Wouldn't they have to take them off at some point? That, or stay in hiding all the time. It's not like you can walk down the street wearing them without someone noticing."

"True," Mind Master said. "When worn, the Trifecta induces their victims' pituitary glands and hypothalami to secrete extra endorphins. In short order, the wearer becomes addicted to the high and wants to wear them without interruption."

"Anything else?" Veritas asked.

"Not that I can think of at the present time, no."

Veritas nodded. "All right. Thank you. I think that's all we need right now."

Mind Master smiled sadly. "I do regret not being more helpful. But perhaps today can be redeemed. Perhaps before you leave, you could see Delphi?"

Veritas marched out of the room. I shrugged to Mind Master and followed Veritas out into the hall. I touched Veritas' arm.

"Don't say it." His voice was little more than a growl.

"What could it hurt?"

He stopped, his back ramrod straight. "Why?"

"She's your mom, Mike," I replied. "Don't you at least want to try to patch things up?"

Veritas crumpled and his shoulders sagged. He nodded and then walked back to the attendant. "We have to see one more prisoner."

"And who would that be?"

Veritas hesitated but then spat out the name. "Delphi."

The door scraped against the bare concrete, a noise that scraped up my back and set my hair on end. I didn't know what to expect. The old pictures of Delphi I had seen made her look dark, almost a wraith. What would she be like now?

This visitation room wasn't much different from the one we had just left. The same high windows in the wall to our left, a large metal table bolted to the cement floor. A cluster of rickety plastic chairs surrounded the table. The only real difference was a large photo of a waterfall taped to one wall. Its corners were wrinkled and torn and its colors had begun to fade.

Then the door across from us ground open, and a woman shuffled in. She didn't look at all mysterious. More like broken. Beaten down. So frail a stiff breeze could have snapped her in half. Stringy red hair hung around her head, partially screening her face. Her green prison jumpsuit draped her body. It hung so loosely on her I couldn't get any clue to her physique—other than that she was very thin. She dropped into a chair and sagged so low she had to prop up her head in her hands.

I considered taking a seat, but something about her kept me on edge. Better to remain standing, just in case she tried something.

Vertias dropped into the chair opposite her. "Hello, Delphi."

She craned her neck. The curtain of hair parted to reveal reddened eyes framed with sallow skin covered in tiny scars. Her gaze locked on Veritas and she froze. I would have expected some change in her expression. A smile. A frown. Maybe even a tear. But Delphi appeared chiseled from granite. The corner of her mouth finally twitched. Her head didn't move but her eyes tracked him. Then her head dropped forward as if a string had been cut, her hair swirling around her.

Veritas sighed and shook his head. "So it's going to be like that, is it?"

"Now what?" I whispered.

"Good question. I guess we see if—"

Delphi giggled. I came around the table and knelt down to meet her gaze, but her eyes were shut and her face impassive. Then she rocked back and forth, her arms wrapped around herself like a hug. Or a straightjacket. She continued to giggle.

Veritas popped out of his chair and started for the door. "That's it. Failstate, let's go."

"No!"

I turned back to Delphi.

Her eyes were wide and locked on me. She tipped out of her chair until her face was close enough I could smell her breath through my hood's material. A strange light blazed in her eyes and she grabbed my shoulders and drawing me even closer. "The scourge! Coming. Have to stop it."

I tried to pull away. "I don't understand. What are you talking about?"

Her fingers dug in tighter and held me in place. She shook me gently.

"Told . . . gave guidance. Siblings. The . . . thrice-moved son. Scourge born of love. Must . . . fight!" Her grip slackened, and she slipped backward into her chair.

I stood. We exited the room, leaving Delphi in a heap.

I tried to say something but Veritas pulled me along the hallways, leading me by my elbow.

We burst out of the building and headed for the parking lot. The cool morning air slipped under my hood and slapped my face.

"I'm sorry," I said.

"Don't be." His voice bore a hard edge.

"Is she always like that?"

Veritas grunted. "No, usually she's a lot more incoherent. At least, that's what Helen tells me."

We set out through the security checkpoints for the parking lot. Once again, I couldn't help but feel out-of-place in my costume. It felt as though Veritas and I were going to a Halloween party that no one else knew about. I didn't know how Meridian or any of the other licensed heroes ever got used to it.

"What made her like that?" I asked.

Veritas didn't answer right away. Tears welled in the corner of his eyes. "I don't know," he whispered. "Come on. Let's go back to the Lighthouse and see what the computers have turned up."

We got into the Reliant and drove through the gate in the massive stone wall that encircled Valley. But as we drove, my mind kept drifting back to the visitation room and the wild look Delphi had given me. It felt as though ropes were slowly tightening around me, slowly strangling me. My only hope was to unravel it all. Hopefully I could before it was too late.

CHAPTER
46

WE EMERGED FROM THE TUNNEL back into the Lighthouse. Veritas hadn't brought up Delphi and I hadn't either, although her words still ricocheted around in my brain. It was as if I could almost braid it all together into a cohesive thread . . . but I couldn't quite grasp the separate tendrils. They continued to slip through my fingers.

We rounded the corner into the Lighthouse and nearly plowed over Helen. She glared at us and then headed for the stairs.

Veritas ignored her and went over to the computer. He jabbed a finger at the screen. "Aha! We have our Madrigal."

Our composite sketch of Madrigal hovered on one side of the screen. On the other side was a blurry photo, apparently taken with a night-vision lens. A man stood in a desert, a long train of people behind him. The man's face was turned partially away from the camera but it looked pretty close to what we had reconstructed.

"Who is he?"

"His name is Juan Madrigal from La Paz, Mexico. He's worked with coyotes out of Nogales to bring illegal immigrants into the country. Probably uses his power to put the Border Patrol to sleep."

A vision of Madrigal romping through the desert with a pack of wild dogs flooded my mind for a moment.

Veritas must have sensed my confusion. "A coyote is a person who guides illegal immigrants into the country."

Oh. I liked the dogs better. "So does that explain how he wound up in New Chayton with the other two?"

"No. Let's see if the cops have found anything interesting at Haruki's house." He glanced in my direction as he tapped at the keyboard. "Dad cracked the New Chayton police mainframe years ago. It helped him stay one step ahead.

"They didn't find anything in Haruki's room and the Takahashi family is still insisting nothing happened aside from your fight. The van was stolen from a rental place near the airport about a month ago. Lots of prints on it, but results and matches aren't in yet. But according to this . . ." He leaned back in his chair. "Huh."

"What?"

"They found a case of syringes and vials in the back of the van. They're running tests to see what inside, but the note here says they suspect narcotics. Plus they found assorted fast food bags and about two dozen used Styrofoam cups from a place called 'Krakatoa.'"

No way. I pushed Veritas out of the way and sifted through the data and found a photograph of one of the cups. Sure enough, the logo was right. Mr. Johnson's coffee shop. "I know this place."

Veritas burst out laughing.

"What's so funny?" I asked.

"Don't you get it? They've had this van for only a few weeks, and they've already filled it up with garbage from Krakatoa. Two dozen coffee cups! They must go there every day or pretty close! And while they may not be there now . . ."

" . . . they may come back at some point." I laughed. We could stake out the shop and capture them. Perfect!

Veritas's fingers flew over the keyboard. The police report vanished and the composite sketch program fired up.

"What are you doing?" I asked.

"We don't know for sure who went to Krakatoa. We'd better have sketches of all three of them ready to show the workers."

Ice snaked down my back. "Workers?" My voice came out as a barely perceptible squeak.

"Well, yeah. Hopefully someone will remember seeing the guy with the serious craving for Krakatoa coffee. He'd be a regular by now. And if he has a usual time of coming in, so much the better."

It was a good plan. We sat down to work on the other two sketches. But all the while, I couldn't help but wonder which Krakatoa employees would be present when we got there.

Veritas parked near a back entrance to the mall in a spot obscured by a big bank of dumpsters. We darted from the Reliant to the door and pressed into the opening. We were still in our costumes. Veritas pulled out his lockpicks, though, which made us look more like villains than heroes. A few seconds later, the door popped open. Veritas pocketed his picks and motioned for me to go first.

I slipped into the plain hallway that stretched around the mall's perimeter. Dull beige doors lined one wall, each labeled in stark block letters: WANTON PALACE, BURGER BLASTERS. We crept past the back doors leading to the various food court restaurants. The thick smell of grease and sugar drifted through my mask. My stomach heaved, but I couldn't be sure if it was the odors or my nerves.

This wasn't a good idea. For all I knew, Elizabeth was working this afternoon, and I had no idea how I'd react if I saw her.

We found the door marked "Krakatoa" about halfway down the hall. Veritas signaled for me to keep quiet, and he pressed up against the wall on one side of the door. He pointed to the other side. I frowned. What was he doing? He was behaving as if he were getting ready to raid the coffee shop. He banged half a dozen times on the door.

The door popped open. "Hello?" Mr. Johnson stuck his head into the hall.

Veritas yanked Mr. Johnson out of the shop. "Hello yourself. We need to talk."

The shock on Mr. Johnson's face matched my own and I froze, unsure of what I could do or say.

"We're looking for someone who's been to your coffee shop a lot in the last month." Veritas shoved the sketches into Mr. Johnson's hands. "Take a look. Recognize anybody?"

The paper trembled in Mr. Johnson's hands. "Are you guys supposed to be heroes?"

"We are heroes," I said in a voice that hopefully sounded reassuring but didn't cause Mr. Johnson to recognize me.

"Just answer the question." Veritas flicked his finger on the papers in Mr. Johnson's hands. "Do you know any of these men?"

"N-no, I don't. But then, I'm not always working the counter. Tell you what, let me go get the workers. Maybe one of them?"

Veritas held him in place for a moment. Then, with a curt nod, he released his shirt. Mr. Johnson wove between us, his eyes down, and darted back into the store. Veritas stuck his foot in the door so it wouldn't close and his body instantly relaxed.

"What do you think you're doing?" I whispered to Veritas. "Mr. Johnson isn't a suspect!"

"I know that, you know that, but fear can be a good motivator to keep people focused."

"Well, maybe. But let's dial it back a little, okay?"

Veritas rolled his eyes and nodded.

A few seconds later, Mr. Johnson poked his head out of the door. "Why don't you guys come inside? We'll stay in the back, I promise."

Veritas nodded and we went into the back of the shop. There was a large walk-in freezer to one side, along with a bank of sinks and an automatic dishwasher. The floor was red tile covered with thick rubber mats. A time clock hung by the door. Several of the employees—but not including Elizabeth—stood in a ragged semi-circle around the door, none of them meeting our eyes. I could practically feel the fear rolling off of them in waves. What had Mr. Johnson told them?

Mr. Johnson turned to his employees. "If any of you have seen these men, please, speak up." Johnson handed the sketches to the closest worker.

The worker, a college-aged man, treated the sketches as if they were poisonous. He barely looked at them and then handed them to the next person. Within a few moments, everyone had examined at them. Veritas went around the circle. He asked each of the workers if he or she recognized the pictures.

One of the girls finally nodded. She pointed to Icy-Ants. "He comes in here twice a week, right before closing. Usually on Saturdays and Wednesdays. Always orders an East of Java to go."

"That's good." I still wanted these people to like us, not fear us. "Very helpful."

"You ever catch a name?" Veritas asked.

She chewed on her lower lip, but then looked up with a timid smile. "He answered his cell phone once. I think his name is Gary."

Gary? It didn't seem to fit an ice-slinging supervillain, but then, most people would consider "Robin" a name for a sidekick.

Veritas retrieved the pictures and nodded to Mr. Johnson. We left the store and headed back down the hallway to the parking lot. Once through, I let out a little whoop. Sure, that had started a little rough, but things had turned out—

"Failstate?"

I froze at the voice. I turned around, and there she was, standing in the parking lot.

Elizabeth stared at me, so luminous I almost didn't notice that she was wearing a jacket emblazoned with the emblem of *America's Next Superhero*.

I did manage to notice that Ben stood next to her, his arm around her hip. His eyes narrowed. I could practically see the smoke from the grinding of his mental gears. Not good. Not good at all.

"What are you doing here?" Elizabeth asked, her voice a bare whisper.

Ben's smile sharpened into a predatory gleam. "That's a good question, isn't it?" He walked up to Veritas and snatched the composite sketches. He looked them over. "Look like some rough customers. Are you sure you two are up to the challenge?"

I tore the paper from his hand. "We're fine. You just worry about your girlfriend, okay?"

I stormed around the corner, hoping that Ben wouldn't chase us. Veritas followed. I had to get away from them. We made it around the dumpster when someone rushed after us.

"Failstate, wait!"

I halted and turned.

Sure enough, Elizabeth stood before me, her mouth working but producing no words. Then she smiled, a cloying grin that would normally have filled me with such hope, such joy. Instead it only hollowed me out even more. "I'm your biggest fan." Her voice was breathless. "Can I get your autograph?"

I wanted to moan. I wanted to shriek. I wanted to take her in my arms and hold her. I wanted to tell her everything. I wanted to yell at her and warn her away from Ben.

Actually, I didn't know what I wanted.

"No." The strangled whisper barely made it out of my throat.

I forced myself to turn away and jog away from the mall.

"I'm sorry about what Ben said!" she shouted. "He wasn't thinking. I'm sure you guys could handle anything!"

Veritas tried to stop me but I ignored him. And I also ignored the sound of Elizabeth crying behind me.

CHAPTER
47

I SLAMMED INTO THE SIDE of the Reliant in a numb haze. Heat built around my face, amplified by the mask. It felt as though I wore a sauna on my head. I wanted to rip off my mask so I could breathe. Who cared if anyone saw my true face? Let them call me a monster. Disqualify me from my license. I didn't care anymore.

"Are you all right?" Veritas's voice flitted around me, the buzz of an annoying insect.

I fumbled with the door handle. Had to get inside, don't break down, not now.

"Failstate, say something."

I shoved Veritas away. I gasped, my breath ragged in my throat, like swallowing razors. The throbbing intensified in my skull.

Veritas touched my shoulder. "What's going on?"

"Just unlock the door."

He wrenched open the door and I fell inside. I ripped off the hood and gulped down cooler air. Veritas clambered into the driver's seat. I hastily started to tug my mask back.

"Don't worry about it. Leave it off." He didn't turn away from me. He didn't even seem disgusted.

I leaned my head against the seat and closed my eyes. "I can't blame Elizabeth. I mean, look at me." I flipped down the visor so my reflection could stare back at me. My hair was bare wisps that poked out of mottled and scarred skin. I sniffed, the nub of my nose twitching over a twisted mouth. And my eyes, dark pools that drained across thickly veined cheeks, stared back at me. "Who could ever want that?"

Veritas didn't say anything. He didn't have to. I understood his secret revulsion all too well. Everyone could sense who I was underneath the mask. My hero name out to be Loser Who Breaks Things. My face only reflected that. Why had God cursed me with this? What had I ever done to Him?

"Look, Failstate . . . Rob. I don't know what's going on with Elizabeth. But if you—"

"Save the pep talk." I slammed the visor shut. "Let's just find a place to stake out the shop. If 'Gary' stays true to schedule, he'll come back for another East of Java tonight. I want to be here to greet him."

Veritas started the car and we circled around the mall. I stared out the window, my fingers rubbing the mask's material. The temptation flared in me to roll down the window and toss it out. Just chuck it all, leave it in the parking lot, and get on with my life. I could wear the necklace forever if I had to. Or maybe I'd jettison that too.

No. First I'd see this through. I owed Lux and Haruki that much. And, since it was entirely possible that this would be

Failstate's last adventure, I'd have to make sure it was a good one.

Veritas snored softly in the backseat. I glanced over my shoulder. He hugged himself, and his chin rested on his chest. I sighed and leaned back in the seat. My gaze roamed over the parking lot.

The setting sun shimmered across dozens of windshields. More cars had pulled in as the day had worn on. Thankfully, none of the drivers had seemed willing to park this far away from the mall, so we hadn't been noticed. Cars raced along the road behind us, their sounds only slightly muffled by the large row of bushes that bordered the mall's parking lot.

A low ache radiated through my lower back. I shifted in my seat, trying to escape the claws that dug into my muscles. Nothing helped. I slid farther down in the seat.

"Problems?"

I jumped. Had Veritas woken up? No, he hadn't moved. I realized that someone was sitting in the front seat next to me. Long brown hair cascaded down her shoulders. Then she turned and smiled at me.

"No way," I whispered.

Lux brushed a stray lock out of her face. I realized she wasn't actually in costume. Instead, she wore a simple school uniform, blue blouse and knee-length plaid skirt. "So why have you forgotten about me?" Her voice was a scratchy whisper.

"What? I haven't!"

"Are you so sure?" She nodded toward the windshield.

I glanced toward Krakatoa and spotted Elizabeth and Ben leaving, draped over each other. I had no idea how they managed to walk at all, as entwined as their limbs were. Gravity should have pulled them down.

I tried to say something, but Lux nodded again.

Haruki exited the shop, looking gaunt and pale, dark lesions peppering his skin. He coughed and the hacking doubled him over. Two people next to him dropped to the ground, limp. Haruki shrugged and kept walking.

Okay, now I knew I was dreaming.

"But I—"

The doors to Krakatoa opened again and a parade filed out, led by Mind Master dressed as a drum major. Krazney Potok followed, riding on the back of a giant robotic spider. Pyrotrack marched out with his Blue Eclipse Boys henchmen. Delphi brought up the rear. She fixed me with a stern gaze and cold iron bands wound around my chest, squeezing me tight.

I turned back to Lux. I hadn't forgotten her. How could I?

Lux smiled at me, her normally radiant skin pale and turning chalky white. Something was wrong. Her expression changed. Blood dribbled from the side of her mouth, and her hair turned stringy. I reached out to her, but when my fingers brushed her arm, she shattered. Worse, her disintegration sent cracks spreading and into the car, radiating through the seat. My surroundings exploded into darkness. The pieces rained down around me.

I was ringed by multi-colored flecks, pieces to an enormous jigsaw puzzle, none bigger than my thumbnail. Each one contained a person in a looping animation. In one, Haruki beat against the barrier that held him inside. In another, Pyrotrack laughed at me. In still another, Elizabeth smiled coyly, beckoning me with a crooked finger.

A low hum built around me and I looked up. Off in the distance, the ground fell away and became a pit, taking the puzzle with it. My throat seized and I scooped up the pieces around me, trying to fit them together. But the tabs and slots didn't mesh. The pieces spilled out of my fingers.

The gaping maw rushed closer and closer, swallowing up more puzzle pieces. The hum became louder and higher and I realized that the sound was actually voices, thousands upon millions of voices—screaming. I had to get the puzzle together before it was too late.

"Here, let me help you." A thirty foot tall Gauntlet towered over me. He smirked, his eyes glinting, as he reached down and picked me up by the scruff of my shirt.

I thrashed, trying free myself. The puzzle slipped through my fingers, spiraling down into the abyss. With a casual flick of his fingers, Gauntlet sent me after them. I fell into the darkness, the puzzle pieces orbiting me. The screams grew louder and louder until I . . .

—Jerked forward in the car seat, my hands shooting out for the dashboard.

"Sorry," Veritas said quietly. "I didn't mean to startle you."

I closed my eyes and leaned back in the seat. I had fallen asleep? The odd visions dissolved, chasing away the fatigue. I couldn't remember the last time I'd dreamed.

"Come on," he said. "They're here."

313

CHAPTER
48

I SQUINTED THROUGH the windshield. The parking lot had mostly emptied as the sun set, shadows creeping across the pavement. The mall's colors snapped brilliantly against the darkening sky. "Are you sure?"

"It's Gary," Veritas said. "A car dropped him off just now and I'm pretty sure there were two people in it. Maybe Madrigal and the Professor."

"Then let's go."

The cool night air seeped through my mask. We jogged across the parking lot. We were only thirty feet away when Gary stepped out of the mall doors and turned to his left, walking along the sidewalk with a gigantic cup of coffee in one hand and a bag in the other. He took a sip and smiled. Such a content grin looked completely out of place on a cold killer.

Veritas nudged me with his elbow. "Go for it."

I swallowed to calm my somersaulting stomach. "Hey, Gary! Can we talk to you for a second?"

Gary turned and his eyes widened. Two heroes in costume often had that effect on villains. The coffee cup and bag dropped out of his hands and he fled. Veritas and I sprinted after him.

Gary pulled out a cell phone and screamed into it. He ducked around a corner of the mall into another parking lot.

Veritas leapt over low bushes close to the mall's wall. Ice shards barely missed his face. I blew past him. Gary cocked his hand back and prepared for another throw.

I marshaled my power around my fist punched him, knocking him to his knees. I grabbed the front of his shirt. "I think it's time we had a talk, don't you?"

A bullet ricocheted off the wall behind me with a loud ping. I whirled.

The Professor stood behind a parked car a dozen yards away from us, the gun rattling in his hands. Madrigal smiled at me, raising a hand, but then Veritas charged. He slammed into Madrigal and dropped him to the pavement.

The Professor stared at his fallen partner with wide eyes, then turned back to me. "H-hold it right there."

"It's all over, Professor," I said. "Just put down the gun and surrender." I allowed myself a feeling of triumph. Veritas and I were seconds away from another stunning victory. All I had to do was—

"Nice gun you got there, Pops. But I've got more."

I knew that voice.

Sure enough, tromping through the parking lot, his armor bristling with his weapons, came Kid Magnum. Oh, no.

The Professor whirled on Kid, then pointed the gun at me again. "This doesn't concern you."

"I'm making it my business." Kid's voice carried his sneer.

"Same here, dude." Titanium Ram stepped out of the shadows of a nearby loading dock.

Veritas glanced at me. "What are they doing here?"

I couldn't answer him. This couldn't be happening. If they were here, then that meant . . .

Gauntlet stepped into view, fists jammed into his hips. "Your reign of terror ends tonight!"

Madrigal pushed himself up from the pavement. "Any of you ever hear of the term 'fair fight?' You've got us outnumbered."

This wasn't good. Veritas and I had had everything under control. But as Gauntlet and his cronies preened and strutted, Madrigal, Gary, and the Professor were clearly regrouping. They stepped closer to each other and gave us predatory looks. I glanced toward the mall. Thankfully, some of the security officers were holding the crowds inside. Things were spiraling out of control too quickly. Someone could get hurt unless—

"Like I care," Gauntlet said. "T-Ram, go!"

T-Ram scraped his feet across the ground. Then he lowered his head and with a war cry, charged Madrigal.

"Madrigal, move!" Gary slapped the ground, and a sheet of ice appeared and stretched along the pavement toward T-Ram.

T-Ram hit the icy patch and went sliding. He barely missed Madrigal, knocked Veritas over, and smashed head-first into a nearby parked car, punching through the grill between the headlights. His arms and legs flailed.

Veritas lay on the ground, clutching his head and groaning. But then Madrigal jabbed a finger at him and he went still.

I took a swing at Gary. He ducked and waved a hand at me. A blast of cold air sliced through my mask. My world went black.

I clawed at my mask and found two inches of ice wrapped around my face. I tried to pry off the ice. Little by little, it ripped free. I tossed the chunk to the ground, and it exploded. I checked my hood with my fingers. How bad was the tear? I couldn't stop to check. Best leave it in place and keep fighting.

Kid Magnum fired a riot-control beanbag at the Professor. The Professor shrieked even though Kid missed.

Madrigal responded with a casual flick of his wrist. Kid Magnum staggered as if struck. His entire arsenal fired at once, bullets and energy beams and flares shooting off in all directions. I dove for cover. Heat flashed over my head. Kid fell with a thud, his arms and legs twitched.

I leapt up to take on Madrigal, but Gauntlet intercepted me. "Get T-Ram unstuck! I'll hold these guys off."

Who was he to give me orders? But what he said made sense. With Veritas, T-Ram, and Kid Magnum incapacitated, now *we* were outnumbered.

I raced to T-Ram's side.

He struggled to free his head from the grill, but the metal had wrapped around his neck like a collar.

"Hold still, T-Ram." I dissolved the metal digging into his neck until T-Ram pulled free. His face was covered in motor oil and antifreeze.

I turned, ready to rejoin the fray, only to discover that Gary, Madrigal, and the Professor were gone.

"Huh?"

I spotted Gauntlet sprawled on the cement, sound asleep and his feet encased in ice.

T-Ram raced to his side. I sprinted through the parking lot, leaping over Gauntlet's prone form, just in time to see a blue car squeal out of the parking lot. I lashed out with my power, trying to hit the vehicle, but I missed, slicing through a cement parking pole instead. The car disappeared before I could catch even a single digit of its plates.

I groaned. Not again! Veritas and I would have had them if it hadn't been for . . . Steel clamped around my heart. My fingers clenched into fists and I spun on my heel, marching back to the mall.

T-Ram helped Kid Magnum to his feet. Veritas leaned against a light pole, shaking his head and rubbing his eyes. And Gauntlet . . .

Gauntlet sat up and shook his head. He took a few deep breaths and smirked. The ice encasing his legs shattered. He kicked off the loose chunks. "Well, they got away, but we'll get them next time."

His words thundered in my ears. I crossed the parking lot and shoved him as hard as I could.

He staggered back a few steps and glared at me. "What do you think you're doing?"

"I should be asking you that! Veritas and I had everything under control until you and your moron brigade came along!"

Gauntlet snorted. "Right. Face it, you needed my help, just like always."

"No, not like always. You have messed everything up, you—" I took a swing at him but missed. Before I could try again, a clicking caught my attention.

Kid Magnum had leveled his arsenal on me. "Careful there, cognit. Don't make me scratch my trigger finger."

"Don't make me strip you again," I said, my voice a growl. "And thanks for almost killing us back there. So great of you guys to 'help' us like that."

"It's all right, Kid." Gauntlet waved him back. "I've had to deal with his bad attitude before."

"Of course he's jealous of you, dude," T-Ram said. "He's a cognit, right? They all wish they could be real heroes like us."

That was it. I whirled on T-Ram. "A real hero like you? Half the time you knock yourself out or get stuck in a wall or a radiator block. And you." I jabbed a finger at Kid Magnum. "You don't even have powers. You just bought a bunch of guns and welded them together. Take off your armor and let's see how well you do, huh?"

They stopped laughing.

I leveled my gaze on Gauntlet. "And then there's you. You're so desperate for approval and affirmation that you've been lying this whole time. You claim to be a strapper, but you and I both know the truth. You're a cognit, just like me."

My accusation hung in the air for a moment. And then T-Ram and Kid Magnum burst out laughing.

"Gauntlet, a cognit?" T-Ram said. "Failstate is desperate, isn't he?"

"Yeah," Kid Magnum said. "I'd like to see a cognit flip a giant robot around like Gauntlet did last week."

But Gauntlet didn't laugh. Instead, his skin had paled. His lips twitched into a snarl. But then the fear was gone. He smirked, his usual mocking half-grin. "See what I mean? He's so desperate to take me down, he's going to make stuff up. Come on, let's get out of here." He strolled away from me, his friends falling into stride.

I stared at the back of his head. I couldn't let him get away with this. I couldn't let him win this time. And I knew how to prove I wasn't lying. Time to force Gauntlet's hand. I dropped down and scooped up a rock. Then I cocked back my arm, ready to throw. "Hey, Gauntlet!"

He turned just as I threw it at his face. I was vaguely aware of Veritas shouting my name, his horror boiling off of him. But I only had eyes for Gauntlet, how he would react.

The rock stopped suddenly, hovering in the air a mere inch from Gauntlet's nose. His eyes flared wide and he took a step away from the floating rock.

"Gauntlet?" Kid Magnum asked.

"See? I told you. He's a cognit!" I stalked forward, the stone hovering between us. "He doesn't have super strength. He only pretends he does. He's telekinetic. He moves things with his mind. He's a cognit. Just. Like. Me."

The rock clattered to the pavement. And I stared into the eyes of someone ready to murder me.

CHAPTER 49

GAUNTLET'S EYES FLARED, and he swung at me. I ducked and fell back, dodging as Gauntlet threw more punches. What could I do? Gauntlet used his telekinesis like armor, to amplify his strength. But even without his power, he had always been strong, much stronger than me. I probably couldn't take him in a one-on-one fight. He knew it. I knew it.

But I had learned a few tricks of my own.

I leapt over some bushes, safely out of reach. Gauntlet ripped a bench from the sidewalk and hurled it at me. I ducked, and it sailed overhead, smashing into a car in the parking lot.

"Okay, come on, Gauntlet," Kid Magnum said. "Enough is enough. You've proved your point."

Gauntlet wasn't listening. He tackled me. His fists whizzed by on both sides of my head. I avoided most of the blows. His fist grazed my temple, and stars exploded in my eyes. When he tried to hit me again, I grabbed his hand and, scissoring my legs, rolled him off of me. I punched him across the jaw.

It was like hitting a concrete wall. My fingers screamed in agony. The jerk had used his power to armor himself. I hadn't even hit him, exactly, just a barrier he conjured.

He shoved my chest, and I was airborne, blasted off him like a grenade had gone off. I smashed into the bushes near the mall's entrance. The branches poked my back. The world jittered in my vision. I staggered to my feet. Scratches burned over my skin. I turned . . .

Just in time to see Gauntlet's fist screaming in at my nose.

Pain erupted through my skull. Warmth spread down my face and into my shirt. Had he broken my nose? Bloodied it for sure.

I forced my eyes open and glared at Gauntlet. He reared back with his fist. But I lashed out with a punch of my own and caught him on the chin. His head snapped back.

Gauntlet threw out his hands. A wave smashed through me, blasting me from my feet again. I tumbled feet over head and twisted—just in time to see the mall's glass doors looming. I tried to marshal my power, wrap it around me, flare it out, break through the glass before I—

I burst through the doors. Shards of glass rained down around me. My power wiped out most of the debris, but it didn't soften my landing. I coughed and my back spasmed in agony. I wobbled to my feet, and shook my head. A dozen shoppers screamed around me. Great. Just what we needed. Witnesses.

Gauntlet strode through the shattered entrance. I backpedaled. I needed to get out of his reach until he cooled off.

No such luck. He chased me deeper into the mall. We emerged into an open plaza, a rotunda underneath a domed roof. The shoppers who had been loitering there quickly fled.

I dropped into a defensive crouch. Gauntlet stomped into the rotunda and smashed a fist at the floor. No one else would be able to notice it, but I saw that he didn't actually make physical contact. Still, cracks radiated out and the tile cracked under his mental assault. Then he cupped his hands, and jagged pieces of concrete burst from the floor. They rose into the air and orbited him.

He sneered at me. "You brought this on yourself." The chunks flashed toward me.

I created a destructive field, enough to shred the smaller pieces. But some still slammed into me and knocked the breath from my lungs. "Gauntlet, stop."

He wasn't listening. He punched and a force slammed into me. It threw me toward one of the stores. The throb in my head erupted and my power ripped through a store's lowering gate. I bowled over a mannequin and two racks filled with clothing.

I groaned and tugged a fuzzy sweater off of my face. My back and ribs were killing me. Had I broken something? This would be a fun discussion at a doctor's office. *How did I get injured? Well, my super-powered older brother tossed me through a mall window.* I wondered how that would look on an insurance form.

The lights overhead flickered and with a pop, one bank exploded in sparks. I tamped down on my powers. But controlling the destructive energy was like hugging an eel covered in Vaseline. I clamped my hands to my temples. Focus. Control.

The storm inside my head abated. I pushed myself to my feet. I had come to rest in a brightly colored store for girls' clothing. Racks filled with the latest fashions surrounded me and pictures of smiling models stared down at the carnage I had created. Two teenage girls in blue vests cowered in the corner of the store. An older woman stood between them and me, her arms splayed out as if to protect them or shoo me away.

I nodded. "Ladies."

The older woman hustled the other two into a back room.

I could still move, walk a little. I'd be sore in the morning, but so far, so good.

Something tugged at my leg. I looked down. Had I gotten myself tangled in an extension cord or a skirt or something? No, nothing was there. Then the tug came again, stronger this time. My eyes widened. Uh-oh. Apparently Gauntlet was—

My ankle wrenched. I landed on my back, and the unseen hand dragged me for the hole in the store's gate. I reached over my head and snagged a clothing rack. Maybe I could use it as a weapon.

But as Gauntlet dragged me through the ruined gate, the rack caught on the edge of the wrecked store grate. I tugged on it, trying to get it free, but it was stuck fast. I strained to hold on but my fingers slipped and I sailed out of the store.

Gauntlet waited for me outside the store. He yanked his arm back, and I flew through the air past him.

I slammed into the wall. Lights exploded in my vision, chased away by darkness creeping in from the corner of my eyes. I rolled onto my back.

Gauntlet spread his arms wide, palms upward. A ripple pulsed out of him. Loose debris kicked up, carried by an unfelt wind, and orbited Gauntlet. Then larger items joined them: a wall sconce, a mannequin torso ripped from a store, a fire extinguisher. Within seconds, dozens of items spun around Gauntlet.

He smirked at me with a malevolent light in his eyes. He took a step toward me, his satellites coming with him. They ricocheted off of each other, settling up a clatter that grew louder by the second. "Why do you always have to ruin things?" Gauntlet shouted. "Liz, my power . . . Dad."

Fire shot through my veins. How dare he blame me for Dad! Time to show him how "worthless" I was. With my eyes, I tracked a fire extinguisher whirling in the cloud of debris. The red canister darted past Gauntlet, coming over his right shoulder. I waited until it dipped, dropping down as near his face as it could get.

Then I channeled my power into a blade, and I sliced through the fire extinguisher, bottom to top.

The pressurized carbon dioxide exploded. Gauntlet threw up his arms to protect his face. His orbiting debris rocketed away from him. The makeshift missiles pulverized the nearby stores. I ducked behind an overturned bench. A garbage can ricocheted off my hiding place.

Time to end this—now! I darted forward into the expanding cloud of carbon dioxide. Before he could react, I channeled my power into my fists and landed two quick blows to his chin. Each hit drive him back.

With each punch, rage mounted inside me. He had mistreated me for years and now, he was going to find out what it felt like to be humiliated.

Gauntlet tripped over his own feet and went. I straddled him, raining down the blows. He whimpered and tried to push me away but I didn't let up. I would end this. I would end him. I would . . .

Then something snapped inside me. My first froze, and I stared down not at Gauntlet but at my older brother. Bruises crept out from underneath his mask. He sobbed, a ragged breath I felt shudder through me. I couldn't do this. As much as I hated the way he acted, as much as he had hurt me over the years, I couldn't.

The rage subsided. Tears welled in my eyes. How had it come to this? How had we wound up here?

Then Gauntlet lashed out.

Pain exploded across my jaw. I flew through the air, and I crashed into the ground ten feet away.

Gauntlet was on me in an instant. He grabbed me by my hair through the hood and slammed my head into the floor. Then he clamped a hand on my throat and drew back his fist.

"I should have put you out of your misery a long time ago."

"Freeze!"

I turned my head far enough to see two mall cops creeping forward, tazers drawn and trained on us. Oh, not good.

"Lie down on the ground with your hands on the back of your head." The one on the right jabbed his gun at us. "Now!"

"Stop!" A new voice rang through the air, resonant with a bass rumble.

The word petrified me. What felt like warm metal cocooned me. Gauntlet and the cops froze as well, statues in threatening poses.

Then a girl dressed in a green apron raced to the cops. "You didn't see anything." Her voice carried an odd warble that bored into my skull and swept down my veins, burning as it went. "You don't know who did this. And you'll go down to your office and make sure that the security tapes are erased. Understand?"

The cops nodded. They tried to holster their tasers, but their arms were so limp, it took them several tries. "We'll go erase the tapes."

The girl watched them go and then turned to us. Tears streamed out of her eyes. "I'm so sorry," Elizabeth whispered. "This is all my fault. Are you okay?"

Although my body relaxed, my mind remained frozen. What was going on?

She knelt next to me and touched my shoulder and my chest, and then she pulled me into a fierce hug. "I can't do this anymore. I can't. I'm sorry, Rob. I'm so sorry."

Fire rushed through me. *Rob?* I pulled away and stared at her. "How long have you known?"

"I've always known."

What? "How is that possible?"

She moved to Gauntlet's side and ran her hands over his face. Sobs wracked her shoulders. Then she lunged forward and kissed him. She broke away and looked at me. "No time. We have to get you out of here." She cleared her throat. "Gauntlet, Failstate . . ." her voice had taken on that odd timbre again, "Move."

My body reacted without any conscious decision on my part. I lurched to my feet and started walking.

Elizabeth led us through the destruction. A young family huddled in a corner, the father draped over his toddler son's stroller. Others hid beneath the tables in the food court. As we passed, Elizabeth spoke to them all, assuring them that they hadn't seen anything, that they'd had a great time at the mall but that they should head on home now. They obeyed. They calmed and jogged out of the devastation, their faces slack and unemotional.

Within moments, we exited the mall.

Veritas stared at us as we came. His eyes narrowed, and he stared through me. "What happened?"

"There's no time to explain," Elizabeth said. "Can you get these two out of here?"

I shook my head, trying to clear it. Elizabeth's instructions clung to my mind like syrup. "No," I said. "We're not going anywhere until you explain yourself."

"I'll tell you everything." Elizabeth pushed me toward Veritas. "But not here. Meet me at church tomorrow. I'll be there, I promise." She ran back into the mall.

Veritas watched her go, his eyes still narrowed into predatory slits. But he motioned for me to follow him. Gauntlet, who still seemed dazed, fell into step with us. I had to push Gauntlet from behind, urging him on, until we got to the Reliant and piled inside. Veritas took the wheel and we calmly pulled out of the parking lot. We merged with traffic and had made it three blocks' down when the police and fire department vehicles sped into the mall's parking lot.

"Feel like going to church tomorrow?" I asked Veritas.

He chuckled, a sound devoid of any mirth. "Wouldn't miss it for the world."

CHAPTER 50

I SPENT THE NIGHT lying on my bed and staring out the window. I tried to will the aches radiating through my body to disappear, but it wasn't working.

What was I going to do? I had broken the first cardinal rule of being a superhero, the one we all knew too well: Ben and I had brawled. In public. We could have hurt or even killed innocent bystanders and caused untold amounts of property damage. Every time I closed my eyes, visions of the wreckage we caused floated in front of me. I had to pay for it somehow, but I had no idea how.

The sounds of Ben thrashing in bed carried through the wall. He had snapped out of his trance halfway home. At first, he hadn't understood what had happened. But as Veritas and I had filled him in, he'd fallen silent, and he hadn't spoken a word to either of us. Even as we'd changed back into our civvies, he hadn't said anything.

329

I understood in that moment how bad things were between us. We hadn't exactly been friends before, but now things were worse. How could we ever overcome this?

And Elizabeth! What was role in all of this? Her voice clung to the back of my mind, stuck there. Just thinking of her caused my legs to twitch and jump. Finally, I had to stop thinking about her.

Thankfully, Mom was already asleep when we'd returned so we hadn't had to explain the bruises that had been quickly forming on our faces. But we couldn't hide upstairs forever. When morning came, we'd have to get ready to go to church and then the interrogation would begin.

Around seven o'clock, Mom's alarm clock buzzed, and she started her morning rituals. Once she was down in the kitchen, I darted to the bathroom and ran through the shower. I checked myself in the mirror.

While the necklace hid my true face, it didn't do much to mask the bruises and contusions from last night's fight. I worked my jaw in a rough circle, examining my face from every angle. I frowned. Given the amount of punishment Ben had given me, I had expected the damage to be much worse. I washed away the blood from my nose, and I considered rummaging through Mom's drawers for some makeup to cover the worst of bruises but decided against it.

I left the bathroom and nearly plowed over Ben. He winced and took a step back. I examined his face. He didn't look much better than me. A black eye, bruises on his chin, and a cut down the middle of his lip. He glanced at my face and then averted his eyes. He mumbled an apology and brushed past me.

Instead of going downstairs by myself, I waited. Better for Ben and me to face Mom together. Fifteen minutes later,

Ben emerged in a simple button-down shirt and nice jeans. He silently motioned for me to go first. Great. How brave of him.

Ben silently followed me down the stairs.

Mom clattered away in the kitchen. My heart hammered harder. Hopefully she wouldn't be holding anything sharp when she saw us.

"Hurry up, guys!" Her eyes widened when she saw us. She rushed to Ben and touched his face. "What happened?"

"Why don't you tell her?" Ben mumbled.

Oh, even better. How could I explain any of this? I couldn't lie to her. Not only would she be able to see right through me, it just wasn't right. "It's like this, Mom . . ." I said. "Ben and I . . . well, we were . . ."

"In a car accident." Ben hung his head.

My head snapped around.

Mom gasped. Her hand flew to her mouth. "You were? Both of you?"

"Uh, yeah," Ben said. "See, I met this new guy from school—um, Sean?—last night at the library, and he offered to give me a ride home. Anyway, we saw Robin walking home, so I asked Sean to give him a ride. Some guy t-boned Sean's van. We just got some bruises, that's all. Nothing serious. The paramedics checked us out and we were good to go."

I stared at Ben, my jaw slack. What was he doing?

Mom's eyes narrowed. She looked at Ben and then at me. Her gaze seemed to drill through my brain and right into my thoughts. But then she nodded. "Well, all right then. Let's go. We don't want to be late." She bustled out of the room.

Ben started for the counter but I grabbed his arm.

"What do you think you're doing?" I whispered. "You can't lie to her!"

Ben snorted. "It's not like we have a lot of choice here, Robin. What are we supposed to tell her, that we caused millions of dollars of damages to the mall? That we're going to get part-time jobs to pay them back? Get real." He shook off my hand and stomped over to the counter.

I stared at the back of his head. I couldn't eat with him. I left the kitchen.

"Where are you going?" Mom asked. "Breakfast is ready."

"I'm not hungry."

I waited for them on the porch, Ben's lie hovering around me the whole time. What could I do? Mom would believe him over me. Well, I'd try to make up for it. I'd find a job, send what money I could to the mall anonymously.

A few minutes later, Ben and Mom came out of the house, and we filed into the van. Our route took us by the mall. The after-effects of our fight had been cleaned up and plywood covered the damaged door.

Mom slowed down as we passed. "I wonder what happened there?"

I looked at Ben. He wouldn't meet my gaze. Thankfully Mom didn't press the issue and we kept going.

As soon as we had parked at the church, Ben practically exploded out of the van. I slipped out and walked for the doors as well, heading off any possibility that Mom might want to continue her interrogation once she was alone with me. I didn't have to bother. She didn't notice me anymore. Instead, she charged up to the main sanctuary and waved to one of her friends.

Once inside the building, I started for the gym. But before I could get there, a hand reached out of an empty classroom and pulled me inside. The hand snaked up and covered my mouth.

"It's okay, Rob, it's just me." Elizabeth met my gaze for only a second and then averted her eyes. Her hair fell around her face like a curtain.

We were standing in a classroom for the little kids. A large mural of Noah's ark sailing under a rainbow filled one wall. Another wall had a dry erase board, smudged and smeared with multi-colored scribbles. Posters of kittens and puppies quoting Bible verses bordered the door. Three tables that came up only to my shins were pushed to one side. Next to those were stacks of kiddie chairs, way too small for a normal-sized person to sit in. No wonder Ben sat in the only adult-sized chair in the room, a plush rocking chair. He looked like a statue chiseled out of stone. His expression was severe.

"All right, we're here," I said. "Start talking."

Elizabeth's shoulders shook. When she looked up, her eyes were dull and bloodshot. "I never . . . That is, I didn't mean to . . ." She closed her eyes and took a deep breath. "Forgive me. Please."

"Just tell us what's going on." Ben's voice was little more than a snarl.

Elizabeth winced as if struck. She sat down in a chair and folded her hands in her lap. "It's a long story."

"Then start with this:" I said. "You know who we both are?"

She nodded.

"And you say you've known the whole time?"

Another nod.

Heat flashed through my cheeks. This wasn't good. One or maybe both of us hadn't been careful enough. If she knew, there was no telling how many other people knew our secret identities.

"How'd you find out?" Ben asked.

"It's part of what I can do." She stared at her intertwined hands. "I get these . . . impressions of people. It doesn't matter how they disguise themselves, I always know who they are. So I went to the first taping of *America's Next Superhero* and got a good look at the two of you. And then I went to the different high schools in New Chayton until I found you. It didn't take long. You two are very . . . memorable."

My heart sank into my stomach. Here I thought I actually had a fan, but she turned out to be a stalker with superpowers of her own. It figured.

"But why?" I asked.

"My boss told me to."

Ben sat up in his chair. "Mr. Johnson?"

Elizabeth smiled, a bare hint of amusement in her eyes. "No, not him. My real boss." She twisted her hands together in her lap. "The one who sent me here to deal with you two."

My legs wobbled underneath me and I fell into a chair. Deal with us?

The door to the classroom burst open. From where I was sitting, I couldn't see who it was.

But Elizabeth apparently could. Her eyes flashed and she stood. "You're in the wrong place." Her voice had taken on the strange bass warble. "You didn't see anything in here. Turn around and walk away."

"Yeah, that's not going to work on me." Mike strolled into the room, his hands shoved in his jeans pockets.

Elizabeth blinked and leaned forward. "Walk away." The tremor in her voice grew stronger.

My legs twitched, and even though I knew she wasn't talking to me, I had the distinct urge to leave.

Mike shook his head. "Sorry. Not happening."

Confusion flitted across Elizabeth's face. "I don't understand."

"Let's just say I understand your power better than you do," Mike said.

The color drained out of Elizabeth's face.

Mike shut the door behind him. "So you two haven't figured out who she is yet?"

I shook my head. So did Ben.

"Think about it. She can control people's minds." Mike waited for a few moments before shaking his head. "Duh. She's Mind Master's daughter."

CHAPTER 51

I TORE MY GAZE from Mike to study Elizabeth's face. I brought to mind our visits to Valley to see Mind Master. There wasn't a great resemblance between Elizabeth and that man, but now that Mike had said it, I knew it had to be true. They had the same violent blue eyes. How had I missed it before?

Tears rolled down Elizabeth's cheeks. "He is my father. And that's why I had to do what I did. About six months ago, I got a message on Facebook from a guy named 'Everard Digby.' He said he knew who Dad was, that he knew I had powers similar to Dad's, and that if I didn't do as I was told, he'd kill Mom and Carson."

"Who?" Mike asked.

"My step-dad."

"Why believe him? He's probably just a harmless crank," Ben said.

Elizabeth shook her head. "No way. For one thing, he knew who my dad is. Mom changed our last name, moved away, did everything to hide our connection to him. So how could he know that? For another, when I didn't respond right away, weird stuff started happening."

"What kind of 'stuff?'" I asked.

"Digby would Facebook me about how much he liked a necklace my grandmother had given me at my First Communion, and the next day I'd discover it was missing. Or I found a teddy bear in my locker and Digby asked me if I liked it. One time he sent me a picture of Mom and Carson asleep in their bed, like he had been standing over them. If he wanted to hurt them or me, he could. What choice did I have?"

"So what happened then?" Mike leaned against a wall.

"I got a message telling me to sit tight. Next thing I knew, Carson got a job offer here in New Chayton, and Digby sent me a message, telling me to *make sure* he took it. So the night we talked about it . . . well . . ." She shrugged. "Anyway, after we moved here, Digby ordered me to learn your true identities, and then I was supposed to . . . well, flirt with both of you, make you jealous of each other. And I . . . I did." More tears rolled down her cheeks. "I'm sorry."

I grimaced. "So you did what Digby wanted and we almost tore each other apart. Why stop us? Why stop the security guards?"

"Because I couldn't go through with it anymore. When I saw how sweet you are, Rob, and as I got to know Ben better and we . . . I just couldn't." She lurched out of her chair and fell on her knees at Ben's feet. "I'm sorry. I'm so sorry."

Ben scowled at her and turned away.

I turned to Mike and raised a questioning brow, asking for a bit of Veritas action. As much as I wanted to believe Elizabeth,

I knew she could be trying to trick us again. But Mike nodded and mouthed the word *truth*.

I frowned. "You don't have any idea who Digby is?"

Elizabeth sniffled and shook her head. "None."

I growled.

"What are you thinking?" Mike asked me.

"Digby has to be the one behind all of this. Haruki's 'aliens,' Lux, this. We're just missing something." I got up and paced the room. "I wish we could go back to the crime scene the night of her murder."

Mike scratched his head. "Maybe we can. Elizabeth, a word."

They conferred quietly. I was struck by the surreal nature of their conversation. Their fathers had been bitter enemies, but now they were planning to work together. Elizabeth finally nodded and they turned to Ben and me.

"Okay, I think we've got this figured out," Mike said. "Rob, I'm going to search your memory like I did before, okay? And Elizabeth will use her powers to create a mental image of what I find and project it to everyone."

"You can do that?" Ben asked.

"I guess we'll find out," Elizabeth said.

Mike pulled Ben out of his chair and steered me into it.

I sat down and braced myself. "I'm willing to try anything at this point. Do it."

Mike knelt down in front of me. "Keep your eyes open and relax."

A subtle pressure built at my temples, pressing inward. I felt like I was falling forward, about to drop from a great height. Elizabeth reached out her hand to Ben. His mouth tightened into a thin line but he took her hand. Then she settled her other hand onto Mike's shoulder, and it seemed that darkness blasted from Mike's eyes and rushed over me.

And I was back in the vacant lot.

In the vision, I took a moment to turn a full circle and drink it all in. It was the vacant lot but it wasn't. It looked like a drawing on a blackboard, all white lines. The only real color came from Ben, Elizabeth, and Mike, spilling from their bodies and onto the ground beneath them. The halo followed them wherever they walked inside the vision. Hopefully we weren't walking in the classroom. I suspected it'd hurt to run into a wall.

"Whoa." Ben walked across the lot.

Where Lux had fallen was a crystalline structure, a glowing sarcophagus. What was that doing there? I didn't want to see Lux's body again, but since everyone was starting there, I moved to join them.

As I approached, colors seeped through the sarcophagus, bathing the others in warm light. Why were they staring? How could they stomach looking at Lux's body? And why had Ben's jaw dropped open?

When I got a good look over Mike's shoulder, I understood.

Lux still wore her mask, but instead of her usual silver costume, she wore a radiant dress, something befitting a fairytale princess. Her hair, rather than knotted and matted, shone and cascaded down her shoulders. There was no sign of violence. She appeared asleep, waiting for her Prince Charming to wake her.

"Is this how you thought of her?" Mike's voice was a low whisper.

My cheeks burned. "Yes." I pressed my hands against the glass and warmth bled through me. "This wasn't here that night."

"I know. Right now, we're experiencing a lot more than what you actually saw. We're overlaying the images with your emotions." Mike took a step closer to me and whispered, "I'm glad she had a friend who cared about her as much as you did."

Elizabeth squeezed my shoulder.

"So we can guess why there weren't any projectiles in her body." I took a step back. "Gary's the killer. He shot her full of projectiles and killed her, but then they all melted."

Mike nodded. "That's what I was thinking too. We should keep looking. There has to be something else."

We spread out. I frowned, looking around the white out-lines around me. Apparently I hadn't been all that observant, or else the details in my vision would be rendered with more clarity. Most of what I saw looked like smudges, little more than hazy clouds of color. For all I knew, I could be standing on the important clue but thanks to my poor memory, it was an amorphous blob.

"Hey, what's this?" Ben stood over a small white mound three feet high.

I knelt down and touched the pile. White spread through it, cold nibbling at my fingers. I withdrew my hand and shook it out. "Snow and ice. I tripped over it when I entered the lot and couldn't figure out what it was doing here. I mean, all the snow from winter has melted, right?"

Ben nudged it with his toe. "Well, we know Gary had been here. Remember what happened when he fell over at Haruki's?"

I nodded. A thin film of ice and snow had formed beneath him.

"So he kind of leaks snow whenever he stands in one place?" Ben asked. "How long do you suppose he would have had to stand here to make this much snow?"

Mike shrugged. "An hour or two."

My head snapped back as the thought struck home. "He had been waiting for her. It was an ambush. He knew she was coming."

My observation hung in the air. Then a deep voice cut through the silence. "What is going on in here?"

The vacant lot vanished, snapping me back into reality. Pastor Grant stood in the classroom doorway, his face reddening rapidly. Mike and Elizabeth, both drenched in sweat, jumped away from each other and Ben stumbled backwards, blinking and rubbing his eyes.

"It was nothing!" I cringed. That only made us sound guilty.

"You kids shouldn't be in here by yourselves. What would your parents think if they knew you were unsupervised?"

Elizabeth smiled and took a step toward him. "It's okay, Pastor Grant, really. Rob just had a hard weekend and we wanted to talk to him in private before we headed in to worship. Nothing bad happened here." Her voice warbled. "Nothing at all."

"Nothing bad happened." Pastor Grant's eyes went slightly unfocused. His singsong tone grated on me.

"We'll be along in just a second, okay?"

"That sounds good to me, Elizabeth. See you in the gym." Pastor Grant turned around and shuffled away from the door.

The minute it closed, I grabbed Elizabeth by the shoulder and turned her around. "What do you think you're doing?"

"Taking care of a problem," Elizabeth said. "What's the big deal?"

I gaped at her and then turned to the others. "I'm not the only one who doesn't like this, am I?"

Ben shrugged. "It covered our tracks. And it is true, we weren't doing anything wrong."

I snarled. "It figures you would take her side."

Ben's eyes flared open. "What is your problem? She's trying to help."

I frowned at Elizabeth. "She's done more than enough already."

Mike interposed himself between Ben and me before either of us could do anything. "Knock it off, you two. You aren't going to brawl here. Ben's right, Rob. It was harmless. Now let's all just take a deep breath and—"

I shoved Mike's hand away from me. I couldn't believe him. How could he take Ben's side after all we had been through? Elizabeth started to say something but I didn't want to give her another chance to control me. Plus, I just didn't care. I stormed out of the classroom and headed for the gym.

The band had already started their set of seven-eleven songs when I entered. Once again, the folding chairs were clustered around the stage. About forty people were swaying and waving their arms. I found a chair at one corner of the audience and slouched into it. Hopefully Mike and the others would take the hint and not bother me. I mouthed the words of the song, reciting them in a monotone drone.

This is ridiculous, God. What are You doing to me? I've tried to do right, to make up for everything I've done wrong, but it's all falling apart. What more can I do? What more do You expect of me?

The worship set wound down and Pastor Grant bounded onto the stage.

"I know we all had a rough week, what with the creeping crud and all. I missed all of you on Tuesday. To make up for it, we're going to go twice as long this morning, okay?"

A few people chuckled, but not too many.

That didn't stop P.G. He guffawed, the only one to laugh at his joke. "If you've got your Bibles, turn to James chapter two. That's where we left off last week."

My seat neighbor, a bright-eyed freshman, offered to share her Bible with me. I smiled but waved her away.

Pastor Grant read something about people showing favoritism to rich people. He snapped his Bible shut and paced. "Here James touches on a real problem that plagued the Church back then and still does today. It rears its ugly head all the time: disunity, disharmony, discord. 'Dis' is a real problem! It puts the Church in distress and can only lead to disaster.

"In James's case, it was because people liked rich people better than poor people and they made that preference known. St. Paul talks about the same thing in First Corinthians, only in Corinth, the problem was that the more talented Christians were looking down on the less obviously talented. Either way, the end result was the same.

"And do you know why that happens? Sin! Sin wrecks our lives. It destroys our unity with each other and with God. It ruins the harmony we should have among ourselves. It wreaks havoc wherever it crops up."

I shifted uncomfortably in my chair. I didn't like where this was going.

"But look at what James tells us. He reminds us that none of us are perfect. None of us can claim to be innocent victims. 'For whoever keeps the whole law and yet stumbles at just one point is guilty of breaking all of it.' Did you hear that! If you break one part of God's Law, you've broken it all.

"Do you see how ruinous sin is? Do you see how serious it is? So what can we do about sin?

"Well, a lot of people think that they can fix it on their own. They do as much good as they can, and they hope that somehow, they can make up for the mistakes they've made, the times they've hurt people, the way they've failed."

I couldn't breathe anymore. P.G.'s words slammed into me, blow after blow. That's what I'd been trying to do: make up for my mistakes. With Dad, Mom, Lux, and now Ben. I had been living up to my name all too well for years.

P.G. laughed, a mirthless chuckle. "But none of those ways work. We can never do enough to tip the scales in our favor. Never, so give up trying! No, there's only one way to deal with the sin that destroys lives: Jesus Christ. His death and resurrection wipes sin out. And it's the only thing that wipes it out. God's grace erases it. And that's why the Church can find true unity.

"Forgiveness allows us to work together the way God wants us to. God's grace levels the playing field. Rich or poor, talented or not, we all matter to God. And we should matter to each other. Because we need one another. So come on, everyone. Get up on your feet."

With a great deal of grumbling, the youth group got up.

"Now I want you to turn to the people next to you and tell them this: 'I need you.' Go on! But keep it clean!"

Mechanically, I turned to the girl next to me. "I need you."

She blushed and mumbled the words in reply. I turned to a boy a little younger than me and repeated the phrase.

"Come on, folks. Mean it! It's the truth, right? We're not as strong separately as we are together. C'mon! 'I need you!'"

Someone touched my arm and I turned.

Mike clasped me on both shoulders. "Rob, I need you."

Heat flashed through me. I grabbed his shoulders as well. "I need you."

A touch at the small of my back. Elizabeth gently turned me to face her, her brilliant blue eyes welling with tears. "I need you."

I tried to say it. I really did. But I just couldn't. "I'm sorry," I whispered.

She ducked her head. "I understand."

Ben hovered behind her, studying his feet.

I crossed over to him. "Ben . . ." I couldn't believe I was going to say this. "Ben, I need you."

The corners of his lips twitched into a nervous grin. "I need you too."

Warmth coursed through me. I closed my eyes and choked back a sob.

Okay, God, I get it. I do.

I threw my arm around Ben's shoulders. "When church is over, we have work to do."

CHAPTER 52

AFTER THE SERVICE ENDED, Ben, Mike, Elizabeth, and I met at the back of the gym. I felt dizzy. The strange rush that had come over me during P.G.'s talk still clung like a warm blanket. I never wanted the sensation to end.

"Okay." My palms erupted with cold sweat. "First things first. We know that Haruki is involved somehow. Was he here today?"

We scanned the crowd filing out of the gym. I didn't spot him, but there were enough bodies he could have blended in.

"I didn't see him," Mike said.

"Ben," I said, "you and Elizabeth go check up on him. Make sure he's okay. When you find out one way or the other, call me and then meet me at the house. Go."

Ben nodded and took Elizabeth by the arm. He led her out of the gym. My stomach curdled. I didn't want the two of them together. A small part of me still wanted her, as stupid as that was. She had used me. She had possibly even brainwashed me.

For all I knew, she could still be messing with me. But she was our only real connection to whoever was behind all this. If she really was sorry for what she did, she could help us track down her boss and bring that individual to justice.

Mike looked at me seriously. "How are you doing with this, *really?*"

"What do you think?" I said. "I'm not happy. I had hoped that Liz and I . . . Well, you know. But that doesn't seem likely now, does it?"

Mike smiled sadly. "No."

I ground my teeth together. Regardless of my feelings, I had to keep going. "We have to find this 'Everard Digby' and bring him down. Any ideas on who he is?"

Mike frowned. "The name sounds familiar but I can't remember from where."

"You don't think it's a scrambled name or anything, do you? Like if we rearranged the letters, we'd know his real name?"

"I dunno." Mike shrugged. "It's worth a try."

"All right, we can both try to think about that. In the meantime, how much of this have you shared with your dad?"

"Not much," Mike said.

"Given how big this is, it might be time to bring him into the loop, especially since the Trifecta is being used. Go home and tell him everything."

A smirk tugged at the corners of Mike's mouth. "Whatever you say, boss. And what about you?"

"I'm heading home. I have some homework to do."

• • •

Mom didn't ask where Ben went, and I didn't offer the information. We rode home in silence.

Once there, I sequestered myself in my room. I fired up my computer and called up a search engine, typing in the name "Everard Digby." It was long shot, and I doubted I'd find any useable information.

Almost immediately, the search engine spit out dozens of results. I frowned and looked them over. Apparently about five hundred years ago, a guy named Everard Digby had been involved in the "Gunpowder Plot," an attempt to blow up the English Parliament and King James I so the Roman Catholic Church could claim England again. What on earth did he have to do with any of this?

I clicked on the first article and started reading, skimming through the details of plots and counterplots, theories and wild conjectures, English names that I didn't recognize. So much for my scrambled name theory.

Wait. What was this?

There was a drawing of men dressed like Pilgrims—black-and-white and old. I didn't see Digby's name listed, so why had it shown up in my search? Instead, in a flowing script, someone had labeled them all as "Bates" and "Guido Fawkes" and "Robert Castelby," all members of that Gunpowder Plot.

My breath hitched in my throat. I had seen this drawing before, hanging in Helen Kirkwood's office in Magnus's mansion.

I clicked back to the article. The man they had caught under the Parliament building was named "Guy Fawkes." Wait—like the person who maintained the "Cape Town" blog? The person who always had all the accurate gossip about *America's Next Superhero,* he went by the name "GyFox."

I leaned back in my chair and stared at the screen. Did GyFox think of himself as a radical revolutionary? I called up the blog. Sure enough, GyFox's avatar was a drawing of Guy Fawkes, the same one from the drawing in Helen's office. I had dismissed GyFox's apocalyptic rants before, but now they glared at me from the screen: dire predictions of how the world would be cleansed by an unstoppable scourge.

But how did he get all his—or *her*, since it could easily be a woman—insider information about the show? It could only be someone on the inside, or at least someone with connections to someone on the inside. The first set of suspects had to be the contestants, the judges, the studio crew, or the producers.

I exhaled slowly. Who would be a better insider than the executive producer and head judge?

Helen?

My fingers drummed on the desk. If it were Helen, it might explain Haruki's involvement. If he somehow generated plagues, as I suspected, and if Helen knew this, she could use him to create one of the "scourges" GyFox was always predicting.

I shoved my chair away from the desk. No way. What I was thinking couldn't be possible. And yet Helen had a picture of the Gunpowder Plot conspirators in her office. Elizabeth's boss called himself "Everard Digby," like one of the conspirators. The insider on Cape Town was named after another. Was it possible that Everard Digby and GyFox were the same person, Helen Kirkwood?

This was ridiculous. It had to be a coincidence. Had to be. Because if it wasn't, then Helen was involved in Lux's death, Haruki's aliens, Elizabeth's mission, and the way Ben and I had been at each others' throats. But why would she do any of that? Why would Helen Kirkwood, Alexander Magnus's right-hand woman, do any of that?

I had to get out of my room, take a walk, clear my head.

I slipped from the house. Mom shouted for me to not go far, that she would start lunch in two hours. I walked slowly, turning over the evidence in mind. Off in the distance, a lawn-mower rattled to life. I waved to one of the neighbor ladies who sat outside while her three kids chased each other around their yard.

Could it have been any of the other suspects besides Helen? I didn't want to rush to judgment and miss important clues about the real villain. But my mind kept flashing back to that drawing in Helen's office.

Why would Helen do any of this? Why would she have had Lux killed? From what Mike told me, she'd loved Elena. There's no way that she would ever want her hurt. Yet it was pretty clear that Gary had been waiting in the vacant lot for her. So someone—someone who knew Elena's plans—had to have sent him.

No, wait a minute. Mike had told me that Elena was always late. Helen would have known that too. So maybe Gary, Madrigal, and the Professor hadn't been waiting for her. If they had been, they wouldn't have bothered to show up on time.

My eyes widened, and I shuffled to a stop. My heartbeat seemed to freeze. They hadn't been waiting for Lux at all.

They had been waiting for me.

I staggered for a moment and leaned against a tree in a neighbor's yard. What would have happened if Lux had been late? They could have jumped out of the shadows. Madrigal could have incapacitated me while Gary attacked, slicing me to pieces just as he did to—

I shook my head to clear it. I had to stay focused. This retroactive fear wouldn't help me. Stick to the facts, find the connections, and bring the killers to justice. I set out again, my strides longer and faster.

So why would Helen want me dead? What had I ever done to her? And why would she want Ben and me to fight each other? What would that prove? Why set an ambush to kill me and then, when that went wrong, lower the bar to simply trying Ben and me into a love triangle? I mean, we'd never been close, but we were still siblings, and . . .

Memories exploded through me in a rush that left me dizzy. I suddenly remembered some of the odd things that Delphi had said when Veritas and I had spoken to her. A coming scourge, something about siblings and fighting . . . No, could it be?

I dug in my pocket and pulled out my cell phone. I needed a fresh perspective. Mike would be able to sort through all of this better than me. I started to punch in his number.

Only to stop halfway through. There was no way Mike would believe any of this. He'd call it a coincidence at best, a wild theory at worst. I couldn't accuse Helen without a lot more evidence.

I quickened my steps. Thankfully I knew exactly where to find it.

Remaining calm proved more difficult as I walked down the halls of Valley. Maybe it was because I was doing so out of costume. I had considered fetching it before coming here but hadn't wanted to waste any time. My necklace provided costume enough for this.

I stepped into the cramped office belonging to the assistant warden and surveyed its dull beige interior. Everything was a different shade of brown: the file cabinets, the bulletin board that dominated one wall, the banged-up desk. Apparently Valley had never hired an interior decorator. A middle-aged man sat at the desk, all belly and thick arms. He hunched over a file and scribbled something inside the brown folder. A plaque on his desk revealed that his name was Morty Hanson. I took a seat and waited. No need to antagonize him, especially given what I hoped to do.

"So what can I do for you?" Morty asked without looking up.

"I need to see a prisoner here. I usually come with someone, and we go right in. But because I'm by myself this time, the folks at the main lobby said I had to check in with you."

"Which prisoner?"

"Delphi."

His pencil stopped in mid scratch. He looked up at me, revealing a round face and narrowed eyes. He rose and stepped to the file cabinets and ran his finger down the front, finally opening a drawer and pulling out yet another file, thick and almost overflowing with paper. He flipped through it for a moment.

"Who are you?" he asked.

I considered lying but figured the truth would work best. "Robin Laughlin. I'm a friend of her son, Mike."

Morty set the file on his desk and crossed his arms over his chest. Then he sighed. "Kid, this isn't a hotel. You can't waltz in here and expect to see just anyone. You have to have a background check, be on an approved list."

Uh-oh. I hadn't thought of that. I tried to speak but the words wouldn't come. What could I do now? "I understand that, sir, but it's an emergency. I need to talk to her about her son."

He glared at me for a moment and then sighed. "Hang on a sec. I'll see if she even wants to see you." With that, he turned and walked out of the office.

The moment I was sure he was gone, I jumped forward and grabbed Delphi's file. I flipped through the preliminary papers that listed things like her real name and her arrest history, until I found what I hoped for: a visitor log.

My finger trembled as it slid down the list. There was the entry showing Veritas and me from a few days ago. But aside from us, the only person who visited Delphi regularly was . . . Helen Kirkwood.

Footsteps echoed down the hall. I slapped the file on Morty's desk again and leaned back in my chair.

Morty stepped inside and jerked a thumb at the door. "She's agreed to see you," he said. "Understand me, kid, this is a one time deal. You try this again and I'll toss you in there with the sharks, got it? You got fifteen minutes."

Morty summoned a guard, who led me down the corridor to the visiting room. He wrenched open the thick metal door and I stepped inside.

Delphi sat slumped in her chair, her head bowed and her hair hanging around her face. I slipped into the seat opposite her and waited for her to respond. She didn't. I glanced at the camera in one corner. Not good. Hopefully the guards weren't listening in. Probably they were.

"Delphi?" I asked. "Do you know who I am?"

No movement. I wasn't even sure she was breathing. But before I could ask again, she chuckled, a breathy sound that set my hair on edge. Her head lolled to one side and she fixed her eyes on the camera. She nodded.

Okay. So far, so good. "You spoke about a scourge. A coming scourge. Does Helen Kirkwood have something to do with that?"

Delphi moaned and clutched at her temples. "Yes. Her. All her. The scourge . . . disease. In your friend. The thrice-moved son."

Ice ran through my veins. I knew it! Haruki was able to create plagues within himself, which explained the strange outbreaks in Japan, Canada, and New Chayton. And I also guessed that the Professor, Gary, and Madrigal were trying to use his power to create new scourges. But why?

"You also said something about siblings. What about them? Do you mean that sibling superheroes can stop the scourge?"

Her eyes snapped open and shook her head. "Not any. Just you."

No wonder someone was trying to drive a wedge between Ben and me—because only together we could stop the scourge! "Did she know about that?"

Delphi clamped her lips shut, twisting them into a pucker. Tears glistened in her eyes. She nodded.

Fire rushed down my arms and legs. All this time, Helen had been plotting against me. How had she maintained her cool when she'd seen me on set or in Magnus's house? How had I missed the signs of her hatred? In that moment, I wanted nothing more than to see her fall—and to be the one to give her the push. "Why would she do this?"

She bit her lip, hard enough that a small trickle of blood dribbled down her chin. "Meridian. All for . . ." She dug her fingers into her temples again. "Him. Wanted him." She sobbed and curled into a ball.

I leaned back in my chair. Why was she in so much pain? Had Helen done something to her to make her like this? "But what do I have to do with it, Delphi? Why is Helen after me?"

She leaned across the table and rested her hand on my chest. I could scarcely breathe. It felt as though she were staring through me, the same way her son did, only I got the feeling that she saw a lot more than Mike ever could. Her head twisted to one side and pain danced across her face. She groaned. "Only you. Stop. End it. Hurry. New Scourge. No time. "

With that, she stood and shuffled to the opposite door. She rapped lightly on the steel and the door groaned open. She offered me one last glance, then slipped out.

I had to get out of Valley as quickly as I could. Helen was planning a new scourge? As I ran for the parking lot, I fumbled with my cell phone and tried to call Mike. But the stupid thing didn't respond. When had the battery died? I shoved it back into my jacket pocket and kept running. I had to get home, call in Mike and the others. Mike wasn't going to like this, but it was time to bring this to an end.

We had to confront Helen.

CHAPTER 53

I SPRINTED FROM the bus stop back to the house. If I was lucky, Ben and Elizabeth would be back from checking on Haruki. Then we could call Mike and finish this.

"Hello?" I shouted as I burst through the front door. "Anyone home?"

No answer. Huh. Mom must have stepped out.

I found my phone recharger on the floor by the coat tree. But when plugged it in and tried to dial out, it beeped. Voicemail message. I considered calling Mike instead of listening, but then realized the message might be important. I punched in the code.

"Hey, uh, Rob. It's Ben. You know how you wanted us to check on Haruki? Well, we did and nobody was home."

What was that smell? Like burnt glue, only more rancid.

"So Liz and I went to the neighbors and asked around." Cars roared in the background, almost drowning out Ben's voice.

I turned a full circle, scanning the hall for the source of the rank odor. It led me to the kitchen. A pot sat over a flame on the stove, smoke seeping from under the cover. Mom must have started lunch. The empty can of cream of mushroom soup on the counter meant tuna noodle casserole again. But why would she have left the stove going?

"Haruki's gone," Ben's voice said. "His folks are in an absolute panic."

I stepped around the center island. And as I did, I saw her legs, twisted at an odd angle. She lay in a crumpled heap on the kitchen floor.

"Mom!" The phone clattered to the floor and I rushed to her side. I pressed two fingers to her neck.

Her heart was still beating. No injuries to her head, nothing that would explain why she was sound asleep. Unless . . .

Oh, no.

"Hello, Robin."

I whirled around. Helen Kirkwood stood over me. Gary and Madrigal flanked her, wearing their Trifecta masks.

"What have you done to my mom?" I asked.

"Nothing," Helen said. "At least, not compared to what we're going to do to you."

With a predatory smile, Gary thrust his hands at me, palm first.

A blast of arctic air slammed into me. I tried to throw my hands up to protect my face but found them stiff and unresponsive. Ice crept up my legs and encased me in its chilly grip.

My fingers fumbled with my necklace. I had to unleash my power, do something. I almost had the knot untangled, but then Madrigal flicked his hand in my direction.

A wave of fatigue swept over me. The room spun and dipped around me. My fingers felt like rapidly inflating balloons. I still worked at the knot. Almost . . . there . . .

Madrigal clamped his hands on both sides of my head.

A wave of knives sliced through me, ripping through my head and down into my feet. I screamed. Chasing the knives was a blast of dizziness and fatigue. My mind ripped free of my body and drifted on a cold wind, circling down, down, down, deeper and deeper into the darkness that swarmed up to claim me. The last thing I heard before it swallowed me whole was Helen's mocking laughter.

CHAPTER
54

EVERY MUSCLE IN MY BODY burned. I had to breathe. Now. Couldn't wait any longer. My back arching, I sucked in air, filling my lungs.

I choked on the relief that swept through me. My head tipped to one side as exhaustion slithered through me. Where was I? The darkened interior of the room I was in didn't offer any clues. The walls were unpainted drywall. The door was made of metal with just a steel plate where the doorknob should have been. No window. Recessed lights but no switch. Nothing to tell me o where I was or how long I'd been here.

I rolled off my cot and fell to the floor. Cold concrete. My body felt enclosed in metal, heavy and sluggish. How long had I been asleep? I got to my feet and stumbled to the door. The plate was held in place with screws. No deadbolt. Maybe I could burn through the plate, dissolve the innards, and get out. I jabbed a finger at the door, expecting the metal to peel away.

Nothing happened.

Oh, right. The necklace. My hand touched my throat, but instead of the hemp rope, I found a metal collar wrapped around my neck, digging into the skin. I tried to slip my fingers underneath it and pull, but I couldn't remove it. I stumbled around the room as I wrestled with the collar. Then light flooded the room.

"I see you've discovered your collar." Helen stood in the open doorway. "We took that bead or whatever it is and welded it into the metal. That should keep you out of trouble."

"How'd you find out about that?"

She smiled. "You'd be amazed how often people overlook my presence. Michael and Elena were quite adept at doing so when they were in the Lighthouse. You had the same tendency."

I glanced over Helen's shoulder. Maybe I could get an idea of where she was holding me. Unfortunately, all I saw was a featureless wall. Was that a bulletin board of some sort? Looked like it. Maybe I could read one of the notices . . . "You eavesdropped when Mike and I were talking?" I asked.

She stepped to her left, blocking my view. "That, and I'm fairly observant. You never wore that necklace as Failstate and yet dear Elizabeth tells me you never take it off in your alter ego. The math practically did itself."

The mention of Elizabeth sent a rush of heat through me. I set myself to charge. But before I could move, Gary and Madrigal appeared behind Helen. I got the message. I backed down.

"So why have you been so anxious to take me out, Helen? Why send your goons to Hogtown? I know you weren't after Lux that night, but me—but I don't understand why. And then, why Elizabeth?" I tried inching to my left to see around her again.

360

Helen's face turned stony. "Because you could stop me. You and only you. I believe you've pieced together most of what I'm doing?"

"Some sort of super plague, brewed inside Haruki. Right, Helen? Or should I call you 'Everard Digby?' Or how about 'GyFox?' So do you take all your aliases from the Gunpowder Plot, or are there other historical conspiracies you steal names from?"

She nodded. "Very astute, Robin. A pity. You probably would've made a good hero after all. What a shame." She once again moved to block my view of the hallway. "When I read your application for the show, I realized that your power could destroy my scourge, even if you claim you have trouble destroying living tissue. I confirmed my suspicions with Delphi." She shrugged. "So I had to make sure you wouldn't be a factor. It's nothing personal."

That wasn't much comfort. I crossed my arms. "So now what?"

"Well, that's where you come in. You see, I have to be sure that my plague will be as lethal as I hope it to be. I also know from dear Michael that you, young man, never get sick, making you the perfect test subject. My plague has to kill everyone—even those with . . . unusually efficient immune systems. Professor?"

The third member of the Trifecta stepped into the room, syringe in hand. His partners grabbed my arms. My feet scrabbled against the smooth concrete. I couldn't break free.

The Professor swabbed my arm and jabbed the needle in. Prickles rushed into my chest and I whimpered.

"That is the lethal portion of the plague." Helen turned to the Professor. "How long does he have?"

"Given my calculations, three days. Four at most."

No! I thrashed against Madrigal and Gary, trying to break free. Maybe I could get through the door, find help. *Please, God. Not like this. Get me out of . . .*

"Good," Helen said. "But don't worry, Failstate. I'm not completely without compassion. You won't be aware of what's happening. Madrigal, knock him out."

Madrigal let go of my arm. I planted my feet and slammed into Gary. I managed to knock him over. I scrambled for the doorway.

I was almost out the door when a sheet of ice snaked across the floor beneath me. My feet went out from under me and I skidded into the wall. I groaned and clutched my head. Had to keep moving. Had to get out of . . .

Madrigal pounced, straddling me. He grabbed me by my temples. Once again, the world spun around me and I fell into darkness. My last conscious thought was that at least I'd see my dad soon.

The pain woke me.

I wanted to groan but my throat was dry. My tongue swollen and clung to the roof of my mouth. I swallowed, and fire erupted down my throat. My head throbbed, but not the way it did when my power was active. This was a dull ache radiating down my back, flaring and receding. I coughed and set off a riot of new pain in my lungs.

Was this what it felt like to get sick? I couldn't remember the last time I had come down with anything, so I couldn't know for certain. But what other explanation was there? Helen's disease had knocked me for a loop and, if the Professor was right, I would die soon.

And if I died—here, and without telling anyone what I knew—Helen's plague would be unleashed, and who knew how many others would die?

Why? What could possibly possess someone to want to do such a thing? Delphi had said it was all for Meridian, but how would killing innocent people cause Meridian to love Helen?

My mind drifted from my cell and back home. Was Mom okay? Ben? Regret welled up within me. I had screwed up so much of my life and theirs. I couldn't do this on my own. I needed Mike's help. Ben and Elizabeth's too. Maybe if I had agreed to work with Ben earlier, we would have unmasked Helen sooner and I wouldn't be trapped here.

Nausea roiled up my throat as I rolled to my side. What could I do? With the bead permanently pressed to my neck, my powers would remain deactivated and I couldn't use them to escape.

I frowned. Wait a minute. If my powers really were shut off when I wore the necklace, why, when I went to bed with it on, couldn't I sleep? Why didn't I get sick when I wore the necklace? Unless . . .

My eyes widened. Maybe the bead didn't shut off my powers at all.

Maybe it only muted them and hid my disfigurement. A tingle danced across my back. If that were true, then maybe I could call on my power anyway. Heat flashed through me. I had to try.

I concentrated, trying to call on my power. I'd do something small. Destroy the lightbulb that hung over my bed.

The itching sensation intensified for a moment but then faded, submerged beneath my aches. I tried again, and got the same results. A groan slipped through my lips. I collapsed onto the cot and tried to pry collar from my neck.

God . . . I'm not going to get out of here without Your help. I don't just need Ben and Mike. I need You. Help me, please!

I felt a gentle prompt, an urge to try again. I did. Deep breath in, slowly let it out. Peace descended upon me.

All right, God. I'm ready. If this is what You want, let's do this.

Pressure built up within me. Fire chased ice through my veins, and ice chased needles. I cried out, a wordless prayer for grace and strength and that whatever storm raged through me would pass quickly.

Then I felt as though I had been thrown head first through a brick wall into blinding light beyond. The pent up fire burst out from every pore in my body. My back arched and I sucked in air, desperate to either stoke the flames or extinguish them. Underlying it all was a deep peace, deeper than anything I'd ever experienced. Strong, unseen hands, carried me up, out of my cell and into a weightless realm of—

Then as suddenly as the storm started, it disappeared. I collapsed onto a cold, hard surface, the chill biting into my back. I shuddered and opened my eyes.

The cot had disappeared, and I found myself sitting in a three-foot deep hole scooped out of the cell's cement floor. My hand darted to my neck. The collar was gone. Incredible! Had I blasted it apart? Melted it? Had God disintegrated it? Then my fingers drifted to my bare chest. My clothes were gone too.

Most importantly: My symptoms were gone. I ached a little, but my lungs felt clear. That dull ache that had flared down my back—my fever, perhaps?— had broken and disappeared. I felt utterly cleaned out.

Healed.

I closed my eyes. "Thank You."

I crawled to the door. Small holes now peppered the metal. Maybe in that . . . whatever had just happened to me . . . I had fried the lock too. I shoved. It swung open. Incredible. I poked my head into the hall beyond. Nobody in sight. Good. Now to get out of here.

I slunk along one wall, hoping nobody would stumble across me. I wasn't sure what would be worse: the humiliation at creeping through Helen's lair naked or being caught trying to escape.

Doors dotted the walls at irregular intervals, most of them marked with numbers and nothing else. But one had a sign taped to it labeled "Wardrobe." The door wasn't locked

A room the size of my whole house was filled with row after row of clothing racks. I blinked. Different costumes hung from the racks: theatrical-grade costumes outfits from different periods of history, plus jeans, sweatshirts, haute couture. There was a little of everything, sorted by gender and size.

I sprinted through the rows. I snagged a too-tight black shirt and a pair of pants with white-and-grey urban camouflage. I found a ninja mask in a bin that covered my head and hung loose onto my shoulders. Not perfect, but it'd have to do.

I left the wardrobe and I found a stairwell that led up. At the top, I emerged into a hallway, one that looked disturbingly familiar. I came to a door labeled "Green Room." I couldn't believe it. Magnus Studios! Helen had locked me in the basement of the building where we filmed *America's Next Superhero*! The exit would be right around the—

"C'mon, Madrigal." Gary's voice drifted around the corner.

I dove into the Green Room. I held the heavy door so it closed silently and held my breath. The room was empty. All of the chairs and couches were gone, as was the cappuccino machine. It felt strange to be in here without T-Ram and the others. Within seconds, Madrigal and Gary walked past the Green Room's door.

"What's he doing, anyway?" Madrigal asked. "He's too obsessed with germ-kid."

"Oh, I agree," Gary said. "But we want to keep the boss happy, right? And given what happened the last time we went to collect from the kid, you can't blame him for checking up on him."

Madrigal grunted. "At least we have him here now, so we don't have to worry about anyone interfering."

I bit my lip to keep from shouting. Germ-kid . . . Haruki was here? Once I was sure they had passed, I crept out of the Green Room and down the hall.

Madrigal and Gary opened double metal doors and stepped through. Those doors led to the finale set. I had never set foot inside and wasn't sure what it looked like. Why would they go in there? Steeling myself for whatever I would find, I slipped through.

The room had to be a hundred feet tall. I felt like I was standing in a high-tech operating room. The walls and floors were metal, burnished so brightly that they shone. In the center was a circular pit at least thirty feet across and a hundred feet deep, one ringed by a waist-high railing. A series of catwalks lined the walls, broken up by gaps with dangling rings in them. Nozzles and other assorted weapons poked out of holes in the walls. Camera placements were marked on the floor and walls out with bright yellow tape. My nose itched at the antiseptic tang that hung in the air. Something whirred and clanged in the pipes overhead.

I spotted a figure sitting just outside the circular pit. It was the Professor. He was hunched over a computer, tapping away at the keyboard. Gary and Madrigal walked around the pit toward their partner. All three were wearing their masks. I ducked behind an open packing crate that had been shoved up against the railing on the opposite side of the pit from the Professor's workstation.

Then I saw Haruki.

He hung in midair over the center of the pit, suspended by an unseen force. As near as I could tell, he was unconscious. An array of grey metal tubes and conduits descended from the ceiling, snaking down and pointing toward Haruki. His eyes were open but unfocused.

I peered over the railing. A series of dinner plates lined the pit's walls, thrumming. Some sort of anti-gravity field?

"How's it going, Professor?" Madrigal shouted.

The Professor shouted in surprise. "I do wish you would be more careful," the Professor said. "I'm engaged in delicate work. A mistake could prove lethal for all of us."

A whirring above me caught my attention. Up in the cluster of tubes hanging beside Haruki, a robotic arm popped out of a tube. Its end bore a needle. It jerked through the open air and paused in front of Haruki. Something caused Haruki's body to slowly rotate around until his chest lined up with the needle. The arm darted forward, jabbing the needle into my friend. Haruki groaned and winced as the arm withdrew, disappearing back into the tube.

"Is he waking up?" Gary asked.

"Better make sure he doesn't," Madrigal said and he pointing at Haruki.

Haruki twitched. Then he relaxed and curled up into a ball.

"So how's it going for real?" Gary asked.

The Professor sighed. "Well enough, I suppose. The plague synthesis seems to be proceeding on schedule. We should have a viable virus well before morning. The real sticking point will be the initial infection. Thanks to the show's hiatus, we'll have to improvise."

What did the show have to do with any of this?

"Have you checked on Failstate recently?" Madrigal asked.

I froze. If they went back downstairs and discovered I was missing . . .

"No need." The Professor pinched the bridge of his nose. "My last blood draw revealed that he was about to enter the final phase of infection. Believe me, none of us wants to see that."

"Well, c'mon. The boss wants to talk to you about infection vectors or something like that."

"Oh, very well."

I hunkered down behind the crate as the three of them walked past my hiding place. Once they left, I darted to the Professor's computer. I didn't see anything that looked like controls for the anti-gravity field. I couldn't make heads or tails of the technical data on screen. But it could be useful. Maybe I could find someone who could decipher it.

I searched through the desk the computer sat on and found a flash drive. I rammed it into the computer. I saved the open files to the drive, then minimized the program and started rifling through the computer's contents. I began the transfer of all the items in the "My Documents" folder.

As the computer worked, I jogged around the pit, examining the railing for buttons or levers, something that might control the field. Nothing. The controls might be in another room.

Back to the Professor's computer. The files had copied. Might as well see what else I could find in its memory. Nothing promising presented itself, but then I realized that computer was tied into a network. Maybe I could see what the other computers contained. I called up the network map, revealing three dozen other computers. I couldn't decipher most of the labels, although one caught my eye. "KIRKWOOD." Helen's terminal!

I double-clicked on the icon, only to be asked for a password. Shoot. What could it be? Offering up a silent prayer, I typed in "Meridian." Seemed like a good guess.

The screen went blank. A red box appeared, warning me of a possible security breach.

Red lights erupted around me, followed by a blaring klaxon. Oh, that couldn't be good. The sirens were loud, but I was still able to hear a skittering sound above me.

Robots. Dozens of little pod-bots crawled from the pipes. They reminded me of the hulks Krazney Potok had used, but where those had been clunky, these were sleek, smooth, and rounded. Their legs were gleaming tentacles. Bright red lights ringed their heads. As one, they all turned to face me.

No way could I take them all out, not while Haruki hung in the middle of the room. I couldn't guarantee his safety. I snatched the flash drive and tucked it into my pocket. Then I darted for the door.

Just as Gary rushed inside. "Hey!"

I bowled him over, and kept going. The sound of skittering robots chased me down the hall.

There! An exit. I barreled through it and emerged into the cool night air beyond. I was in the employee parking lot behind the studios. No telling if the robots would keep chasing me out of the building, but to be safe I tore across the lot and used my power to burn through a security gate. I risked a glance over my shoulder. No pursuers.

Then I smashed into a stopped van.

I fell backward onto the pavement.

The door swung open and the shocked face of a middle-aged woman appeared over me. "Ohmygosh, are you okay? What were you doing, running out into the street like that?" She looked up at the studio behind me and her eyes widened. "Wait, are you Failsafe?"

I nodded and sat up

Her smile turned radiant. "I love your show! But . . . is this a new costume?"

I nodded again.

"Look, son," she said, "you gotta say something. Are you okay?"

"I'm fine." I looked over her enormous van. "Could you give me a ride?"

CHAPTER 55

MY RESCUER TALKED my ear off all the way across town. Her constant drone soothed and annoyed at the same time. It meant I had escaped but it also made it hard to think.

Where could I go? Helen had already attacked me in my house, so I couldn't go home. Helen would probably know where Elizabeth's apartment was, so I couldn't go there either. And Mike's home was definitely out. I finally had my rescuer drop me off near the one place I prayed Helen wouldn't look.

A few minutes' jog brought me to Mount Calvary Christian Church. Relief surged through me. Here I could find food, telephones, pretty much everything I'd need.

The doors were locked, as I expected, so I checked the windows. None were open. I used my power like a knife to slice through the latch on one window. It dropped open and I clambered through. Great, now I was breaking into churches.

I found that I had broken into one of the Sunday school rooms. Tiny chairs were stacked along one wall, drawn and finger-painted artwork lined along another. I headed out of the room and directly for the kitchen. Once I got something to eat, I'd figure out my next move.

The skin along the back of my neck crawled. Was someone behind me? I whirled just in time to see a metal baseball bat coming down at my head. I sliced through the bat close to the grip.

Good idea, maybe, but poor execution. The severed end cracked me on the forehead. I stumbled back, clutching my head.

"Get out of here or I'll call the cops!" Pastor Grant's eyes were wide and his legs shook. He looked about ready to either attack me with the stub of a bat in his hand or run. Neither would help me.

"Pastor Grant, it's okay. It's me. I'm Rob Laughlin." The words were out of my mouth before I could think about them.

P.G. blinked a few times. "What are you doing in that costume, and how did you cut my . . ." His eyes widened for a moment. "Rob . . . is there something you should tell me?"

I sighed. Too late to back out now. "I'm Failstate, P.G."

P.G. collapsed against the wall. "Wow. That's so cool!" Then he seemed to recover his responsible adult mood. "Where have you been? Your mother is worried sick!"

Mom was worried about me? Why? "How long have I been gone?"

"Two and a half weeks."

The room spun around me. P.G.'s declaration slowly strangled me. My breath came out in ragged gasps. I stumbled down the hall toward the kitchen. I had to sit down.

"Did you run away, Rob? Is that what's going on? I mean, I get that things can be rough sometimes, but that isn't the answer. I'm glad you came here for shelter, but you really have to go home."

I shook my head. "No, no. I didn't run away. It's . . . it's a long story."

"Is Haruki with you? His folks are freaked out too."

"No." I had to tell him. "Look, P.G., you'd better sit down."

He ushered me into the fellowship hall and took a chair. I sat across the table from him and sighed. The story spilled out: my power, my secret identity, Helen's plans, all of it. To his credit, P.G. listened to the whole story without interrupting.

But by the time I was done, his jaw hung slack. "That's . . . that's . . ."

"That's why I can't go home," I said. "If I do, Helen might hurt Mom."

P.G. nodded. "Okay. Let's call the cops. They'll take care of this." He left the fellowship hall.

I slipped into the kitchen and raided the fridge. All I found was a stale blueberry muffin and a can of soda, but I wasn't going to be choosey.

A few minutes later, P.G. walked back into the fellowship hall, scowling. "No good. They didn't believe me. Now what?"

I leaned back in my chair. "Can you call my brother and my friend Mike?"

"Why?"

I hesitated. Sharing my secret identity was bad enough. I didn't want to expose Mike and Ben as well. "Just tell them I'm here."

P.G. nodded. "I think I have their numbers on file. Consider it done. Anything else?"

I frowned. "What time is it?" What *day* was it?

P.G. glanced at his watch. "About midnight."

"Hey . . . what are you doing here anyway?"

He shrugged. "I come to the church late at night sometimes to pray. Tonight, I just had this feeling that I had to be here."

I chuckled. "Thanks, P.G."

"Don't worry, Rob. We'll get through this."

I hoped so. I really did.

CHAPTER 56

GAUNTLET BURST THROUGH the fellowship hall door. He paused when he saw me, then charged. He grabbed the front of my shirt and slammed me into the wall. Tears glistened in his eyes. "Where have you been? Do you know how worried Mom and I have been?"

I didn't fight back. Best to let him rage a little, let it out.

"I've been tearing up half of New Chayton looking for you!"

"I'm sorry. I was captured." I squeezed his shoulders. "It's good to see you too."

He stared at me, his lips twitching. Then he pulled me into a crushing embrace, so hard and sudden that the breath popped from my lungs. That's when I saw Elizabeth standing in the doorway, her eyes wide.

Some of the old hurt surfaced. Part of me wanted to order her out of the church, cut her out of my life completely. But I

375

needed her too. I hadn't said it the last time I'd seen her. Now I understood. It was time to forgive.

I smiled at her, and she smiled back shyly. I turned to Gauntlet. "Were you able to contact anyone?"

He smirked. "You could say that."

Titanium Ram, Kid Magnum, Prairie Fire, and Blowhard walked into the room.

"What are you doing here?" I asked.

"We take care of our own." Kid Magnum rolled his arms, and two miniature cannons popped from his shoulders. He looked around as if ready to take on a horde of robots. "Besides, I figure if Gauntlet is really a cognit, they can't all be that bad."

T-Ram nodded. "No way we were going to let you twist in the wind, kid."

Tears stung my eyes. They were here, even after the way I had treated all of them. And it was so great to see Prairie Fire again. Sometimes when heroes get voted off, they duck out of hero work for awhile. Glad to see her back in the fight. Don't know if I could've done it if I'd been in her shoes. "Thank you, guys. I . . . I don't know what to say."

"How about you tell us who we're going to squarsh!" T-Ram punched a fist into his open palm.

Then Veritas entered. His gaze roamed over me, as if he were assessing me for injuries. Then his eyes narrowed, sharpened, and darted to mine. "Tell us everything. And don't spare any details."

I motioned for the others to take a seat. As they settled in, I tried to collect my thoughts.

"For the past two weeks, I've been held prisoner at Magnus Studios . . ." I glanced at Veritas. Here went everything. "By Helen Kirkwood."

Veritas's head snapped back as if I'd punched him. Gauntlet's jaw dropped open. T-Ram barked a denial, more incoherent grunt than word.

Kid Magnum shook his head. "I never liked that broad."

Veritas propelled himself out of his chair and began to pace in a tight circle. Then he turned on me. "You're sure."

I opened my arms. "What do you think?"

His gaze darted over me, and he groaned.

"No offense, Failstate, but why would Helen kidnap you?" Blowhard asked.

"Because I'm the only one who can stop her plan to unleash a scourge that will kill just about everyone on earth."

Stunned silence descended on the room.

"She wants to make a what now?" T-Ram asked.

I leaned on the back of a folding chair. "There's this kid that goes to school with . . ." I glanced at Gauntlet . . . "me. His name's Haruki. Turns out that he can create diseases in his body. I don't know how it works, but Helen is using him to brew some sort of plague or something. She's got these goons working for her, and she's controlling them through some tech that Krazney Potok and Mind Master created."

"The Trifecta." Veritas's voice was so weak I barely heard him speak.

"Right." How could I explain this next part without revealing who Veritas's mother was? "She found out that I can somehow stop this plague, and so she sent her boys to kill me. Only they accidentally killed Lux instead." I glanced at Elizabeth. Should I tell them about her involvement? No, probably too risky, especially given Kid Magnum's short fuse. "And then two weeks ago they ambushed me in my home and took me prisoner. I escaped and broke into the finale set. It's crazy. There's this anti-gravity pit, and I saw Haruki. I overheard what they said, and I was able to retrieve some data." I held up the flash drive. "But we have to do something about this, guys."

Prairie Fire frowned. "Why would Helen want to kill so many people?"

Once again, I was walking through a minefield. "I'm not totally sure, but from what I understand . . . she's doing it for her boss."

Veritas collapsed into his chair.

"You mean Magnus is behind this?" Blowhard asked.

"No, no! Nothing like that! I think it's . . . some sort of weird attempt to win his affection."

Gauntlet leaned back in his chair.

"That's just weird, dude," T-Ram said.

That's when P.G. bustled in. He froze in the doorway. His gaze skipped from me to the others and then back to me again. "Uh . . . can I . . . Any of you want coffee?"

"Not right now, P.G. Thanks, though," I said.

He nodded and left the fellowship hall as quickly as he'd entered. Oh, boy. I had a feeling he and I would have to have a long talk when all of this was over.

"Look, speculating about her motives right now is irrelevant." Blowhard said. "You said you had downloaded some data? I'm a microbiologist in my other life. Let's see what this 'Professor' is working on."

I tossed him the flash drive, and we headed to the church offices. We found P.G. in his office. It was a small room, painted baby blue. A large set of shelves filled one wall, loaded with at least a hundred books. A laptop computer sat on an armature that held it above P.G.'s desk, which was almost completely buried in papers.

"Mind if we borrow your computer, P.G.?" I asked.

His eyes goggled again, but he nodded and quickly got out of the way.

Blowhard fired up the computer and started sorting through the files. At first, he mumbled technical jargon I couldn't decipher, but as he kept reading, he fell silent.

The rest of us waited. Gauntlet took a seat in a chair opposite the desk. Elizabeth stayed close to him. T-Ram looked over P.G.'s shelves, idly tapping the books' spines. Kid Magnum removed his wrist plates and fiddled with the cannons. I hovered at Blowhard's shoulder and tried to read his reactions.

After twenty minutes of reading, the color drained from Blowhard's face. He finally leaned back in the chair and blew out a shaky breath, the force of which shoved the desk back two feet. "This isn't good," he said. "This Professor is a genius. I've never seen anything like this before. It's bioterrorism, that much I can see. He's somehow engineered a virus with three distinct infection phases."

"What's that mean?" Prairie Fire asked.

"Well, most viruses have a simple goal: survival. When a virus takes control of a cell, it rewrites the cell's genetic code so that it will do nothing but produce copies of the virus. The virus the Professor created does the same thing but . . . its life cycle is a bit more complex. At first, this virus would replicate like crazy. And it's extremely communicable. If an infected person breathes on you, you'd probably be infected.

"After a certain number of replications, the virus goes dormant. As near as I can figure, this dormancy is supposed to last somewhere around two or three *years*. And then, when that time period is up, it'll go active and become a world-killer, a pandemic unlike anything we've ever seen before."

Sparks danced over Prairie Fire. Kid Magnum clicked his guns back into place.

"How bad are we talking?" Gauntlet asked.

"According to the Professor's projections, the virus would have a mortality rate of 99.99 percent."

"Hold on," Kid Magnum said. "Ninety-nine-point-nine-nine percent of what?"

"Of humans," Blowhard said. "This virus is designed to kill nearly 100 percent of the entire human race."

Veritas groaned and wrapped his arms around himself.

It felt like fog filled my brain. "You mean . . ."

"By my rough estimate," Blowhard said, "when all is said and done, there'd only be six million survivors worldwide." Blowhard leaned forward in the chair. "The last time the global population was that low was around 8,000 B.C."

Silence descended on the office.

"One thing I don't get," I said. "Everything hinges on Haruki. Helen's whole plan revolves around him. How did she even learn about Haruki?"

"A little deductive reasoning," Blowhard said. "According to these files, she heard about some strange outbreaks that had happened in Aso, Japan, and then Swift Current, Sasketchewan. My guess is that Haruki's body somehow transforms immunization vaccines into a more virulent version of the diseases. The Japanese and Canadian governments consulted with the CDC, who in turn passed the buck to the VOC. Helen could've learned about 'Patient Zero'—Haruki—from the VOC and then and run her own investigation. I mean, how many people move from Aso to Swift Current?"

"How did Helen think she'd spread this disease?" T-Ram asked.

"I can't say for certain." Blowhard scrolled through some more files. "Maybe it's something in the soundstage they've set up for the show's finale. Maybe that structure Failstate saw would infect whoever was in the final round. Plus everyone in the crew and the studio audience. Helen must have thought that would be enough to spread the plague. And a lot of us get around quite a bit."

"That . . . that makes sense." Veritas's voice was barely more than a whisper. "Mr. Magnus was planning a victory tour for the winner. Fifteen cities, autograph sessions, media interviews. I think he was even trying to get an audience with the President."

A chill swept through me. With that kind of exposure, the virus would have spread through most of America and probably beyond, and that was just from what the winner would do.

"But now that the show's not on and the finale's not even scheduled," Blowhard said, "who knows what she'll do with it. Maybe she'll drop it in the water supply or convert it to aerosol form and spray it into the jet stream."

T-Ram turned back to the bookshelf and braced himself against it. Blowhard rubbed his chin thoughtfully.

Kid Magnum cleared his throat. "We're out of our league here, folks. We're not licensed heroes. Let's call the VOC. Maybe we can get Etzal'el or . . . or Dr. Olympus to come in and handle it."

"We don't have time," I said. "I heard the Professor say that the virus would be ready well before morning. I think they're planning to harvest it tonight. It may have already been done. If we wait, Helen could disappear with the virus. No, we have to do this."

Nobody met my gaze. But then Gauntlet took a step forward. "I'm with you." I nodded, but then he punched my arm. Same place every time!

"Me, too," Blowhard said. "She has to be stopped before that virus gets loose."

"I'm all in, baby," T-Ram said. "But hey, before we go, you think we should take some zinc or something?"

I stared at him blankly. "What?"

"I've got some zinc supplements here. It's a great, all-natural way to boost your immune system, guys."

"T-Ram, we're facing a pandemic that could wipe out billions of people," Blowhard said. "I don't think that a little zinc is going to help all that much."

"Couldn't hurt," T-Ram grumbled. He pulled a pill bottle and shook a few tablets into his hand. He downed them and smiled at me. "Ready for anything now! Just point me in the right direction!"

I winced, remembering how T-Ram had smashed past Krazney Potok's robot and into the warehouse wall. I'd better make sure he had a partner.

Prairie Fire nodded silently. We turned to Kid Magnum.

He bowed his head and sighed. "Die all, die merrily."

I turned to Veritas. "What about you?"

Veritas stared at the computer screen for a few moments, not even blinking. "I don't want to believe this. It's . . . it's impossible. Inconceivable."

"It's the truth," I said.

"I know. That's what makes this harder." He met my gaze, tears welling in his eyes. "I'm in."

"Good."

"So what's this plan?" Kid Magnum asked. "We can't exactly go to the studios and knock on the front door."

"Actually, I think we should. We just need to make sure to get their attention."

"And how do we do that?" T-Ram asked.

"We give them the right bait." I looked at Veritas.

Veritas frowned, but then his eyes widened. "Oh no. Not that."

I shrugged. "You said it came with a remote control. That would get their attention, wouldn't it?"

Veritas groaned. "Yeah, it would but . . . Oh, never mind. Okay."

I turned to the others. "Once we've got their attention, the rest of you will hit the front door. That should hopefully draw off the pod-bots. But you'll be in for a tough fight."

"We can handle it." Kid Magnum snapped up his arm, his barrels whirring.

"What about me?" Elizabeth tucked a strand of hair behind her ear.

"I have a job for you," I said, "one particularly suited to your talents. Plus it'll keep you safe."

Elizabeth started to protest, but Gauntlet squeezed her hand.

I turned to the others. "All right, let's get going. When we're done, the world will be a safer place."

Someone cleared his throat. We turned around and saw P.G. standing in the office door. "May I make a suggestion?" He stepped into our circle, his eyes wide and his shoulders hunched. It was strange. Normally he seemed so gregarious, so larger than life. But standing in this gathering of heroes, he looked small. And yet, there was a dignity and confidence about him that made it seem that he towered over all of us.

"Sure, P.G.," I said.

"I don't know what you guys face," P.G. said. "So I don't have any suggestions for tactics or strategy or anything like that. But I do know one thing: 'Unless the Lord builds the house, its builders labor in vain. Unless the Lord watches over the city, the watchmen stand guard in vain.' Would you all mind if I prayed for you?"

Prairie Fire's head dipped immediately. Veritas folded his hands and closed his eyes. One by one, the heroes assumed reverent postures. Everyone except Kid Magnum. He crossed his arms over his chest with an audible clank. But he nodded anyway.

P.G. raised his hands, his eyes closed. "Father God, mighty Lord of Sabaoth, these young men and women are about to go into combat. Guide them with Your wisdom. Shield them with Your strength. And by Your grace, uphold them where they are weak."

Warmth descended upon me, rushing from my scalp, down my back, and then shooting out through my chest, arms, and legs. I felt as though Someone drew near to me, so near I could feel strong arms supporting me. Instantly I felt as if I were back in the studios, held captive, and feeling God's power flow through me. A distant rush surrounded me, like thousands of wings humming in the night.

If P.G. noticed anything strange, he didn't let on. "May their individual talents and skills blend together as You intend. Just as You watched over the Israelites, just as You gave victory to David, even as Your angels protect us now, give these heroes success. In Jesus' precious name. Amen."

Murmured "amens" rippled through the room.

The sensation faded but in its wake I still felt supported.

Gauntlet clapped a hand to my shoulder and give me a gentle squeeze. "Let's do this."

I nodded. Time to show Helen why she shouldn't have messed with the Laughlin boys.

CHAPTER 57

MAYBE USING THE SEWER hadn't been such a good idea. The cold water nibbled at my feet through my boots and based on what I was smelling, I didn't even want to think of what was in the water with us. But, as Veritas had pointed out while we were planning, there wasn't any security down here. Who would be stupid enough to break into Magnus Studios through the sewers?

The meager light of my flashlight barely illuminated the walls, so I kept my hand on Veritas' shoulder as we sloshed through the musty water. Gauntlet grabbed the back of my shirt. I could only assume Blowhard followed behind him.

Veritas came to a stop. The pale green light of his cell phone lit his face from below, revealing the metal rungs of a ladder attached to the wall. I squinted up. Light filtered through the holes in the manhole cover above us.

"Are they in position?" I asked.

Veritas fiddled with his phone then nodded. "T-Ram reports a security guard in a booth."

"You two ready?" I whispered over my shoulder.

Gauntlet's grip tightened ever so slightly.

"Isn't there some other way?" Veritas said. "Maybe T-Ram could—"

I leaned in close and lowered my voice. "We need a big bang, right?"

He kicked at the water. "Right."

"Then it's now or never. Send them in."

Veritas sighed. He tapped at his phone and tucked it away.

Off in the distance came the squeal of tires, followed by a boom. Sirens wailed in the distance. I wish I could have been there to watch as the Reliant and T-Ram assaulted the main entrance to the studio, smashing through the wall side by side.

"Let's go." I motioned the others to move forward.

Gauntlet jabbed a hand over his head. With a pop, the manhole cover slid aside. Gauntlet leapt up the ladder and disappeared through the hole. I went next.

Gauntlet helped Blowhard and Veritas out of the sewer. I checked on the others. Prairie Fire and Kid Magnum had joined T-Ram. Good thing, too. The pod-bots boiled out of the buildings, skittering across the pavement toward the heroes.

With a loud cry, T-Ram charged the largest robot in the field, one the size of a horse. He smashed through its center and stomped across a dozen more. Lightning danced across Prairie Fire's hands. She pivoted and unleashed a storm of bolts that fried clumps of pod-bots. Standing over them on top of the wreckage of Veritas's Reliant, Kid Magnum fired into the boiling mass of robots with his entire arsenal. He looked like a Fourth of July fireworks display on the ground. They were holding their own, but robots kept coming. If my team didn't move fast, they might be overwhelmed.

I slipped back to the others, who had gathered at a set of metallic double doors on the other side of the building.

Veritas ran his hands over them for a moment and then nodded. "These right here."

"Ready?" Gauntlet asked.

I nodded. I sheared through the doors' hinges. Before the doors could drop, Gauntlet grabbed them in a telekinetic field and lifted them out of their frames. He gently set them down against the wall. We stole through the opening into the darkened room beyond.

We had entered the Chamber. My stomach lurched. How long had it been since I had competed—very poorly, as I recall—in this room? Weeks? The memories rushed back: the obstacles, the fear of being eliminated, the relief when Prairie Fire had been sent home. I shook my head to clear it. As menacing as the Chamber had been during the tapings, now it seemed almost sad. Sheets covered the studio cameras and the lights overhead glowed feebly, barely enough to light the black-walled room.

Veritas popped open the doors on the other side. A quick check revealed the hallway outside the Chamber was empty.

Now I took the lead. We bypassed the dressing rooms until we came to the doors of the finale set. I checked with my companions, then I cracked open the door and peered inside.

Things appeared pretty much as they were when I'd left this room. It was the large soundstage where the set for the finale had been built. The Professor still stood at the computer console, sweat glistening on his forehead. Madrigal and

Gary still paced nearby, their postures tense. Haruki still hung suspended in midair over the pit.

A distant boom shook the building, sending the lights swaying. Gary stiffened and turned toward the direction of the sound.

The Professor stumbled as another tremor rattled the floor. "Those heroes could ruin everything! I'm extracting the plague now."

Large metal arms that ended in funnels dropped from the ceiling and positioned themselves on either side of Haruki's body.

I turned to the others. "We have to get in there now."

Gauntlet grabbed the door. His fingers crumpled the metal, and he ripped one off its hinges with the squeal of tortured steel. Gauntlet threw the door at Gary.

It struck him in the chest and knocked him off his feet.

Madrigal whirled, only to get bowled over by a blast of wind from Blowhard.

Veritas, Blowhard, and Gauntlet charged into the room to grapple with Gary and Madrigal

That left the Professor for me. He drew a gun and leveled it on me but I was ready for that. I sliced the barrel right down the middle with my power. The Professor stared at his ruined weapon, and I tackled him.

He clawed at my face to twist my mask around. Two could play at that game. I slid my fingers under the edge of his Trifecta mask and pulled.

"No!" The Professor's voice pitched up into a shriek. He tried to push my hands away.

Out of the corner of my eye, I spotted Haruki hanging in the anti-grav field. Seeing my friend like that steeled my resolve.

I kept prying. The hooks in his skin didn't want to give. But slowly, one by one, they popped free, drawing blood from each wound. The hooks flailed inward as if alive. It reminded me of a centipede. I shuddered but tightened my grip and yanked until the mask came off.

The Professor's back arched and he screamed, a heart-wrenching cry that knocked me off of him. Then he collapsed to the ground, unconscious.

"What did you do?" Veritas spun me around.

I looked over his shoulder. Madrigal and Gary lay on the ground, a metal door wrapped around both of them. I glanced at Gauntlet, who merely shrugged. I chuckled. Show off.

"What. Did. You. Do?" Veritas shook me a little and then ripped the writhing mask out of my hand.

"What? The mask was controlling him. I figured if we could get him free of Helen's control, he could shut down—"

Veritas threw the mask on the ground. "Great theory, but you should have checked with me first. If the mask is forcibly removed, it wipes the wearer's memory of everything he did while wearing it."

"You mean . . ." I looked at the Professor. He was unconscious.

"That's right," Veritas said. "He's worthless to us now."

"Uh, guys?" Blowhard knelt by the computer and tapped at the keyboard. "I could be wrong, but if I'm reading this data right, Haruki's about to release the plague."

CHAPTER 58

I RUSHED TO Blowhard's side. "Are you sure?"

"I think so." He pointed to the jagged line of a graph. "See the spike? The plague's ready to be collected."

"Then let's get him out of there."

Something exploded in the distance. The Reliant? Kid Magnum's arsenal? We had to get out of here and fast!

Blowhard pecked at few more keys and then rose. "I don't think we can. I can barely make heads or tails of this system. And even if we could get him out of that anti-grav field, what would we do about the plague? It might be best to let the machine collect the virus. Maybe that would remove it from Haruki."

Veritas shook his head. "There's no telling where the machine will send the plague. By the time we track those pipes, Helen could grab the canisters or whatever it's stored in and escape."

"Has anyone seen her yet?" I asked.

Gauntlet ignored my question. "So what do you suggest we do? Just stand here and run the risk of catching whatever 'scourge' Haruki's got in him?"

The computer pinged and Blowhard leaned over it. "We're out of time. The virus is being released right now."

I paced at the edge of the pit, staring up at Haruki. He looked so helpless, his arms limp in the anti-grav field. There had to be something . . .

"What about your power, Failstate?" Veritas asked. "Maybe you could destroy the virus as it's released?"

I balked. Sure, I had already destroyed the virus once before—in a room not far from right here, actually. But that had been God, not me. Even if I could do it again, I'd have to channel so much destructive energy at Haruki that I could hurt him, maybe even kill him.

Gauntlet grabbed me by the shoulders. "You can do this. I know you can. Tell me how I can help."

Peace settled on me like a thick blanket, the same sensation I's felt when P.G. prayed. I remembered Delphi telling me that only I could stop the scourge. I looked up to Haruki. "I need to get up there."

Blowhard walked around the perimeter of the room. "Maybe we can find a ladder or something . . ."

"That won't do any good," Veritas said. "I'm guessing your power would eat through whatever you're standing on, right?"

I hadn't considered that. I glanced down the pit, a gaping maw that descended at least a hundred feet. "And there's a good chance that if my power spikes, I could fry the anti-grav generators. We could both fall."

"No, you won't," Gauntlet said. "Trust me. I won't let that happen."

He took a step back and raised his arms.

I floated up from the floor. Invisible hands carried me up to Haruki. Using his telekinetic power, Gauntlet pushed me through the anti-grav fields to Haruki. A tingle rushed over my skin, and it felt as though every hair on my body was standing on end.

Haruki's skin was practically transparent, all veins and black lines. His hair was matted to his head and green pus oozed from cracked lips. His head lolled to the side.

I touched his shoulder, and his eyes popped open.

"*Are*! What's going on?" He struggled, and then seemed to realize he was wrapped in cables and up in the air. "Aagh!" He spasmed and thrashed.

"Whoa, whoa!" I said. "Settle down, Haruki, I can help you. We'll get you down. But first, are you okay?"

"My head hurts, kind of." He tried to look around, but the motion caused him to flip in a somersault. His arms flailed. "What's happening?"

"Just relax and hold still. We're going to get you out of this." I hoped I sounded more confident than I felt.

I closed my eyes. In my mind's eye, I pictured my destructive field flowing from me and wrapping around Haruki.

God, I can't do this on my own. But I know You can do this through me. If this is what's supposed to happen, let's do this.

And fire exploded through me.

I ground my teeth together. Mentally, I saw the virus erupting from Haruki's skin—and then being shredded by my field. The destructive cocoon wavered, shrinking and expanding, dropping dangerously close to Haruki's skin far too many times. Had to maintain my focus, keep it under control.

My weight shifted and I fell. I jerked to a halt two feet lower. My concentration broke for a split second and sparks exploded from the overhead lights.

I rallied my power and kept the field up. Gauntlet must've slipped. He had to be more careful than that. I glanced down at him.

Sweat soaked through his mask. His hands trembled, but he kept them pointed in my direction. The rebuke died in my throat. This couldn't be easy for him either. I don't think he'd ever used his powers like this before.

"You're doing great, Failstate!" Blowhard shouted from the computer terminal. "It's working! According to these readings, Haruki's released two thirds of the viral load. You're almost there."

Easy for him to say. I was being hollowed out. My field wasn't just destroying the virus, it was also eating me away from the inside out. I closed my eyes again and tried to fall deeper into my power.

God, I don't know if I can keep this up for much longer. Let Your will be done.

The blaze inside me intensified. My back spasmed and my hands jerked upwards. I stretched them toward Haruki. My breath exploded in ragged bursts. The air both burning and freezing inside my lungs. Spots danced and collided with bursts of light in my vision. Had to hold on. Just a little while longer.

"That's got it!" Bloward's words sounded like little more than an echo in the distance. "The plague's been completely eliminated!"

With an almost audible pop, my field broke. The tension drained from my limbs. "I can't . . . I can't . . . I think I got . . ." My throat felt like it was full of glue.

"Bring 'em down!" Veritas jogged along the edge of the pit and pointed at a spot on the floor.

I felt like a leaf floating in the air, drifting to the floor. Strong hands caught me. My head lolled to one side. Veritas caught Haruki out of the air and carefully set him on the floor.

Gauntlet set me on my feet and held me up. "I am so proud of you. You did it." He hugged me.

I stood there, surprised at the sudden embrace. But then my arms wrapped around him, and we held each other tight. When he finally let go, my knees buckled and I almost fell.

"Let's get out of here." My words slurred.

Blowhard and Veritas helped Haruki while Gauntlet held me up. I stumbled out of the studio and headed for the Chamber, the others following me.

Gauntlet and I entered the Chamber first. I saw that the overhead lights were buzzing and snapping, and swaying. I frowned. Tremors shot through the floor. What was . . . ?

The far wall exploded and bricks rained down around us.

I turned back to the door where Blowhard and Veritas were helping Haruki. "Keep Haruki safe!" I shouted. "Gauntlet, shut the doors!"

Gauntlet slammed the Chamber's door shut with so much force that he put a massive dent in it. We backed away from the ruined wall. I scanned the smoke that billowed into the room. What had done that?

I got my answer as a woman's mocking laughter echoed through the room.

Helen.

CHAPTER 59

HELEN WAS WEARING A ROBOT.

She towered over me. In her mechanized suit, she had to be at least fifteen feet tall, peering out through a thick plexiglass window. Her arms and legs were like moving girders, lined with wiring. Thick metal plate covered her abdomen and chest. Her metallic arms ended in pinchers, her legs in clomping boots. Red Cyrillic lettering lined her limbs and carapace. The whole get-up clanked and *wheeshed* like a steam engine as she stomped into the Chamber.

She charged at Gauntlet and me. Gauntlet knocked me down, and her claw sliced through the air where my head had been. He rebounded and threw a punch. Helen caught the blow on her forearm and responded with a swing of her own. With a loud crack, Gauntlet stumbled backwards.

The blood pouring out of my brother's nose snapped me back to reality. I rolled to my feet and tried to summon my power. If she wanted a fight, I'd give it to her. I'd strip that clanking monstrosity right off her, and then we'd see what would happen. I threw open my hands and willed destructive energy in her direction.

Nothing happened.

No, not again!

I threw my hands at her and squinted as hard as I could. A thin strip of paint peeled off her left shoulder and vanished. That was it.

I stumbled backward a bit. Oh, no. I didn't have my power. I was facing down a robotic villain unarmed.

Very funny, God.

Maybe, when I exerted myself like I did in the finale set or in Krazney Potok's warehouse, I used up my power and it took me a while to regenerate. If that were true, then I just had to hold on for a little while and hope it came back soon.

Helen took a swing at me. I dodged, and her arm punched through the floor, splintering the wood, and leaving her stuck.

Gauntlet leapt onto her back and pounded at her armor. But he didn't even dent the plating. She reached around and grabbed him. A flick of her wrist sent him careening into a brick wall.

Gauntlet legs wobbled beneath him. He shook his head a few times and tried to take a step forward, but Helen grabbed him by the head and slammed him face-first into the wall. Gauntlet's body went limp and she tossed him aside.

Gauntlet wasn't moving. Not good.

"And now I get to squash you, you pest." Her voice, though tinny, still carried its usual chill.

I looked for some kind of weapon. The only thing I could see were broken planks from the shattered floor. I grabbed a plank and hurled it at her head as hard as I could. It bounced off the clear plexiglass and didn't even leave a scratch.

She laughed. "Like you could hurt me."

I summoned some bravado. "Oh, I don't know about that. Haruki's safe, and your virus is destroyed. We've neutralized your boys and my friends out there are taking out your robots. I may not be able to crack open that shell you're wearing but you're done."

The claws scissored over my head. I dodged and grabbed another chunk of wood as I rolled and lobbed it at her. It pinged off her back, again without doing any damage. She whirled on me. She was surprisingly agile in her robot suit, but I was still quicker. Maybe I could use that somehow.

"So," I said, "is there anything you didn't steal from Krazney Potok? Your security robots, that hot mess you're wearing, the Trifecta. Don't you have any original ideas, Helen? You're just a pathetic wannabe, aren't you?"

She took another swing at me and grazed me. I hit the floor and stars exploded around me. I recovered in time to roll out of the way of her thick boot, which barely missed me.

"I will destroy you!"

I dropped behind a stack of crates. "Like you destroyed Lux?"

She went still for a moment. "That was an accident! Those idiots . . . I loved her! She wasn't supposed to be there, you were!"

I ignored the guilty sting that pricked my mind. "You have a funny way of expressing your love. Killing your boss's daughter, who you say you love. Trying to wipe out humanity, what—to get Meridian to love you? I don't wanna know what you'd do if you really loved someone."

"Don't you get it? I do love him. I'm doing this for him! My gift to him!"

"Wait . . . you were doing this for Alexander Magnus? Really? I hope you kept the receipt, because I don't think he's going to like what you got him."

She whirled. Red headlights blazed from the suit and swept over the walls of the Chamber. "Oh, but he will. I was going to fix the world for him. He was always working, always fighting, always struggling. Against crime, against evil. So I was going to make things easier." She swung at me, an easy blow I dodged.

"By killing billions of people?"

"Of course. The world is broken, boy, can't you see it? So many people, so few resources. But what if I could take most of them away? Things will be simpler. More peaceful. Everyone would have enough. We could start over. All of us." She giggled. "And he'd finally see me. He couldn't ignore me anymore."

"Right. You know, I'm pretty sure he still wouldn't have noticed you even if you were the last woman on Earth. Which you might have been."

She shrieked and threw back her arms. Then she charged. I dodge, but she smashed the crates I hid behind and caught me around my neck. She lifted me and slammed me into the ground. Needles exploded in my chest and across my back.

But I still chuckled. Because I felt something: The faintest hint of a throb started behind my eyes.

"You don't know anything!" she said. "Do you know what it's like to always be in the shadows, always in the corner? Do you know what that's like?"

Better than she knew, but I didn't say anything. I focused on the minuscule sensation, urging it on, fanning its flames.

"Delphi was the key. She told me how I could win him, how I could finally help him retire. No more missions. No more undeserving women like his wife or Delphi. No more living vicariously through his children. It would be just him and me. Together. Finally. The way it always should have been." Her grip on my neck tightened. "Except you've ruined everything!"

"Sorry . . . for the . . . inconvenience." My voice was little more than a wheeze. "Just like . . . I'm sorry . . . for this!"

My power flared and washed over both Helen and me at the same time. The claw around my throat dissolved.

I fell to the floor and scrambled backward to get away. But then my power faltered, and its assault stopped.

Helen's other claw clamped around my leg and flipped me over. Her armor was still mostly intact. My power had burned holes through it at random points, though. Her faceplate was cracked, just enough to reveal the insane light burning in her eyes. "Enough of this!" She raised the suit's severed arm high overhead like a club.

"Failstate, stay down!"

Gauntlet leapt from the ground and punched her faceplate.

She stumbled back and dropped me. She swung at Gauntlet but he grabbed her good pincer and ripped it clean off. Then he caught her arms and wrenched them behind her in a shower of sparks and the shriek of twisting metal.

He turned to me. "Finish this!"

I clambered up the towering robotic suit. Helen stared out of the faceplate at me, her eyes wide with fear. I cut through the cracked faceplate and marshaled my power around my fist. "Mom always told me never to hit a girl," I said. "But then, you attacked my mom, so I don't think she'll mind." I smashed her across the jaw.

Her cranium bounced off the back of the armor and she was out. Gauntlet danced out of the way as the hulk collapsed. I clung to the robot's chest and rode it to the floor, and then rolled off and to my feet in front of Gauntlet.

Gauntlet smirked at me for a moment, then he applauded, a gentle golf-clap. "Not too bad, cognit."

"Feel like joining our club?" I asked.

Men in charcoal grey suits poured through the ruined wall, weapons drawn and ready. The man in the lead flashed his badge. I laughed. I never thought I'd actually be glad to see Agent Sexton from the VOC.

Sexton looked down at Helen. "That's Kirkwood?"

"That's her, sir," Gauntlet said. "She arranged the whole thing."

"Good job, boys." Sexton holstered his weapon. "But we'll take it from here." He turned to his companions. "All right, let's get the scene secured and get these dirtbags in custody. You two," he indicated us. "Over to the command center. We'll want to talk to you."

I hesitated. "Do you know what happened to Veritas, Blowhard, and Hurki?"

Sexton shooed me out of the room without answering.

We left the building and headed toward the flashing lights that filled the streets. Police, fire fighters, EMTs, and more VOC agents swarmed over the scene. Several of them clustered around our assault team. As near as I could tell, they were all fine. Prairie Fire sat cross-legged on the ground, holding her head in her hands. Kid Magnum flashed me a thumbs up. Except . . . where was T-Ram?

Then I spotted him. His head was stuck in a brick wall, his body flailing as he tried to free himself. Why was I not surprised?

An ambulance crew swept past me, pushing Haruki on a stretcher. I jogged alongside, wanting to make sure he was okay. He was enclosed in a clear plastic bubble. He smiled weakly at me and waved.

I returned the gesture. "Are you okay?" I shouted, hoping he could hear me through the plastic.

"Thanks to you," he said. And then he was gone, shoved into the back of an ambulance.

Someone touched my elbow. Veritas smiled at me weakly. "So is it over?"

I nodded. "Yeah. It is. Helen's down. The VOC has her. Haruki?"

"Blowhard says there shouldn't be any trace of the virus in him. We thought about breaking the computer to destroy their data, but the VOC will need it as evidence. Besides, maybe they can use it to figure out how to cure Haruki from making any more diseases." Veritas lifted his fist. "And I did some poking around after getting Haruki out of the building. I think this is yours." He pressed something into my hand.

I looked down. The red crystal sparkled at me.

"Apparently you didn't destroy that, after all."

I bit my lower lip and smiled. I never thought I'd actually be happy to see that stupid crystal, but an enormous sense of relief surged through me. I tucked it away in my pocket. It would be good to be able to take this mask off and have a normal life—whatever that might look like for a superhero.

Veritas smiled at me, then stumbled over to the building and collapsed against it.

"Are you okay?" I asked.

He ruffled his own hair so it stood straight up, and then nodded. "I will be." He looked around. "This is all a little surreal, isn't it? I mean, where'd all these people come from? I thought they couldn't be bothered."

"You can thank me for that." Elizabeth had somehow slipped past the security cordon. She smiled, her eyes sparkling. "The VOC didn't want to listen at first, but I can be pretty persuasive."

I laughed.

She took a careful step forward and then hugged me. My arms wrapped around her in spite of myself.

"I'm so sorry, Rob," she whispered. "I wish I had never hurt you."

"It's okay," I said. "I forgive you."

She pulled away and then rushed past me. She threw her arms around Gauntlet. My brother hugged her fiercely. I watched them for a few moments and swallowed the pang in my chest.

Veritas patted me on the shoulder. "You can't win them all."

I groaned. "That's just a stupid cliché."

"Doesn't make it any less true."

CHAPTER 60

WE TALKED TO THE VOC for close to six hours. At first, their questions seemed skeptical, even mocking. But as more and more evidence was recovered from the studios, they became less hostile. By the time things wrapped up, they were actually treating me politely. They even took us down to the cafeteria and bought us breakfast. Which was good, because by now it was six in the morning.

I was finishing my orange juice when Alexander Magnus arrived, dressed in a tan trench coat and a black suit with no tie. He conferred with Agent Sexton by the doorway for a few moments. About halfway through their conversation, the color drained from Magnus's face and he collapsed into a chair. That must've been the part when he heard who was behind all this—and why she'd done it.

Eventually Magnus recovered enough to come over to the table where we sat. He crossed his arms and stared at us, his face stern. Was he going to sue us for doing so much damage to his studios? "So in the middle of the night," he said, "I get a call that a bunch of vigilantes are battling robots at my studio. For the life of me, I couldn't imagine what was going on. But from what Sexton tells me, you all played a part in bringing down a dangerous domestic terrorist." A smile split his face. "I'm very proud of all of you."

I relaxed. No lawsuits, apparently.

Magnus went around the circle and shook hands with each of us. When he reached Veritas, he clasped him on the shoulder, and his smile grew a bit brighter. I might have been mistaken, but I think a glow flashed across his face. Then Magnus turned back to the rest of us.

"I'm glad you're all here, because we've got some business to discuss. I've been trying to convince the networks to let us back on the air, but earlier this week, they decided to pull the plug entirely. We're cancelled."

I groaned. The others leaned back in their chairs.

"So what does that mean for the vigilante license?" Gauntlet asked.

There was something in his voice, a hunger. I glanced at him. He leaned forward, his eyes bright and that all-too-familiar half-grin on his face. Oh, great. His change of heart hadn't lasted long.

"Well, I checked with the VOC and my lawyers. The VOC is more than willing to let one of you have the license and, according to my lawyers, the best way to handle this is to go with the results of the last vote. So I've got a production assistant pulling the data. In a few moments, one of you will be a licensed hero."

I ground my teeth. A fair decision, but I knew what would happen. Gauntlet would win. I closed my eyes and swallowed my mounting frustration. My envy wasn't right. It wasn't what God would want. As much as it pained me to admit it, Ben was a good hero. He had proved as much last night.

A few moments later, a twenty-something young lady scurried into the cafeteria. She passed a piece of paper to Magnus. He looked it over and blinked. He shot a questioning look at the woman. She shrugged.

Magnus cleared his throat. "According to the last votes we received before the show went on hiatus, the winner of the license is . . . Titanium Ram."

Silence. And then I burst out laughing. Soon Veritas joined me. Gauntlet looked a bit frustrated, but even he smiled.

I turned to T-Ram and stuck out my hand. "Congratulations."

He blinked several times and then turned to Magnus. "Dude, I don't want it!"

Magnus's head snapped back as if struck. "Excuse me?"

"I'm sorry, Mr. Magnus, but I'm done. I may have a thick skull, but I ain't stupid. I can read the writing on the wall. I'm retiring. Gonna go into homeopathic medicine instead."

I stared at T-Ram and then turned back to Magnus.

The billionaire's face purpled a bit. "All right. Well, if you're not interested, then we'll just have to—"

"I've got an idea." Gauntlet rose from his chair and jammed his fists into his hips. "Why don't we vote? We've seen each other in action, especially tonight. I think we can figure it out on our own."

Magnus crumpled up the paper. "Well, the VOC may not like it, but I think they'd be willing to work with us. You have a nominee?"

"Yeah, I do."

Here it came. He'd somehow manage to sound humble as he nominated himself. What a peacock.

Gauntlet stood back from the table and spread his arms wide. "I nominate . . . Failstate."

I knew it. He would have to—

Wait, what?

My brother smiled at me, pride shining in his eyes. "While the rest of us were too full of ourselves, he never lost sight of what really mattered. And he was the one who rallied us to take down Helen and save everyone. Time after time, he kept pointing us in the right way, toward the main things. If anyone deserves the license, it's him."

Was this a dream? I could hardly believe what I was hearing.

"Sounds about right to me," Blowhard said.

"Absolutely," Kid Magnum added.

A pang twisted in my stomach and I turned to Vertias. How was he going to handle this? Would his dad be disappointed with him? But he just nodded.

Magnus's eyes narrowed. Then he looked over the group. "Everyone good with that?"

Nobody objected. Magnus stepped over to me and took my hand, pulling me out of my chair. "Stop by my office later and we'll make it all official. Congratulations." He leaned in close and whispered, "I'm proud of you, kid. You're gonna do great, I just know it. But come on by the Lighthouse for some more lessons in the ring, eh?"

My throat constricted. I blinked away tears beneath my mask. "Thank you, sir." I hesitated for a moment. "If you don't mind me asking, are you okay, sir?"

Magnus sighed. "No. I had no idea Helen felt that way about me. Well, that's not true. She mooned after me when she first started working for me, but I thought she got over it when I married Carissa. But thanks for asking, kid. I'll make it."

He released my hand and glanced at the young woman. "Okay, let's go. We've got some phone calls to make and I don't have an assistant to help me. Congratulations. You just got promoted. Let's go."

Magnus strode away. The young woman fell in behind him. Before they could leave though, Magnus held out a hand and stopped her.

"But first . . . you married?"

She nodded, her eyes wide.

Magnus nodded grimly. "Good. C'mon."

And then the other heroes swarmed me, slapping me on the back, offering me congratulations of their own.

Eventually Veritas shook hands with me too and for a moment I could only mouth a few words, trying to find the right platitude. "Veritas, I . . ."

He shook his head. "It's okay. This is for the best. But if you ever need any help . . . ?"

"You'll be the first person I call."

Then Gauntlet stepped in close. He balled up his fist and prepared to hit me on the arm. I winced, ready for the pain. But instead, Gauntlet stuck out his hand. I shook it, only to be pulled into a tight hug. "Good job, Rob," he whispered. "I'm proud of you. And I know Dad would be too."

I hugged my brother tightly and then finally broke away. "I couldn't have done it without you."

"True," Gauntlet said, his eyes sparkling.

My brother threw his arm around me and we headed out of the cafeteria. We made our way through the crowd of emergency workers, most of whom barely acknowledged our presence. We left the studio and I stopped as the sunrise blazed between buildings, painting the city with hues of orange and red. I smiled. A brand new day, a bright future.

But I still had one more mission to complete.

EPILOGUE

MY STOMACH FLIPPED as we pulled up to the curb. I rubbed my hands across my pant legs, trying to wipe away the cold sweat.

"Are you sure you want to do this now?" Mike asked.

I looked out the window and nodded. " If I don't talk to her now, I'll lose my nerve and never do it."

"Do you want me to come in with you?" Ben poked his head between the seats. "Moral support?"

My fingers crept over the door handle but I couldn't bring myself to push the door open. "I'll be fine."

"Cool. That means I'll get to stay in the sweet car."

Elizabeth smacked him as he settled back into the seat. I smiled in spite of my accelerating heartbeat. When Magnus had learned what happened to the Reliant, he had given the keys to his BMW to Mike. Once again, I was thankful that Mike had found my bead, which was now held against my neck by a length of dental floss. At least I wouldn't have to worry about wrecking the interior. Given how my nerves seemed ready to boil over, my power would have spiked.

411

Elizabeth reached from the back and rubbed my shoulder. "We'll be out here if you need us. Now go on."

I smiled and squeezed her hand. Taking a deep breath, I pushed the car door open and started up the sidewalk to my house. My heart slammed into my ribs and ricocheted off my spine. I ground my teeth together and forced my feet to keep moving.

God, in some ways, fighting Helen was easier than this. You haven't failed me yet. Be with me now too.

The house loomed over me. I swallowed and climbed the stairs, quietly opening the front door, and slipping inside.

"Mom?"

Something metallic clattered in the kitchen. Mom rushed out of the kitchen but paused in the hallway.

She looked like she had aged ten years. Her hair was pulled into a frizzy bun and dark shadows ringed her eyes. Her lower lip trembled and she covered her mouth with her hand.

I braced myself. Would she yell at me? Throw me out?

She ran down the hall and threw her arms around me. Words poured from her mouth. "Robin, where . . . I mean, you were . . . so worried . . ." Her embrace tightened and then she broke away. Her hands came up to the sides of my face. "Where have you been?"

"I'm sorry, Mom, I never meant for this to happen." I couldn't look her in the eye. I tried to dip my head, take a step backward.

She wouldn't let me escape. "Do you know how worried I was?" Her voice didn't carry accusation, only barely suppressed panic—and relief.

Hot tears stung my eyes. "I know. I'm sorry. I'm sorry for everything. For disappearing, for the way I've treated you and Ben, for what happened to . . . to Dad."

Her fingers dug into my cheeks, and she looked at me fiercely. "Why are you sorry for that?"

"Because if it hadn't been for me and . . . and what I do . . . you two wouldn't have been fighting that night and then he wouldn't have . . ."

"Oh, Robin." Her hands fell away and she took a step back. "It never has been. Your Dad and I . . . we were in a bad place. If anyone should apologize, it's me. I put you in the middle of our arguments and I shouldn't have."

I tried to say something, but she wouldn't let me. "No, I need to say this. When you disappeared, I realized how badly I've been treating you. I haven't been as loving toward you as I should. I haven't supported you the way you needed. I've blamed you for things that aren't your fault. I'm sorry that it took me this long to realize it. But when I thought I had lost you the same way I lost . . ." Her voice hitched. "Do you . . . Can you forgive me?"

I couldn't hold it back any longer. Sobs burst from me. Bitter, wracking anguish, years of continual self-blame . . . all of it came gushing out. I wanted to nod to let her know I forgave her, but I think I just cried helplessly, the same way I had the day Dad died. Mom held open her arms and I fell into them and held on tight.

Minutes—years—elapsed as I cried out my pain. Finally, I could attempt words again. "I love you, Mom."

"I love you too, Rob." She held me up and rubbed my arms. "I'm so glad you're home and safe. Are you all right?"

I nodded again, wiping my nose on my sleeve. At that point, I didn't care if it was sanitary or not.

"Good." She put an arm around me. "I think we have a lot of catching up to do. Tell you what. I'm going to clean up my mess and grab us a few sodas, okay? Meet me out in the garage."

"The garage? But you never—"

"Don't you think it's time we changed that? Let's see exactly what your powers can do, shall we?"

This time I could nod, but just barely.

She squeezed my shoulder and headed back for the kitchen.

I leaned against a wall and closed my eyes. *Thank You, God. I couldn't have done any of this without You.*

I turned back to the front door and waved out to my friends to let them know I was okay. And then I headed for the garage, glad that I had finally come home.

ACKNOWLEDGMENTS

You meet a lot of interesting people on the journey to fulfill a lifelong dream, and a lot of them have helped me along the way:

To my darling wife, Jill. You gave me the seed for the idea, the time to create, and the support to keep working. That this book is in the hands of someone other than family and friends is because of you. You are absolutely my hero now and always.

To my sons, for inspiring me in countless ways and for showing me what Failstate's costume would look like if designed by a five year old.

To my "Brain Trust," Joel and Chris, for your invaluable help in fine-tuning Failstate's and Gauntlet's powers and relationship. Your encyclopedic knowledge and willingness to serve as a sounding board during my brainstorming sessions were invaluable.

To my family, for letting me tell bizarre stories in my childhood. Look where it got me!

To the members of the American Christian Fiction Writers Scribes group, your tweaks and encouragements kept me going.

To Sharon Hinck, for helping me wrestle this monster into a readable form and helping it to shine. I can't even begin to thank you for all of your hard work and help. You are truly a blessing to the Christian fiction community.

To Jill Williamson, for believing in my book so much that you would pitch it for me.

To Amanda Luedeke for taking a chance on a new writer. I appreciate all of the hard work you put into this project, including the "disapproving looks."

To Jeff Gerke, a great friend, editor, and visionary. We are all lucky to have someone as brave as you fighting the good fight. And I promise to beware the cardinal sins from now on.

To the crew of Marcher Lord Press, for being such a great and supportive family.

And most of all, to God—Father, Son, and Holy Spirit—for creating me, redeeming me, and giving me gifts. Without You, this book would have never been written. May it exist solely to give You glory. "[You] must increase; I must decrease." (John 3:30)

You've read the book.
Now listen to the song!

Christian recording artists **Tangled Blue** have recorded "On What Has Now Been Sown," the song played at Mount Calvary. And because you've read the book, you can download a copy of the song for free!

Visit John's website at www.johnwotte.com to download your copy of the song. And then be sure to check out Tangled Blue at www.tangledblue.com.